THESE BLUE REMEMBERED HILLS

MICHELE DEPPE

DEDICATION

A story about sisters,
for Adora and Audra.

Into my heart an air that kills
From yon far country blows;
What are those blue remembered hills,
What spires, what farms are those?

That is the land of lost content,
I see it shining plain,
The happy highways where I went,
And cannot come again.

From *A Shropshire Lad,* by A.E. Housman, (1859-1936)

CHAPTER 1

On the crest of a great hill stood the aptly named Hilltop Farm. The farmhouse was expansive and newish, a stalwart three-storeyed toast-coloured brick. Across a pebbled yard were a trio of much older stone-and-timber barns, skirted by acres of rolling pastures, a thick wood and distant blue peaks.

There was also a near-to-overflowing ditch out by the road, as it had been a sodding wet spring in the Midlands. Overwhelmed with showers, the ground swelled into grey pools at the lowest places and turned the lawn around the farmhouse into a saturated green sponge.

A young woman emerged from the farmhouse. The door closed with a crash behind her as she skipped down the shallow steps of the front porch and strode toward the largest barn which housed her goats. Mollie Purslow's long legs were shrouded in heavy corduroy trousers, tucked into green gumboots. A woollen jumper peeked out beneath a dark blue tweed coat. These sensible clothes had been her father's.

Reaching the barn Mollie paused. Standing on the stone floor at the barn's entrance, she turned and gazed at the Long Mynd, the craggy backbone of lofty hills to the east. The dawn had left behind a thin azure sky, gilded with weak sunshine. Mollie closed her eyes for a moment. The air felt balmy against her face. Inhaling deeply, she savoured the sweet smell of hay and the soul-lifting fragrance of April. Shedding the tweed coat, she hooked its collar over a dusty light switch inside the barn door.

Mollie felt fizzy with excitement. Things were only going to get better. After doing the milking, she'd be off to enjoy a rare day spent with her best mates.

Entering the barn, Mollie's mood soared ever higher. Her favourite doe had given birth to a pair of healthy kids. Despite the regularity of this miracle, Mollie was in awe each time she met her new little goats. The doe, Primrose, had licked her offspring to a clean shine and they bleated at Mollie with soft baby voices.

Mollie slipped into the generously-sized pen. 'Well done, Prim,' she said, carefully approaching the reclining mother and her kids. Mollie sunk to her knees in the thick bedding, giving a cuddle and performing an amateur vet-check on each baby goat. Both were girls, a welcome addition to her small goat's milk and cheese enterprise. The larger girl had a pretty, mocha-brown coat swirled with white Swiss markings and a face contoured in chic black. The smaller baby was a sharp contrast; very dainty, with fur as white and shiny as a pearl.

Mollie freshened the bedding with piles of barley straw and forced herself to leave Prim and her babies. She'd have to do the morning milking by herself, with her sister off at an early dental appointment. Mollie's boyfriend, Rhys Davies, was due at half-eight to finish the feeding and mucking out of the remaining goat pens.

She worked efficiently, talking to the goats and moving them through the milking parlour. It was a routine Mollie could perform in her sleep. Some mornings she felt as if she had.

She was almost finished with the washing up when her boyfriend arrived. She smiled at Rhys, her gloved hands submerged in bleach water bobbing with milking equipment. She raised her lips to his. He kissed her, then said in his swoon-worthy Welsh accent, 'I'm happy with this weather, I am.'

'Me, too.'

'Going to bother with those girls, Jenny and Natalie, are you?'

'You know I'd rather be with you.'

'You'll put on something decent, huh?'

She giggled. 'They wouldn't come with me if I didn't. Don't sulk, Rhys. I do dress for you, sometimes.'

'Sometimes.'

Mollie drained the huge sink and gave the equipment a thorough rinsing in fresh water. 'We're going to Telford to get our hair cut. Then out to lunch. We may even see a film. Go shopping. Or not. Since we don't really have any money to spend, it's just as likely we'll sit in a park and enjoy the sun. It'll be great fun.'

'And that's all that matters.'

'I couldn't go if not for your help. Thank you.'

'Have a wonderful day, love.'

Mollie was drawing off her gloves and felt him stuff something crisp and light into the deep pocket of her father's old trousers.

'Rhys?'

'Just a bit extra.'

She shook her head, but was thankful for the money.

Mollie paid him another kiss and dashed out of the barn into the sunshine.

THE DAY MOLLIE spent with her friends had gone, more or less, as predicted: first the hair salon; then buying lunch at a chip shop, to be eaten on the lawn of a near-by park. Then a half-hearted browse in some shops, which were bursting with bright, over-priced summer clothing that wouldn't do for working on a farm and were far too dear for their meagre budgets. They went for an ice cream. Late afternoon, the girls drove from Telford toward

Church Stretton, a busy market town larger than their own sleepy village of Marris Mynd, situated further south-west.

It was late now and growing chilly. They'd giggled over glasses of wine on the brick patio of Giovanni's Italian restaurant. Wiping tears of mirth from her cheeks, Mollie sighed and looked beyond the strings of fairy lights draped around the dining area. Green fields ran up to the edge of a distant forest. Behind the wood rose the beautiful hills of Shropshire. It was a lovely, romantic view. Her thoughts strayed to Rhys and she wished she were here with him.

Mollie turned her attention back to her friends. Jen and Natalie were sharing the last of the tiramisu. 'Today's been heaven,' Mollie said. 'We all of us really need more time away from the farm.'

'Definitely,' Jenny groaned.

Silence fell. They'd each need a good night's sleep to slog through tomorrow. There would be catch-up work to do, especially now that the rain had finally blown away. Over their dinner, they'd questioned Mollie about how things were going with her handsome Welshman. Neither Jenny nor Natalie had dated much since they'd all left school.

'Do you think you'll marry Rhys?'

Mollie was forking in the last bite of pasta with carbonara sauce and savouring the creamy flavour of Parmesan. 'Good cheese, that, even if it isn't from a goat.'

Jenny rolled her eyes. 'Don't avoid the question, Molls. We live vicariously through your romance with Butty, you know.' She used the Welsh term for friend with affection.

'Yeah,' Natalie agreed. 'I am lucky if I get to see romance on the telly. As soon as I sit down, I fall asleep. An old lady at twenty-one.'

Mollie fidgeted. Ordinarily she loved talking about Rhys because she was besotted with him. But she was keenly aware of her mates' discontent with their own love lives. 'Well, he hasn't asked me, yet. But maybe later this year. Rhys is rather fond of Christmas. Anyway, I have other things on my mind.'

'Yes, we know, Mollie,' Jenny snapped. 'Goats, goats, more goats. You'll lose your man if you don't mind him better,' she said, reminiscent of her mercurial moods and sharp tongue that had been legendary back at school.

Natalie blushed and looked away. She preferred to stay neutral and hoped Mollie and Jenny would stop arguing.

Mollie bristled. 'So, I'm ambitious about my goats. And why not? If we're going to slave our lives away then we may as well create something that's worth it, don't you think? And as for Rhys, he's working sun-up to sundown on his father's dairy, not waiting around for me to finish with my goats.'

Jenny's face softened at the rebuke. 'Fair enough,' she replied, changing the topic by proposing they try for an actual holiday next year. 'Before we all drop of exhaustion.'

'It's easier during the winter when the goats are dry and–'

'No, Mollie. No consideration given to cows or goats. The important bit is that we're going somewhere warm!' Jenny corrected herself. 'No, not warm. *Hot.* I want to bake on a beach. Perhaps Spain.'

Natalie smiled. Mollie said, 'France would be rather nice.'

Jenny chuckled. 'Because you'd like to check out the cheese being made in France, no doubt. You're pathetic, Mollie, really. Besides, we ought to figure where we're going to get the dosh. European luxury holidays don't come cheap.'

Mollie raised her glass. 'Well, then. I declare this to be the most profitable year we've ever had. Here's to high prices for milk, crops and goat's cheeses!'

'Cheers!'

Jenny immediately soured again. 'And if we don't come into a lot of cash, we'll at least be sending you and Rhys away on your honeymoon.'

Mollie felt warmth spread up her neck. She'd like nothing better.

At half-past eight, the girls paid their bill and piled into Mollie's ancient Land Rover. Confined in the darkness of the vehicle, each grew thoughtful.

Finally Mollie spoke. 'You know what's rather odd? I found at times today that I wanted to jump up and be off to work. Not that I *wanted* to be back at the farm, working–'

'But rather that you're so used to the constant push to try and get it all done! I felt the same. Sitting, having a laugh, somehow seems wrong.' Jenny's voice betrayed more animosity than Mollie felt.

'Honestly?' Jenny continued. 'I'd be off in a heartbeat, if I imagined I could do anything else.'

'Really?' Mollie hoped that Jenny's resentment would dissipate and she waited for Natalie to chime in.

She didn't.

'Nat? You're awfully quiet. What about you? Didn't you feel it was a bit difficult to relax?'

'Yeah, Nat. You didn't say a word about our holiday.' Jenny stared over her shoulder at their friend seated in the back. Mollie glanced in her rear-view mirror. Natalie's face was swallowed in shadows. She hoped that Jenny's terse attitude hadn't upset her.

Natalie's reply was scarcely audible. 'I'm leaving.'

'What!' Jenny shrieked.

The vehicle was climbing a steep, twisty track. Mollie swerved slightly. Had she heard Natalie correctly?

'When were you going to tell us?'

'I'm not going straightaway, Jen, so don't get your knickers in a twist.'

Mollie's eyes darted once again towards the mirror. She'd never known Natalie to stand up to Jen.

'It's just that my dad's found a way to send me to university.'

Mollie's throat tightened. Natalie was one of seven children.

That her father had committed to help fund her education was not only exceptional, but ever so loving. Mollie's own dad had been marvellous and supportive. She missed him, now, as keenly as ever.

'Congratulations, Nat. We're really so happy for you, aren't we, Jen?'

Mollie glimpsed Jenny's frown.

'Well, at first I wasn't able to decide, you know? Farming's all we've ever done,' Natalie twittered, sounding slightly out of breath. 'Then I wasn't able to come to a decision about the uni. And finding affordable housing around a campus is madness. Trying to figure it all out, over the years, well, I'd rather sort of given up. Then last year my mum got talking to Mrs Hayward in the village. You've met her, the new vicar's wife? Mrs Hayward had all sorts of ideas. Mum said she was very knowledgeable; she'd been working at a university before and she answered loads of questions.'

Jenny snorted. 'All right, then. So, Mrs Hayward is a helpful busybody. You've blathered on Nat, but haven't actually told us a thing.'

'I was coming to it!' Natalie cried.

Mollie pulled the vehicle into Natalie's drive and parked beneath a monumental oak tree. The farmhouse was lit within, the very picture of a busy family home. The window to the front room was open and a television could be heard.

'After speaking with Mrs Hayward, I took a few distance learning courses,' Natalie said. 'And I'd made up my mind about what to do.'

'You've been going to school online? And you didn't say anything?'

'Let her finish, Jen.' Mollie shifted in her seat. She had meant to turn and face Natalie, in a show of support. Her hands were planted on the steering wheel instead. Like Jenny, she suddenly found that she didn't want to hear the details of how she'd leave them either, but there was nothing to be done about it but to listen.

Not everyone stayed in the village, Mollie reflected. Not everyone remained close friends.

Natalie thinking about her plans, she was refreshed with excitement. 'The thing is, I am going to be a nurse! I've just done the entry requirements and have my fees paid up to begin this autumn. At the University of Wolverhampton. But I'll be going, actually, at the end of next month. In May. To move into a shared house. And naturally I'll need to find a job.' Natalie gave out an incredulous laugh, unable to believe her own extraordinary news.

Mollie unclipped her safety belt, turned and clamoured up the back of the driver's seat, leaning over it to give Natalie a proper hug. 'That's amazing, Nat! I am so proud of you!'

Jenny remained forward facing. 'Me, too. Even though you didn't see fit to say a word.'

Undaunted by Jenny, Natalie told them of her luck in securing a room close to campus. Her housemates were also nursing students. 'Thanks to Mrs Hayward's suggestions, most of that got settled online as well.' Natalie chatted for another half-hour, then got out of the Land Rover. They waved their goodbyes as Mollie turned the vehicle in the wide farmyard and made her way back out to the road.

'Fancy that.' Jenny sighed. 'Never said a word.'

'Will you *stop*?'

'Oh, that's fine, Mollie. You have your Welshman and your goats and you don't mind if our Natalie leaves, do you? You've got your rosy life all planned as well. You don't give a moment's thought of what'll become of me. Had you even realised it's been four months since we've gone out? Not even a text from you or Nat since the holidays. You don't give a toss about me.'

'Jen, don't be ridiculous.'

The short distance to Jenny's family's farm stretched on, with Jenny giving Mollie the silent treatment. 'I don't know what you'd like me to say, Jen. I've been busy, not to mention that I've not heard from you, either. Look, we ought to be happy she's leaving. Peoples' lives change, you know. Even Natalie's. Yours will, too, even though you're not sure how it possibly could at the moment.'

But Jenny had hit upon a truth. Jen's life seemed to be shrinking, whereas Mollie's future seemed bright and beautiful. She couldn't imagine her life changing much, except for the better.

CHAPTER 2

Mollie woke moments before her phone alarm began chirping. She wasn't a morning person, but she was a keeper of livestock. Which meant she rose at an unholy hour, day in and day out, regardless of her deeply reluctant feelings about doing so.

Thankfully, Mollie's younger sister was a cheerful sort and could be counted upon to make their coffee. Even better, Willa postponed unnecessary conversation until at least half-six. Coming up to seven, the sun would be well on the rise, the milking nearly done and Mollie would be sufficiently caffeinated. She could then think about being sociable with someone besides a goat.

She yawned, then forced herself from her warm bed, standing slowly and stepping into her father's old clothes that had been draped over the wooden chair. Her mind's cottony musings turned to all of the healthy baby goats born this spring. She smiled, gratified at the way her little herd grew each year. Unlike many modern farmers, Mollie allowed the kids to stay on with their mothers, instead of snatching them away to be bottle-fed. A stressed out mum and orphan babies didn't add up to the kind of animal husbandry she wanted to practice. That's not how her father had run his dairy, so neither would Mollie. Besides, by some miracle of nature the mothers were cunningly able to 'hold back' enough milk for the wee ones and Mollie only relieved the mums of excess milk in the mornings and evenings. Win-win.

A few minutes later Mollie stepped outside. Her eyes watered from the chill and the injustice of opening too early. She held a steaming thermos of coffee, courtesy of Willa having left it on the dresser in the kitchen. Mollie gazed ahead and saw her sister. Willa's petite form was encased in a puffy, bright green gilet and her blonde ponytail swept sideways across her back as she paused to slide the barn door open. Walking fast on long legs, Mollie caught her up. Without speaking, the sisters parted ways. Mollie flipped on the lights in the milking parlour. She rolled up the sleeves of her dad's old tattersall shirt, washed her hands and arms, put on gloves and readied her equipment. She poured grain out for the first group of seven does that would soon scramble into the milking parlour, eager for their breakfast.

Within a minute – she and her sister had perfected their timing – Willa had let the first group out of their pen. Into the parlour trotted the goats and each found her place in front of a small pile of grain. Mollie closed an individual collar around each goat's neck, while speaking reassuring nonsense.

'It's going to be a sunny, lovely day, goatie girls! Lots of good pasture time this afternoon, with hours to have a tea and chat!' Sometimes she made herself laugh. And sometimes the goats would sneeze a complaint, as though they knew a bad joke when they heard one. Mollie cleaned them underneath with solution and did test squirts, to make sure the milk looked right. Then she fitted on the automatic milking apparatus and went to her writing board to record milk yields. Time clipped along while Mollie repeated the process. After Willa had sent in the ninth group of goats and Mollie had finished with them, she did the washing-up, while Willa continued tidying the pens.

Cleaning up the milking parlour, Mollie reflected on how yesterday had been such a lovely day; one for making memories with old friends, laughing together and, ultimately, sharing secrets. But as Natalie had left the vehicle, Mollie had felt an almost tangible shift. Natalie had turned and looked back at she and Jenny and gave a sad wave. A gesture of farewell.

Mollie had only made sense of it all this morning. Their friendships had been foundering and, last night, had completely collapsed.

It was doubtful Natalie would ever return to live in Marris Mynd. There was no work for a nurse in their small village. Natalie wasn't the only one who'd known that they hadn't really been close friends for a very long time now; Jenny had sussed it out a long time ago.

But when, exactly?

Mollie had been caught up in her work, in seeing Rhys at every opportunity. She simply hadn't noticed her childhood friends were slipping away.

Why hadn't she thought to suggest a good luck party for Natalie? Surely there was something to be done. She should ring Natalie and offer to get together.

On the other hand, what was there left to say? It had all felt so awkward. And then there was Jenny. She wouldn't tolerate Mollie trying to smooth over everything. Mollie knew there was no fixing it. They'd never, the three of them, be close again.

LATER, she met with Dean Scott, their veterinarian and long-time family friend.

'Hello, Mollie,' Dean said as he came into the barn. 'Looks like you have another couple of healthy babies there.'

She was in the largest pen with the does and kids. 'Yes! Aren't they gorgeous?'

With practised grace, Dean folded at the waist and passed

between the rails of the pen. He stretched out and scooped up a baby goat. 'This little one is a real princess, isn't she?'

Mollie had a cross breeding programme that produced goats in a variety of colours, but this was her first completely pure-white kid. 'I think you've just named her, Dean. She's got a placid, regal temperament to match, don't you think?'

'I do,' Dean said, laughing as he returned Princess to the straw, where she wobbled about on unsteady legs. 'I reckon she's one of Primrose's best.'

'I most certainly agree.' Mollie counted herself lucky to have a vet so keen on goats when many vets focused their attention on cows, or specialising in horses or sheep. Dean had been one of her father's dearest friends. He'd helped Mollie convince her mum that she could carry on raising her father's goats. Dean had understood that even at the young age of eleven, Mollie had shared her dad's love of animals and she'd displayed a tenacity that convinced Dean that she could cope. Dean's support of Mollie had been well-founded; she'd kept the business going and growing – with the help of her benevolent sister, Willa, who'd toiled along with Mollie simply because Mollie had asked.

Mollie followed Dean around the barn as he made his rounds and asked him to check the rot she'd found on Billy-Goat-Gruff's hooves. Gruff was Mollie's male breeding goat, father to the majority of the kids born at Hilltop Farm and thus one of her most valuable – and most frustrating – goats. Like many of the British Toggenburg breed, Gruff was rich brown with white markings and mischievous to the core. When he was a kid, Mollie had to bribe him with raisins in order to get near him. One of Mollie's best milking nannies, Primrose, had refused for the last two years to allow Gruff to come near her. Two years ago, when Mollie first paid a neighbour for a breeding with their buck, Prim had rewarded Mollie with triplets.

'I wouldn't give you the satisfaction, mate,' Dean said, expertly stepping around the muscular goat to avoid receiving one of

Gruff's famous head butts. Mollie held Gruff's collar and tried to distract by lightly scrubbing his chest with her fingers. Dean checked Gruff over and looked at each foot.

'He'll be fine,' Dean said. 'No temperature. His feet do look particularly soft because of all the rain, but nothing worrying. I was able to pull some off with my fingers and his hoof looks good beneath.'

'Okay. Thanks for checking him.'

They left Gruff's pen, as the billy showed off by snorting and trotting around.

'Well, that's me off home for my tea, then,' Dean said dusting his hands on his jeans. 'Had an early start at 3:45 this morning.'

'Really?' Mollie said, walking to his truck with him. It was the same tan-coloured van she'd known for over ten years now; it had been brand-new the spring her father had passed away. Dean walked to the back of the van, where he kept various vet supplies under lock and key. He opened this now and stowed his bag away.

'Yes, I was over at Aquarius Farm. The show jumpers, you know.' Dean wasn't one to gossip, even with someone that he'd known as many years as Mollie, but he gave his funny 'la-tee-da' look and they shared a laugh. 'Those people up there certainly do seem self-important. I'm glad they've usually got Kevin Sowder at hand. It was a false alarm and that's all I should say. You must be the right age to have gone to school with Miss Courtney, eh?'

'Oh, yes,' Mollie answered. 'She was on her high horse even then, though she was still riding ponies.'

Dean laughed and walked to the front of his truck. 'Call me if you need anything, all right?'

'I shall. Thank you.'

Mollie waved as Dean left the farm. As his vehicle went out of sight, she chided herself for having forgotten to ask after his new grandchild. Perhaps Jen was right. She thought too much about goats.

CHAPTER 3

*H*er sisters were away from the farm. Mollie enjoyed being alone with her mum, so she sped into the house intending to take a leisurely lunch with her. She toed off her boots in the boot room and came through to the large farmhouse kitchen. Lisa Purslow was standing at the cream-coloured Aga, ladling soup into a bowl.

'I reckoned you'd be in as soon as Dean left,' she said to Mollie with a smile. 'Tomato soup with toasted cheese, your favourite.'

'As long as the cheese is mine, you're right.'

They gathered the dishes and took their meals to the table where Lisa had laid out plaid mats and matching napkins.

'Smells divine, Mum. Thanks.'

'You're most welcome, love. Even with the sun shining, it's chilly enough to appreciate soup today.'

Indeed, the April sunshine was pouring in the many windows above the sink and gleaming off the white-painted fitted kitchen cupboards. A trio of ceramic pots in bright hues lined the windows, planted with primulas. The golden wood floor was scattered with colourful rag rugs and Gus, a black and white cat, dozed on the padded bench along the wall, opposite the chairs occupied by Mollie and her mother.

Beyond the kitchen was a large room, with a generously proportioned brick fireplace. The room was filled with much used comfortable furniture, a television, a low table stacked with books and magazines. A half-folded blue and green woollen throw, used to ward the chill from Lisa's feet while she knitted in the evenings, was laid over the back of the sofa. Several water-colours hung on the walls, mostly featuring flowers. In a large carved frame was a photograph of three pretty girls. Mollie was the image of their father, tall with shiny dark hair. Mollie was shown flanked by her younger sisters, Willa and Phoebe, both of them with the same pale blonde hair, average height and slight build as their mother. There was a bookcase, lamps and a large armoire set at an angle in one corner, which housed family items such as photo albums, the children's saved papers and drawings from school, board games, unfinished art projects, puzzles and some baskets of miscellaneous things no one had ever got round to clearing away.

Mollie abandoned her spoon and drank the last little bit of soup from her bowl.

'Mollie, do try to slow down. The food's not going anywhere.'

'Sorry. You're quite right. I always feel I have to get on. It was a bit of a challenge to do nothing yesterday.'

'Was it? I've never had that problem on a day out. How was your time with Jenny and Natalie?'

Mollie took a huge bite of sandwich and answered with a full mouth, doing her mother the small courtesy of hiding the lower half of her face behind her napkin. 'Mmm. This cheese is delish. After the salon, we did some window shopping nearby. Had lunch. Ate some ice cream. And then we wanted dinner at Giovanni's. It was warm enough to sit outdoors, which was heaven.' Mollie swallowed. 'It was a fabulous day. Until it wasn't. You won't believe the news.'

'Your hair looks nice. I like seeing you in a fringe again.'

Another bite of sandwich. 'Thanks.'

'It sounds like you had a lovely time. What news?'

'Natalie gave us a proper surprise. She's been keeping a massive secret.'

Lisa stopped spooning soup and pulled a face.

'Not *that* sort of secret, Mum. She doesn't even have a boyfriend.' The last bit of sandwich down, Mollie popped out of her chair to put the kettle on.

'Well, what sort of secret then?' Lisa asked.

'Nat's been taking distance classes online. Her mum interrogated Mrs Hayward about colleges and universities–'

'The vicar's wife knows about colleges?'

'Yes. And the short version is, Nat's moving away next month to attend uni.'

'Really? Wolves?'

'Yes. She wants to be a nurse. Her father is helping with fees and she's sorted out a place to live with two other girls. She begins at school in the autumn, but she's going early to find work.'

'That's wonderful. I imagine Jenny was quite jealous.'

'As always, you can trust Jen to make a mess of it. I've told her before that she mustn't blame other people for her own misery. Anyway, she never listens, so now I don't bother.'

'Do you mean to say that you had a row, or that you gave each other the silent treatment?'

'Mostly the latter. You're quite perceptive, Mum.' Mollie laughed. She took her dishes to the sink.

'Oh, I don't know that I am. I've known Jenny since she was quite small. She and Natalie are more like your cousins than friends.'

'Not any more.' Mollie's misery was apparent.

'Oh, sweetheart. I know it's difficult when we grow up and thus grow apart. But Natalie's always wanted to do things different to her own family.'

'Well, she's getting her wish. My wish would be that she takes Jenny with her.'

They laughed at this. The kettle came to a boil and shut itself off with a click. Mollie dropped two teabags into mugs, covered them with water from the kettle and brought them to the table.

She settled into her chair and asked her mother, 'How are things going at the library?'

Lisa sighed. 'Things don't look good. The village council has now said that we'll close very soon.'

'Oh, Mum! I had no idea it was as bad as that.'

'Well, it is. Our village isn't able to support a library these days. Really, considering how small Marris Mynd is, it's sort of amazing we've had a library all this time and the many years before I came on. It's all down to 'less footfall'. Which simply means less visitors, leastways not enough to keep us open.'

'It's the most beautiful little library.'

'It is. I've loved working there. It's been nearly eighteen years now!'

'Yes, I was a toddler when you began, going to Mrs Hansen's house to be looked after, wasn't I? Isn't there anything that can be done?'

'Not really. I do have meetings to attend, through what remains of April. Make no mistake, the library will close. But there's lots of decisions to be made and we must tidy things up and organise the schedule for the mobile library to make visits to our regular patrons.'

'One of those vans, that take books to people confined to home and such?'

'Yes, exactly. I can't leave some of them entirely without books and other resources. Especially our elderly. They're not coming on with downloading electronic books and all of that. And I've wondered where some of them will go now to socialise.'

'Yes, particularly Mr Anderson and Mrs Crook.' Mollie referred to a pair of elderly people that accidentally crossed paths at the library every Tuesday morning at ten. Their modest courtship had brought smiles to the librarians and their neighbours for years.

'Mr Anderson's just going to have to ask her on a date,' Mollie surmised. They laughed, but the thought of the couple had made Lisa sad. Mollie reached out and took her mother's hand. Lisa used the other to wipe away a stray tear.

'What will you do?' The gravity of Lisa's unemployment dawned on Mollie. What do librarians do when they become redundant? Mollie's family couldn't manage on her earnings, yet. The goats paid for themselves and brought in a bit of extra money, but not enough to adequately support herself, her mum and two younger sisters. Lisa's job had meant economising to make ends meet, but it had been steady and seen them through. And it'd provided good benefits and a local authority pension scheme for her mum's future.

'Don't worry, Mollie. Something always turns up.' Lisa put on a brave smile. 'A change might even be the best thing, mightn't it?'

IT WAS ONLY a minute after Mollie had returned to the barn when Lisa received an annoying phone call. Lisa's insides curdled when she saw the caller's name on the screen. Edward Purslow. Her brother-in-law. She considered not answering, but that was childish. Grant's brother wouldn't have the satisfaction of her avoidance, lest he think he was winning at his little game.

'Hello.' She forced herself to sound casual. Friendly, even.

'Lisa. Edward. But I suppose you already knew,' he sneered.

She pretended otherwise. 'Oh, hello. How are you? How's Mel? Are her daughters visiting this summer?'

'Doing well. Yes. She's out shopping with them now.'

Edward responded with a long-suffering tone. Making small talk, particularly about the welfare of other people, had always bored him. He was alone in the house and Lisa guessed he'd taken some days off work, technically to 'see the girls', but he wouldn't have spent much time with them.

'And how are things at Hilltop Farm? Still unprosperous?'

'Edward–'

'Look, Lisa. Let's come straight to the point. We've been through this in years past, but I should think with Willa's university tuition coming round that you'd be a bit more logical. And it won't be long until young Phoebe will follow.'

She didn't want to correct him. Telling Edward that Willa had no plans to go to university would simply give him more leverage in his attempt to shame her.

'It's simple, Lisa, even you can follow along. Allow me to pay you a small fortune for my brother's farm. You and the girls can find somewhere closer to shops and cafes and have bags of cash to spare. Where's the difficulty?'

'As I've said before, Edward–'

'My brother paid for it, so it should've come back to me. He would never have obtained the farm in the first place without Father's co-signature. I'm Father's heir, therefore–'

Undaunted, interrupted, speaking over him. '...The farm is our family home. Grant's life insurance paid it off. I'm raising three daughters by myself with no substantial cash inheritance from your late father, or my late husband. Enough to pay taxes and carry on, that's all. I'll never understand why you think the farm ought to have come to you!'

Edward assumed a more conciliatory approach. 'Alright, calm down. Let's forget the past, shall we? The thing is, I'd like very much to have a country property. In fact, my eldest step-daughter is carrying her first child. London's wonderful, but we'd like to offer the girls and their families a place in the country. A retreat, if you will.'

'And there are hundreds of country homes on the market, Edward. With locations much closer to London. Why this one?

Why does it vex you so very much that we're here? I've never understood.'

'Well, because Grant chose that farm and I've little else left of my brother. You'll agree it has lovely views.'

She sighed, exhausted by this row that had been carrying on for years. For a mad moment, Lisa thought it mightn't be the worst thing. She could demand a very dear price from her brother-in-law. Then she remembered Mollie.

'Mollie is doing a lovely business with her goat's cheeses. She'd be heartbroken to have to sell them.'

Edward cleared his throat. Lisa was suddenly aware of his excitement. She realised that this was the first time she'd shown any weakness and he was instantly aware he'd made progress. Perhaps he had; Lisa wasn't sure at the moment. Maybe having lost her job was clouding her judgement.

Edward's voice took a persuasive edge. It reminded Lisa of his late father, Arthur, who'd always sold more jewellery than most of his competition combined. Edward was quite the salesman, too, in the City.

'Yes, Mollie is an enterprising young woman.' His voice was warm, doting. Lisa knew that Edward probably couldn't name Mollie's age, her chosen subjects at school, or the names of the friends she'd had since childhood. Edward and Mollie were virtual strangers.

Edward pressed on. 'I've given a lot of thought to our Mollie. About what would work best for her. And I think I've got a cracking idea.'

His voice was benevolent, as though he were Father Christmas, hand-crafting precisely the right gift for Mollie, who'd been a very good girl. It was all a bit nauseating, but Lisa couldn't help being intrigued. 'All right, Edward,' she said. 'I'll bite. What's your idea?'

'Mollie should be allowed to stay on. We would only be able to enjoy the farm on holidays, at weekends. Someone needs to be there to keep the house occupied. In fact, we'd be in her debt for managing the place on-site. My budget would run to providing a salary for her. And of course, the property could finally be looked after in the way my brother would've wanted, with help you haven't been able to afford, such as a gardener and a man to maintain the farm as a whole. I'm sure Mollie's done well looking after the barn and the few pastures nearest the house where her goats graze, but my brother purchased over, what was it? Twenty acres? Thirty?'

'Forty-two.'

'Right. As *you* said, quite a lot for a single mum to maintain.'

Lisa hadn't said that, had she? 'That's kind of you to think of how you could secure Mollie's future, Edward. But she doesn't need your help, as she already lives here and we really don't need a gardener.'

Edward was careful not to ruin the tiny bit of headway he felt he'd made. He took great effort to hide his indignation, but Lisa noted how quickly he ended the conversation after she'd effectively said 'no'. Again.

They rang off. She sat there for a moment, bobbing between feelings of triumph at standing up to him and confusion in wondering if she wasn't foolish for not taking him up on his offer.

She'd been shaken during this round of their endless negotiations. Edward wouldn't probably ring again for a while and she'd only be forced to actually see him this winter at her mother-in-law's house, where he never broached the topic. Lisa hadn't been facing unemployment in all the years Edward had been harassing her to give up the farm to him. Perhaps she ought to give his proposal a thought. On the other hand, she didn't believe for a moment that Edward would pay Mollie or any member of the family to live here as they had been doing. Selling off the goats on some feeble excuse would definitely be Edward's first move and that would simply crush Mollie. But perhaps Lisa's inability to put food on the table would be worse. At the moment, Lisa couldn't imagine what sort of other work she may be able to get when the library finally closed its doors.

She sighed and let her worries go. That had always been her way and so far life had worked itself out. She wondered what had come in the post earlier that morning and decided to go have a look.

Willa Purslow and her younger sister, Phoebe, arrived home from school ravenously hungry.

'If you're thinking of being a chef, why can't you feed me something? There's *never* anything to eat in this house.' Thirteen-year-old Phoebe stood with her hands on her hips and waited for her older sister's response.

'All right,' Willa conceded. 'Actually, I'd like to try a couronne. Remember? The fruited, twisted bread from the baking show on telly last night.'

Phoebe wasn't pleased. 'I don't like fruitcake. That looked disgusting. Why not something brilliantly normal, like a loaf of good bread?'

She sighed. Her younger sister made quite a career of being a demanding little Miss, clearly because she needed attention and reassurance. Willa patiently explained. 'Because, Phebs, with the time added on for proofing the loaf it'd be a few hours and naturally you'll have died of starvation by then. How about I do something simple. Scones?'

'Perfect.' Phoebe was already tapping on her phone and drifting upstairs to her room, her hunger temporarily forgotten.

Willa gathered everything needed for scones. Flour, baking powder, butter, sugar, eggs, milk. She took her favourite mixing bowl, a heavy white ironstone with a blue stripe circling the top edge, from the bottom shelf of the dresser. Measuring the dry ingredients, rubbing in the butter, beating the eggs in a measuring jug – it was like a meditation. Peace settled over her and the familiar noises of the house were companionable; the hum of the refrigerator, birds singing outside, the sound of Phoebe's music playing upstairs. It was amusing that Phoebe's tastes were as yet undeveloped; she couldn't grasp Willa's adult tendencies to experiment with challenging recipes which produced complex flavours. But Willa wouldn't hold it against her. Phoebe was growing up so quickly that it was staggering.

She'd just brushed the tops of the scones with egg and put them in the Aga when Willa heard her older sister coming into the boot room; the door slamming behind her.

Mollie appeared in the kitchen a moment later. The air fairly crackled with her agitation. 'I thought you said you'd help me in the goat shed?'

'I will. Phoebe was hungry and I was in the mood for a bit of quick baking–'

'Willa, there's no excuse. Phoebe's perpetually hungry anyway. I can't believe you're in here messing about when we have a dairy to run. Real work, remember?'

Mollie's dark eyes were intense. Willa tried to recall if their father had been this way. Mum had said often enough that Mollie was like him, but Willa couldn't summon many details. There was a shadowy memory of a tall man, the sensation and thrill of his swinging her above his head and making her laugh. A deep, masculine voice reading to her. Nothing more. She was jealous that Mollie remembered. Willa had been only four when he died and she'd asked her mum – now and then, over the years – to tell her again about their father. Her mother related the basics, beginning with, 'Your father and I met at university. I was only eighteen and we fell in love straightaway. Daddy was a bit older and reading physics. As you know, Granny and Grandpa raised your father in the city, but he had a strong interest in agriculture from early on. He'd spent his gap year on a farm in Scotland.'

Willa tried to imagine her father, Grant, not as he was in old photographs, but as a living person, moving about, laughing and talking, but it was nearly impossible.

'We married young. Your father got his degree in engineering and worked for a while. We had Mollie and later I finished my librarianship qualification. We saved as much money as possible and with your grandfather's help, bought our own small holding, here at Hilltop. Mollie was three by then.'

Willa remembered being shy of asking her mother what had happened *later*. When at last Willa decided that she must know, but simply couldn't ask Mum, she got the inspired idea of asking Granny. It'd never occurred to Willa that her question may give Granny pain; Willa hadn't quite figured out at that young age that Grant was Granny's oldest boy. He was simply their father and Granny was simply their granny.

But her grandmother wasn't angry or tearful when Willa asked the first time, nor the dozens of times over the years. Granny pulled Willa up into her lap and hugged her as she sketched the details as best she could.

'It had rained and rained that April,' Granny began. 'Your father had taken out the tractor for some reason and gone out in the steep fields behind the house. Hours later he hadn't returned.'

Willa looked at her grandmother, but she didn't continue.

Willa prompted. 'Why not?'

'Because Grant, because Daddy, had a terrible accident, love. Later that morning, Daddy's friend came by to look after Daddy's sick cow. You know the veterinarian, Mr Scott?'

Willa nodded. Granny meant Dean, whom she'd never called Mr Scott in her life.

'He and Daddy were great friends you see. Mr Scott found

your father beneath his tractor. Somehow it had turned over and Daddy was stuck beneath it, in a stream of water. He'd drowned, sweetheart.' Granny kissed the top of her head. Willa nestled close to her. By that time, Grandpa had died, too, because Granny said his heart had broken. She'd explained a heart attack in words that Willa could understand.

Willa set the timer for her baking scones and turned back to her sister. Mollie would surely resemble Granny, as Granny had looked when she was young, because their father was the very image of his mother and Mollie like them both. It was obvious that Granny had also been wilful, irascible and keen on getting her own way. Granny Phoebe had certainly mellowed, but there were suggestions in her grandmother's temperament that put Willa in mind of her sister. But Mollie's love of the farm and of animals was, without question, inherited from their father. That was the other thing Mum had always said: Mollie adored Daddy. Followed him everywhere. Was the son he never had. It was no wonder why Granny got a strange look on her face sometimes when Mollie came flying in from the barn. Often, Mollie was even dressed as her father had been. Literally.

Willa remembered their mother's exasperation. 'Mollie, you're already three inches taller than me,' she'd said, as though it were Mollie's fault. In an effort to keep the fast-growing teenager in trousers to wear around the farm when she wasn't in school uniform, Lisa had gone through an old cupboard in the attic, bringing down with her some old things from Grant's college days. Mollie put them on and loved them. They were warm, she said and gave her room to move around. And there were no worries about ruining them, because they were her father's old castoffs anyway. Only Mollie had never given them up.

Willa wasn't sure if Mollie's resemblance had left she and Phoebe outside of Granny's deepest affections, but there was nothing that could be done about it. It certainly seemed, sometimes, that Granny favoured Mollie. Willa could be quite wrong though and wouldn't want to think uncharitably about their grandmother. She'd been very generous to all of them.

'Why are you looking at me that way?'

Willa sighed. 'I know you're saving for new labels for your cheeses, Mollie, but don't you sometimes want new clothes?'

'Not really. And I'll be wearing my other things soon enough, when it becomes too warm for these.' Her annoyed look meant she was done wasting time talking. In a few long strides Mollie was back in the boot room slipping on her wellies. 'Bring me a scone when you come,' she called out as the door shut behind her.

Then Willa heard the door open again. 'Willa?' She turned as Mollie's face appeared around the corner.

'Hmm?'

'Could you help me with something?'

What could she possibly need now? She was already Mollie's milkmaid every morning. Tender-hearted and curious, Willa answered, 'I suppose.'

'It's just that, you're brilliant in the kitchen, you know. I wondered if you could help me make Rhys's favourite pudding? He loves cheesecake and I thought with your help, I could give it a go.'

What a surprise.

Mollie smiled. 'Maybe it would be fun?'

Her sister could be annoying, but Willa loved an excuse to bake and a cheesecake was something different.

'Yes. We'll make the best he's ever eaten.'

They grinned at one another and Mollie left again.

Willa stood by the cooker, leaning against the cabinet, waiting for her trusty tomato-shaped timer to buzz. She thought of how Phoebe was also like their granny, in her tastes. Phoebe thrived on visiting grand houses, like the one granny lived in; she loved the vibrant shops, going to the theatre, buying clothes. Willa knew that young people have the capacity to change a great deal, but she didn't think her younger sister probably would. As soon as

Phoebe was able, she'd leave them for what she always referred to as 'civilisation'.

Only two more minutes. Willa put the kettle on, knowing Mollie would also want a thermos of tea alongside her scone.

Her thoughts turned again to how like Granny her sisters were. She could clearly see her sisters for who they were and could imagine how they'd be in the future. But she didn't seem to have a clue as to the person she herself would become.

The timer buzzed and she opened the oven door to the fragrance of hot scones.

Her boyfriend had shown up unannounced, wanting to go on a leisurely walk.

'I'm heating milk right now, Rhys,' Mollie mumbled. She stood over a large, scrupulously clean double-boiler. 'You know I can't leave it. Give me ten minutes?'

Rhys's jaw tensed. He glanced at his shoes and hooked his hands over his hips. 'Take all the time you need, Mollie. Take all day. I'm sure I don't care.'

She'd never seen Rhys act so childishly. What on earth was wrong with the man? For now, she'd have to forget him and get on with the task at hand. She checked the industrial-use metal thermometer that hugged the side of the bain-marie.

Mollie patiently warmed the goats' milk through. She stirred it gently, using a large metal spoon with an exacting lapping motion that Phoebe called 'dog drinking', whilst the temperature rose very slowly to thirty, or, easier to see on her slightly scratched dial thermometer, eighty-six degrees Fahrenheit. Stirring was one of the few slower activities she ordinarily enjoyed. But not since Rhys had burst into the dairy, wanting her to drop everything.

The goats' milk was sufficiently warm. Mollie added her special blend of cultures. Through years of trial and error, she'd found that the powder rennet used by loads of cheesemakers did well enough, but it could also make the cheese a bit like a jelly. Her secret was combining teaspoons of dry mesophilic culture with the tiniest drop or two of liquid rennet for firming the milk into a perfect curd. The culture would roar into life and nibble away on the milk sugar, turning it into lovely lactic acid. The acid would react with the rennet and coagulate the milk solids. In about twelve hours, she'd rival Little Miss Muffet with a luscious amount of curds and whey. The whole process made Mollie feel like the coolest sort of mad scientist.

She was able to step away now, but she tidied up the area first and then went to find Rhys. He was leaning against his pickup truck, which had bits of hay stuck to the side where he'd been moving bales and feeding cows. His father's dairy farm outside of Marris Mynd was one of the largest in the county and the Davies owned a part of another large farm further south, so work was carried out over miles, keeping Rhys on the move.

Rhys didn't acknowledge her approach. He stood looking toward the Long Mynd, lost in his thoughts. Her man was tall, dark and one of the most fit she'd ever seen. Mollie smiled at him. She reached up and rubbed his muscular shoulders. 'I'm glad you've popped round. I was thinking about you this morning. Willa baked that blueberry bread that you like.'

'She gave me a slice.'

'And that put you in a better mood, did it?' Mollie laughed and kissed him. He seemed out of sorts.

'How's the cheese making going?'

'The milk yields are still high, so I'm working long hours to keep caught up.'

'Anything you want to ask me?' Rhys said quietly, looking at his work boots.

'I can't think of anything. Why?' Mollie laughed.

'I didn't think so.' His voice was tetchy.

It wasn't like Rhys to be so prickly. And now he was opening the door to his vehicle, obviously intent upon driving away. Mollie laid a hand on his arm.

'Rhys? Have I said something wrong? I thought you wanted to go on a walk.'

He smirked and slightly shook his head, as though he ought to have known better. 'I've changed my mind about the walk, Mollie. Too much to do this evening.' He trained his eyes on her and added, "I work too, you know.' He shook her hand free, got in the truck and turned the ignition.

Mollie was speechless. She'd always been proud of what a hard worker Rhys was, so it was odd that he seemed intent on reminding her. He backed the vehicle abruptly, then lurched forward and down the drive. She called out goodbye, but he hadn't heard.

CHAPTER 5

*L*isa Purslow hoped she wouldn't be late for her appointment. After years of chiding her daughters to be punctual, she was cutting it fine. She'd been a bit distracted of late with the library's closing and her never-changing schedule had become an ever-changing schedule, with no two days the same.

She sighed with pleasure as she drove through a tree tunnel of white blossoms. Another beautiful spring day. Warm, sweetly-scented breezes engulfed her through the windows. It'd been a long while since she'd driven this direction on the A49 through south Shropshire, toward the Welsh Marches, the border threading between England and Wales. Her destination was Bucknell about ten-minutes shy of the medieval Welsh town of Knighton. Lisa remembered it as a charming village, with sheep grazing to the north-west, a river that meandered close by and possession of the essential three-P's – a pub, post office and a place of worship. Hearing the name again had brought a smile to her face. When Mollie was quite small, she'd learnt that Bucknell meant 'he-goats' hill', in Old English, so she'd wanted Grant and Lisa to up sticks and move there.

The lovely surroundings aside, Lisa thought the obscure village was an unusual place to meet with Mr Ferrington. Mr Ferrington was recommended by Councilman Andrews as 'a solicitor with a lot of sense', from whom she should seek out advice. This seemed a good idea. Perhaps someone from a different walk of life might have fresh ideas for saving the library, or at least helping the remaining programmes provide the most benefit.

Expecting a stuffy, dark little place smelling of ale, Lisa was pleasantly surprised when she swung into the car park of the Lord Marcher's Tavern. There were several dining rooms. She enquired and was shown to a table in the conservatory, a lovely sun-drenched room with a double height ceiling. A gentleman with tanned skin, clear blue eyes and prematurely grey hair was on his feet in an instant, making her welcome.

'Lisa Purslow, how do you do?'

'Michael Ferrington. Please, do make yourself comfortable. Would you like a drink?'

'No, just a peep at the menu, thank you,' Lisa directed both these comments to Mr Ferrington and the woman from the bar who'd helped them meet up.

Lisa picked up the menu. The only problem was, she'd forgotten what food she liked. The man was utterly gorgeous and she was having a time of it trying not to laugh at her good fortune. Ridiculously, the longer she pretended to read the menu, the more giggly she felt and her expression probably gave hints. What must he think?

Lisa ventured a glance and found that he was looking at his phone. Relief helped her relax. He was so courteous. Or, perhaps he wasn't. Maybe he was one of those people who couldn't stay off their phone. At any rate, he looked incredibly fit for his age. His light blue eyes were amazing against his deep blue shirt.

Then he was looking at her. And talking.

'...Or perhaps you don't care for driving? I wouldn't have

minded driving in your direction, but I have several appointments further south today and the rest of the week I'll be away.'

'Oh, no, not at all,' Lisa stammered, catching the general drift of his comments. 'I enjoyed the drive, the weather's so beautiful.'

A waitress came into the conservatory dining room for their order. Whatever Lisa had decided upon had flown her mind. She picked up the menu again and ordered the first item that came to her eye. 'Cheddar and pickle sandwich please, with coffee.'

Mr Ferrington ordered, and nodded away the waitress and turned to look at her.

'I am really not sure why I've come,' Lisa began, laughing self-consciously.

'Oh?' His brows raised but his smile was warm and relaxed. She'd look for a wedding band, but it would be too obvious at the moment.

'I meant to say, Councilman Andrews said he knew you, but he really didn't advise me on an agenda. I think he was a little confused about what's happening with the library. You see, our library in Marris Mynd is closing. I am afraid we've tried everything. A new digital infrastructure, coordinating our hours with community transport, fundraising and even co-location with an artist gallery and parish council offices. I apologise,' Lisa said, taking the moment to flick her eyes down. No wedding ring. 'I'm running on a bit. You've probably been told all of this already. Obviously, I would be open to your advice. But I think, now, it's really a matter of providing mobile library services... tackling rural isolation, as it were.'

'Yes, *rural isolation* can be a problem, can't it?' His tone was conspiratorial.

Lisa felt flushed.

He glanced at her. 'I am sorry that Tom Andrews didn't better explain, but I suppose he had his reasons. You see, Mrs Purslow–'

'Lisa, please.'

'Michael, please.' He leaned forward. 'You're here on business of a more personal nature.'

Lisa's mouth flew open in surprise and they laughed.

Just then, the waitress brought their food. She placed Lisa's rather off-putting plate in front of her – there was nothing wrong with it, but Lisa hadn't eaten pickle since she was a teenager and hadn't wanted any since.

She smiled at him. *Michael Ferrington.* Rather a sophisticated name. She turned it over in her mind. It suited him terribly well.

They each took an obligatory bite, enjoying the tension of this luncheon that had taken on the vibe of a sexy cat and mouse game.

'Mmm. They do a lovely curry,' Michael said. 'How's yours?'

'Unappetizing.'

'Order something else.'

'It's not their fault that I've only just remembered how much I dislike pickle.'

Their eyes lingered on one another.

Michael came clean on their reason for meeting. 'It so happens that Councilman Andrews is married to my cousin, Sally.'

'Is that so? Sally's lovely. I don't often see her. She keeps terribly busy with their sporty boys and their pharmacy shop.'

'Yes, she does. We're cousins on my mother's side. Sal's not too overwhelmed to be a busybody, though, and she's told me she's concerned about you. "Nothing for her in Marris Mynd" she said, "But you'll think of something suitable, Michael". She's labouring under the impression that I know everyone.'

'That's really lovely of Sally. And, I admit, I've been a bit concerned. The idea of re-entering the job market is intimidating. And Sally's quite right, there isn't a lot of opportunity around our village, short of helping my eldest daughter with her career choice.'

The waitress came again and gave Lisa a quizzical look. 'Are you finished, madam?'

'Yes, thank you.'

'May I have a slice of lemon tart and a rhubarb meringue pie, please.'

'Of course,' the waitress said, setting off with a bemused look.

'I hope you don't mind. I can't very well send you back to Marris Mynd having had two bites of a sandwich. Whichever dessert most appeals is yours, I like them all.'

Another gorgeous smile. Lisa fluttered inside and tried to ignore it, but she couldn't wipe the smile from her lips.

'Do you play golf?'

He laughed. 'What?'

'You have the look of a golfer. A bit of sun on your face, a sense of fashion.'

'As it happens, I do. And when you're not closing down village libraries, do you get out on the green?'

'Heavens no. Clubhouse windows would go crashing.'

Their desserts arrived and Lisa took the rhubarb pie. They'd added vanilla ice cream, which she hadn't eaten since last summer. It had sounded delicious since Mollie had mentioned having some and she couldn't have been happier with Michael ordering it for her in his confident way. It was lovely to have a man look after her, even if it was only puddings-on-a-whim.

'What else do you do, when you're not golfing?' Lisa asked, taking a sip of coffee.

'Well, a number of things, really. I consult for companies. I help develop business plans, sort out problems with finances, help clients approach the right people when it's time to construct a new building or refurbish one. Even staffing issues, networking mostly, which is where Sally thinks I could be of benefit to you.'

'Could you benefit me?' Her cheeks burned. She felt as though she were asking for something indecent.

'I believe so,' he said, lustily polishing off the last bite of his lemon tart. 'My friend, Sam Lloyd, may need someone with your qualifications. Although you may find it rather boring, I don't know.'

'Libraries are generally perceived as boring, but I don't find them so. Please, tell me more.' She had sounded so smooth and self-assured. It was shocking as she felt silly and flustered.

'Alright. Sam Lloyd is a professor and author of text books. He needs a support person to help him properly cite research, organise computer documents and take over some of the admin duties. Some of these things have been handled in the past by students and they've not been up to standard. He's willing to pay a good wage as he hopes to release two textbooks on biology and chemistry topics in the next twelve months. Other professors review the science bits, so no worries there.'

'Sounds challenging. But it also sounds like something I'd enjoy.'

'One bonus may be that you can trade files from home, if you have access to a reliable computer and connection? I know Sam has done that before with students.'

'That would be lovely. I've enjoyed a short commute to the village for so many years that I was sort of dreading the possibility of a long one.'

'So, it would be all right to give Sam your contact information?'

'Yes, of course.' Lisa opened her bag and wrote down the information on an envelope.

'And may I have your number?' he asked. 'For my personal use?'

'Certainly.'

DURING THE DRIVE HOME, Lisa recalled every entrancing detail of the meeting. Her stomach squeezed with an odd sort of guilt feeling. She already knew she'd keep this luncheon a secret from her daughters. She'd actually been a bit *flirty*. It had been a very long time since she'd felt so feminine, so alive.

The romantic part of her life had died along with Grant. She'd now carried on over a decade as a grieving widow, single mum and an underpaid librarian in a village that didn't use its library.

She could reflect on this with more strength now, because she felt a jubilant distance from the life she'd been living. Not only had she the hope of securing a new job with Michael's friend, but a single afternoon with this intelligent, charming, handsome man had somehow reenergised her life. She smiled and chuckled a bit. The very odd thing was, she didn't even mind whether or not Michael Ferrington rang and asked her for a date. Certainly it would be lovely if he did – but, this inward transformation she felt wasn't really about him, he'd just been a catalyst. The unexpected experience of meeting him had thrown a switch somewhere deep inside her. She'd come to a sudden decision that things would be different. Not only might this be a start at a new career, but, as a woman, she would no longer be satisfied with simply being a mum. She wanted more. As of an hour ago.

Lisa laughed at herself, and gloried in the wind whistling through her hair as she drove back to her new life at Hilltop Farm.

CHAPTER 6

Newly-born Princess ambled after Mollie in the goat pen. Mollie finished feeding and watering, then turned to give little Princess a cuddle. Princess wagged her tail and bleated with delight. 'What a sweet little goatie you are!' Mollie kissed the goat's face. Princess licked a piece of hay from Mollie's hair and attempted to chew it. 'Aww, look at you, Princess! You're munching!'

It was in this happy state of baby-goat-love that Mollie's boyfriend found her.

Rhys came to the fence and gave Princess a rub behind her ears. 'Who's this, then?'

'The Princess of Hilltop Farm.'

'You'll not want to be tellin' our Phoebe that she has competition.'

'My sister wouldn't care for the title, since our farm is not part of the civilised world.'

'Ready?' Rhys, shaking his leg impatiently.

'You're awfully keen today. Just give me a minute. I have to feed the dog and then we can be off.' Mollie came from the goat pen and walked towards the house, with Rhys taking up Princess's place at her heels. The border collie stretched out on the wide porch by the front door had belonged to Mollie's father. Grant had named him Tarrant, Welsh for thunder, and he'd lived up to his name by greeting strangers with a booming bark. He was a smart dog, though, and remembered the visitors he'd met and approved. He greeted Mollie and Rhys by standing up and said hello with a sweeping tail and a big grin. Mollie disappeared into the house while Rhys sank down on the steps to stroke the dog's blue merle coat, a striking blend of white and grey, with random blotches of black. The dog focused his light grey eyes on Rhys and slumped against him. A moment later, Tarrant slipped from Rhys's side and lay on his back, inviting Rhys to rub his tummy.

Mollie reappeared and emptied a scoop of dog food into Tarrant's dish, which he acknowledged with a slight roll of his head, not wanting to disturb Rhys's pampering. She then went back into the house, came out with a fresh dish of water for Tarrant and a picnic hamper in the other hand.

Rhys gently dumped Tarrant onto the porch and began sweeping away dog hairs. 'I can't believe you've actually cooked me a picnic.'

'I didn't. We're stopping at the pub to fill it up. But I did ring Jake with a take-away order and I have fresh scones. And a surprise for pudding.'

'Willa's been baking.'

'Of course. You ought to be chuffed there're any left. Phoebe attacked the scones and ate three. I hid these before she came down this morning.'

They settled into his grey Nissan pickup truck. He drove down the short track to the road and turned right. The road wound this way and that, in curves that Mollie could negotiate with her eyes closed, so many times had she ridden her bike or driven this way toward Marris Mynd. She looked out the window and appreciated the beautiful spring. In the week since she'd enjoyed a day away with her friends, the earth had fairly erupted in flowers. They passed gardens bursting with pink and purple trees, creamy magnolias and stands of tulips in orange, yellow and red. Rounding another bend, hedgerows blocked the view, enveloped in fresh green with white flowers gathered at their brambly feet. Mollie saw a pasture dotted with sheep, several little lambs frolicked with their mums and far beyond lay a woodland with a carpet of bluebells so thick and bright as to be seen half-a-mile away.

Coming into the village, Rhys drove past the vicarage, where a green-leafed climbing rose adorned the doorframe, soon to be covered with a huge spray of pink roses. Mollie saw some late daffodils clinging along the protective wall of the Holy Trinity church, where cherry trees cloaked in white-pink bouquets stood on either side of the wide double-door. Opposite the church was the library where her mum had worked. It was a lovely old chocolate-box Tudor building with a massive stone fountain in the garden alongside. She'd often played on it and stolen a coin or two, while waiting for her mother to finish work.

Mollie sighed in contentment.

Rhys usually admired the views with her but today he sneered. 'You don't get out much, do you?'

'No, but I am grateful when I do.'

'How's your mum?'

'She's fine. She's better than fine, actually. I thought she'd be rather devastated when the library closed, but she seems to have needed the change. In fact, some professor called Sam-something has already offered her a position helping him with textbooks.'

'Really? That's wonderful.'

'It is. I'm rather impressed at her snapping up another job so quickly. And, if I'm honest, relieved that my goats aren't responsible for all of the bills. Someday, but not yet.'

Rhys retrieved their take-away steak and ale pies from Jake at the pub and five minutes later they'd left the vehicle parked in a lay-by. Mollie chose a level spot to unfurl an old plaid rug on the grass. The sun's warmth was surprisingly toasty and Mollie pulled off her dad's old cardie and rolled up the sleeves of a shabby long-sleeved T-shirt. The view was amazing, even given Mollie's familiarity, or perhaps that rendered it even more beautiful. The Shropshire hills rose sharply in the distance, mossy coloured and daubed with dried-up purple heathers along the crowns, with swaths of emerald grass running steeply down into fields sprinkled with bright wildflowers.

'Not only is it warm, we've hours of daylight left, now.'

Rhys didn't answer. He settled down on the rug and opened a beer. Mollie handed him a fork and he tucked into his pie.

'Hungry?'

'Mmm.'

Mollie was as well. They ate without talking, two hard-working farmers with hearty appetites. Rhys finished first and opened the hamper looking for scones.

'What's this, then?' He was pleased. 'You made this for me, did you?'

Mollie grinned from ear to ear. 'Last night, with loads of help from Willa, yes. Because it's your favourite.' Although it was cracked a bit across the top, Willa had said the cheesecake was an excellent first effort. 'It's been so hard not to taste it! I am beyond proud of myself.'

'As you should be,' Rhys said, sticking a fork right in, not waiting for a piece to be cut and served on one of the blue enamelware picnic plates Mollie'd brought along. 'That's very good, that is! I could eat it till I'm sick.'

Rhys's hard-won compliment was terribly gratifying. They finished and then put the hamper aside. Mollie unfolded her long legs and began to crawl over to sit close to Rhys.

But he straightened his arm, catching her shoulder. 'No, Mollie. I need to talk to you.'

She was worried by the note of seriousness in his normally-buoyant voice.

'I've been in love with you for a long time, you know, Mollie.'

Her heart flip-flopped. *He couldn't wait till Christmas to propose!* She wondered where he'd secreted her engagement ring. And she wondered how long he'd planned this moment and she was chuffed she'd added something special by making his favourite pudding. Her mind flew ahead and she imagined telling Jenny and wouldn't even mind when Jenny couldn't be happy for her. On second thought, she'd better tell her mum, first.

Mollie's hands flew to her face at the thought of showing Mum her ring and she giggled into her palms.

The stern look Rhys gave her squelched her laughter. He wasn't wearing the expression of a man about to propose. *Something was wrong.* Her hands stayed where they were on her face, helping to protect her from whatever Rhys was about to say.

'But the truth is, you've not loved me the same way.'

Mollie's hands dropped to her lap. She was too shocked to protest. Rhys took advantage by rushing on.

'I know, you're fond of me. You like the idea of having a boyfriend and all of that. More's the pity, Mollie, but you have more passion for making cheese and keeping goats.' He looked up and levelled his eyes with hers. 'You know it's true.'

'But Rhys, it's just that we've not been able to get serious, financial circumstances being what they are. Now that I know you're keen–'

'That's not the way it works, love. You've known all along I was head over arse for you. I can see that you just don't feel the same way.' His accent was getting stronger, his voice a husky tone that Mollie didn't recognise. He flung a hand in her direction, dismissing her. 'It's not worked out, look you. I've no intention of rowing about it.'

Mollie felt hot tears fill her eyes. She pleaded. 'I've never had a boyfriend, not a real one, Rhys. Until you. I suppose I've, I don't know, not been paying attention. Please, give me another go. I do fancy you like nobody else, I do love you, Rhys, I swear it. I can't believe you're accusing me of not having feelings–'

'Too late for all that, isn't it?'

Mollie smeared tears away with the sleeve of her old T-shirt. 'What? No, of course it's not, I–'

'I've met someone else.' Rhys looked away, studying the horizon.

Mollie drew her knees up to her chest and began to rock back and forth. Rhys can't have just broken up with her. He'd always been so kind. He'd treated her the way her dad would've wanted a boyfriend to treat her. Mollie studied his profile. His was the face she'd never tire of seeing. They'd talked about their future, they'd wanted to farm together. His parents seemed to adore her, as much as her own mum thought so highly of Rhys. Maybe she hadn't been focused like a laser on him, but she loved him as much as she'd felt capable of loving anyone while still cultivating her dreams.

'Please. Don't let's do this, Rhys.' She released her knees and reached out for him. He allowed her to grip one of his forearms with her hands.

She couldn't keep her voice from quavering. 'No one else is right for you but me.'

'I beg to differ.'

He'd said it so coldly that it was hard to recognise this man as her Rhys.

Mollie lashed out. 'You made a date with me for this evening, we've been together an hour. You did that because you wanted to spend time with me. Why not just say what you thought you needed to say in the goat shed and be off?'

'We needed to eat. We needed privacy. And I didn't want to disrespect your goats.'

'Oh, for heaven's sake.'

'No, Mollie I mean it. You know as well as I do they get stressed out and I wasn't having that on my conscience as well.'

Ridiculous, yes. But it was true enough. The goats sometimes didn't give the proper amount of milk if she'd fussed at them. As a fellow farmer, he wouldn't be responsible for causing her a lack of income, especially when her mum hadn't begun her new job.

However kindly his action was meant, it was clear that Rhys had given more consideration to the goats than herself. 'You sat here and ate my picnic.'

'I paid for it, love.'

'But I made you a cheesecake. Do you know how hard that was? It took nearly three hours, Rhys.'

He said nothing. She let go of his arm. She was freezing. He had felt so warm when she'd released him and there'd be no snuggling up to him now. Or ever again.

They silently gathered up the picnic things between them, returned to his vehicle and got in.

Nearly home, she thought. In a few minutes, he would be gone and no longer hers. Hot tears streamed down her face. It occurred to her then, what she needed to ask. Must ask, no matter how upsetting the answer may be.

'Who?'

Rhys shot a look. Then he answered. 'Courtney Williams. Also known as the girl you despise from Aquarius Farm.'

'Why?'

'I am not answering that, Mollie. It's not a game based on points. You have your merits, she has hers. Hers suit me better. She's very keen on me.'

'You can't have any sort of future with her! A wealthy girl who doesn't work. Doesn't even know about her own horses. And doesn't have a thought about anything but doing her hair and putting on make-up. Who can't make a cheesecake.' Mollie laughed bitterly at her joke, sounding like a lunatic. She was trembling. He hadn't turned on the heat in the truck.

'You've no idea what she thinks about, Mollie. You think you know her, but you don't.'

'I suppose I am guilty of thinking I knew you too, Rhys.'

He sighed. 'Yes, I suppose you are, Mollie.'

MOMENTS LATER, she stood in the driveway of Hilltop Farm, watching the tail lights of Rhys's truck disappear down the road.

CHAPTER 7

ollie awoke an hour before dawn the next morning. She closed her eyes against tears as the reality hit her full-stop.

Rhys had dumped her.

She lay there for a few minutes, remembering. She'd come into the house, where her mum, Willa and Phoebe were putting away the shopping.

'It's over.'

They'd exchanged looks, not understanding what Mollie meant. She wasn't able to speak again. There was a tremendous pressure bearing down on the front of her throat. Mollie looked at her mum, willing her to understand.

'Mollie–' her mother began.

In a heartbeat, Willa dropped a box of teabags on the floor, flew across the kitchen and wrapped her arms around Mollie. 'I'm so, so, sorry, Molls.'

Mollie heard her own voice in response, howling like some wild animal. Her body shook within Willa's tight embrace and she sobbed without sound until she sucked in a vast amount of breath and panted against the floods of tears.

There was commotion. She heard Phoebe asking questions of their mum, then heard her little sister verbally abusing Rhys in every way she could think of.

At some point, Mollie finally exhausted herself and Willa pulled away, her hair sticking to Mollie's wet cheek as she came swimming into view. Mollie's head pounded and she cupped her forehead with her hands, trying to make it stop.

'But what could have gone wrong?' Lisa asked, stroking Mollie's back. Mollie shuffled to the table and sat down. Phoebe had taken an adolescent interest in the drama of seeing her eldest sister made completely miserable and sat beside Mollie, scooting her chair very close. Mollie wanted to swat her away, but didn't have the energy.

She'd tried her best to put it in words.

'He said I didn't love him. That he loved me, but I didn't…' She hunched in her chair. Phoebe had put an arm around Mollie's shoulders, sending her chest painfully into the table's edge.

'Don't,' Mollie said, shrugging off her little sister. 'I can't,' she'd said, unable to talk any more. Willa came with tea and tablets, just before Mollie's head surely would've burst.

They'd been lovely, of course. Mollie knew that she could sometimes be maddening, headstrong and terribly focused on her own activities. And her mum and sisters and even her granny, Phoebe the Elder – for whom her sister, Phoebe the Younger, was named – understood her and loved her in spite of herself. Mollie realised not everyone could claim such strong support and she was grateful for all of these lovely women in her life.

But the truth came home to roost this morning. It was what her mum and sisters *hadn't* said. No one had disagreed with the accusations Rhys had used against her.

It must be because he was right.

She must certainly be disgustingly selfish. The revelation hurt. Tears of shame, hot and plentiful, streaked her face, dripped off the bridge of her nose and were absorbed in the soft bedding. She sniffed hard and felt her head throb again.

More the question was how had Rhys managed to stay with her as long as he had?

He was kind, brilliant, so fit and good to look at and a very hard worker. He'd been understanding, funny and affectionate without being smothering.

Rhys'd been perfect. And she was so horrible that she'd lost him.

Even her own family was on his side, she saw that, now. Because he was good and right; and she was mean and small. Her stomach clenched with sharp pangs of humiliation.

Her view had been so distorted. Now she saw all her relationships more clearly. Jenny was someone she'd bullied; Jen had no faults, except that she'd made the mistake of being friends with Mollie. Even sweet Natalie had had no impulse to trust Mollie and talk with her about going off to university.

She turned her face into the pillow and wept.

Later, Mollie slipped out of bed and into her dad's old clothes. She made her way to the barn without her usual thermos; she was earlier than Willa and she felt too unworthy a person to bother making herself a cup of coffee.

The sky was black as she made her way into the barn and flipped on the yellowish lights that were suspended over the goats' pens. In the daytime, the pens were flooded with sunlight through the roof windows her dad installed when he updated the big barn. The goats blinked at her curiously. One or two whined at the early interruption of their rest. She walked the aisles between the pens, looking but not really seeing, and then wandered out the back of the barn.

She crossed the cobbles into the older, smaller barn. Her father hadn't remodelled this shed, which was over a hundred years old, the inside was shadowy and dark. The barn housed Billy-Goat-

Gruff, in an escape-proof, large stall that gave out to his own pasture. She flipped on the old light switch and was surprised when he didn't bleat at her. It must be an earlier hour than she'd thought. Ordinarily, he'd be instantly mouthing off.

Gruff was lying down in the far side of his stall. Mollie slipped into the stall, expecting him to awaken and then stand on his hind legs, with his front feet perched on a board in the fence. She stuck her hands in her pockets for a treat for him, but felt nothing but flannel. She'd promise to bring him dried fruit later.

Surprisingly, Gruff still didn't stir. Mollie squatted down beside the mischievous goat and stroked his neck.

Then she knew. It felt as though an electrical current buzzed through the nerves in her hand and Mollie quickly pulled back from the animal's hard neck. Gruff was cold. Unmoving. *Dead.*

WILLA FOUND HER SOMETIME LATER. Mollie hadn't been able to get herself into the house; she'd been light-headed and then had fallen onto the porch in front of the boot room door. Her arms were still around her father's border collie, Tarrant, when Willa happened upon them.

'Mollie! Are you alright?'

Her mouth felt unbelievably dry, as though coated with dirt. 'Gruff… is… gone.'

Then she watched as Willa had gone to the barn, probably to make sure there wasn't some mistake.

Mollie's thoughts were disjointed. She sighed and Tarrant whined in sympathy. Dean – the world's best vet – had just seen Gruff a week ago, so why he'd died was anyone's guess. But Gruff's death, coming just hours after Rhys broke off with her, made her feel as though she had emotionally drifted out on a sea where no one could help her. Worst of all, she knew she deserved it.

Willa returned from Gruff's barn and said nothing. Mollie was thankful. She couldn't answer questions. And there was nothing comforting to be said this morning that would make a bloody bit of difference.

Mollie was dimly aware of Willa going back into the house. A few minutes later, her sister came back out to the porch. She set a cup of steaming, sweet, strong tea down beside her. Mollie knew the tea would help the dizziness, but she couldn't seem to release her arms from the endlessly patient dog, who was warm, breathing and had been loved by her dad. It was better to loose Gruff than Tarrant. But losing Rhys was worse than anything.

Willa disappeared inside the house again. A few seconds later she heard a chime from her phone. She knew then that Willa had texted Mr Seabury to come for Gruff's body. She wouldn't have to see him again. She sighed, thankful for small mercies. On the strength of this, Mollie let go of Tarrant and took a sip of tea.

The tea was restorative and also sent her to the loo. Being on her feet helped Mollie to get going again. She must do her work, she must try to be selfless; she must try to press on instead of crying like an idiot. Wordlessly, she followed Willa out to the barn and they began the morning milking. Group by group, Willa released the goats from their pens. They ran, eagerly bleating, poking their heads through the metal stanchions to nibble grain and be milked. Mollie tried to talk to them in her usual happy voice, but kept going quiet without realising it. Luckily, the goats didn't seem to notice, so her distress must have not transferred to her hands.

The milking finished, Mollie set on feeding. When Mollie collected her rake to begin mucking out, she stopped and leaned on it, exhausted. Willa had been working feverishly and was nearly done. Mollie turned and looked around the barn and suddenly noticed voices in the room beyond the parlour. Then she knew that Willa had asked their mother and Phoebe to help finish up the sterilisation of the equipment. Now that she was aware of them, she heard Phoebe's excited voice, talking a mile a minute. She heard her mother comment, heard them laugh together. Mollie was cowered by the kindness of her family. She sunk down on a bale of straw.

Willa came, took the rake from her hand and sat beside her. Finally, Willa spoke gently.

'I am so sorry, Mollie, but you do remember what day this is?'

Mollie thought.

The first day of being without Rhys? The day that Gruff died. To date, one of the worst days of my life.

She shook her head.

'It's the day of the Corbett's party, up at the big house. Remember?' Willa waited for a response. She didn't get one, so she prompted her sister. 'You're meant to supply the cheese trays.'

Mollie considered this. She couldn't care less about her obligation.

'I know it's the last thing you want to do right now, Molls. But it's such a big opportunity. Half of south Shropshire will be there, you know? Loads of people who haven't had your delicious cheese before. Passing trays about was the best marketing you could imagine, you said. Please say you can manage, Mollie. I'll be right there with you, we all will. You said before it could open all kinds of doors for you, with vendors and such. Not to mention, Lord Ranson has paid well, not only for the cheese, but for us to cater.'

Mollie agreed. She just felt so muddled that she couldn't quite think what to do about it. She mumbled, 'Alright.'

'Let's get you into the house. Something proper to eat, if you can. Then we need to get dressed, all right?' Willa was doing her best to galvanise Mollie. 'We'll get the sliced cheese and trays and everything together, so all you'll need to do is get yourself ready. Let's go and show them up at the Hall that you're a talented cheesemaker and worthy of their trade.'

Expressionless, Mollie looked over at her sister's smiling face and allowed Willa to give her a hand up from the bale.

THE SUNSHINE WAS DAZZLING, as were the elegantly dressed, esteemed visitors gathered by Lord and Lady Ranson at Myndcroft Hall. The annual Spring Party had become a tradition, always held on the last weekend of April for the past three hundred years or so. It was the same each spring: there would be loads of food and drink served while a live orchestra played. Neighbours caught up on news, friends issued invitations for the summer months and conversation turned to weddings, graduates and holiday plans.

After several hours of small talk, circulating cheese bites and accepting gracious compliments, Mollie longed to flee the garden and its perfect white marquees for the seclusion of the big house. Known by the Corbett family since birth, Mollie had no qualms about sneaking into Myndcroft Hall for several minutes of precious quiet. She turned to make her way to the specialty food marquee with the intention of putting down her tray. She met her mother and Phoebe there, chatting with the vicar's wife, Mrs Hayward.

'Oh, Mollie, how are you holding up, love?' Her mother reached – for Mollie was quite a bit taller, especially in a pair of wedges – and she clasped Mollie about the shoulders.

'Fine, Mum,' Mollie replied with an embarrassed smile at Mrs Hayward. The vicar's wife was perhaps in her late thirties and looked beautifully exotic. Her black hair was long and gently wavy and she wore a coral dress of fine silk that would do nicely for a classy actress at a movie premier. *Who is this woman, really?* Mollie wondered.

'Mollie, your cheese is lovely,' purred Mrs Hayward. The fact that Mrs Hayward doubled as an advisor for Natalie's career at university only added another layer of mystery that Mollie couldn't fathom. 'I especially like your herbed camembert-style. Very creative to craft a goat's cheese that's traditionally made from cow's milk. How is it so sweet?'

Lisa squeezed her daughter's shoulders, as Mollie was daydreaming and hadn't replied.

'Oh. Um, the goats' milk reflects their diet. Ours eat a lot of sweet pasture grass and so our cheese is less "goaty" in flavour.'

Smiling and nodding, Mrs Hayward waited for Mollie to add further comments, but she had run out of inspiration. She looked at her mother, who could see that Mollie had done her best.

Her mother smiled at her in an encouraging fashion and released her shoulders.

'Lovely to see you, Mrs Hayward.'

Mollie made for the big house. Her plan was to enter through the back, cross the drawing room, make her way down the long gallery, cross the wide main hall and then turn right. There was a massive cloak room. The loo was truly worthy of being called a rest room, in the sense that, in addition to the small grouping of toilets, there was a large room in which ladies could loll about on sofas, or sit in front of lit-up mirrors to touch-up their make-up and chat. She counted on the room being unoccupied; there were other toilets more easily accessible, so her chances were good.

Mollie entered Myndcroft Hall through the large doors of the drawing room that were open to the garden. She smiled as she walked past two elderly ladies, seated at the far end of the room in a pair of floral love seats that swallowed their small, curved forms so that only their little bird shoulders and smart spring hats could be seen. One was talking non-stop, employing the volume of the nearly deaf; her companion reclined with her hatted head tipped back on a rose coloured cushion, gently snoring away the warm afternoon. Seeing their repose, Mollie relaxed a bit and pondered how and where the vicar had met his glamorous wife. She turned a corner and encountered a trio of people standing in the middle of the hall by the grand staircase, having an amicable conversation.

As recognition dawned, Mollie froze. A tall young man that Mollie knew, but couldn't remember, was chatting with Rhys.

Mollie's Rhys.

And standing next to *her boyfriend* was his girlfriend: Courtney Williams, socialite and star equestrian of Aquarius Farm.

CHAPTER 8

For a seemingly eternal moment, no one spoke.

'Well, hello there, Mollie,' Courtney purred. She twined herself around Rhys's arm. She dipped her head toward him in a territorial gesture and a section of her blonde hair clung to his broad shoulder. Mollie noticed that his back seemed to go rigid at Courtney's touch, but he stared at Mollie vacantly and said nothing and neither did the man they'd been speaking to. Courtney flitted on, her voice mocking and treacly. 'We were just talking about how wonderful the party was last weekend at the Evanses, but of course you weren't there. How goes it with your... *cheese*, is it?'

'Pardon me.' Mollie walked towards them but clung to the far wall. She eased along the edge of the highly polished hall table, watching the laughter in Courtney's eyes and feeling cold emanate from Rhys. At last Mollie found the door for the ladies and slipped in. With fumbling fingers, she pulled the lock on the door and let out a jagged breath. Time to pull herself together. She'd never imagined that Rhys would be here today; he'd never attended before. There were people from the village who came, people who didn't come and Rhys's family, for whatever reason,

56

never had. Actually, she should have expected Courtney, but Courtney's presence without Rhys would've been neither here nor there. It was seeing them together that had knocked her sideways. Now Mollie was left with a picture of the two of them that'd been seared into her mind.

How could Rhys have been so uncivil? He'd never been rude. At least, not until the last twenty-four hours.

Mollie sunk down on one of the petite, French-styled sofas in the ladies' lounge. Had Rhys also been at the Evanses party? Was he hobnobbing with Courtney's posh crowd now? It didn't add up. The Rhys Davies she'd been dating for the last eight months was a pragmatic, hard-working, farmer. Not the sort of bloke to sashay around swimming-pools and drinks parties, inspiring jealousy amongst Courtney's girlfriends. Why couldn't Rhys see that Courtney was making a fool of him?

She sighed and gazed around. The wallpaper here had fascinated her since she was a child. The motif was enormous, with black scrolls that repeated between large, gold, feathery plumes. Her eyes danced along with the sweeping patterns. She remembered being in this room with her mum, for some sort of Christmas party for the village children. Her mum was trying to give aid and repair Mollie's hair after she'd been running about like a little delinquent and caught her head in a garland of Christmas holly. It had scraped her neck, making her cry and leaving a scratch that stung when her mother wiped the blood away with a wet cloth.

Mollie's grandparents had been friends with Lord and Lady Ranson for many years and they were, of course, her neighbours and therefore known more casually to Mollie as Alex and Colleen Corbett. Mollie smiled as she recalled Colleen apologising for her 'fearsome holly' and handing her a present. It was a little knitted stocking, probably an ornament proffered from one of Colleen's Christmas trees. A sweet wrapped in bright foil had been secreted inside the stocking. Mollie had been delighted and with a 'thank-you' had popped the sweet into her mouth and wriggled off her mother's lap to rejoin the fun.

She let a full five minutes pass before gathering sufficient courage to leave the comforting sofa and mesmerising wallpaper. She unlocked the door and quietly made her way back to the main hall, trying to remember another route should she find Rhys and Courtney still lingering about. They weren't there.

Mollie stepped into the hall. The tall young man, the one who'd been speaking with Rhys and Courtney, reappeared from the other side of the staircase. She realised now that she knew him. It was the young man of the house, Lord and Lady Ranson's son, Oliver Corbett. He'd gained weight, in the muscular way that young men who've grown up do.

'Oliver!'

'My apologies if I surprised you just now.'

'No. Well, yes, you did, but…'

'Are you all right, Mollie? It's just that you went rather pale a few minutes ago and obviously Courtney Williams was trying to make a point. And rather unkindly, it would seem. I was a bit concerned.'

Mollie grasped for a tactful way to explain. Not finding one, she simply blurted out, 'Rhys just broke up with me. Last night, actually. It was the first I knew of him and Courtney being together. Seeing them together was gut-wrenching.'

'Yes, definitely a bit harsh. I am so sorry, Mollie. Why don't you come and sit with me in the library. Let me get you a drink?'

'You're so kind, Oliver. But I really ought to get back to helping my mum and sisters. I've got my cheese samples circulating, you know.'

'Yes, I heard that from Courtney. She filled me in when you left. But to her chagrin I was rather impressed. Sounds like you're making a success of your father's dairy. He'd be proud.'

Oliver's unexpected compliment blurred Mollie's vision.

'Oh, Mollie, again, I am sorry. Not at all the right time to mention your father. Please, come along through. I'm sure your mother can spare you for a few minutes.'

Mollie followed him passively into the dim library that smelled faintly of Lord Ranson's cigars. The walls between the bookcases were lined with dark wood. She eased herself into the deep embrace of a leather club chair by the fire. Oliver went to a small bar in the corner, behind the massive desk. He poured a small Scotch, neat, and returned to where Mollie sat and handed it to her. She took the small crystal glass from him and without thinking, knocked it right back.

'Well, that went down a treat!' she exclaimed, with a hand on her throat. They laughed and she handed the glass back to him. He asked, 'Another?'

'Oh, no, thank you.'

Oliver poured himself a drink and settled on a high-backed leather chair opposite her. He crossed his long legs and shifted a small cushion from his back to the side of the chair. There was a little Yorkshire terrier embroidered upon it, with a blue bow around its neck.

'It looks like Fitz, doesn't it? I remember your mum loved to do needlework. I suppose it's one of hers.'

'Yes, I am sure it is,' Oliver said, picking up the cushion and handing it to Mollie for a better look. 'He was a great little dog. I don't think we'll ever have another Yorkie at Myndcroft. Another dog couldn't live up to him, you know?'

Mollie laughed. 'I suppose not. He was such a fierce little individual. Loved to go shooting with our dads, even though he was too little to do anything but sit on someone's lap.'

Oliver smiled at the memory and took a sip from the tumbler in his hand.

'I am trying to remember when I saw you last, Oliver. I think it was before you left for university.'

'Seems right. We went to see family in London for most holidays, so I've not been back that often.'

Mollie felt calmed by Oliver's presence and sitting in this secure, centuries-old room. Chatting with him came easily. She hadn't known Oliver very well, he was several years older, with Mollie being closer in age to Oliver's sister. She asked, 'What have you been doing with yourself?'

'Reading chemistry, mostly. I came away with a masters in biomaterials engineering this year.' Oliver looked a bit embarrassed. 'Next I'll be reading for a doctorate.'

'Oh, right – as you do,' Mollie teased. 'No, really, Oliver sincere congratulations. And rather you than me. I felt lucky to escape school at sixteen after GCSEs. My youngest sister won't have that option, I guess.'

'Ahh. The new "Raise the Participation Levels" policy, keeping students until age eighteen. Shouldn't surprise you that my father had a hand in bringing that policy forward. Do your sisters have particular interests?'

Mollie smiled, thinking of Phoebe. 'Oh, yes, the youngest, Phoebe, has strong interests in boys, fashion and leaving the village at the soonest opportunity. But Willa, well, I have to say I don't really know. I think she's wicked smart, like our dad. She got A-star grades in everything. Willa's nineteen and could be off any moment, so I plan to use her as free labour for my goat operation as long as possible.' They laughed. Then Mollie asked him, 'Do you enjoy it? All of this higher learning?'

Oliver leaned back in the chair, which had cradled generations of his family during long hours of reading and conversation. 'Honestly, it's expected, you know? I am a bit at sixes and sevens at the moment, with regards to the future. What I'll actually end up doing with my life. I don't like spending tedious weeks indoors, doing endless research. And I'm not a city person. Actually, I'd like to come back home.'

'I hope you do,' Mollie said.

They sat quietly for a moment. 'This certainly won't be the longest party we've had.'

'Why?' Mollie asked.

Oliver tipped his head towards the window. 'It's raining quite heavily.'

Mollie reluctantly stood to her feet and Oliver copied her movement.

'I hadn't even noticed. I'd better go and help my mum.' She stuck out her hand. 'Thanks for looking after me, Oliver. It was really decent of you.'

THE PURSLOWS ARRIVED home from the big house utterly soaked. It had taken herculean effort to quickly wrap all of the brochures about Hilltop Farm Cheese before they became drenched and to bundle trays, cocktail sticks, napkins and the few remainders of cheese into their old vehicle.

When they arrived home, Mollie gratefully abandoned the kitchen items to her mum and sisters. She trudged upstairs to take off her damp dress and dry herself. She stepped into her father's old trousers, put on a flannel shirt to ward off the chill she felt from sopping wet hair and headed to the barn to do the evening milking.

No one had asked where she'd disappeared to before the downpour had squelched the event. Her mum related some hopeful news about speaking with a Mr Abbott, who'd very much like to carry Mollie's goat cheeses in his three shops, in and around nearby Shrewsbury. Mollie listened, dutifully expressed gratitude and felt nothing at all.

It was unlikely her family would find out that she'd seen Rhys unless she put them in the picture and she had no intention of doing so.

Oliver had seen everything. He had cared for her and helped her regain her composure. And that had been enough.

Willa hadn't come to help with the evening milking and Mollie didn't care. She circulated the eighty-seven animals through in groups and they happily followed her lead out the other side and into their respective pens, where she'd fed them a proper meal after the milking was done.

It was her first day without Rhys. And it hadn't been *completely* devastating.

At least, not until it was time to check the goats for the evening. She'd absentmindedly cleaned the equipment, did the sweeping, tidied away the fresh milk and checked her schedule for making cheeses tomorrow. She'd begun making the rounds, turning off lights, looking closely at the baby kids and their mums and then crossing from the main barn into the small barn.

Only, Billy Goat Gruff was no longer there.

Mollie felt a yawning, hollow pain cross her chest. She missed her dad. She missed Rhys and then remembered him and Courtney standing together. He hadn't even spoken to her. She stood for a few minutes, trying to come to terms. Feeling much older and defeated by it all, Mollie turned and made her way to the house. She dreaded facing the people who cared for her. All of their kind attention couldn't pull her from the sucking, dark emptiness she felt.

CHAPTER 9

The week following the garden party at Myndcroft Hall slipped by and early May brought Granny to visit over the bank holiday weekend. 'Phoebe the Elder' arrived, much to the thrill of her namesake, at the leisurely hour of ten on Saturday morning.

Phoebe was waiting by the front porch. She was up and running towards the silver Bentley the instant she heard Granny's vehicle.

'Granny!'

'Hello, darling. I think you've grown since I last saw you. What's this?'

'I finally got them pierced, Gran.' Phoebe pushed her earlobes with her fingers to afford her grandmother a better look. 'Care to guess what I'd like for my birthday?'

'Phoebe, don't be so rude,' Lisa admonished, as she and Willa came from the house. 'Hi, Granny! How was the drive?'

Granny had travelled about an hour-and-a-half from what her youngest granddaughter referred to as 'the *massive* city of Birmingham', home to Grandmother Phoebe for over fifty years. She'd grown up in Coventry, where her father had become wealthy from his investments in Daimler and other automobile manufactures. Phoebe had moved to Birmingham when she married Arthur Purslow, a successful jeweller. The young Purslows had set up house before the birth of their sons, Grant and Edward, on a prestigious avenue in Sutton Coldfield and hadn't moved house since. Over time, the estate was absorbed into Birmingham's suburbs. Its location had given Arthur Purslow not only the status he craved, but a reasonable commute to his shop, located in the city's century's-old jewellery quarter in Hockley. The still thriving business – despite Arthur's passing and Phoebe appointing new management– provided motivation enough for thirteen-year-old Phoebe to have gotten her ears pierced.

Phoebe loved to visit Granny in Birmingham. Her favourite were outings in the cool, bohemian suburb of Moseley, full of shops, pubs and parks. There Phoebe picked up bits of lore about Tolkien, the author, one of Moseley's most famous past residents. Phoebe trotted out nuggets of literary wisdom in conversations, attempting to impress. In truth, Phoebe had never enjoyed reading.

Dealing with Granny's overabundance of suitcases, Willa followed the others into the house. She wondered how Mollie was getting on, but she'd given up trying to connect with her sister. It didn't pay to follow her about and ask questions, only to have Mollie shrug her shoulders. Mollie was working hard as usual, but was otherwise withdrawn.

The women came into the house, talking and laughing. Granny always brought with her a sense of excitement and a sprinkling of fairy dust. Willa passed the others in the kitchen, taking Granny's cases all the way to the guest room.

The farmhouse at Hilltop Farm was rather sprawling and whilst the guest room was modest compared to what Granny was accustomed to, she'd have her own spacious bed, sitting area and an en suite bath. Willa marched up the stairs and toward the back of the house, her hands cramping with the weight. Finally she made it to the furthest bedroom. The walls were chalk white; a white chenille rug covered much of the wooden floor; and the white bedspread was punched up with a dusty plum folded duvet and co-ordinating pillows. Willa, ever attuned to details, had found some sweet-scented violas and cut them for a little aqua-coloured glass jug she'd found in the kitchen. She'd come upon the flowers yesterday, smelling them before seeing them, where they carpeted the ground in the shade by the side of the house. Her mind had been humming with possibilities for them. This morning she'd had the inspiration to make a tall, white, butter-cream-iced cake. She scattered crystallised periwinkle, yellow and purple violas over the top. It had turned out beautifully and was now setting in pride of place on the Welsh dresser in the dining room, to be eaten this evening. Even more intriguing to Willa was that her cookbook had said that the posies could be used to create violet-coloured marshmallows. She planned make those as soon as she had time, but hadn't any ideas, yet, as to what to serve with them.

She hefted the largest suitcase up on a banded rack so that Gran wouldn't have to reach to the floor to access its contents. Straightening up and putting her hands at her aching back, Willa gazed out of the bedroom window. It was a gorgeous view, the green pastures running away to the steep, green Shropshire hills, which were blanketed in places with dried, fuchsia-coloured heather. The spring sky was pungent blue against the hills and the sun kissed everything with gold. It was true that Granny's manicured gardens were beautiful, but, like Mollie, Willa had a strong affinity for these landscapes of home. Abandoning her reverie, Willa turned and made her way down the stairs.

Conversation was in full flow, but no one had thought to put the kettle on. Willa filled it and flicked the switch, then went to greet Granny with a big hug, not minding if she interrupted Phoebe's account of how boring last Saturday's party had been.

As she leaned over and gently hugged her grandmother, Granny patted Willa's cheek.

'It was one of those totally country affairs, Granny,' Phoebe continued recounting the day. 'All the men talking about shooting things, all the women talking about doing lunch and garden teas and me, ready to fall off my feet from passing Mollie's cheese bites around.'

'How are the Corbetts?' Granny asked Lisa.

'They're fine. Alex asked after you. They need a new car and plan to look you up for lunch when they come to Birmingham.'

'Oh, lovely.'

'And then it rained buckets, Granny,' Phoebe resumed her complaining. 'We were all positively soaking.'

'Oh, my. Did that happen very early on?'

Lisa answered, before Phoebe could insist that it rained nearly the whole day. 'Really, things were winding down at that point. Most people made it to their vehicles without getting damp-through, but we had all of the kitchenware to pack in, most of it beneath the tent. So, it was a lovely party as usual.'

They spoke about Granny's recent trip to Europe and she wore a bemused expression when Phoebe made Granny promise to never leave the country again without her. Granny then said, 'I suppose Mollie's doing something with those goats?'

Willa answered. 'The dog has been a terrible mess. Mollie's had to bathe Tarrant today, it couldn't wait, Granny. I expect she'll be in, soonest.'

'Always busy, busy, our Mollie,' Granny said, obviously proud of her granddaughter's industry. Then she noticed the downcast faces. 'What's happened?'

Lisa drew in a long breath. 'Mollie's young man, Rhys, has broken up with her. It's hit her harder than we would've imagined.'

'But that's awful. They were an adorable couple. Did he have a good reason?'

'I personally wouldn't call Courtney Williams a good reason.' Willa was usually one to see the good in every person, but her loyalties fell in with defending her older sister.

Mollie's youngest sister wasn't as reliable. 'She blew him off all of the time, Granny. He got bored of it.'

'Phoebe!'

'Well, Mum, it's true! It's her own fault. And Courtney Williams dresses like a girl, Gran. You should've seen how lovely she looked at the garden party.'

Willa and her mum looked at one another in surprise. Willa asked, 'Courtney was there?'

'With Rhys, of course.' Phoebe rolled her eyes at her daft family.

Willa should've realised that Courtney Williams wouldn't have missed one of the biggest social engagements on the calendar, but somehow it never had occurred to her. They'd never cared before whether she was there or not, since Courtney wouldn't lower herself to count the Purslow girls amongst her acquaintances.

'Do you reckon Mollie saw them together?'

'How would I know? There were like hundreds of people, weren't there?' Phoebe was clearly put out with all of the attention directed at Mollie.

'Mum, I feel that Mollie must've seen them together,' Willa said. 'Although she was much the same through the day, she seemed particularly gutted after she came back from the big house.'

'How could you tell? We were all drowning.'

Willa shot Phoebe a warning look.

Granny asked, 'What do you mean, "much the same through the day"?'

At that moment, the subject of their conversation could be heard entering through the door of the boot room beyond the kitchen. Mollie appeared, her front covered in a sagging damp shirt and her hands red, presumably from scrubbing the dog. She was wiping herself off with a towel and went over to kiss her grandmother. 'Hello, Gran,' she said quietly.

'Mollie, we've just been talking about you.' Granny was never one to mince words. 'I am so sorry to hear about your young man.'

'Rhys? Thank you, Gran. I am sure our Phoebe told you I didn't deserve him. And she's right.'

'Oh, Mollie, that's not true.' Lisa sprang to her feet to hug her daughter while Phoebe wore a smug expression. Lisa smoothed Mollie's dark, glossy hair from her face and whispered comforts.

Willa had so often found it hard-going with her bossy older sister. All the same, she missed the old Mollie terribly. Willa studied her sister's slumped posture, her indifferent eyes, and she was afraid for her.

SHE FOUND Oliver Corbett waiting for her on the large flat rock, just as he promised when she'd sent him a message fifteen minutes ago. Mollie could no longer cope with a house full of gabbing women. It was too early to start the evening milking, so she'd gotten a questioning look from Willa after she'd made her excuses.

Ordinarily, Mollie loved Granny's visits. Not for the same reasons that Phoebe did, as Phoebe was in awe of Granny and besotted by Granny's wealthy, city lifestyle. Mollie's connection was more intrinsic. She felt linked to her father when Granny was near. She looked quite a bit like Granny which was not surprising as Mollie's father, Grant, had resembled Granny, too. Today the bond somehow added to the heaviness she felt.

The sun was shining, but there was a cold bite to the air and the wet shirt she still wore was chilly. She crossed her arms about herself, the damp material feeling miserable against her skin. Mollie climbed up and sat beside Oliver on the rock and looked at the exquisite view.

'So you made your escape. What's happening at the house?'

'My grandmother's visiting.'

'You adore your granny Phoebe.'

'Yes. But I can't talk to them. Just with you.'

Oliver and Mollie sat in silence. He wasn't upset at her being sad. Oliver rubbed Mollie's back. She could feel the heat of his hand through her wet, threadbare shirt. It was reassuring. 'You're shivering.' Oliver scooted across the rock closer to Mollie, held her around the waist and she dropped her head on his shoulder. The heat from his body warmed her and she felt safe. She drew strength from being here with him. Minutes passed.

'I know a secret about your grandmother.'

'You do?' Mollie didn't really care. But it was easier to answer, to be the one listening.

'Once upon a time,' Oliver began. Mollie lifted her head and gave him a weak smile. 'There was a very pretty girl. You look quite a bit like her, actually. Only you're in colour and she was sepia toned. Can you imagine her?' Mollie remembered old pictures of her grandmother, wearing grand hats and having her blue eyes appear pale grey in the old-fashioned photos, putting Mollie in mind of Tarrant. Granny would hate being compared to a dog, Mollie thought. But it was in the sense of colour value.

'The young pretty girl fell in love with a dashing soldier named Charles. But Charles was a second son, so he didn't inherit. And there was an annoying possibility that Charlie would soon be off to war.'

'Your great-uncle?' Mollie's emotions still felt flat, but in her thoughts, she was astonished.

'The same. So, the pretty girl dumped Charlie the Soldier. Soon after, it became known around the county that she'd met a boring, wealthy young man who was decidedly ambitious. His father was setting him up with his own jewellery shop, where he was sure to make his fortune. The bonus was, being the eldest, he would perhaps be spared from being called up, should there be war.'

'I had no idea. Not even an inkling.'

'Could've made us cousins, had she chosen Charlie Corbett instead.' Oliver smiled at her and she smiled more easily this time.

'Who told you that story?'

'My grandfather. To make it even more juicy, *he* confessed to having been in love with Phoebe as well. But she loved his brother, Charles.'

'And what happened to your great-uncle? I can't remember.'

'He came to rack and ruin. Perfect ending for a romantic story, I should think. Quite the drinker, he died young. Somewhere in Spain, actually.'

'Oh, how awful for him!' Mollie said.

'Not the happiest story, or the most gracious picture of your grandmother. But it hasn't made you feel worse, has it?'

'No, not at all. I don't know why, but somehow it's cheered me up considerably. How'd you do that?'

'I've probably taken a course. I can't remember, but it feels as though I've sat for everything. Years and years of it. But do you know what else?'

'What?' Mollie asked.

'Just watch them together. My grandfather's still attracted to her. He acts differently when Mrs Purslow's around. A bit, well… flirtatious would be too strong a word, but it's quite comical.'

'Really? I hope your grandmother doesn't mind.' Mollie put her head back down on Oliver's shoulder. It was almost time to do the milking, but she wanted to savour the minutes. All too soon, she'd have to return to real life and she dreaded what else could go wrong.

She had the inexplicable, sinking feeling that something else would.

CHAPTER 10

$\mathcal{L}$isa Purslow enjoyed her mother-in-law's visit, but for the first time in their relationship, Lisa had not been exactly forthcoming about the goings-on in her life. Grant had been gone for eleven years, yet Lisa felt she wasn't ready to share with Phoebe that she'd met a lovely man called Michael Ferrington.

It was an odd feeling, to say the least.

Neither had Lisa told her girls. There was enough romantic drama at Hilltop Farm with Rhys breaking Mollie's heart so suddenly and so it seemed unwise to mention her unexpected re-entry into the dating world. Sally Andrews, Councilman Andrew's wife, who'd artfully arranged the match – and indirectly lined up a job for Lisa, as well, had never said a word about Michael when they met in the village. Lisa appreciated Sally's discretion and respected how Sally had gone about minding her own business after giving Lisa a push in the right direction.

And so it was that Lisa had lied to Granny and the girls, in order to meet Michael this evening.

She felt awful about it, but she was desperate to see him. Of course it didn't really matter, as Granny would enjoy having some time on her own with the girls.

Lisa learned that Michael didn't live in the village of Bucknell where she'd met him, but in the opposite direction, in Ludlow. This evening she visited his home for the first time. It was a newly-built modern flat, well appointed, perfect for a bachelor. Michael had surprised her with extravagant gifts, scent and jewellery, that, if she were honest, she'd rather not receive. The gifts were too difficult to hide from her girls. Not to mention she found it hard to express her thanks in a way that felt adequate for the money he'd spent.

'I'd forgotten how much I love digging deep into texts,' Lisa explained to Michael over a cup of coffee in his open-plan kitchen. 'At first I thought Sam was such an intellectual that I wouldn't be able to follow anything he was asking me to do!'

Michael laughed with her about this. 'And then you found out why he's considered a brilliant teacher.'

'You're quite right. He explains what I'm meant to do so clearly, that I find myself able to navigate these technical papers and to pull out the citation he's looking for. Which, I think, actually ends up saving us both a lot of time. I couldn't really do this job without Sam's help. He's a most lovely man.'

'We played golf yesterday. He told me you hadn't taken any work home yet. I hope I don't have anything to worry about, where you and your new boss are concerned?' Michael was smiling, but Lisa sensed an undercurrent. Was he actually jealous of Sam Lloyd?

'Or perhaps you're just that desperate to get away from the farm?'

She was relieved. He was interested in her family, in how her household functioned. In other words, he was truly interested in her.

'I love being at home, actually. ' Lisa paused to think. 'I was at the library so many years, with a very set routine. I imagine it gave me confidence to show up at Sam's office on a regular schedule.' She smiled at Michael. 'Not to mention, it's given me a convenient way to meet you for secret lunches.'

Michael took her hand and kissed her palm, but looked at her reproachfully. 'Lisa, I want to meet them, you know.'

'But it's so simple this way.'

'Yes, I know. But your girls are a large part of your life.'

'Oh, Michael. I am not sure if I am ready. Is it so important to meet them?'

'Yes. Want to know why?' He kissed her on the lips.

'Why?'

'Because seeing you once or twice a week has been great. But I won't be content with that. If I meet your girls, just once will do, they'll immediately see what a nice chap I am. Then we can arrange to go away on weekends.'

'I can't remember the last time I was away on holiday.'

'See? The idea appeals to you.'

It did appeal. But she felt uneasy. It was all happening so fast. 'It's been a really long time for me, feeling this way about someone.'

'Me, too.'

'And I must consider the girls.'

'We are. They're old enough, Lisa. Surely you don't want them finding out months after the fact and feeling lied to. That's not right.'

Guilt burned in her tummy. Speaking of lies, she'd told the girls she was meeting a "colleague" this evening. 'I wasn't thinking of it that way. Of course you're right. They'd feel they have a right to know. My youngest, Phoebe, is thirteen now. She's becoming very interested in boys and relationships. Not *my* relationship of course, that will probably disgust her. But my baby's growing up!'

Michael hugged her. 'I understand completely. It's hard to start letting them go.' He'd told her that he had a son, Tyler, now at university. Michael and his wife had divorced three years ago. As he spoke, he stood very close, his hands caressing her arms.

'You'll have to tell me what sort of things the girls like. I'll pave the way with birthday gifts and so forth.'

She ignored his comment. Girls always needed things, especially hers, but she wouldn't feel comfortable about giving Michael shopping inspiration. They weren't spoiled and would simply appreciate him because was important to her. So she said, 'I'll look forward to meeting Tyler as well.'

'Ah, well, we'll have to wait and see,' Michael said, disappointment deepening his voice. 'University claims most of his time. I try not to interfere.'

Lisa smiled with compassion. She'd been glad that Mollie had wanted to stay home. It was selfish, but she so enjoyed Mollie's companionship and energy. At least she had, until Mollie had recently become a shadow of herself.

'Now you've had the tour. We can come back and relax later. How about we go downstairs to dinner,' Michael said, pulling her out of her thoughts. There was no shortage of restaurants within walking distance of his home. And she would joyfully follow him wherever he wanted to go.

COURTNEY WILLIAMS barely noticed when Rhys left her pool party. Outwardly she behaved attentively. She walked with him to his vehicle. Kindly told him she wished he could stay longer. She kissed him goodbye.

But she was eager to return to her guests and he knew it. He slid into his pickup and made his way down the tree-lined drive and through the gates.

Her friends weren't a bad lot. None were from the village except Courtney. They lived in posh places with names Rhys had never heard, like Bray, or Alderley Edge. They knew each other from the schools they attended and the social circles of their families. Rhys wasn't one to practise reverse discrimination. The fact was, he'd had some good chin wags with the men and their girlfriends were decent. He'd even been invited by one of them to fish in Scotland. If there was one among them that he wasn't all that comfortable with then, admittedly, it was Courtney. She was usually lovely to him and even lovelier to look at, but she'd been so full of herself she'd embarrassed him. He hadn't realised it, or seen the full scope of her behaviour, really, until he'd seen her alongside some of her friends. It was the contrast that'd made it obvious. Rhys surmised that Courtney's arrogance was something deeply ingrained in her. Her mother behaved the same way.

Leaving the party, one thing was certain. He'd really made a hash of his relationships.

Pulling into the yard at his parents' dairy, the summer sky was streaked with orange. He'd begged off the evening milking and he felt guilty about it. His brothers only asked for time off for really important things, like being best man at a wedding. Rhys felt a small comfort in that he wouldn't be disrupting their schedule with that monumental fuss anytime soon.

He went into the house and found his parents seated at the kitchen table enjoying their Saturday evening. Each had a slice of homemade pie, alongside white ironstone mugs filled with coffee. The house was empty of his brothers, who were down the pub, or with a girlfriend, or both.

'Rhys, *bach*. How was your party?' His mum had already popped up from her place at the table to cut him a piece of pie. Rhys took his usual chair and rubbed his face.

'Lush. Courtney's mates are a friendly lot. Not at all what you'd expect. I reckon they work as hard as we do, just in different circumstances than what goes with cows.'

His father's knowledge of how "the other half" lives, was based on his vague association with Lord Ranson, and Huw knew that his lordship blew hot and cold in his tolerance of common folk. 'What sort of work do they do?' he asked.

'Let's see now. I met a banker. A bloke whose father owns pharmaceuticals. A couple who were still getting degrees. A few medics – one was a surgeon for your bones but I always forget what they're called.'

'Osteo,' his mother supplied, forking a bite of pie into her mouth.

'Here's one for you, Da. One of 'em, name of Ferguson, has a whisky distillery business. He invited me to fish in Scotland with him and his father.'

'I'd be going in a tick, were I you, I would,' Mr Davies said, taking a long swallow of his coffee. He wiped his mouth across the back of his wrist and settled back into his chair.

'I don't think I'll be going, Dad.'

'Why ever not?' his mother asked. 'Your dad would give you a long weekend for such a grand experience, wouldn't you, Huw?'

Rhys's father groaned his agreement.

'It wouldn't seem right to me to take up Ferguson on his invitation when he most likely made it because of Courtney, not necessarily on my own merit. I'm only sayin' he doesn't know me, does he.'

His mother said, 'Oh, son.'

His dad failed to see the problem. 'What's it to do with her whether men go to go fishing? Men know each other because they fish. 'Twas ever thus.'

Rhys leaned heavily on his elbows. 'Because, Da, Ferguson was welcoming me to the fold, as it were. A nice enough gesture. But not one I'd act upon that soon.'

'Well, you must know better. You certainly seem to be working your way through girlfriends of late.' His father was irritated by indecision. Everything in Huw's life had been rather straightforward. Rhys's father was a fourth generation dairyman and he'd married his childhood sweetheart. Things had come along nicely.

The only adventure was leaving Wales, but Rhys knew his father had inherited this farm by way of a distant relative, so there wasn't much risk in coming to Marris Mynd.

'I'll get myself sorted. And there are plenty of pretty girls, eh Dad?' Rhys grinned. His father snorted and smiled back.

CHAPTER 11

Phoebe enjoyed her granddaughters, but she knew she'd sleep soundly after spending a rousing evening with them. When Lisa had come home she was sitting with the girls at the large dining room table, where they were playing cards. She and young Phoebe were in a team together, naturally and were winning against Willa, who was virtually on her own since Mollie's mind was obviously elsewhere.

As soon as Lisa had peered around the corner, she had known. Lisa had a man. And something about it wasn't quite right.

How Phoebe was so certain about this wasn't important. In her seventy-one years, she'd come to accept that much of what she knew was gathered by intuition and confirmed by gut feeling. She was seldom wrong.

Phoebe changed into her silk nightdress and then went into the bathroom to cream her face. More's the pity that Lisa felt she couldn't speak with her. Many friends had confided in Phoebe about their love affairs and allowed her to help steer their course. She was seldom mistaken in her advice and she could probably help Lisa see her situation clearly, whatever it was.

She climbed into the big downy bed and put a book in her lap.

She sat with her hands folded on top of it, rather than begin reading. Phoebe heard someone plodding up the stairs. Willa.

A knock on the door and then it opened. There stood her middle granddaughter, balancing a small tray in her hands.

Phoebe smiled. 'Oh, dear girl. You remembered.'

Willa shuffled in, closing the door behind her. At least one of them was going to speak with her about something that mattered. She adored her youngest, her namesake, but thirteen-year-old Phoebe was completely consumed by her friends and her phone.

Putting the tray on the bedside table, she looked sheepishly at her grandmother for permission. That was Willa. Unfailingly polite.

'Sit down, my sweet. Look at this. Steaming hot cocoa and you've treated me to a chocolate biscuit as well. Pure luxury.' She leaned forward and patted Willa on her rosy cheek, then flicked a strand of Willa's long blonde hair over the girl's shoulder. 'Thank you, darling. But you ought to be having a cup with me.'

Blushing, Willa smiled. Phoebe knew she hadn't even thought of serving herself. What a dear girl, always on task, serving others, happy in the background. It was Willa's gift and her way and Phoebe wouldn't feel regret for her, because these attitudes brought Willa pleasure, too.

A bit of an icebreaker was needed. 'I was glad that Mollie spent the evening with us, weren't you?'

The girl nodded. Her brow was furrowed in thought.

'Does she talk to you, Willa?'

'No. But she's talking to someone.'

'Oh?' Phoebe took a sip of the hot cocoa. It was deliciously rich. Never one to do things by halves, Willa had made it properly on the Aga, not from a microwave-mix. She'd even put a fresh dollop of cream on the top. Bliss. 'Who's Mollie talking to, then?'

'I followed her one day,' Willa began. 'She met with Oliver Corbett. They sat on the big rock overlooking the valley. Mollie seemed to be able to chat with him quite freely.'

'That's very interesting. I suppose we shouldn't be shocked. Although he's been away and you girls haven't always travelled in the same social circles, she has known Oliver all her life. As you have.'

'Yes. I was surprised. But not *worried*. If that makes sense?'

'Absolutely. Corbetts are rather good in a crisis, my dear. I've put them to the test once or twice.' Phoebe retreated into herself for a moment. 'Oliver always seemed the nicest sort of boy.'

'He is.' It was not lost on Phoebe that Willa's cheeks were glowing.

'Still,' Willa continued. 'I wish she'd talk to me, instead. I only want to help. She seems so… unreachable.'

'Perhaps it's because Oliver's also a bit distant – in the sense that he's rather removed from the situation – that Mollie is able to share her thoughts with him.'

Willa chewed her lip. 'I hadn't thought about it that way. But what do you think is the matter, Granny?' Willa's eyes brimmed with tears. For all of her finely-honed instincts, Phoebe hadn't realised that Willa was so distressed about her sister.

Phoebe stroked her granddaughter's corn-silk hair. 'Oh, Willa, you mustn't worry, child. I won't pretend that Mollie isn't suffering a sort of depression. However, we should be very encouraged.'

'How do you mean?' Willa sniffed. Phoebe handed her a Kleenex from the bedside table.

'I think it's a good sign that Mollie is able to talk to Oliver. If she were lying in bed all day, not able to speak to anyone, then we'd have cause for greater alarm.'

'She's hardly eating, Granny.'

'Well, that's true. And she's lost weight. But what jilted girl hasn't, my love? In her own headstrong, absurd manner, Mollie really loved Rhys. It's to be expected. And it wasn't but a fortnight ago.'

'I've been so worried.'

'Well, my pet, you can do an important job by Mollie.'

Willa looked intently at her grandmother. 'What's that?'

'Most of the time when people have something awful happen, it takes a while, a bit of moving forward and then a few steps back, but they recover. But on occasion they get rather stuck. Can't stop thinking rubbish thoughts. Their sense of loss has become a habit, you see. Then they really are in trouble.'

'So, you're asking me to keep an eye on Mollie.'

'Yes. And keep trying to help her look for the bright side of things. Much of life happens inside our heads. And it's up to each person whether or not one's own mind is a pleasant place to live.'

'I suppose you're right, Granny,' Willa chuckled. 'You always are.' Willa tipped forward for a kiss. She stood up and retrieved the tray. As she pulled the bedroom door closed she said, 'I'll see you in the morning, Granny.'

'Sleep well, my darling.'

ON HER WAY to her car this morning, Granny had said her goodbyes and then suddenly invited Phoebe to accompany her to Scotland in a few months, to visit with friends in St Andrews. Occasionally, Granny randomly invited one of the girls – never all three at once – to have a special treat. She was very firm that the other two sisters should be gracious, saying, 'Life isn't fair, my darlings. But your turn will come, if you don't complain about your sister's good fortune.' They never knew when Granny might take them on a holiday, or send them a special package, or have them come to visit her at home, but they found her to be fair when they took the long view.

Willa had a simpler, but genuine reason, to be delighted. Discussing Mollie's depression with Granny had lifted a weight from her shoulders, re-energising her creativity. Willa knew her mother had been concerned as well, but Mum was a laid back sort of person, one to just let things be. Willa tended to fret and

Granny had understood. And by talking about it, Willa wasn't the only one attuned to the situation. If action was needed on Mollie's behalf, Granny would be ready and know exactly what ought to be done.

Thus, Willa had been busy this afternoon, assembling something special in the kitchen. When finished, she'd taken her creation to the dining room and no one was allowed to peek. Following dinner, Willa was ready to unveil her new idea.

'Mollie, you'll be so pleased, I just know it.'

Instead of saying something funny or sarcastic, Mollie just looked at her blankly. When would her sister return? Willa remembered what Granny had said: give her time and remind her how to be enthused with life. Willa put on her best smile and invited her sisters and mum to the dining room.

There on the table stood Willa's creation: upon a crystal pedestal stood a three-tiered white 'cake' made of large rounds of goat's cheese. She'd decorated the cake with herbs, purple flowers and clusters of ripe, green grapes. On the very top was a small bridal couple, purchased long ago at a car boot sale. There were decorative, tiny black signs attached to wooden picks and stuck into the various rounds of cheese, identifying each flavour. Circling the tiered rounds of cheese, on separate glass serving platters, were fresh breads, sliced meats, thin biscuits and bottles of wine. It was a veritable feast.

Lisa said, 'Oh, Willa that's beautiful! Very inviting. The ultimate cheese, wine and fruit party, isn't it?'

Willa clasped her hands together, thrilled with her mother's reaction and perception.

'Can we eat it?' Phoebe asked, plucking a grape from the food montage.

Mollie stood motionless.

'Don't you see, Mollie?' Willa said, putting a hand on her sister's statue-like arm. 'It's a sort of wedding cake, but made of cheese. For people at a wedding banquet, or wedding breakfast, or parties of any type, really, whenever someone wants to serve guests your goat's cheese in an attractive, upscale way. We could even partner with other dairies for cows' cheese, to add more variety.'

Mollie still said nothing.

Willa maintained her composure. 'I think they'll sell like mad, Mollie and they're so simple for people to self cater. We can just provide the cheese rounds, other foods and instructions in a box for them to pick-up at the nearest retailer. It was you who gave me the brilliant idea, you know! When you asked me to help you make *cheesecake* I thought, hold on, there's an idea, so I looked online–'

Mollie's eyes filled with tears. Willa berated herself. Why had she carelessly reminded her sister of the dessert she'd worked to create for Rhys? *Stupid, Willa, very stupid.*

But it was impossible for Willa to retrieve her words. Mollie had left the room.

Phoebe had left too and come back with a plate.

'I didn't mean to upset her, Mum.'

Lisa gave Willa a hug. 'I know, sweetheart. It's not your fault. I reckon Mollie's thoughts are never far from Rhys and it was just an unfortunate comment. She'll be all right.'

'Did you make these cracker things?' Phoebe asked, crunching them down with slices of meat. 'They're really good.'

'Yes. They're seasoned to complement all the other flavours. They're actually very simple to bake.'

'It's a wonderful idea, Willa. I think they'd go down a treat.'

'I agree, Mum, but I've got to have Mollie's help to offer kits like this. The price should be based on the quantity of people they serve. There's £80 worth of cheese here and then the cost of fruit, meats, and of course, my baking, if a person chose all of the extras. Or maybe we'd go with packaged crackers. It's hard to calculate all the pricing and we need to figure out what to offer. I am going to go find her.'

'Willa.'

She turned to her mother.

'Just don't expect too much of Mollie right now, alright? I don't want you to be disappointed.'

'I have to try to reach her, Mum.'

Willa searched the barn but didn't find her sister. She went to the outbuildings where her father's old farm equipment was stored. No one. She walked about the garden; the lawn surrounding the house was bordered with blossoms of lilac, blown down from spring-blooming trees. She made her way down to the farm's small pond. Mollie wasn't there. Willa walked back toward the house, wondering if Mollie had perhaps made another of her secret trips to the big rock to talk to Oliver Corbett. If so, she probably shouldn't interrupt, as Granny thought he was doing Mollie a lot of good. Then she remembered a spot she hadn't checked: the small barn, where Mollie used to visit Gruff when he was alive.

She was there.

'Hi, Mollie.'

Mollie looked up.

Willa didn't want to frustrate her sister, or risk having Mollie push her even farther away. But the truth was, she'd would rather have Mollie bossing her about than be given the silent treatment.

'I wasn't sure, you know, what you thought of the wedding cake… Mollie?'

'It was grand. You're very creative, Willa.'

Willa blushed. Mollie wasn't one to give compliments very freely, leastways, not without adding how one could do a bit better. Mollie had always thought that she was being helpful, not realising that she'd ruin the praise by saying something negative. But Willa had always known Mollie meant well and she'd catalogued Mollie's compliments in her memory. More than once, when Willa wanted to give up on something, she'd remember

Mollie's encouragement and even some of her criticisms, and she pressed on.

'Thanks, Mollie. I am so glad you liked it.'

Mollie went to the window of what used to be Gruff's stall. Willa climbed into the space and followed her. They looked at the view together.

'Do you think we could sell them? For weddings and bridal parties, to start?' asked Willa.

Mollie sighed. 'I suppose. If you'll let me know how many cheese rounds you'll need.'

Willa thought this was the best vote of confidence that Mollie could give the idea. She was keen to do all the work and show Mollie how people would want them. 'All right, then. I'll figure things out. Perhaps Mum would like to help me. I'll need to let our retailers know and perhaps I can run an ad where brides would be likely to see it, or something.'

'Sure,' Mollie said. Her voice was quiet, but otherwise normal, Willa thought. Willa suddenly felt as though she were intruding on her sister. She'd best not outstay her welcome.

'I'll see you in a bit, Mollie.'

There was no reply as Willa turned to leave.

CHAPTER 12

*L*isa Purslow phoned her boss, Sam Lloyd, on a Thursday morning.

'Oh, hello. I was just wondering where you'd got to, since you're ordinarily here about half-eight.'

'Yes, I know, Sam. I hope this wasn't one of those rare days that you actually needed me in the office. My youngest daughter, Phoebe, isn't well. She's usually set on convincing me that she's a proper adult, but today she's behaving like a clingy toddler. I think it's best I stay close to home, after running a few errands this morning.' She'd felt quite relaxed in making her request, but now she was holding her breath. Some people, she'd found, were magnanimous about making offers, until you decided to take them up.

But Sam was as kindly as ever. 'No worries,' he said. 'In fact, take a personal day if you'd like. That's the beauty of a salaried position, isn't it? We're well ahead on deadlines at the mo. Why not take a long weekend?'

'It'll be a very long weekend, indeed, if Phoebe doesn't feel better!' Lisa joked. 'Thank you so much, Sam. I really appreciate the flexibility.'

'Not at all. Take care, alright?'

They rang off. He was such a lovely man.

Lisa went upstairs to check on Phoebe, peering in at her from the corridor. She was dying, she'd said, but Lisa came and went completely unnoticed, so absorbed was the head-phone wearing Phoebe by her computer. She knew there was some truth to Phoebe's claims, as Lisa had heard her being sick early this morning. Lisa felt sorry for her, but also felt a flicker of gratification that her youngest daughter still needed her mum. She pushed aside anxious thoughts of what it would be like, alone in this large farmhouse, when the girls left to make their way in the world. Having promised to go to the village for something to settle Phoebe's tummy, Lisa grabbed her handbag and started out the door.

Warm sunshine revitalised her spirits as she walked to her car. May had been a continuation of April's beautiful weather. Turning right from the farm drive onto the main road, she was in the village within a few minutes. Passing the vicarage she saw Mrs Hayward, elegantly tending to her roses while wearing something long and shimmery, suitable for a Hollywood film star of another age. Lisa waved and smiled. What an interesting woman Mrs Hayward was. Lisa ought to invite her to tea some afternoon and get to know her better. There were many things she ought to do, but mostly she just covered the necessities.

Again, the thought crossed her mind, of her girls making their exits out of her life. She'd thought when she had them that she'd have Grant when it was their time to leave the nest. Perhaps Michael would be there for her? Thinking of him helped her cope. Surely he knew what it was like; Michael has said his son Tyler was caught up in his own life at university. She hadn't realised it at the time, the pain he must be feeling. Michael had been trying to let her know he shared her feelings. Lisa hadn't understood, being secure in the fact that her girls were still at home. She must be badly out of practise at relationships to have been so obtuse.

She parked her car on the street opposite the chemists. She crossed the road and entered the shop and was immediately absorbed in the colourful spring displays. Lingering by the gift merchandise, Lisa realised it had been ages since she'd purchased something just for fun. She looked at the shiny pottery, sniffed several candles and ran her fingers across the fine embroidery of the tea towels. She moved on to an area of personal items. A row of clean little linen bags, their openings gathered by a thin, twisted cord caught her attention. She picked one up. The brand was French. *Coté Bastide.* There was a paper label laced through the cord that had script resembling romantic handwriting. *Ambre Sells de Mer.* Bath salts, with a special sort of fragrance. She brought the sample to her nose and a heavenly scent enveloped her. The rich oriental notes drifting from the linen bag were enticing. Mrs Hayward may have two-dozen fragrant roses in her garden, but Lisa would have *this.* An emotional impulse purchase? Definitely. And worth every penny? Without a doubt. Feeling smug, she made her way further into the shop, into aisles of headache tablets, reading glasses and children's suncream with animals on the bottle.

Considering which preparation might do Phoebe the most good, Lisa hadn't heard Sally Andrews at the end of the aisle.

'Good morning,' she'd said and Lisa had jumped.

'Oh, Sally. I was totally absorbed.' She described Phoebe's complaints and asked Sally for a recommendation.

'I've had a number of mums come through in the past few days; it would seem there's a nasty bug circulating at the school. I'd choose this one.'

'Thank you. Fortunately, it's been a very long time since we've needed anything. They change the labels, making it that much more confusing.'

'Yes, you're right.' Sally looked about; she seemed to be checking they were alone in that part of the shop. She lowered her voice. 'I apologise if this is none of my business. But I've heard that you're seeing Michael Ferrington.'

'Well, yes,' Lisa blushed but she was excited to finally speak of him to someone. She'd almost mentioned it to the girls after Granny had gone, but the timing hadn't been right. Mollie was still having difficulty coping with her break-up from Rhys, and Phoebe was feeling poorly. 'I have *you* to thank, Sally.'

Sally seemed uncomfortable and she crossed her arms.

Lisa carried on. 'It was a bit awkward at first, Michael and I were not quite sure why we were thrown together. But it was a lovely bit of matchmaking on your part.'

'Oh, dear. I think there's been a huge mix-up.'

'What?'

Sally's voice became professional and a smile spread over her face. 'I can check on that, if you'd like. Would you mind to come into my consultation area for a moment?' Peripherally, Lisa caught sight of Mrs Conniff, a woman from the village known for not minding her own affairs.

Lisa fell into step behind Sally and her heart began to pound. Something was wrong.

They went behind a screen, where Sally had set up a small desk and several chairs. There was a sink with a cabinet and shelving that housed a bit of medical paraphernalia, a weight scale, blood pressure cuff and an area with hypodermics for those requiring flu jabs and other horrors. Perhaps Phoebe should've had an inoculation?

Sally offered her a chair and turned to a small table at the back of the room. She filled a kettle and flipped the switch. She turned toward Lisa. 'I am sorry to bring you back here, as no doubt Mrs Conniff will wonder what's brought us to the "Embarrassing Problem room".'

'Thank you for your quick thinking, Sally. What is it?'

'I've always liked you, Lisa.' She stopped and smiled. Lisa had always felt comfortable with Sally as well. They'd led busy lives raising families and their paths hadn't crossed often enough to claim a close friendship. 'I had only your best interest at heart and that's why I meddled. But it would seem that my efforts have backfired in the worst possible way. I suppose it serves me right.'

'I don't understand.'

'I didn't intend… no, let me say it this way: I never would've thrown you together with Michael Ferrington, except that I trusted him to keep his word. Naturally, he betrayed my trust. I ought to know better. And now you've been caught in the middle.'

The kettle boiled. Sally stood from her chair and went to make them tea. Lisa sat quietly, realising that Sally was quite upset.

She put a steaming cup of builder's tea in front of Lisa. It was served in a beautiful patterned mug. Under other circumstances, Lisa would've asked if the darling mug was from a range sold in the shop. Only it wasn't that sort of visit. Lisa was beginning to feel distressed and her hands felt rather clammy. She put her palms around the mug of hot tea and took a deep breath to steady her nerves.

Sally sat down across from her, leaning forward on her elbows, but not making eye contact. 'I'm making a real hash of this. Perhaps I should just come straight to the point and seek your forgiveness later.'

'Okay, Sally, though I can't imagine being cross with you. I know you've only tried to help.'

'That certainly makes what I have to say worse,' Sally said with a woeful smile. She spoke with measured tones, the same she might employ when she was being a caring pharmacist, telling a patient some dreadful possibility, before referring them on to a doctor.

'Sam Lloyd is a great friend of ours; a dear, dear man. He's widowed, I don't suppose he told you? No. He wouldn't have. I wanted so much for you to meet him, but he's extremely shy about meeting anyone new.'

Lisa thought Sally's comment didn't really ring true. She'd been working with Sam in the office and had seen him encounter a number of people, including strangers. He'd always seemed relaxed, with an easy, outgoing personality. Lisa wanted to ask Sally about this, but she knew she must allow Sally to finish.

'Of course, Michael Ferrington is a friend of Sam's. I asked Michael if perhaps he would talk to Sam and suggest that Sam consider a casual meeting with you at some sort of public do, like an event in our village. Low pressure, you know the sort of thing. For unfathomed reasons, Sam actually likes Michael and I thought if another man helped him along, perhaps Sam would feel more confident.'

'But…' Lisa was still in the dark. And she felt a small flare of temper when Sally expressed disbelief that Sam would *actually like* Michael. She interrupted Sally. 'Michael did help make the connection. He arranged for Sam to interview me and I am working for Sam now.'

Sally looked wretched and took a long sip of tea. Lisa absently sniffed her bath salts. It was a childish thing to do and she was glad Sally didn't seem to notice.

'Alright,' Sally said. She uncrossed her arms and leaned back in her chair. 'Hopefully all will become clear. You haven't seemed to realise that I was thinking of you and Sam *together* – not as work partners. You see, Sam's wife, Angela, passed away about the same time as your Grant. Well, naturally, Michael has expressed sympathy for Sam. He said Sam wants to meet someone, but he feels hopeless at dating. Michael agreed to put you and Sam in touch. Michael told me, *three weeks ago*, that he'd been dating a very nice lady. It was his idea to suggest to Sam that the four of you go for dinner. You with Sam; Michael and his girlfriend.'

Lisa was aghast.

Sally let her sit with the truth of the situation for a moment.

'I don't know who he was dating three weeks ago, but perhaps they weren't serious and he hasn't seen her since.' Lisa replied. 'He told me he hadn't really dated in ages.'

Sally shook her head, but Lisa carried on. 'And it seems lovely that Michael wanted to help Sam, even though it turned out a bit differently. I mean, isn't it lovely that you're on good terms with someone who divorced your sister not so very long ago? Surely that says something good about Michael's character?'

Sally tutted. 'You think we're on good terms? And you believe Michael Ferrington is a wonderful person, do you?'

'Well, isn't he?'

'He divorced my sister when she was six months pregnant with their son, Tyler. He's never taken any interest in his own son. The divorce he referred to in his conversation with you was likely his most recent divorce.'

'Most recent?'

'Yes. His fourth.'

'Oh my.'

'Uh-huh.'

Lisa felt tears well up in her eyes. 'I feel such a fool.' She wondered if she were coming down with Phoebe's bug. She felt quite sick.

Sally reached out and laid her hand on Lisa's shoulder. 'Don't. Michael is quite the operator. You weren't to know any better. All I can say is how very, very sorry I am.'

'Sally, I don't blame you.'

'You should. What was I thinking? You're very attractive, Lisa, and I should've realised Michael might snap you up for himself. I've just rather forgotten how he thinks, you see? I was thinking only of Sam and how Michael ought to be a decent enough person to want to help a friend. But I was wrong.'

'I've been terribly wrong, too, though. Things got a bit… out of hand. I went to visit Michael at his flat, you see.'

'You mustn't blame yourself for the weak moment, Lisa. I imagine you've been lonely for a very long time.'

'Yes. And it's all been rather exciting. But I'd only known him two weeks, Sally.' Lisa felt mortified.

'Michael has that effect on women. It's just that, well you must understand. He dates. *A lot.* And when Michael does commit, well, he's not very jolly good at it. I think his longest marriage lasted about two years.'

Lisa felt her chest tighten and was afraid she'd sob. Then the thought crossed her mind that she wasn't the only person messed about by Michael's meddling. He'd used his friend in an appalling manner. 'Does Sam know what's happened?'

'No. And I won't fill him in. It's up to you, Lisa. You'll decide how you want to handle the situation without any more "help" from me. But at this point I just couldn't, with a good conscience, fail to put you in the picture. It was a family member of ours that saw you and Michael, obviously on a date, at a restaurant in Ludlow. I hope you'll forgive me. Initially, I knew if I tried to suggest dating you that Sam would shy away before you had a chance to say hello. He's done that before, you see. But he really is the sweetest man and I thought, well, I could see the two of you together.'

'He is a dear. I've so enjoyed working for him. I said as much to Michael and he behaved in an oddly cagey manner. Now I understand why. Rest assured, Sally, I appreciate your telling me.'

Sally nodded.

'I probably ought to get back to the shop; I've only got one other person in today.' Both women stood.

'You know, Sally, I'm not sorry this happened. I've come out of it with a lovely job. That has meant a great deal, because I was totally at a loose end when the library closed. You're not to worry, or feel badly; I don't hold you accountable in the least for Michael's dishonesty.'

'You're a star, Lisa.' They hugged. 'I hope that we can chat again soon and have more cheerful things to discuss. Good luck.'

Lisa gathered up her bath salts and Phoebe's medicine and went to pay for her purchases.

DRIVING BACK from the village really wasn't long enough for Lisa to process all she'd learned from Sally about Michael Ferrington.

She remembered their first kiss. He'd kissed her in a darkened alley outside a restaurant where they'd just dined. 'You probably think I'm rather clumsy,' he'd said, stroking her hair. 'It's been such a long time since I've dated.'

'I'm out of practise as well,' she'd said, smiling as he stepped closer. 'I haven't been on a date in over a decade.'

Tasting passion after so many solitary years was heavenly; Lisa was sure that she was falling in love. After all, Michael had told her he'd been married before, too, and gone through a bitter divorce. He knew what it was like to have to struggle on in life without a partner. Wasn't it lucky they'd found each other?

Lisa sped up the hill, sending Phoebe's medicine bouncing off the car seat and on to the floor. To think this was the very same man who told Sally he'd been dating a wonderful woman the day that Sally had given him Lisa's phone number. He'd actually told Sally that Sam and the very lonely Lisa, would be welcome to join him and his lady on a double date.

'What a liar!' Lisa yelled, slamming her hand on her steering wheel.

Arriving back at the farm, she sat in her car, fuming. Later, perhaps, she'd feel hurt and broken-hearted. But at the moment she was furious.

She'd break it off with him. *Now.*

Lisa dug in her handbag and retrieved her phone. She rang him. Michael's voice messaging invited her to leave her name and number. She left much more.

It was rude way of going about it, but he'd been rude first. She told him she knew about his not keeping his word to Sally. About the recent girlfriend and multiple marriages he'd failed to mention. How she knew that he'd manipulated the situation in order to date her himself and keep poor Sam out of the loop.

'What a nasty piece of work are, Mr Farrington. Don't contact me ever again.' Lisa disconnected the call, then fished on the floor of her car for her daughter's medicine.

CHAPTER 13

Yesterday, she'd put the final part of her scheme in place. Mollie popped by Mr Seabury's farm and asked if his youngest daughter, Charlotte Seabury, would like to help out at Hilltop Farm. Charlotte was Phoebe's age but quite a different sort of person, meaning that she was hard-working and uncomplaining. Charlotte readily agreed and seemed to think helping Willa with the milking would be great fun. Mollie smiled weakly at the overly-keen girl and thanked her and spent a few minutes talking with Charlotte's mum.

All that was needed to do this morning was to leave a note behind.

There wasn't any choice, after what'd happened a few days ago. Mollie had been doing all right. Keeping to herself perhaps, but functioning.

It was early in the afternoon, when her mother went to run errands in the village. Mollie had checked on Phoebe, who was home from school and feeling poorly. Her sister was asleep, her computer still on her lap. Mollie moved the PC to her desk and covered Phoebe with her duvet. She walked to the small office out in the barn to put her paperwork in order.

Mollie was somewhat concerned about buying a new buck –
in regards to both the cost and finding the right breeding goat –
but, as with most things right now, it was a vague worry. Practically speaking, she had a few more months to sort out the
problem and hopefully she'd be in a better frame of mind then.
She'd just begun to start on a project, but heard someone in the
barn entrance.

Quite unexpectedly, Mollie had a visitor. It was Natalie.

Mollie sat still in her chair, transfixed by the change in Natalie's appearance. For her part, Natalie might've been in a disguise.
Her long hair had been cut short into a sleek style that cupped
her jaw and made her beautiful eyes emerge. She'd done something to her eyes as well; she was wearing make-up and her
brows had been elegantly shaped. Not to mention, she'd traded in
her usual great, stomping gumboots for a pair of heels and a
simple dress.

'Nat?'

'I know. My new student ID. What do you think? I got quite a
few looks in the village. No one knew who I was!'

'You look lovely.'

'I wish I could say the same of you, Molls. You've lost weight,
love.'

'Yeah.'

Mollie stood, came around the desk and hugged Natalie. Then
apologised. She'd left dirt and straw behind. 'I'm sorry.'

'It's only a cotton dress, Mollie. It'll wash up. Why don't we go
into the house, though? Surely you've got time for a cup of tea?'

'Okay.'

Mollie felt self-conscious, imagining what Natalie must be
thinking of her. They'd known each other so well, for so many
years, that no small, subtle changes in Mollie would go unob-
served. Feeling defeated and so very tired, Mollie followed Natalie
into her own house and allowed her guest to get their tea. Natalie
knew her way around the kitchen at Hilltop Farm. She put the

kettle on, collected cups, and opened the dresser drawer where a tin of biscuits was always kept.

Mollie sat at the back of her kitchen table, watching her friend and thinking jumbled thoughts. She was glad that it was quiet and that it was sweet Natalie visiting her today, instead of Jenny, who'd be full of abuses about Mollie's blue mood.

Natalie brought the tea and biscuits and joined Mollie at the table.

Mollie made an effort. 'So, when are you leaving?'

'Tomorrow morning.'

Mollie looked at her, asking for details without speaking.

And Natalie answered. 'I am still excited. I can't seem to find it within myself to feel afraid, or nervous. And I don't regret it. Actually, it's more like I can't wait to get there, move in and start working. I found a few job adverts online and I've applied. I have an interview next week, to work in admissions at the hospital. I really want the position. Even though it's nothing to do with nursing, the pay is good and I'd literally be "in the door" so to speak.'

'I am so happy for you, Nat.'

'No, you're not, Mollie,' Natalie said softly. 'Because you're simply not happy at the moment.'

Mollie took a drink of her tea. She was having a difficult time getting into the flow of conversation with Natalie, whereas Oliver just seemed to be able to turn on her words like a switch. She didn't have a clue what to say next.

'What are you thinking, Molls?'

'I've been talking to Oliver Corbett. It's helped a lot.'

Natalie looked at her, considering this information.

Mollie added, 'It's nice to talk to you, too.'

'But not quite as nice,' Natalie said, smiling.

Mollie found her smile as well.

'You'll be okay?'

Mollie despised herself. She answered with as much energy as she could muster. 'Yes, of course.'

They sat quietly, sipping their tea. Mollie didn't really have a taste for it but it gave her something to do.

Natalie spoke gently. 'You know, Mollie, out of the three of us, you've always been the really smart one. You've a knack for figuring things out, for figuring how to push ahead with life. But I think, right now, you've sort of lost your way, haven't you?'

Mollie didn't bother nodding.

'So, if you don't mind too much, I want to give you a bit of advice. I really think you ought to go away. Not perhaps for a whole week. And it certainly wouldn't need to be anywhere special. A place to take you out of your everyday life. What do you think?'

Mollie knew Natalie was onto a good suggestion. 'Do you know, Oliver said exactly the same.'

'Well, if Oliver said!' Natalie teased. 'Would you maybe want to come with me? I am sure we could work something out with my new roomies?'

Definitely not. How to say it?

'Alright, I can see that's not on,' Natalie said, reading her. 'And no wonder. Moving in with us would be a bit like staying here with your mum and sisters.'

Mollie appreciated Natalie's understanding.

'I think I ought to go to my gran. You remember visiting her house in Birmingham, don't you?'

'How could I forget? The closest I've come to staying in Buckingham Palace.'

'It looks a bit smaller, now that we're not nine years old.' Mollie realised she'd said that quite spontaneously. She'd said it just like herself. 'But I could go anywhere. I'll decide at the station.'

'Just the idea of it is doing you a world of good. I can see that.'

It was true. She'd made a plan; things could be different, instead of the constant slog of dragging herself from bed to barn and back again. It wasn't an emotion that she could put a name to, but the fact that she actually *felt something* made for a nice change. Oliver would be proud of her, and knowing that she could tell him she'd taken his advice would be as though she was giving something back. And it was a response to Natalie, too, who was trying to be supportive.

'I don't want to tell them where I am going. In fact, I don't know where I'm going. I couldn't actually ring Granny.'

'You don't have to, Mollie.'

'This is the new Natalie.'

'Yes.' Her friend laughed and to Mollie she already looked like a successful nurse, living in a big city and loving her life.

Natalie said, 'Let them know you've gone and you're okay, but I know what you're thinking: your mum or Willa mightn't think it's best. Plus, it'll create bad moods if Phoebe thinks you're getting a treat from Granny. And you've already been a burden enough, right?'

'How well you know me. How well you know all of us.'

'You're right, though. It won't pacify Phoebe knowing that she's going to Scotland later, when you're with Granny now. I do think you ought to ring your grandmother, though. You know that's where you'll end up.'

Mollie looked at her quizzically. 'Perhaps. There are other destinations in the world.'

'My train doesn't leave until late tomorrow afternoon. I'll pick you up early in the morning and take you to the station.'

'Thanks, Nat. We'll say our goodbyes now, won't we?'

'I don't really want to do that. Just think of me coming home at Christmas, alright? But I am going to miss you, Mollie.' Mollie and Nat walked out of the house. They hugged and shed a few unwanted tears and then Natalie got into her mother's vehicle and drove away. Mollie stumbled back to the house, and threw some clothes into a rucksack to take along on her as-yet-undisclosed trip.

The same morning was one of utter confusion for Willa.

'"Startled" was a bit of an understatement,' Willa told her mother, who'd decided to work at home because Phoebe wasn't well. 'I came out of the house, half sleepwalking, and up springs Charlotte Seabury from the bottom of the porch. I might have sworn and I managed to spill coffee down my front.'

'I think she meant for you to see this note. It was by the coffee.' Lisa went to the dresser in the kitchen. She read Mollie's words aloud:

I need a bit of a break. I've asked Charlotte Seabury to help Willa with the milking and everything else. Don't worry.

'Have you looked to see if her big bag is gone?' Willa asked.

'No, but that's a good idea.'

'Mum?'

'Yes?'

'Are you okay?'

'Of course, darling.'

'I don't mean about Mollie. It seems you may have had something else on your mind. Even though you're obviously happy, I've been worried. I know that sounds absurd.'

Lisa crossed the kitchen and hugged Willa to her, kissing her cheek. 'No, you're just terribly perceptive, Willa. I know you need to be off to school, so I promise we'll talk about it, later.'

'Mum! How am I supposed to function all day with that bit of vague foreboding?'

Lisa laughed. 'The short version is, I met a man. We dated very briefly. We're no longer dating. But I'm fine.'

'And your new job?'

'I really, truly love it. Furthermore, we're not to worry about Mollie. She's a grown woman and she hasn't had more than twenty-four hours away from this farm in the last two years. She simply needs a break. Okay?'

Willa kissed her cheek in reply and left.

THE NEXT MORNING Phoebe was well and went to school.

Lisa woke with a terrible headache. It was grey, both outdoors and inside, and Lisa felt drained by bleak emotions.

As she took some tablets, she decided to quell her grief by getting dressed and going in to the office. She'd face Sam and be the friend to him that Michael was not. And she'd be an even better employee, somehow. There seemed to be scores to settle and though it made no sense, this is what helped Lisa face the day.

And what propelled her right into another muddle.

Perhaps Mollie's note should've concerned Lisa more than it did. But after a sleepless night, relentlessly reviewing every moment she'd spent with Michael Ferrington, she didn't have the emotional reserves to mourn Mollie's love life too. She knew from Mollie's note that her daughter merely needed space and Lisa was happy to indulge her. Especially after a bit of discussion, when Willa compassionately agreed to keep things going while Mollie was away.

So, this morning found Lisa less angry. But far more humiliated.

Lisa had believed Michael's lies without reservation. She'd been so appreciative at the gentle way he'd woken a dormant part of her life. He'd wanted to meet her children. He'd even managed to connect her with a wonderful job.

In turn, she'd given herself to him. Body and soul.

Her behaviour repulsed her now. How easily he'd been able to take advantage of her. How quickly she'd forgotten her personal code of conduct; how eager she'd been to be loved.

She checked her lipstick in the rear-view mirror of her car, got out and walked toward Sam Lloyd's rooms at the college. Coming in, she put away her handbag and laid the mail she'd collected on her desk. The office was pleasant. It was a rather large room, with a big window overlooking a lawn with some old trees. There was a walking path for students at some distance away, and beyond the lawn, another old building owned by the college. She'd brought in a houseplant in a cheerful pot and set it in the middle of the spacious window. Opposite her desk was a large bookshelf filled with books of interest to Sam, a twin of the other bookshelf in his office situated beyond her own.

A broad shelf on the wall served as a little hospitality station. She went to the electric kettle, filled it with fresh water from the water cooler and then flipped it on. Lisa could hear Sam's voice coming from behind his office door and gathered that he was in telephone conversation with a colleague about the agenda of an upcoming conference. She knew Sam had been asked to speak and realised that she'd never sat in on one of his classes or speaking engagements. Perhaps after their chat today he would invite her.

A shiver of nervous energy passed through her. He may be one of the kindest men she'd ever met, but it was still quite a risk that Lisa was about to take.

The kettle came to a boil and she made them both a cuppa, using a matching pair of mugs sporting the college logo. The teabags were running low; she kept meaning to bring in a box. Sam was forgetful about details like that and she'd assumed those sorts of tasks as part of her job, buying the odd box of staples, calling the repair person when the printer needed servicing. She was well paid and hadn't minded, and she enjoyed Sam's compliments of how she kept their shared space running smoothly. She realised, now, that his garden-variety, daily gratitude had always made her feel more special than an expensive bottle of scent, a typical gesture from Michael.

But she determined she wouldn't think about *him* any more.

With a cursory knock on the door, she entered Sam's office

and he greeted her with a smile. He picked up the mug of tea she'd made for him, and raised it to her in a toast, while saying, 'Yes, I see,' to the person on the phone. Lisa quietly left his office, closing the door behind her.

It was almost an hour later when she heard him end the call. Lisa sat up straighter in her chair to stretch her back. She'd made good progress this morning on helping to construct one of Sam's indexes. His office door opened.

'I must admit, I do miss your making me tea when you choose to work at home. Why does it always taste better when someone else makes it?'

'Would you like another cup?' Lisa offered.

'I would, actually, if it's no bother.' Sam sat in one of the three chairs in front of Lisa's desk that were sometimes occupied by students waiting to speak with him. He sighed. 'Lots of work, planning a conference. Somehow I always get roped in.'

'Will this one take place locally?'

'No. I'll have to spend the weekend in Northumberland next year. In January.'

'Oh, dear.'

'Yes, exactly. The only place I really fancy in early January is my reading chair, in front of my own humble fire.'

Lisa smiled. 'I've got one of those spots, too. It's also close to the Aga, so one can warm both sides at once.'

Sam laughed. 'Sounds delightful.'

He took a sip of tea and Lisa gathered her courage. 'Suppose I have an idea? Hopefully one that appeals more than freezing for academia.'

Sam raised his eyebrows but said nothing. Lisa wasn't sure his mind wasn't still on conference planning, but she must carry on or she'd lose her nerve.

'I'm going to a gallery opening. My friend, Tracy, does lovely watercolours and she and some other painters are having a little show close to the campus. I wondered if you might want to join me. Maybe go for supper afterwards?' She hadn't planned on adding the bit about going for a meal, but there it was.

Sam stopped, tea held high against his chest, mid-way to his mouth. 'Oh, my!' he said, obviously surprised. Lisa knew at once she'd made a mistake.

He lowered his tea, then raised it again and drank some and then said, 'I apologise. I don't think I could, actually.'

Lisa whimpered out a reply. She didn't seem to have enough breath for any decent volume. 'No problem.'

'I hope it won't, uh…'

'No, no. Of course not.' *Of course it matters. It may feel awkward between us for a fortnight. Or maybe an entire month!* She smiled broadly and flung her hand as though sweeping away a crumb. 'It was just a passing idea. Something I thought you may like to do. You seem to work so much.' *Wonderful.* Now she'd just criticised her boss regarding his work habits. She hoped her disappointment and embarrassment wasn't as obvious as it felt.

Sam drank the rest of his tea. He rubbed his hands together and said, in an altogether different voice. 'What have you got for me regarding the manuscript?'

'Two more chapters done, and I'm just finishing the index of the other,' Lisa replied with a forced cheerfulness. Why did she feel so gutted? It wasn't as though she was carrying a torch for Sam. She'd never even considered him as a potential date until Sally explained what'd happened with Michael's opportunistic actions. Had Sam known that she was dating Michael? If that were the case, no wonder he'd immediately turned down her invitation. Or, perhaps it was his policy that he simply never dated anyone from work. Either way, it certainly hadn't gone to plan.

Sam spoke with her for a few more minutes, confirming work details. He seemed uncomfortable, and then made his excuses and left the office. Lisa was thankful that he wasn't expected to return for the rest of the day.

CHAPTER 14

The day wore on at school. Willa would sit for her final exams soon and have her results by August. Following that, she hadn't a clue. She'd tried speaking with her mother, but her mum had been a bit preoccupied. Perhaps now that Lisa wasn't seeing the mysterious boyfriend any longer, she may have some new inspirations for Willa, beyond, 'What would you *like* to do, darling?' Willa was the sort of person that much preferred collaboration of thought. Not that she didn't think for herself, but she wanted someone to talk to about everything.

People at school seemed to have very definite plans. She'd been in the top stream, yet she felt totally daft. The staff seemed to have overlooked the fact that she wasn't heading anywhere, and she hadn't known what to do about it; she wondered if she was meant to make appointments with a counsellor or something. Not wanting to draw attention to herself, she'd simply done what was in front of her. The next step, of course, was to complete her GCSEs and leave school. Perhaps she'd just milk goats for Mollie and read fabulous books in the evenings for the rest of her life. It wasn't like she'd be breaking any laws.

Added to her angst was Mollie's strange disappearance this morning.

Willa had wanted to talk to Mollie, or try, but now Mollie had done a runner. For some reason, her sister's departure had made her feel nervous. Life was already all over the place; Mollie ought to be at home.

Then Willa had had a corker of an idea.

She'd go ask the one person that may know where Mollie had gotten to and what her leaving meant: Oliver Corbett. After all, Mollie was her sister. Her lifeline, really. Willa had a right to know.

One of the mysteries of Mollie's departure was that she'd left behind their ancient vehicle, indicating that someone had picked her up. Willa was sure Mollie wouldn't have wasted her hard earned cash on a taxi to the bus station.

After school, Willa quickly changed from her uniform into a pair of jeans, a jersey and some sneakers. She then changed her mind entirely and slipped into a soft, cabled jumper dress and a pair of flats. She retrieved the keys from the hook where they hung in the boot room. It was a rainy, cold day, and the interior of the old Land Rover smelt of wet dog. The worn windscreen wipers needed replacing, and Willa moved about, trying to see past the wide smear on the glass.

As she neared the Corbett's estate, it occurred to Willa that perhaps she wouldn't find Oliver at home. Perhaps *he* was the one who'd taken Mollie away? They could be together.

She considered this. She and Mollie hadn't seen much of Oliver since he moved away to university at seventeen. Once, she remembered they'd been thrown together with him and a number of other young people at a party. It was the New Year. Had he been a fresher then? Willa couldn't remember. The point was, Mollie had been reacquainted with him for only a month. Had they fallen in love and Mollie hadn't been able to explain? Willa felt she wasn't sure who Mollie was any more.

She turned into the black iron gates of Myndcroft Hall. The long drive was bordered by forest for a quarter mile and then subtly gave way to open parkland with ancient trees. The lane swept to the left and began the climb to the top of the hill where the massive old house was situated. There was available parking for dozens, and so Willa just stopped somewhere along the perimeter and stepped out, leaving her keys in the ignition. She saw no one about, so decided to go to the front door and see if she could be heard with the knocker or bell. If not, she'd go around the back, and could probably find Mrs Jenkins in her kitchen.

Willa knocked. Then she rang. Just as she was about to turn away, Colleen Corbett opened the great door.

'Why, hello, Willa! Do come in, darling. You look cold. I hope the rain stops soon.' She chirped all of this friendly greeting while taking Willa's coat. She led her visitor past the grand staircase and toward the drawing room at the back of the house, where a large fire was lit.

'Oh, this does feel lovely, doesn't it, Willa? The oil heater works in our old pile, but somehow I'd forgotten to turn it on. We've had such a long spell of warmth, haven't we?' Willa shuddered and hoped her hostess didn't notice. Oliver's mother carried on. 'Well, do settle there, Willa, and I'll see if I can trouble Mrs Jenkins for some tea. She's been doing a spring clean, so if I am not back straightaway, you'll know I am taking a moment to prepare it for us. Alright then?'

'Yes, thanks so much, Colleen.'

When Lady Ranson had left the room and could be heard clicking down the corridor, Willa stood up from the floral sofa with its deep, lovely cushions and went to stand by the fire. She held out her hands. Within several minutes, the fire had done its work, and her fingers were quite toasty, but Willa didn't draw them back. There was something glorious about having them too hot, even though her skin would be dry later. She wondered about this and supposed she was in an extreme sort of mood. What else would prompt her to behave so rudely, showing up unannounced, to enquire as to whether Lady Ranson's son had carried off her morose sister? Maybe living with Mollie made her crackers in her own right. She hadn't been sleeping terribly well; feeling the pressure of ending school and not knowing what to do had stirred her thoughts during the long nights.

She returned to her previous perch on the sofa and took in the room. She loved it here. The room was long and had many windows and doors leading onto the wide terrace, allowing an uninterrupted view of the dark, rain laden clouds. The lawn where they'd had the spring party was empty and stretched at an incline up towards the horizon behind the house. Beyond, the Shropshire Hills looked like grey-stone sculpture. The house was a true family home; cosy, with lots of furniture, books, carpets and rugs, so that one didn't feel overwhelmed by the modern, wet world outside. There was a table in front of the fire littered with newspapers, a few magazines and a curling birthday card; it all reminded her of her own home and endeared the Corbetts to her. They were very unpretentious people in their own way, though Alex, Oliver's father, did have his 'Lord Ranson' moments –when he was quite authoritative and impressive.

'Here we are!'

Willa had quite forgotten that Colleen Corbett was coming with tea and so relaxed had Willa become that she could've dropped off for a nap. Stifling a yawn added to her embarrassment. She was completely without manners, sleep deprived, and had foisted herself on this unsuspecting neighbour. Willa could've cried.

'Are you okay?'

Willa looked at Colleen and couldn't lie. 'No, I am not. I am so very sorry for troubling you like this. I'm sure you were quite busy, going about your day, and here I am. I've been completely obnoxious, turning up at your door, rain soaked and ridiculous.'

'Oh, Willa. Don't be so hard on yourself. Mrs Jenkins had me feeling quite guilty over the state of my sewing room, so I'd determined to give it a good clean. You can't imagine how relieved I am that you've given me an excuse to stop.' She laughed sincerely and good-naturedly and Willa adored her for it. 'I was talking about you to your darling mum at the Corbett's garden party. She said you're due to sit for your exams soon. You've always been so bright, Willa, that I can't imagine you've even had to study for them.'

Willa blushed at the compliment. 'I feel fairly prepared. And *really* ready to leave school!'

'Oh, I remember being the same way. When the end came, I wasn't at all sad. You see, I wasn't really one to have lots of friends and didn't go about crying over how I'd miss everyone. I'd wanted to get on.'

This was the opposite of how Willa had imagined Colleen Corbett – whatever her unmarried name had been.

'I feel the same way.'

Colleen quieted and Willa felt it was the moment to confess why she'd come. She took a sip of tea for courage. It was strong and black, just perfect for helping Willa gather herself.

'I came to see, well, I wondered if Oliver was home today?'

'Yes, he is. Shall I go get him?' She looked ready to shoot away at Willa's command and discomfort washed over her again.

'I've been such an inconvenience. I am so sorry.'

'No, perhaps I ought have asked you in the first place if you wanted to see Oliver–' Colleen spoke without conviction, though, as she knew Willa and Oliver were more in the category of long-familiar acquaintances rather than close friends.

'You see, Mollie's left home, without much information, and I happen to know that she's been talking to Oliver a bit since he's come home. So, I thought–'

'Of course. See, there you are, Willa, being clever again. He probably can help to put your mind at ease. You just enjoy your tea and for heaven's sake, help me eat that cake. I'll see if I can run him to earth.'

Willa sighed in relief but felt acutely embarrassed that the lady of the house had just popped up to do her bidding. Now she was gone, Willa thought of all sorts of kind and proper things she could've said to Mrs Corbett. Asking about her daughter for example. Or thanking her for the lovely time they'd had at the party. But she'd said none of this, and it was down to Colleen's graciousness that Willa didn't remove herself immediately due to overwhelming shame.

She reclined her head back on the sumptuous cushion. It was a very odd thing to feel absolute self-consciousness over one's bad manners, and to be so relaxed and sleepy at the same time. A few more minutes passed. Then she heard a noise in the corridor that brought her to her senses. She sat up and took another sip of tea.

Oliver had come alone.

He was dressed in jeans and a long sleeved T-shirt, and his cheeks were rosy as though he'd been outside in the cold. Looking at him now, she felt as though she'd never laid eyes on him in her life. He was gorgeous, and taller and more heavily-muscled than Willa remembered. When had he become so handsome? Willa felt immobilised. She hadn't actually thought this through and now it was too late. She'd called on Oliver, meaning to ask him personal questions. Her humiliation seemed to have not hit bottom, yet, and she just continued falling, falling, falling, since she'd been received in this house, despite the kindness – or in part, because of it – that she'd been shown.

'Hi, Willa. Lovely to see you. There were so many people at the party I didn't have the opportunity to speak to, and you were one of them.'

'Really?' *Think of something else to say, Willa. Now.*
Nothing came.

'Yes. Of course you probably know that I'd seen Mollie, and

she'd told me how well you've been getting on at school. She's so proud of you, you know.'

Oliver had mentioned Mollie, giving her a perfect segue into the reason she came. Willa realised this, but still hadn't quite recovered her composure. Oliver was… rather distracting.

'Oh.'

He was sitting in the chair where his mother had sat and was leaning towards her, forearms resting on his knees. He looked down at his hands. An awkward silence fell between them.

She cleared her throat. 'I've come to ask about Mollie.'

'Have you?' Oliver looked at her with eyes that were more green than blue. Willa knew she needed to think about their colour later. She glanced at her teacup. It was empty. Her throat was dry.

'May I?' Watching her carefully, Oliver responded by picking up the teapot, leaning further, coming closer. Willa put out her hand, which was trembling, as evidenced by the cup rattling slightly on its saucer.

'Willa, you're shaking.' Mercifully, Oliver took the teacup from her. Willa had a passing thought of how dearly the china must cost and was thankful to be relieved of it. He put down the teapot as well and took Willa's breath away by coming to sit directly beside her on the sofa.

He said, softly, 'I hadn't realised you were so upset.' He reached out and took Willa's hands in his. She was glad she'd practically roasted them on the fire so as not to be cold and damp and off-putting. She looked down at her hands, so small in Oliver's. She couldn't believe how lovely this was.

Oliver said, 'You mustn't worry about Mollie, all right?'

Willa looked up at him. He was very concerned about her.

'I'd thought perhaps she'd run away with you, and that your mother might have information about where you'd gone.'

His brows flew up in surprise. He sort of laughed. Worse, he dropped her hands as he said, 'No.'

Willa felt the need to defend herself. After all, she'd asked a logical question. 'But I know Mollie's been talking to you. In fact, you're the only person she's spoken to, it would seem, about anything. So, naturally–'

'Oh. Yes, you're quite right. I am sorry, it's just that, well, it wasn't like *that*. Mollie and I are mates. Wait – what did you mean about running away?'

Willa told him. 'She's gone. There was a note about Mr Seabury's daughter coming to help me with milking the goats. We have lots of relations, but they're mostly inhospitable. Not the sort to help out.'

'Even your grandmother?'

'We all adore her but Granny sort of relates to us on her own schedule and her own terms, if you see what I mean. She wouldn't encourage us to show up unannounced and in a crisis. Besides, Mum thinks Granny may be away at the moment.'

'If she is home, then perhaps your grandmother is a bit more generous than you imagine? I really don't think you ought to worry, Willa.'

'But we've no idea where she is and her phone is turned off.'

Oliver sighed and said, 'I'm afraid that's my fault.'

Then he explained and Willa knew she was right, after all, in coming to talk to Oliver about Mollie's whereabouts.

OLIVER SAID TO HIS MOTHER, 'Come with me?'

He'd snapped the lead on the dog's collar, and was setting out on a walk. The rain had finally ceased after lunch, although the sky was a strange greenish colour and overcast to the point of looking as though it was early evening at half two. His mother pulled on her ancient Barbour and she followed him outside.

They crossed the lawn in front of the house then picked up a track alongside the wood, as it was muddy beneath the trees.

Feeling generous and having missed talks and walks with his mum since being at school, he came right to the subject at hand.

'Mollie's done a runner.'

'Really? That seems so against her character. Surely she's the most responsible girl. Carrying on with the business after her father died. How many eleven- or twelve-year-old girls do that? And stick with it, these many years on?'

'Oh but then she got talking to me, didn't she.'

Colleen laughed at him. 'Whatever did you say to her, Oliver?'

'I saw myself in her. You know how completely crushed I was when Arabella broke things off. I knew I had to get on with my life and I was doing my best. But I told Mollie what really helped was to leave for a bit and gather some perspective.'

'And she was open to that?'

'Not at first. She quoted at me, you know, the one about wherever you go to escape yourself, there you are. I suggested that, for me, it wasn't about trying to run away from my problems. Or even from seeing Arabella, for that matter. But that some physical distance and a change of scenery sort of took me out of my head. That's the problem, she's been ruminating. She has lots of hours to think about Rhys Davies.'

'So, obviously she took your advice.'

'Yes.'

'But her family thought she was missing?'

Oliver paused and let the dog off his lead for a run in the meadow. 'Not missing, exactly. Mollie did leave them a note. Being the sensible girl she is she'd even lined up farm help. She just failed to say exactly where she was going. And when they asked Charlotte Seabury how long Mollie had hired her for, the daft girl said she hadn't a clue. Mollie hadn't said and Charlotte hadn't thought to ask.'

Colleen looked at her son with an enquiring expression. Oliver recognised the look as a means of asking permission. 'You've been here at home most of the time since you returned from uni. I guess I am a bit confused as to when you had a conversation with Mollie. Care to enlighten me?'

'Unwittingly, I ended up right in the middle of the drama.' Oliver explained to his mother how he'd been speaking to Rhys and Courtney when Mollie came into the house on the day of the party. 'She saw them together and was obviously gutted. Courtney's such a bore. So, I waited about and invited Mollie to come into the library with me for a few minutes. It gave her a chance to calm down a bit.'

'You told her to leave then?'

'No. I've met her once every few days since then. Up on the rock. Just for quick chats, a hug and a bit of sympathy. Do you remember, after Arabella, we'd gone to London and I spoke to you about her? But I hadn't talked to anyone else. Some of my best mates at school didn't even realise that we'd broken up.'

Colleen nodded.

'Mollie was the same. She couldn't talk to everyone. Only me.'

Oliver's mother had other questions, but dared not ask them. She felt assured regarding Mollie. But she also had an inkling that Oliver wasn't disclosing everything he had on his mind with regards to the Purslow family.

CHAPTER 15

$\mathcal{M}$ollie was in unchartered territory with Granny. Her grandmother very nearly slammed the door in her face.

'I'll not be a party to this, Mollie. Running away is inconsiderate to the extreme. You shall ring your mother immediately. Then we'll have a talk about whether or not you're to stay here.' With that, Granny turned and marched off.

Mollie wanted to call after her and ask what she was supposed to tell her mother, since she didn't know if Granny was kicking her out. Mollie used the phone in Granny's hall. No one answered at Hilltop Farm, so Mollie left a brief message that she'd found her way to Gran's house and that she'd phone back later. She spoke as though they knew that was her destination and perhaps she'd just forgotten to write it, slightly appeasing her conscience.

Natalie had dropped her at the station early this morning. Mollie wanted to leave but still felt upset at having to take this step. She'd looked at the wodge of notes pulled from her carryall. Oliver had given her a generous amount of cash to make good on his advice. But when standing in the Church Stretton station, faced with the myriad of possible destinations, she lacked the energy to be creative. Besides, Oliver had insisted her grandmother would understand and take her in.

Oliver may have been wrong.

Mollie made her way, dripping, into Granny's perfectly clean home. She'd walked a half-mile in pouring rain from the Four Oaks train station to Granny's house on Bracebridge Road. She toed off her squishy, filthy trainers and left them on the hall rug by her soaked nylon bag. She shuffled down the slippy wooden floor in her drenched socks, looking for her grandmother in various rooms as she passed by. She came to the kitchen feeling slightly dizzy and remembered she hadn't eaten since yesterday.

It was then that she spied Granny across the bricked patio, busy in her conservatory. She grew all sorts of beautiful plants there and had loads of fresh arrangements throughout her house. Mollie wondered if this meant she might be allowed to stay; perhaps Granny was fashioning a little nosegay for one of the spare bedrooms. Doubtful, though; Granny was deadheading an Asiatic lily with undue violence. Mollie couldn't recall having seen Granny so angry as when she opened the door to find her dripping on the doorstep. Things in Granny's world were ordered, but, more than this, she was committed to the notion of Manners. One was to Consider Other People's Feelings at all times. Which meant that one didn't Show Up Completely Unannounced at Other People's Homes.

She plodded in wet stockinged feet and went meekly to her grandmother in the conservatory. The heavy, sweet scent of gardenias permeated the air, reminding Mollie of her father's funeral flowers. She'd hated gardenias since.

Granny turned and looked her up and down. 'Why haven't you gotten out of those horrible clothes? Not that you're going to put on anything less horrible, but at least your others would be dry.' Mollie thought of her saturated bag and doubted this was true.

'Why are you standing there like a dolt, Mollie? Get a move on.'

The disdain in her grandmother's eyes reached through the fog. Since the day of the garden party, Mollie had felt detached. Talking to Oliver had been the rare thing that seemed to anchor her to humanity. Otherwise, she'd seemed to move into this strange role of being an observer.

But just now, unexpectedly, Granny had stuck a pin right through Mollie's numb layer of defence.

Her torso seemed to bob back and forth, her mind ignorant of what was happening to her. Her face contorted as her hands grabbed her stomach, wadding up the generous pleats of her father's trousers in her hands. A strange sound came from her mouth and Granny's confused face swam out of focus. Then Granny's arms were around her, squeezing her wet clothes into Mollie's spasmodic body. By the time Mollie realised she was weeping, she couldn't stop.

The sobbing lasted for a while. After some minutes Granny led Mollie dumbly to the kitchen and pushed her onto a tall stool at the kitchen counter. Mollie's head had gone down on her crossed forearms. She was so tired. The sobs gave her a sore tummy and left her feeling unable to sit. Granny pressed a tissue into one of her hands and Mollie carried it to her nose. Mollie guessed she'd need another box of those.

Time slipped by. Granny was in her study making phone calls. Mollie still sat collapsed over the kitchen counter. She thought about Rhys Davies. She wondered if he would propose to his new girlfriend this Christmas and if Courtney would invite her to their wedding just to be completely odious. Even now, she didn't think Rhys would allow that. He was still a man to be admired in Mollie's eyes; it was her fault she'd lost him. She rolled her head onto one side, scanning the room. Granny was coming back down the wide passage towards Mollie. Mollie felt very fragile and hoped Granny wouldn't scold her again for having a breakdown in her otherwise shipshape kitchen.

She didn't. Instead, 'I've run a hot bath for you, darling. You've caught a chill.'

'Yes. I suppose.' Mollie feebly raised her head. It pounded against the effort.

'Go on, then. Get in the bath and after that, come down for some Scotch broth.'

Mollie didn't move, her eyes filling with tears again.

'Thanks, Gran.'

Granny leaned over and kissed Mollie's damp forehead, which bore an imprint of her sleeve. 'Now go.'

Mollie did as she was told. She'd traded her numb feeling for something worse. She felt as though every nerve fibre was exposed. The bath was too hot, too cavernous, too wet. When she finally coaxed herself in to the hot water, the air above felt like a biting draft, unbearably cold; the lights of the bathroom, blinding. Mustering her courage, she pulled the plug, towelled off, and stepped into another pair of her father's old trousers and a heavier shirt this time, made of cinnamon coloured wool. She plodded downstairs, wobbly from the hot bath and fasting.

Granny was sorting through her mail in the hall. Mollie saw Granny scrutinising her and realised she ought to have dried her hair. She followed Granny into the kitchen, took her perch once more and spooned down the delicious soup in silence. The broth acted as a tonic, nourishing her from the inside out. Sitting up, her head stopped hammering and eased into a dull ache. The kettle sang. Granny added lots of sugar and milk to a large mug of tea and stood it in front of Mollie, who gulped as eagerly as a lapping puppy.

'Your father always drank scalding hot tea, too. I've read that it's bad for one's oesophagus.'

'But it feels so good. Warms me right through.'

'Good. You're going to need it.'

Granny was still being firm, but more maternal about it now. 'Because we're going shopping. I simply can't allow my granddaughter to go stomping around in my dead son's clothes. It's really macabre, Mollie, and isn't going to help you get over your loss.'

'But–'

'No. I know what you're going to say, Mollie. Firstly, I haven't taken you on any of the trips your sisters have enjoyed with me. I'm not likely to get you away from the goats again anytime soon, so I've decided to send you home next week with merchandise. Secondly, you needn't panic, as I am prepared to kit you out for working at the farm as well. There are several shops that are major stockists of all of the country brands. Tough-wearing, serviceable clothing. I'll take your opinion into consideration, but you *will go* and you *will try them on*. Understood?'

Her grandmother's disappointment in her appearance sliced at her tender feelings, but Mollie was drained of tears. She followed her grandmother to the car and then suddenly it seemed they were getting out of it. The drive had been a blur, but now Mollie felt like a hunting dog, keenly attuned to the sharp noises of the busy streets and the pungent smells of the restaurants. And the need to escape into the closest wood.

True to her word, Granny took her first to a shop selling country wares. Mollie knew such places existed, but she'd never actually been in one. There were signs about the shop and she recognised them as being the same as the labels in her father's old clothes, the same ones, in fact, that she stood in at this moment. She glanced at a movement to the left; it was herself, reflected in a glass. Mollie almost gasped at the strange picture she made; a tall, thin girl with lank, drenched hair, in shabby, rough clothes that were clearly for a person of another sex, two sizes larger than herself. Surely there were people living rough on the street who looked more presentable than she. How had Rhys loved her in spite of her looking like a dog's dinner?

A plump lady with a tight bun on the back of her head approached them, all smiles, mostly at Granny. 'Hello, ladies, can I help?' she sang. Mollie thought she looked rather like an itchy tree trunk. She was square and squeezed into a tweed suit, her tyre shaped skirt gracing sturdy calves. Mollie wanted nothing more from this annoying woman than to be left on her own. Looking away to withhold eye-contact, Mollie noticed a table a few steps away. It was laid with dozens of soft, lofty jumpers, folded and queued in neat rows. Granny followed Mollie's sightline and announced to missus Sausage-in-a-Tweed, 'We'll begin with these.'

Mollie held a V-neck in a yummy plum colour against herself. It was softer than a baby goat.

'I think that will do nicely for you.'

'No, Gran. It's cashmere.'

'Willa will teach you how to care for it. Surely you go somewhere besides the barn, Mollie. If not, you should. Take the black one, too, and another in the blue.'

The saleswoman rushed forward to take possession of Mollie's commission-heavy cashmere. 'I'll just start a little collection for you over here, shall I?' The woman fairly cooed and Mollie remembered times past where she and Jenny would've exchanged a look of disgust.

Mollie submissively followed her grandmother through the shop, stepping into clothes behind the velvet red curtain, exchanging sizes, having trousers and jackets measured, being marked as to be let out for Mollie's height. At last they were at the till. The plum jumper was being shuffled into tissue paper and joining what seemed to be half the inventory of the shop: trousers, a waxed jacket, a hooded down-filled coat, shirts with collars, even a knitted hat and a pair of leather gloves, all constructed to hold up against weather, dirt and years of use. They would come back for the trousers, and the rest would consume half the space in Gran's boot, where they now stood crammed in shopping carriers. For the present, Mollie was back in the clothes she'd brought from home. She'd admitted to herself that it was difficult to put them back on, having had tried on similar, comfortable items in her own size. However, even if she wouldn't be wearing her father's clothes any longer, she had no intention of letting them go. She'd carefully store them away in his old attic office.

'We'll stop for a late lunch.'

Mollie's appetite had returned with a vengeance. The sunshine made an appearance as well and Mollie stood squinting for a moment, until she realised her determined grandmother had sped off from the car toward a cafe in the next block. Mollie caught her up and they were thrust into a revolving door which opened into a noisy eatery. Immediately a girl led Granny to one of the best tables by the window with a flower basket showing through from outside. A moment later, another efficient girl, who looked a few seconds too long at Mollie's clothes, took their orders for sandwiches and drinks.

'Gran, thank you so much. I didn't think you'd want to buy me work clothes.'

'Who do you think bought the ones you have on?' Mollie looked up to find her grandmother smiling.

'Probably from the same shop?'

'As a matter of fact, yes. They're costly initially but they wear like iron.'

'I always thought you were rather disappointed by Dad's choices. You know, him wanting to be a farmer.'

'Well there you're quite wrong. He was completely enamoured with agriculture, and with your mother. I was happy for him. For them. I remember there was a local farm open several times a year for "dairy days", offering visitor tours of the farm and of the milking operations. People were encouraged to ask questions of the farmer. Grant went back twice. He was hooked. After graduating from university, he told me that he'd never forgotten those beautiful blue hills. That was the place on earth he most wanted to be.' Granny smiled at the memory. 'When Hilltop Farm came up for sale, the timing was perfect. It was Grant's dream coming true, right on schedule.' Granny's voice was thoughtful. 'I'll be honest, Mollie. Your father realised it was a harder life, in terms of physical work and less financial reward, but in other ways it was much easier because he loved it all. He loved the independence, the animals and raising his family in the countryside.'

'I love it, too.'

Granny reached out and squeezed Mollie's hand. 'Yes, I can see that you do. And you're making a go of it, my girl. Stick to getting what you want out of life. You mustn't let yourself simply float out to sea, because of a love affair gone awry.'

Mollie wanted – needed – Granny's insight on this. She wouldn't let on that Oliver had told her about Granny and his great uncle, but she replied, 'It sounds as though you speak from experience.'

Granny gave her a penetrating look, and Mollie's gaze darted to her plate.

'I do speak from experience. All I can say is, you'll live. And when the right love comes along, try not to let it go for anything in the world.'

Mollie glanced up but this time Granny's eyes were downcast. There was a brusqueness in the way she stabbed her fork into her garnish that indicated she was navigating some strong emotions. They were quiet for the remainder of the lunch, each woman deep in her own thoughts.

CHAPTER 16

The next day was full of more shopping and Mollie resigned herself to accepting Granny's generosity. She felt happy about having clothes that fit and were farm-worthy, so she'd cooperate with Granny regarding the fashionable bits. Fortunately, they got through the worst in the morning, which was shopping for smalls. Mollie figured she now owned more bras than her mum and sisters combined. Then Granny was appalled to learn that Mollie didn't actually have a handbag and carried her money and keys in her trousers like a man. Why should that be such a shock, Mollie thought, when she'd been wearing men's trousers?

They were in the midst of looking at handbags, with Mollie not caring for any of them, when one of Granny's friends materialised from a nearby display of shoes.

'Phoebe! Oh, imagine seeing you here,' said the gushing woman, wearing a bright pink tracksuit that Mollie wouldn't be caught dead in.

'Hello, Delores. How's Fred?'

They embraced and grasped hands as one or the other emphasised different pieces of news. Mollie lingered over some belts that she rather liked.

'And this is my granddaughter, Mollie!'

Granny was reaching out to her, ready to squeeze her by the shoulders and present her to her friend.

'Oh, how lovely.' Delores's eyes grew large. 'I don't suppose Mollie shall still be with you on Saturday?'

Granny said, 'Why, what's happening then?'

'I am simply desperate for someone to model for our fashion fundraiser. Mollie would be perfect. So tall! Of course, we'd need you to do a fitting, dear, just to make sure we have the proper outfits for you. In fact, that's why I am here this morning; one of our other models did fine with the clothing but she didn't have a decent pair of pumps.'

'Mollie would be delighted, wouldn't you, darling?'

Mollie felt her blood pressure rise and her cheeks burn. How dare her grandmother commit her to such a horrible undertaking? She considered walking right out of the store and onto a bus, as Granny walked away, chatting on and on with the despicable Delores.

She suddenly didn't care that Granny understood her feelings, or that she'd kitted her out with enough country clothes to be the best dressed farmer for the next decade running. Mollie despised prissiness, make-up, and doing anything with her hair besides wearing it in a ponytail. She'd positively refuse to do this.

What on earth was her grandmother thinking?

Then Mollie had a thought: perhaps Granny was just putting the woman off and somehow she'd made excuses in the interim. Granny could be infuriating and headstrong, but she wasn't daft. Mollie couldn't even walk in heels, not to mention behaving like a fashion model was enormously stupid. Granny must surely have another plan.

Calming herself, she tried on one of the rustic looking leather belts over her father's trousers. It looked great with the corduroys, and there was a handbag that sort of matched. These would tick another box on the very long list of 'necessities' that Granny planned for her. She just hoped some jeans were part of Granny's 'priorities' as hers at home were looking the worst for wear.

Granny had returned, acting as though Delores didn't exist.

'Oh, that's a smart belt and handbag you've got there. I think they're both suitable. Well done, Mollie. It isn't that difficult once you get in the spirit of things, is it?'

She had taken the items from Mollie and was handing them to a salesperson. 'How about a few pairs of jeans and some tops?' Granny said with a smile. A syrupy sort of smile.

'Gran?'

'We'll discuss it later. Stay focused. There's a myth in the world, Mollie, it's called multitasking. It isn't really true that people can do all sorts of things at once. At the moment, you are shopping. Head in the game and all of that.'

Perhaps her grandmother secretly worked for the government. She couldn't have merely kept her housekeepers in line and her garden free of slugs all these years? She was positively a force to be reckoned with.

Obediently, Mollie trailed her from one department to the next, trying on jeans, tops, jackets, even a casual dress. She hated the dress and it came off before Granny saw it on her.

'Did it fit?' Granny asked from outside the changing room.

'Well, yes, but–'

'Then you're having it.'

Mollie had stopped caring about an hour ago. She'd even put on a happy face regarding a pair of sandals with a jewel on each foot. The more efficiently she cooperated, the sooner it would be over.

Eventually it was.

It was over tea that evening at home that her grandmother finally came clean.

'This is how it will be, Mollie. I shall tell you all of the details and I am sure you'll find that you can rise to the occasion.'

'You mean you actually agreed to me modelling for that bloody woman?' Mollie hadn't ever used that tone with her grandmother. But if there was a first time for everything, then *this* was the time to rebel.

Granny suddenly looked pleased. No, that was too mild a word. Thrilled.

'Look at you, Mollie. You're back, darling.' She came to Mollie and hugged her where she sat at the dining room table.

Mollie softened. 'Oh, Gran. I think you're right. The modelling thing, all of the shopping, just being here. It was like Oliver said, I needed to be taken out of my head. I feel ever so much more like my old self. But I'm warning you, Granny. I shall hate every moment if you make me do modelling. Just the thought edges me towards suicidal tendencies.'

'That's lovely, darling.' Granny said. Did she hear nothing? Granny became all businesslike. 'I did tell Delores you'd model, and so of course you'll not do anything to jeopardise my word. It's simple: you'll put on five outfits and walk around a dining room showing them whilst women eat lunch. I've insisted that you're not to wear heels; they may imagine you've had an injury or something, say nothing about it. The whole thing will take two hours of your time and it's for a good cause.'

Mollie crossed her arms in front of her. 'A dining room?'

'Yes.'

'Not up on a stage. No one but lunching ladies? No men?'

'Right. And the people serving the food; Delores's help back-stage. You'll do it.'

It was more of a statement.

'Yes, Gran. I'll do it. Only for you.'

'Excellent. And now here's a detail that'll wipe that scowl from your face.'

Mollie couldn't help but laugh. It seemed an odd sort of noise. She hadn't laughed spontaneously in a while, except at Oliver, and that was more of a chuckle. But her Grandmother's terse observation amused her.

'What's that, Gran?'

'You'll be paid three hundred and fifty pounds.'

'*What?*'

'I insisted you receive what the girls from the agency get and that's the pay.'

'Oh, Gran! I really need the money. Thank you.'

Mollie's grandmother grinned, rather like the cat with the cream, and said, 'If you do well, there are more assignments. Or whatever they call them. *Should you want them.*' Mollie wondered how rich people ever made money for their charities when they spent so much on fundraising efforts.

'I'll be able to get my new cheese labels! And look into buying a new buck to replace Gruff.'

'What about staff wages?'

'What are you talking about?'

'It seems to me, Mollie, that Willa does an awfully lot for you. There's very little in it for her. She may decide to do something differently in future. Then what would you do?'

'Has she said something?'

Granny pulled a face. 'No, dear. Mollie, if you're going to be in business for yourself, you need to learn to look ahead. Labour is always an expense. You treat Willa abominably. And you know your odds of getting Phoebe out to the barn are nil.'

'I'll give it some thought.' Mollie felt tremendously encouraged. 'I feel as though I've been away a year. I can't even remember what date I was meant to submit my cheese for the awards this year.'

Granny patted her and squeezed her hand. 'You'll catch it all up when you go home next week. If you've missed the competition then there's plenty else to do.'

'I suppose.' Mollie sighed.

'Another bit of advice, Mollie?'

'Please, Gran.'

'Do consider actually wearing your new clothes.'

Mollie blushed. She'd hung up all her new things, admired them, and thanked her grandmother profusely. But she sat, now, on her grandmother's silk sofa, taking tea in her father's work clothes.

CHAPTER 17

Willa was apprehensive about her sister's homecoming. She'd worked diligently on a special surprise for Mollie, and hoped to inspire her sister. Restless, Willa got up from the table to put the kettle on. 'Maybe we should've gone with Mum to meet her at the station.'

'Oh, right,' Phoebe snorted. 'It's massively unfair that Mollie's been at Granny's for an entire week. But she deserves a home-coming party as well.'

'You know what Gran would say if she heard your moaning.'

'I know, but it's true. Maybe I'll decide that I am in a horrible mood because a boy said something hideous to me, then Granny will have to take me in for a week.'

'Phoebe, give it a rest. Please.' Truth be told, Willa felt a twinge of envy when she thought of Mollie's holiday in Birmingham. It was difficult not to, when staying at their grandmother's was like entering another world – one of wealth, leisure and freedom from responsibility. Mollie's timing had been awful; Willa felt secure in her preparedness for her exams, but she still had to go through them.

'Do you suppose Granny took her shopping?'

Willa snapped at her little sister. 'If she did, do you know of anyone who needs clothes more than Mollie? She's spent every penny on building up her business, which is a bit more admirable than trying to impress people.'

'I do not try to impress people,' Phoebe countered. 'I'm simply impressive.'

'And incredibly humble. Why don't you take yourself off somewhere else so that I can study?'

It was then that the kettle clicked off and simultaneously they heard car doors shutting outside the farmhouse. Willa and Phoebe shared a worried glance. They scuttled into the kitchen. As the back door opened, Willa went to the kettle, ready to make the drinks. Mollie was the first to come in, bearing her old rucksack and a vast number of shopping bags.

'I *knew* it! Granny's bought you a shedload of new clothes!' Phoebe turned on her heel, presumably to go to her room and share the grief of her situation with her friends online.

Willa instantly knew by looking at her sister that she'd come back to them, not just from Birmingham. She stepped forward and reached up on her toes to hug Mollie's neck. 'I've missed you,' she said into Mollie's hair. 'Welcome home.'

'I've missed you too, Willa.'

'Sorry about Phebs. You know how jealous she is.'

'Yeah. I've brought her some hair stuff from that one salon and a Tolkien T-shirt.'

Willa smiled. 'Good plan.'

'Did the kettle just boil?'

'Yes, Mum.'

While Lisa made herself some tea, Willa couldn't wait another moment. 'I've made you some presents.' It was as exciting as Christmas. She disappeared for a moment, and then brought Mollie several gift bags, which she stood on the kitchen table. 'I couldn't wrap them together. You'll see why.'

Willa shared an excited look with her mother, who seemed

very happy and relaxed. She and Mollie must've had a nice chat on the way home.

Mollie untied a loose ribbon that bound the handles of a light blue gift bag with matching tissue paper. She lifted out a small white box. 'It's like a Chinese takeaway packet. Is it lunch, Willa?' Mollie pressed together the folds of the box. It opened to reveal several chocolate truffles.

'You're crafting chocolates now?'

'Not just any sort, Mollie. These truffles are filled with a bit of your creamiest goat's cheese. Go on.'

'Oh, Willa. I don't know.'

Willa could see that Mollie thought the combination of chocolate and cheese was revolting. Nervous, Willa began chattering, explaining that although it took about two hours to make a batch, most of the time was in waiting for the filling to chill, and then another half-hour for the outsides of the chocolate to firm.

Mollie hadn't made a move to taste a truffle. Their mother obviously sensed a row beginning to develop, for she suddenly took her mug of tea upstairs to her room.

Willa felt a nasty quiver in her tummy. 'They're really quite simple, Mollie. And use little cheese or milk.'

The sisters stared at one another. Mollie sighed and set her jaw. Willa watched as Mollie popped an entire truffle into her mouth, quickly, before she lost her nerve. Mollie chewed slowly. A smile spread across Willa's lips; she could tell that Mollie was savouring the rather odd flavours.

A foodie at heart, Mollie gave her professional opinion. 'The sweetness of the chèvre balances well with the acidic, dark chocolate. It's really not half bad.'

Willa grinned from ear to ear. She'd spent hours practising making the truffles, and she'd worked up several different flavours. She hadn't the nerve to give Mollie the whole range, so she was allowing her to start with tasting the most basic. 'So, it's balanced. Did you notice it's both moist and dry? But the real question is, did you like it?'

Mollie laughed. 'Yes. I'd call them *unusually* delicious!'

Willa's hands flew to her face. 'Really? Honestly?'

'Honestly. Oh, for heaven's sake, Willa, calm down, it's only a truffle. You've made me feel like Mary Berry!'

'I'm so relieved you like them.'

'To be honest, I'd never have believed that was an edible combination, had you not forced me to try them together,' Mollie said, quite her usual bossy self again.

'Here's the other gift, Mollie.' Mollie picked up the pink bag and brought out a clump of white tissue paper. She unwrapped a bar of soap that wore a paper collar, which she read aloud. 'Hilltop Farm Goats' Milk Soap, with Honey and Oatmeal.' Mollie sniffed the soap and said, 'That smells nice. And it's rather a hefty size, isn't it?'

'Yes, I wanted it to be a good value for money.'

'What do you mean? I thought this was a gift.'

Lisa came back downstairs and into the kitchen. Willa thought she'd returned because she hadn't heard yelling. Perhaps she was premature.

Trying to keep her head, Willa said, 'Well, they are gifts for you. But also, maybe, products we could offer besides cheese.'

'And what happened to the yield while I was gone? Did you make any cheese for our customers who are waiting? Or did you use up all the milk doing art projects?'

Willa felt her cheeks burn in indignation. 'That's not fair, Mollie.'

'They're my goats and it is a fair question.' Mollie crossed her arms and stared at her. Their mother remained silent.

Willa had a fleeting thought: perhaps she preferred her sister depressed.

One of the top dog breeders in the county had been buying some goats' milk to nurture their puppies and Willa reminded her sister of that change in distribution. 'For the soap, I used a little of the goats' milk that's no longer going to the Dixon's puppies. The cheese came from Mum, you gave it to her, and it was here in the house. I didn't *steal* from you, Mollie.'

She saw Mollie's mouth soften a bit and she dropped her arms. 'I am sorry, Willa, I shouldn't have said that. I feel a bit out of control of my goats right now, like I've abandoned them.'

'Anyone for a cup of tea and a biscuit?'

The sisters answered in chorus. 'Yes, Mum.'

'Alright, I'll put the kettle on again. In fact, I'm having an apple as well. I feel peckish,' Lisa announced, to no one in particular.

Mollie pushed the gift bags aside and shuffled through some pieces of mail that had arrived in her absence.

Willa slowly made her way to the table, truly needing a cup of tea. The aftermath of arguing left her a bit shaky and out of sorts, whereas it always seemed Mollie could immediately change her mind, mood and physiology. She'd hoped that she and Mollie could have a serious discussion about the truffles, the goats' milk soap, and perhaps even the tiered cheese-round wedding 'cakes', but that conversation would have to wait.

Phoebe came floating down the stairs, phone in her hand. She dropped herself into a chair between Mollie and Willa and said, 'Isn't there cakepud?'

'Aren't you stuffed from all that lasagne you ate?' Lisa asked.

'That was two hours ago, Mum.'

Lisa brought a plate of shaped cookies to the table, iced in pink frosting.

'What are these?' Phoebe said, already having one in her mouth.

'Nigella Lawson,' Willa said. 'They're called Rosewater Hearts.'

'But I thought there was ice cream cake.'

'No, I took that to a neighbour who was having a birthday.'

Phoebe felt injured. Biscuits were okay, but were nothing to an ice cream cake, which was one of her favourites. 'Which neighbour?'

'No one you know very well.' Willa drank her tea, hoping the moment would pass.

Her mum helped it on. 'Aren't you going to show us what Granny bought you?'

Mollie shot her mother a look. 'No. I'm not having Phoebe weeping all over the place.'

'Give me a bit of credit,' Phoebe said dramatically.

'Really?' Mollie snapped. 'You've just gone sulky because Willa baked biscuits instead of cake.'

'Girls.'

'Alright.' Mollie rose from the table, took a deep quaff of tea and walked over to the litter of shopping bags. She pulled out pairs of jeans and several tops. One of the tops was a floral print, with some crocheted edging around the hem. Phoebe flew out of her chair and took it from Mollie, held it up to herself and went into the hall where a mirror hung on the wall by the front door. She returned and said, 'You're so tall, Mollie, that this is a dress on me. And it would look so brilliant!'

'Or maybe it's a shirt for me.'

'You're so cruel.'

Mollie relented. 'Just don't stain it, all right?'

Phoebe giggled and took a photo of herself, holding the garment in front of her. Then she eagerly waited for Mollie to unveil other items she may want to permanently borrow. She was vastly disappointed.

'It's all goat clothes.'

'Yes, I am afraid so, Phebs.'

Willa said, 'Granny is really the coolest, isn't she?'

'Yes, she can be,' Mollie agreed, looking at the farm clothes. 'She also offered me quite a bit of "tough love" while I was visiting.' They all laughed. 'But, if I am honest, it did me quite a bit of good.'

They finished their tea and Mollie said that she needed to make the rounds.

'I've only just checked the goats before you and Mum arrived,' Willa said.

'Well, I'm going to check them, again.'

'You don't trust me, do you?' Willa was still stinging from Mollie's rejection of her goat soaps and truffles as possible new product ranges for the business. She knew that Mollie merely wanted to visit her goats, and she regretted accusing her.

Mollie simply gave her a reproving look, and rose above the temptation to begin another row. 'If you must know, I'm also going to chat with Oliver and let him know everything went well at Granny's.' Mollie crossed the kitchen and went out through the boot room.

Willa sighed and took her tea things to the kitchen. Lisa was putting the leftover biscuits in the tin.

'I'm sorry, Mum.'

'I know, sweetheart. Strangely, you and Mollie sometimes have the same sort of dynamic between you as your father and I did. Only Grant was more gracious at rubbing along with people than Mollie has been lately. Just try to be patient with her.'

'I am only trying to help.'

'I know, darling. It's just that Mollie isn't very open to creativity lately, and you've had a lot on, what with sitting exams and running the milking. I think you're overtired.'

'Maybe,' Willa conceded. 'But I'm done at school as of this week and she'll have to acknowledge my part in the business. I know she's done the lion's share, but I did put in my money from Gran and I don't take any pay.'

Lisa gave her a hug. 'You're a gem, Willa. Mollie appreciates you, and it'll all come right.'

Willa loved her sister. All the same, her mother was making excuses for Mollie. Why couldn't Mollie stop being so stubborn so that they could move forward. Logically speaking, Mollie had always been this way, caring more about how their father would've conducted every detail of the goats' care and the income that they generated. But perhaps it wasn't healthy, the way had Mollie acted like their father would return and be thrilled that she'd kept things exactly as he'd left them? Willa had no such feelings for what her father may or may not want; perhaps she hadn't loved him? It was all so muddled. Willa knew she ought to focus on the silver lining, but at the moment she was busy clearing up Mollie's mess of gift bags and tissues.

CHAPTER 18

Colleen Corbett sat at her desk in the morning room, reading a proposal for rehabbing one of the estate outbuildings that suffered storm damage. Just as the hall clock was chiming eleven, Oliver interrupted her. He'd come into the room with a tray and set it on the circular table by the window. Surprisingly, there was a tall cake, plates and utensils.

'But wherever did it come from?' Colleen asked her son.

'Come join me. I didn't make tea as I've never liked it with ice cream.'

Astonished, Colleen chuckled, set aside the paperwork and removed her glasses. 'Did you say ice cream?' She made her way to the table where Oliver held out a chair for her.

'Yes. It's an ice cream cake. Those were always my favourites, remember?'

'I do, but it's been years since we've had one.'

'Well, someone else remembered, too.'

He sliced the cake and gave each of them a generous portion. She thought of her waistline and objected. 'I think we could've shared this.'

'Live a little.'

He seated himself and took up his fork. They tried a bite.

His mother said, 'Very well done. But if you're expecting me to guess where it's come from, I'm going to disappoint you. I can't imagine.'

'Willa Purslow.'

'Willa? She made this or did she pay someone?'

'She's an excellent cook. Apparently, according to Mrs Jenkins, Willa brought it in last night and asked her to put it in the freezer. Willa said I was to have it for my tea on my birthday. Mrs Jenkins asked me if she should bake something else for me – her nose was a bit out of joint since she's always made my birthday cake. Mother, are you listening?'

Colleen wondered, was young Willa carrying a torch for Oliver? It seemed ridiculous.

'You'll have to discourage her, of course.'

Oliver didn't answer for a moment. Then he said, 'It was a lovely gesture. I can't think of a time, in recent years, when someone that wasn't on our payroll actually made something for me. And you can't accuse her of pushing in; she didn't even put in a personal appearance and expect to share it with us.'

'One must ask why, Oliver.'

'One realises she was being kind, Mother,' Oliver answered good-naturedly.

'Kindness from eighteen-year-old girls is usually suspicious when conferred on handsome young men home from university.' She knew she shouldn't fuss, but she couldn't help herself.

'I am flattered and I appreciate Willa's talent. It's by far one of the best birthday presents I've ever received.'

Revelation dawned. 'You're fond of her.'

'I am.'

'Oliver!'

'Mother!' he said mockingly. She couldn't help but laugh along with him.

He teased her. 'Are you a snob, Mummy? Are you going to tell me I ought to fancy someone from university? Whose parents are a bit higher up the social ladder?'

She couldn't let *that* go by. 'You know better than that, don't even joke. I was thinking of her age. She's a girl, a teenager. You're twenty-three today.'

'She's pretty.' Oliver grinned at her, suggesting a bit of mischief where Willa Purslow was concerned.

Colleen suspected he was a bit carb intoxicated after the vast quantities of chilled sugar he'd just consumed. And she knew he was enjoying having a go at her; he'd spent too much of his time at home this week. But this should be nipped in the bud.

She put down her fork and pushed away her half-eaten and melting slice of cake. 'You're not the sort to behave like a heart-breaker, Oliver, but it seems you need a reminder. Do be careful with her. She was so very upset when she came over to speak with us about Mollie. It's easy to see that she's a very sensitive girl. Very sweet.'

'Just the sort of girl you'd want to keep.'

'Now you're worrying me. Have you been carrying on with her in secret?'

Luckily, Oliver took little pleasure in being truly boorish. He leaned back in his chair and courteously answered her question. 'As it happens, no. I haven't seen her since that afternoon. But I have to say that I was rather stunned, and pleased, that she's done this,' he said, waving a finger towards the cake. 'And now I'll have to think of a way to thank her.'

Colleen smiled politely but she was becoming frustrated. Was he serious about the girl or had he become more of a flirt than she'd realised? Whatever the case, none of the local girls could compare to the lovely Arabella. Of course, Oliver and Arabella had gone through a rough patch when they were much younger, but those first years of university were always difficult and not the time to try for a time-consuming relationship. Oliver would someday realise this; Colleen only hoped it wouldn't be too late.

'Mother.'

'There's really nothing to discuss, Oliver. I'm sure I didn't intend to pry.'

'I know she's a bit young but I'd like to take her out. That's not exactly proposing, is it? And she's lovely. You must agree?'

'Oh, Oliver. I suppose she is.' She made an attempt to regain her sense of humour, and added, 'The truth is, when it comes to the Purslow girls, I much prefer Willa to Mollie.'

Oliver laughed aloud. 'No worries on that score. Mollie's a mate, nothing more.'

'I really need to get on with reviewing these bids, darling. Your father and I are planning on your birthday dinner at the club this evening, as always, assuming you're free. I only wish your sister were home this summer so that she could be with us.'

'I miss her, too, Mum. Thanks for breaking your diet with me. Willa's ice cream cake is better than anything you could've ordered at the club.'

'Agreed.' Perhaps he'd see some of his friends this evening, Colleen thought. He'd make some plans with other people, and forget about Willa Purslow.

HE TOOK the ice cream cake back to the kitchen, covered it and returned it to the freezer. Oliver then went into the hall, called up his dog and set out for a walk. He'd been rather casual in speaking with his mother about Willa, but secretly he was rather concerned. He knew, in only spending a few minutes with Willa Purslow, that it wouldn't take much of a push to fall head over heels in love with her. She was intelligent, sweet and loving. Just the sort of girl that's nearly impossible to find.

He walked out and up the hill behind the house. The sky was clear and blue. The sun had warmed the grass. Oliver's dog was zig-zagging with delight, scenting something here and then over there, sneezing and joyfully trotting with his nose to the ground.

Oliver followed him, his head bent down as he climbed the steepest part of the path, using big, ground-covering steps. The exertion felt good. He thought about the many girls he'd met at university. Like Willa, they were also very bright, of course, but so often he found them to be hard-edged. Competitive. Easily angered. And dare he say it, spoiled. And always they had something they were trying to prove to him. He thought of Gabrielle, one of his partners in the lab. He'd thought of her as his equal since the moment he met her. They'd worked on experiments and discussed hypotheses and worked well together. But every so often, when he needed clarification and asked a straightforward question, she assumed he was somehow attacking her. He found it all very confusing and spent days trying to sort things out with her afterwards, despite having no idea why she was so deeply insulted. He'd said to her, 'Gabrielle, I am not tracking with your thoughts on this. Help me understand.' It was as simple a plea as he knew how to make, yet she was still keen to find him guilty of some sort of discrimination.

Oliver came to the top of the hill and took in the beautiful view; the familiar line of the ridge of Long Mynd, rocky in some places, green in others, sharp against the deep blue heavens and crested with white clouds. He looked down at the smooth rock, where he was meant to check in with Mollie in a few minutes.

He breathed in deeply and savoured the smell of sun on earth. None of those university girls would suit. Neither would living in an overcrowded city, instead of here.

Willa, he imagined, was different than the other girls. She was smart and creative, pretty and interesting, without being so bloody 'permanently offended'. Not to mention, he was undeniably attracted to her. She came without all of the pretence and designer labels. Willa's clothes were very simple and she wore just a touch of make-up. Often, her long hair was swept up in an easy ponytail.

Oliver smiled. She was simply gorgeous.

RHYS WAS LEARNING that his new girlfriend had definite ideas about how their relationship should work.

'Why don't you want to spend the summer with me?' Courtney bellowed.

They were standing in the middle of the main barn at Aquarius Farm, where Courtney was having a colossal tantrum. The tall horse behind her was growing nervous, and Rhys gave a look to a passing groom. The groom, having seen this sort of outburst from his employer's daughter before, discreetly removed the hunter from the barn aisle and led the horse into his stable.

'It isn't that I don't want to be with you, but I've got work to do, Courtney. I can't drop everything in my life to watch you at horse shows. Who'd help my dad run the farm, then?'

Courtney crossed her arms in front of her, ready for battle. 'Well, my dad will pay you. You can be my fitness trainer. Would that work?'

Rhys found this latest row especially hard going. He'd been irritated with Courtney for days and avoiding this conversation. He was giving up women, that was for sure and certain. But for the moment, he'd have to sort this out with her as best he could.

'It's not entirelyabout money, love. It's about my family and running our farm. I'm a part of that. You knew that when you came after me and asked me out. You've known it every time I've had to put off going to a party with you because I was needed to work or milk cows.'

Courtney turned on her heel and walked rapidly down the barn aisle.

Rhys came after her. 'Courtney? Don't you want to talk this through?'

'What's there to discuss, Rhys? You're putting *cows* over advancing our relationship. The same as Miss Mollie put goats above you. Wow, it's really tough to come second to livestock, isn't it? I'd not realised how badly she made you feel until now. Now you've treated me just the same.'

'Mollie wasn't rude to me, Courtney. We just live in a different world to yours.'

'Oh, wasn't she? You told me she expected you to work for her all of the time, to do for her goats and such.'

'And what's the difference, I wonder, in helping her with her goats or you with your horses? It does seem to me I've gone now from the pan to the fire, I have.'

'Don't confuse me with Mollie. I am inviting you to stay with me at posh hotels and go to nice barbecues following an afternoon horse show. To sip champagne in the competitors' tent. I am asking you to be my guest and travel around England, France and Italy where I am competing this summer. At no expense to you. In fact, I'd pay you to come. That's hardly the same as asking you to milk a goat, Rhys.'

'That's all very generous, cariad. Truly it is. But a man must do his work, look you.'

'You could work for me,' Courtney hissed. 'You're choosing to break up with me, instead.'

'I am so sorry,' Rhys said gently.

'No, Rhys, I'm sorry. I'm sorry that I thought you wanted a different sort of life. I thought you were fit and loads of fun. I was madly attracted to you just because of who you are and I looked over all the other differences. My father thought you were quite intelligent, a young man that he could've given a start in one of his businesses. But no, you're not having it.' She huffed, thoroughly put out over his depth of ingratitude. 'You're having quite the spring, aren't you, lover?' Her acid smile revealed her utter contempt. She turned away and this time Rhys knew he was being dismissed.

Striding quickly to his pickup he couldn't wait to get away. He wasn't so lucky as that, as Mr Williams came into view. He was arriving home from a day at work. Rhys was angry, but he had no cause to be churlish with Courtney's father.

'Rhys.'

'Yes.'

'What's wrong, son? You look a bit out of sorts.'

'Courtney and I have had a bit of a falling out, Mr Williams. I won't be coming back around.'

Mr Williams stood for a moment, studying him. 'It's not as serious as all of that, surely?'

'I am afraid so. Now, if you'll excuse me, I've work to do.'

Unexpectedly, Mr Williams laid a hand on his shoulder. 'Best of luck to you, Rhys. No hard feelings?' The two men shook hands.

The brief conversation did a lot to calm Rhys down. He felt respected by Mr Williams, and that was something he craved. His own father valued him, although he never said so, and he was always made to feel that there was nothing special about a man doing what he ought to do.

Rhys drove himself to a lay-by and parked his vehicle. He walked towards his best thinking spot, a rock with a view that made a bloke feel he was just that bit closer to God. But when he came near, he saw that his thinking rock was occupied.

He stared for a while at Mollie, sitting close and cosy with Oliver Corbett, Lord Ranson's son from the big house. So, she'd decided to climb the social ladder this summer as well. Rhys felt his gut twist with resentment.

Corbett could never understand his Mollie the way he did. Or love her as much.

CHAPTER 19

*L*isa was thankful for her flexible work schedule in more ways than one.

Since she'd invited Sam – she couldn't bear to think of it as asking him on a date – and had been turned down, the atmosphere in the office was different. Mostly because two obliging people were trying so hard to make sure that it wasn't at all awkward. Which made it very awkward indeed.

As an excuse, Lisa said that she was using her daily commute time to work on plans for this year's arts festival in the village. Sam quickly gave his blessing and wished her well in the preparations. Best of all, it was true since she was one of the main coordinators of the event. Many of the same volunteers turned up each year, which helped tremendously, yet public undertakings always had challenges that would arise. Plus, all of the planning, following up and confirming always took more time than one would imagine.

This morning an arts festival council meeting was being held in Lisa's old library. She still had the keys and was the first to arrive. The books had all gone by means of sales, distribution to mobile libraries, and donations to larger collections. Some of the large tables remained and a few pieces of office furniture. Village events were still held in the old Tudor building and this year it would accommodate a dozen more artists who'd agreed to come, since they could display their fragile pieces indoors. There were glass artists, ceramicists, a doll maker, and a woman who sold miniatures depicting musical instruments.

Marris Mynd wasn't bothered by many tourists. The village was too small to offer any interesting amenities. Although it was situated in a designated area of natural beauty, it was a bit too distant from the more popular walking and biking trails, and there wasn't a bed and breakfast or interesting shopping for at least eight miles in any given direction. Once or twice a year, though, that all changed. What Marris Mynd did have was a lovely summer arts festival, which featured numerous artists that came out of their creative hibernation and set up stalls full of ceramics, paintings and fibre art. There was lots of live music, a pop-up farmers' market and Jake hired a dozen extra people to extend his pub's reach to include a great white marquee tent, serving up delicious food to locals and visitors alike.

Lisa walked into her old office and sat at her empty desk. She'd been passionate about being the library's director. She missed helping young students with school projects; teaching older people how to use a computer and watching their surprise at its technical capabilities. She had loved inviting storytellers to come and sprinkle their fairy dust over their tiny audiences sitting cross-legged on the floor; and the parents, who also enjoyed being told a story. She felt nostalgic for the tidiness of the books being returned to their shelves, the community services involving having an expert come to speak, or issuing helpful advice in the library newsletter.

'Hello?'

Lisa was startled by Colleen Corbett's voice. Colleen was responsible for organising the provisions for the music productions, including the electrical support, stage set-up, lighting and hospitality for the performers who often were graciously invited to stay at the big house.

'Through here, Colleen. I was just sitting at my old desk, lost in memories.'

'I hope I didn't disturb you.'

'Oh no, of course not.'

Colleen put her handbag and a folder stuffed with papers onto one of the large round community tables where the meeting would take place. 'I didn't get a chance to speak with you at the garden party. How do you like your new job? I mean, I know it doesn't hold a candle to running the library, how could it? But I hope you're content working for Sam Lloyd?'

'Oh yes, I really enjoy editing and research. It sounds as though you know Sam?'

Colleen nodded. 'Yes, I was friends with his wife, Angie. I am sure you knew she passed away?'

'I'd heard that. Sally Andrews knows him, too.'

'Yes, we'd attended a few dinners and things together. So many years ago now.' Colleen smiled. 'You and Grant had three little ones to take care of along with the farm, so it's no mystery why you missed some of those times.'

Lisa laughed. 'Yes, in those days I would've hired a babysitter for the girls just so that I could properly clean my house. A night out wasn't even a thought!'

'Sam probably told you that he'll be coming, since Ursula is participating?'

'Ursula? No. Actually, he's been rather busy, and I've been working from home to spend more hours pulling together last minute details–'

Lisa was interrupted by a trio of other volunteers coming into the library. Colleen turned to greet them and the opportunity was lost for further chat.

As soon as she was home, Lisa wasted no time sifting through the lists of artists, food vendors, farmers, and even the auctioneer, looking for the mysterious Ursula. Finally, Lisa came across a contract: a woman named Ursula Schwarz was scheduled to play the violin during the village tea on opening afternoon, which followed the church service on Sunday. There was a note made by Colleen, 'Referred by Mrs Hayward, the vicar's wife'. Of course, Mrs Hayward, the woman capable of networking on any level.

Lisa grabbed her laptop and searched 'Ursula Schwarz'. A biography from a music college in Paris appeared. There was a small black and white photo, showing a beautiful, dark-haired woman with a sombre expression holding a violin. Lisa was impressed, despite the fact that she didn't understand the jargon and hadn't heard of the many awards Ursula Schwarz had earned as a classical musician.

Ursula hailed from a place called Schaan. Feeling dreadfully parochial and uncultured, Lisa needed to look-up the city as well. She learned that Schaan was the largest city in Liechtenstein, 'a German speaking micro-state bordered by Austria and Switzer-land'. Well, good on you, Frau Schwarz.

But why was Sam Lloyd coming to her performance at their village festival?

Well, she thought. That's rather obvious. Look at the woman. The question is, how long have they been seeing each other and why didn't Sally Andrews know about her?

At least she could suppose that Ursula Schwarz was the reason Sam had turned her down for a date.

Rhys had been doing quite a lot of thinking since he broke with Mollie. Before, he was desperate to latch on to any money making scheme that may support them, because he'd wanted to marry Mollie. Without that pressure, Rhys was more objective. He only wished that he could talk to Mollie about his plans, even if she weren't going to be a part of them. Very practical and sensible, that was Mollie. A good planner.

He felt a stab of hot anger trickle in his chest: and more concerned with her own business, always. That was Mollie, too. She'd only cared about his dreams so long as they supported hers. And apparently Oliver Corbett was a better bet for her these days. Funny how she'd wanted to get back at him by snaring a posh bloke that was in Courtney's set. The whole thing was comical, but not very funny.

Rhys had a long think about his own creativity and commerce. Suppose he had a bit of land? Rhys wouldn't have cows. He was weary of his family trying to make a living on low milk prices. His dad had begun sending twenty per cent of the total milk volume to the continent because they'd pay him something resembling a living wage. Here in England, the superstores took the profits, instead of the farmers. It was a lucky thing that Rhys's family owned their land outright or they would've had to shut the dairy by now.

Farming economics aside, Rhys was more interested in working the land. He had a passion for farming veg and even for creating beautiful flower gardens. There were lots of gardens open to the public in the region, but not one of them was anywhere near Marris Mynd; if there was, there may be a few more tourism dollars spent in the village. The idea excited him and he liked planning out the particulars in his mind.

Rhys finished milking with his father. After a hot shower he put on a fresh short-sleeved shirt and jeans and drove to the pub. The pub was noisy inside and there was a game of darts under-way, with bets on who'd win it. He already knew, and so did everybody else, that you couldn't beat George Webber, but almost on a weekly basis someone tried.

Rhys bought a cider. He went out back to an unoccupied picnic table, straddled in and leaned over with his elbows planted on the table top, thumbs drumming along with the tune that was floating out from inside. He thought about the upcoming arts festival, when some of the best local bands would give concerts here at the pub.

Rhys was lost in his thoughts when he felt the slight breeze and bump of someone sitting down beside him. A woman. He'd have preferred talking to a bloke about farming and having him sit opposite. Especially since the woman was Mollie's friend, Jenny, a girl that Rhys had never particularly liked. Natalie was a sweet girl and Jenny a sour one.

'Hello there, handsome,' she said, a bit wobbly. He remembered another thing he didn't like about Jenny. She sometimes got stuck in at the bar and got incredibly drunk.

'Jenny.'

'Penny for your thoughts,' she said, taking a long drink of a locally brewed pale ale that girls seemed to always like. Rhys didn't care for the strange fruity smell of it.

'They're far more expensive than that.'

Jenny smiled at him and Rhys had a sickening feeling. She leaned close, pressing her breast against his bicep. 'I can think of something nice to trade.' He gently put a hand against her shoulder and pushed her away, saying nothing.

She laughed. Her breath was disgusting. 'Heard some news you may like to hear, Rhys.'

He dreaded this too. It'd be about Mollie. And try though he might to be disinterested, he wasn't. He still had an appetite for all-things-Mollie.

'Oh? What's that, Jenny?'

'Mollie's living quite the high life. I had it from my younger sister that she's become a model. Got paid a bloody fortune for being as tall as a house and wearing a dress. Do you think she put on her dad's trousers afterwards?'

Mollie, modelling. Rhys could imagine that quite easily. She was the most beautiful girl he'd ever seen, even wearing baggy clothes and no gloppy make-up on her face. She'd never been heavy, but he saw her at a distance about two weeks ago, walking about the village with her mother. She'd lost weight and he supposed she was as skinny as those models in London. That made him sad. Mollie had looked tired and there was a slump about her shoulders that had never been there before.

'You hadn't heard that, had you?' Jenny taunted. 'I could tell you more but what would be the point. You finally came to your senses and broke off with her. And guess what, Rhys? So did I.'

'What're you saying, Jen? You've been mates with Mollie since you were little ones.'

'Yeah, but she's been treating me poorly, too, Boyo. I say we're better off without her.'

'What did Mollie ever do to you? I expect she's put up with a fair bit from you.'

Jen snorted bitterly at his remark. Rhys looked at her red-rimmed eyes and waited. He expected her to be hateful but her mood changed instantly. Suddenly her eyes were brimming with tears.

'She never mistreated me, Rhys. She just isn't capable of loving other people,' Jenny slurred. 'Always thinking of herself, that's our Mollie. You know the sort of thing, don't you, love? With friends like that, tearing you down real subtly like, you don't need enemies, that's what I say. How about you, Rhys? Did she lord it over you that she already had her own animals, her own living? Didn't really need you, did she?'

Rhys's stomach did a lurch hearing Jenny's poisonous words. The problem was, there was a part of him that wanted to hear. Jenny was like the vinegar you put on badly done, greasy chips – that bit of sharpness made swallowing them down a lot easier, and some days, rotten food was better than nothing.

'I suppose you're right, Jen,' Rhys said, even now a bit surprised that he was sitting here palling up with her against Mollie. 'I am not sure Mollie ever thought much of me. At least, not any further than her own plans, you know?'

Jenny pushed close to him again and this time he didn't push her away. 'A man needs respect, Rhys. Some women don't understand that like I do.' She was rubbing his neck and shoulders now, and it felt damn good. But he also felt a bit slimy, like he needed another shower.

'Hey, mate, mind if I push in?'

Rhys was startled but relieved. His close mate, Neale, was sitting down and giving Jenny a nasty look.

'Neale.' Rhys shot his hand across the table to shake Neale's hand, the effect of which unsettled Jenny, causing her to drop her arm in order to keep her balance on the bench. 'Are the lads coming? Jenny here was just leaving, there'll be plenty of room.'

Neale nodded.

'Yeah, whatever, Rhys,' Jenny spat. She was unsteady getting herself away from the picnic table, but Rhys would just as soon watch her fall over than lend a helping hand. Now that the moment had passed, he was more disgusted by Jenny than ever.

CHAPTER 20

It was a lovely Friday morning. Willa was amazed at how quickly the weeks were flying by; the summer term had ended and Phoebe was on holiday. The arts festival began tomorrow morning in Marris Mynd. She reviewed her baking list for later today: four dozen small custard tarts, four dozen biscuits, and a three-tiered cake for a Coffee Concert to be held at ten on Saturday. Willa considered asking Phoebe to help her, and then decided against it. She and Mollie had nearly given up trying to guilt their younger sister into helping with the goats, making cheese, or anything useful. Phoebe took ages to accomplish basic household chores, wasting time checking her phone, complaining, and always needing to eat something.

Finally the morning milking concluded and Willa left the barn with Mollie. 'What a gorgeous morning,' Willa said, looking across the clear, azure sky, and feeling the sunshine on her cheeks. 'I wish I could sit outside and read.'

'Why can't you?'

'I told you, Mollie. I volunteered to bake for the opening day concert tomorrow. Want to help?'

'Want to be able to eat any of it?'

'You're not that awful at baking.'

Mollie chuckled. 'I most certainly am.'

Willa hoped that Mollie wouldn't remember the cheesecake she'd made for Rhys, but fortunately Mollie was distracted by a black sports car climbing up the drive. The driver steered it away from the house and parked to the side, where the vehicle wouldn't be in the way.

'Anyway,' Mollie said. 'I've just gotten a better offer than ruining all of your tea treats.' She turned and smiled brashly at her younger sister and sauntered towards their guest.

Willa's heart felt like it was visibly pounding beneath her shirt as the driver got out of the car. Oliver Corbett. He was wearing dark sunglasses, a jersey with his school logo on the front, a pair of long denim shorts and dark canvas trainers. She trailed Mollie, looking forward to saying hello to him before Mollie and Oliver spun away in his sleek car. Mollie's border collie, Tarrant, followed on as well, on a mission to ensure that the visitor wasn't a threat. Oliver dropped his fingers, allowing Tarrant a sniff, and Oliver must have passed inspection, as Tarrant then turned and ambled back to the front porch.

'Well hello, stranger,' Mollie said familiarly. Oliver met her halfway and they hugged casually.

'You're looking the picture of health today, Mollie. Good to see you.'

'Thank you. Sorry I haven't been around the last few days. There's been so much work to do. It's lovely that you've come by.'

Oliver shoved his hands in his pockets and glanced at his shoes. Then he looked at Willa, in a way that could've sent Willa into a full-on swoon.

'Actually, Mollie, I am here to see your sister.'

Mollie had the poor grace to assume that Oliver was teasing her. 'Oh, aren't you a funny boy? Well, that will teach me to ignore you, I suppose. Since you don't have a clue about how Willa spends her time, I can tell you that while you're taking me out to breakfast, she'll be busying herself making custard tarts.' Mollie laughed, as though this comment were actually amusing. Willa wished for the ground to open up and swallow her sister whole.

Oliver brushed past Mollie.

'Custard tarts, huh? Those sound good, but they'll be nothing next to my birthday cake.'

Mollie followed, keen to re-enter the conversation, still under the impression that Oliver had come to visit her. 'I am sure that your birthday cake was amazing, Oliver,' Mollie said, with an uncomprehending glance at Willa. 'Where did you have your dinner? At the club? But I must confess that my sister is actually quite handy in the kitchen. Honestly, I've not had anything in a restaurant that rivals what she makes at home, even in Birmingham.'

It was all becoming too embarrassing. Willa cut in with a quick, 'Thank you, Mollie.' Couldn't Mollie just quietly take herself off, just this once?

Oliver hadn't taken his eyes from Willa's face since he'd come to stand in front of her. Willa hoped he wouldn't see the blush she felt creeping across her cheeks. Focusing on this fact was increasing her anxiety. Not to mention what effect looking into his eyes had on her.

'Do you have to begin baking this minute?' Oliver asked Willa. 'I had the lovely idea of taking you to breakfast before Mollie swooped in and claimed credit.'

'I didn't take the credit,' Mollie said from behind Oliver's back. She took a few steps and joined them. 'Great minds think alike and all that. I'll go get some money since Willa's grown roots.' Mollie's long legs were striding toward the house and Oliver followed her. Willa wasn't sure what to do, so she casually took an interest in looking at the trees beyond Oliver's car. She knew Oliver had overtaken her rather thick, self-centred sister. Willa heard his voice.

'Mollie.'

'Yes?'

'I wasn't joking, you know. Not to put too fine a point on it, but I am actually here to see Willa. Sorry this has become a bit awkward. I hadn't thought, or I would've rung first.'

Willa relished every word, but was deprived of seeing Mollie's face. Willa didn't want to feel catty, but it was tremendously satisfying to have Oliver put Mollie in her place. After all, Mollie had brought it upon herself; Willa had done nothing.

At least, nothing besides delivering a cake through a back door. That was over a week ago and she'd given up hope that there would be a note from Oliver in the post or even an email. Willa suddenly felt a creeping concern: perhaps she should go into the house and get some money? Perhaps even though Oliver wanted to only take Willa to breakfast, maybe the invitation was meant as a friend and not as a date? A plan flew into her mind: she'd just realised that she was wearing barn clothes. She'd go in and change, and then she'd return with her handbag, ready to pay for her meal if necessary.

Mollie answered Oliver in a mocking sort of fashion. 'Oh! Mr Corbett, you're quite correct. I hadn't realised you were here to call on my little sister, since we've been *good friends* as of late. Please, don't let my uber-rudeness stand in your way of an intimate breakfast.'

Willa felt her cheeks burn with shame. But Oliver wasn't put off by Mollie's immature response. He walked back over to Willa and she looked up at him.

'My apologies.'

'No worries. Won't you come inside? I'll only be a moment to change.' There, she'd sounded quite normal and controlled. *Well done, Willa.*

They turned and Willa saw that Mollie had already entered the house. Willa hoped they could get away without further humiliation.

Willa walked with Oliver towards the farmhouse. The door

stood open. Mollie's boots had been kicked off in the centre of the boot room, defying anyone who'd wish to walk in. Willa ignored Mollie's mess and climbed the steps towards the front door. She took a deep breath as she walked in, remembering that Lisa had left during milking for a last minute meeting with the festival committee. That meant there wasn't anyone to remind Mollie to be on her best behaviour.

Smiling at Oliver, Willa zoomed up the stairs and into her room. She snatched her favourite outfit, changed and plucked her handbag from her shelf. She noticed Phoebe's bedroom door was still closed. Going back down the stairs, she heard voices. Mollie was with Oliver.

When Willa came around the corner into the kitchen, Oliver was standing with his arms folded across his chest, listening to Mollie. Whatever she'd been saying, Mollie broke off when she heard Willa arrive and she turned around with a serious face. Willa decided that she didn't even want to know what Mollie had said.

'Ready to go then?' Oliver said, dropping his arms and smiling.

Willa smiled in reply and they left the house together. As they drove towards Church Stretton, Willa's anxiety melted into a surreal sort of calm. She enjoyed Oliver's car. It was fun to be sitting low and going at a nice speed, the shadows and bursts of sunlight sliding over the windscreen and shading them in patterns of dark and light. It was a bit chilly and Willa pulled on the light jumper she'd brought along.

'Cold?' He reached out and turned a switch on the dashboard, and comforting heat caressed Willa's legs and torso. Their quiet was companionable and Willa realised she was no longer nervous. Excited, but that was quite different to being afraid. As soon as they'd left Mollie behind, Willa felt like a different person. It was as though her own life came to the fore, no longer eclipsed by her sister's words, moods, and physical presence. She sensed that Oliver hadn't felt overwhelmed or the least bit cowered by Mollie;

in fact, he hardly seemed to notice her behaviour except when he let her know she'd totally misread the reason for his visit. Willa thought back to Oliver's face in the kitchen, when Mollie was having a private word. Even then he wore the expression of courteously listening. Mollie was such a gale force in their home – in Willa's life – that it was refreshing to see an outsider come along who was unaffected by her.

Somehow Willa knew that after today Mollie wouldn't have the same control over her life as she'd been wielding in the past. Willa mightn't always be alone any more, and that fact changed everything.

CHAPTER 21

The morning had been productive. Despite the last minute problems that always arise, Lisa and the other arts festival volunteers had managed to put everything right. She felt that she'd lived through an entire work week in one morning though, and would murder for a cup of tea. Lisa walked into the house and put her folder and handbag on the dresser in the kitchen. Two of her daughters sat at the kitchen table, looking glum.

Phoebe perked up. 'You'll never believe what's happened, Mum!' She loved being the bearer of news, and her flair for the dramatic usually meant that the news was in some way undesirable.

'Good morning to you, too, Phoebe. Would anyone care to join me in a cup of tea?' Lisa didn't know if Phoebe would ever fundamentally change, some women never grew out of a love of histrionics, but Lisa certainly wasn't going to reward it. For the same reason, she ignored Mollie, who hadn't even bothered to look up at her arrival. Things must not be too dire, for she noted that Mollie was eating a large bowl of porridge with enthusiasm. Perhaps, thought Lisa, I'm just in a prickly mood.

'Willa's gone on a date with snooter boy.'

Now that was a bit surprising, Lisa had to admit. 'Really?' She despised giving Phoebe such satisfaction, but Willa hadn't ever had a boyfriend, or even a single date. And now she was out with Oliver Corbett? Lisa looked at Mollie for substantiation of the claim. Apparently Mollie was going to be above it, or perhaps she was just depressed again?

Putting the kettle on, Lisa reflected on the news. Willa was eighteen; she certainly didn't need Lisa's permission to go for a meal with a boy whose family they'd known for over twenty years. Or probably sixty years, if one wanted to count them among Granny's friends. In fact, Lisa had just parted ways with his mother, Colleen. She doubted that Colleen knew about the social engagement between their children, or she'd have said. Lisa smiled. Perhaps that's why Oliver chose this morning to call on Willa, while his mother would be out of the house. Oliver had left home at a very young age to attend boarding school, and was now a university man. Lisa knew that Oliver did as he pleased – but why not carry out his agenda with the least fuss? Yes, that sounded like him. She'd always liked Oliver. He was respectful, good-natured and undoubtedly intelligent.

Lisa stirred milk into her tea and joined her daughters at the table. Mollie finished her porridge and popped up to wash the sticky bits out of her bowl and set it in the dishwasher. She then turned and, without a word, left the house via the boot room. When would she ever get over her tendency to be so absorbed in her thoughts? At Mollie's age, she ought to be able to ask Lisa how the meeting had gone, or *something* bordering on civil behaviour.

'She thought Oliver was coming to see her, since they'd been meeting secretly,' Phoebe supplied. 'But then she realised he was here to see Willa and he enjoyed telling her so, Mollie said. She's gutted.'

Then a detail registered with Lisa. 'Did you say they'd been meeting in secret?'

'Yes.' Phoebe smiled, loving the intrigue. 'Willa told me a couple of weeks ago. Mollie and Oliver would sit on the flat rock overlooking the valley and she told him her problems and cried on his shoulder, or whatever. Willa told me that she was glad.' Phoebe wound a length of her hair around her finger, the picture of contentment. 'Then we wondered if it was Oliver who told Mollie to run away, because Mollie even had extra cash for expenses, and Oliver's rich. And Mollie couldn't have planned to go away on her own, because other than goat stuff, she's been acting as though she's brain dead since Rhys broke up with her.'

Lisa took a big swallow of comforting tea. How did so much happen under her own roof and escape her notice? She supposed it was another side effect of dating Michael, breaking up and then approaching Sam. Guess Mollie wasn't the only person with an inward focus. Phoebe's phone chimed and she began texting. Lisa picked up her mug and went to speak with Mollie.

Lisa found her in the milking parlour, vigorously cleaning the windows with a rag and a plastic spray bottle of lemony smelling cleaner.

'I just heard from Phoebe about what happened this morning.' Lisa spoke gently, and hoped that Mollie would open up to her. She'd read in an article recently that people can slip back into feeling blue when they don't talk things out.

'I don't want to talk about it.' Mollie finished the window she'd been working on, and moved to the next. She wasn't rubbing quite as hard on this one. Clearly she was beginning to tire.

'You should, Mollie. You mustn't keep your feelings all bottled up. It hurts all of us to see you fed up, to see you mope around as though you've not got a friend in the world.'

'I'm not moping, I'm working. And I did have a friend in the world, but my sister took him away from me.' Mollie's voice wasn't sharp, it was just a simple statement.

'I am sorry about that, sweetheart. But how long had it been since you've spoken to Oliver? Perhaps he thought, like we all have, that you're doing much better. Maybe Willa didn't take him away, but that he wanted to spend time with her for some reason.'

Mollie suddenly laughed. Raucously. Lisa was taken back by her merriment, but unable to resist joining her.

'Mollie, why are we laughing?'

'Because you said, "He wanted to spend time with her... for some reason". Like you couldn't possibly think why any boy would want to pay any attention to Willa. That's quite funny, Mum. And my feelings exactly. She's as boring as watching paint dry.'

Despite herself, Lisa was laughing. 'But I didn't mean it like that.'

'Yes you did. That's why it was funny.'

Lisa grinned and crossed her arms. 'No, honestly, you know I wasn't criticising Willa. But I suppose it is different to think of Willa being in a relationship. She's always been so studious, so serious. Anyway, I'm not out here to discuss Willa's love life.'

'Or her total lack of one.'

'The point is, Mollie, I can't imagine that Willa or Oliver mean to cause hurt. She's just not capable of going to those lengths, and my guess is that you were both a bit embarrassed.'

Mollie brought the rag down from the window and thoughtfully turned it over in her hands. 'No. You're right, Mum. She was as surprised as I was.'

'Well, then, why must you be so sulky? I can't believe you have romantic feelings for Oliver.'

Mollie took up rubbing the window again. 'Of course I don't carry a torch for Oliver. And of course it's laughable to think of Willa's carrying on, doing anything from spite.'

Lisa waited.

Mollie dropped the rag and bottle of cleaner on the floor and turned to face her mother. She drew in a deep breath, and kept her eyes cast down. 'This'll sound really odd, Mum. It's just... I'm not the person you all think I am. It's so incredibly annoying, always knowing everyone thinks the worst of me.'

'What are you talking about?'

'Wasn't it you who taught us that if we had nothing nice to say than we ought to keep our mouths shut? If Willa is quiet, no one bothers her, they just imagine her great mind is at work. If Phoebe is quiet, we're all relieved for the silence. But if I am quiet, everyone must pursue talking to me until I say something cross, and then it's, "Oh, see there! We knew Mollie was in one of her moods!" I know I am not naturally sweet like Willa or bubbly like Phoebe, so I have a hard time connecting with other people when I am unhappy. I acted a fool, thinking that Oliver came here to see me. Why aren't I allowed to just want to forget it? Honestly, Mum, I'm simply trying to act adult and keep my negativity to myself.' Mollie ran her fingers through her hair and swiped away a tear. 'Especially lately, when there's been nothing anyone can do. None of you can make Rhys love me again.'

Lisa crossed her arms, upset at being taken to task. Everyone had done their best not to upset Mollie and this was her thanks? 'You're not being exactly fair, Mollie. I don't expect you to be like anyone else. Remember, you were deeply upset, crying hysterically–'

'Yes! I was, Mum. I acted like any other girl who's been dumped. I admit, I haven't been the poster child for cheerfulness. However, no one will give me any grace.' Mollie's eyes welled with more tears. 'I try to be more mature than my younger sisters, but they clearly think I am such a mess, Mum, and you do, too. And it hurts. Everyone seems to want to have a go at me until you get a reaction, then when I defend myself, you're all self-satisfied and say, "There's Mollie acting horribly again, I told you she's still upset." I mean, why are you out here, asking me all these questions, instead of just letting me be?'

'Well, because I was worried. You didn't even acknowledge me when I came into the house.'

'I'm sorry,' Mollie said. 'I wanted to leave before Phoebe started rehashing everything. I'm just trying to stay above it and be busy at whatever I can think to do next.'

Lisa took Mollie into her arms. 'I suppose I wasn't sure what you meant at first. But I do see what you mean. We've sort of slipped into certain roles, haven't we?'

'Yes. And I realise I've done that, too, Mum.' Mollie ran her hands through her hair and crossed her arms. Then she brightened. 'Willa is taking on a new role, this very minute. It was massively insensitive of me to be offended when I realised Oliver came here for her. She's actually on her first-ever date, and it's about time!'

'You're sure she and Oliver weren't going as friends?'

Mollie threw her head back with a lusty laugh. 'Oh, no. Certainly not.'

Lisa laughed too, and they hugged one another, swaying and giggling.

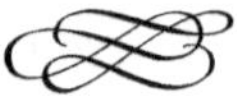

CHAPTER 22

*P*hoebe squealed as Lisa turned carefully out of the drive. 'Careful, Mum!' She balanced a large box of custard tarts on her lap and raised one side of it to keep the box level as they wound down the hill toward Marris Mynd. The two eldest girls sat in the back of Lisa's car, holding other boxes of treats.

'I'm feeling a bit hungry, Willa. Do you mind?'

'Mollie Anne, if you eat one crumb of those biscuits, I'll bake a pie just to throw at your face!'

'Make it an apple.'

The Purslows arrived in the village and brought Willa's baked goods into the reception hall of the library. After depositing the refreshments with others on a long banquet table, they found themselves with a half-hour before the Coffee Concert would commence. Lisa saw Willa blush and turned to see Colleen Corbett coming from Lisa's old office, carrying a roll of tickets to be issued for the concert.

'Good Morning, Colleen.'

'Oh, hello, Lisa. Girls. I'm going to take these out front. You said that we have seating for eighty, is that right?'

Lisa confirmed the number, then casually she asked Colleen, 'You know, I didn't recall meeting any of these musicians in previous years. I suppose it's down to my memory–'

'No, you're quite right. They're a group from France and they were scheduled to be in Ludlow yesterday and then Shrewsbury later this month, so they agreed to come here. Several of the string quartet from last year have retired, so I was pleased to have someone else to sign on.'

'I don't suppose you went to the other performances?'

Colleen looked a bit puzzled – and no wonder, Lisa thought.

'No, I didn't attend any of their concerts last week, but they did send a recording,' Colleen said. 'They're very good. I don't have any concerns about them.'

'Of course, I am sure they're excellent. I just thought, well, I think my boss… he may be friends with the violinist.'

Lisa felt three pairs of eyes immediately join Colleen in staring at her. *Uh-oh.*

'Anyway, it's not important.' Lisa could see Mollie smiling wickedly.

Things went from bad to worse as Colleen decided to change the subject. She made a cordial smile in Willa's direction, but Lisa noticed she didn't actually look at her daughter.

'So, I understand that you and Oliver had a little outing yesterday. Did you enjoy yourselves?'

Willa was past blushing now, her face completely flushed a healthful shade of pink. 'Yes, thank you. It was interesting to hear about the research Oliver's been doing in the medical lab. Not that I followed it all, exactly.'

'Quite.'

Lisa was shocked to hear the slightly clipped note in Colleen's voice. Probably every mother who felt their child was getting short shrift was capable of bad behaviour. Lisa had to admit that Willa seemed a bit young for him. But Colleen had never been a snob; surely she simply had the same reservations about Willa being too young for Oliver. Whatever her motivations, it was clear that Colleen meant to intimidate her daughter. Bored with the exchange, Phoebe and Mollie wandered away.

'I think his work – well, not just Oliver, but the whole team, really – could benefit so many people all around the world,' Willa marvelled. 'I mean, there haven't been these sorts of advances for prosthetic limbs for many years, don't you agree?'

Lisa couldn't help but smirk. Colleen's attempts were completely lost on her sweet daughter. Enthusiastically praising Oliver's altruism had not been the desired effect.

'Well, he's certainly put you in the picture, Willa. Would you excuse me, please?'

'Yes, of course. Have a lovely day!' Willa would've hugged Colleen in parting, given half the chance. Lisa decided not to caution Willa but to simply let things take their course. It was a method that had served Lisa well, most of the time, anyway. And Willa needed to learn to negotiate her own way.

Lisa was about to have a test in the same sort of manoeuvring. Sam Lloyd, and a woman that Lisa recognised from photos, had just entered the library.

SAM LLOYD WAS HAVING DINNER. With a large helping of second thoughts.

'I will work two mornings each week, teaching masterclasses,' Ursula said crisply, before taking a sip of wine.

Sam looked at her, trying to see her as he once did. But he could only see Ursula shaded by Lisa's perspective. Introducing the two women following the concert was awkward at best. Sam had turned nearly all the way around in his seat, scanning the crowd. He saw Lisa coming in just before the performance began, taking a chair by another woman in the back. Afterwards, when Ursula had descended the stage to meet and greet, Lisa very kindly approached them.

'Hello, Lisa,' Sam said, kissing her on the cheek. She looked beautiful and fresh, wearing a summer dress with a floral design that resembled a watercolour painting. Her hair was pinned up and she wore a more vibrant lipstick than usual. He turned to Ursula and said, 'This is my tremendously competent assistant. She's the reason my research notes resemble any sort of organisation.' Lisa smiled, appearing to have no ill feelings about his refusal to go out with her. And she'd never looked more beautiful.

Sam suddenly came to himself and turned to look at the other woman standing next to him. He couldn't have remembered her name for all of the tea in China. A moment passed and Sam froze.

'I'm Ursula Schwarz.' She shook hands with Lisa.

'Yes, of course,' Lisa said, her voice warm and friendly. 'I'm one of the festival organisers, so Sam knows that I am already well-familiar with your name. My friend, Colleen, told me about the wonderful recording that was sent ahead.'

Sam was grateful that Lisa had covered for him in that awkward moment. But she'd done that often enough at the office, too. Only she wasn't there so much any more. He'd missed her.

'I hadn't heard the solo piece you played before,' Lisa said to the violinist. 'But I am not much of a classical music aficionado.'

'Many people do not know it,' Ursula said with authority, her words pronounced in a concise German accent. 'It is one of Morton Feldman's pieces. He has been called, what is the correct word for a sort of fantastic weirdness?'

'Eclectic?' Lisa supplied.

They discussed the unique composition while Sam wondered if Lisa was also here with a companion. Surely not or he would have surfaced. On the other hand, if he lived in Marris Mynd then he may also have responsibilities in keeping the festival running. What sort of man would he be?

'Sam?'

'Yes?'

'Isn't it true?' Ursula was insistent.

'Of course.' He adjusted his glasses; they always seemed to go slippy when he was nervous.

'Well, I hope you'll have a lovely time in France,' Lisa responded. She looked downcast. Sam panicked.

He said, 'But I haven't discussed our publishing schedule with Ursula yet. That really has to be the determining factor.' He smiled and laughed slightly. Both women stared at him. 'Uh, well, Ursula, I am sure you could use some refreshment. Perhaps Lisa can show us the way.'

'Oh. Yes, of course,' Lisa said.

The trio of new friends left the main room of the library, each lost in thought.

CHAPTER 23

Following the concert, Willa left while her mother stayed on to meet the performers of the string quartet. As she passed the reception area on the way out of the library, she was astonished at how many of her baked goods had already vanished. Perhaps people who weren't attending the Coffee Concert had nipped in and taken some refreshments? Oh well, Willa thought. She was a baker, but it was up to her mum and other committee members to act as security around the cakes and tarts.

Oliver had told Willa that he'd be cycling for a few days up in the Shropshire Hills with his friend Patrick, who lived in Ludlow. Willa remembered that Oliver had always been a keen cyclist, often taking week-long riding excursions. She wondered if she ought to learn. Of course she knew how to ride a regular sort of bike. But those lightweight, road-going, clip-in-your-toes varieties were an entirely different kettle of fish. She'd watched the Tour de France on television and been horrified when there was a pile-up of riders, men writhing in pain and nearly falling off some mountain in the process. Maybe she'd just let Patrick be Oliver's companion for that sort of thing. Willa also had to come to terms with the fact that Oliver may have other plans until it was time for him to leave. And then she may not see him again for a long while once he returned to university for the autumn term. The coursework for his doctorate degree sounded very challenging.

She hoped to find Mollie on her own so that she could explain about the ice cream cake, which was probably the true reason Oliver came to be at their house yesterday. He'd said more than once that it was a lovely gesture, not to mention a delicious cake. The whole household had been treated to a piece, but Oliver had eaten three. This response was amazing to Willa and she wanted to natter with Mollie. Her sister was actually her best friend, despite their differences in temperament, personality, goals, and – well it sometimes seemed that she and Mollie differed in their opinions about *everything*. But Willa's closest friend at school had seemed to 'outgrow her' – her words – and become caught up in her new life with other friends. So, Willa had no one else to tell.

Willa saw some people she'd known at school, incredible to think that was actually 'past tense' now; they said hello. There was a group of men standing around a stall displaying hand-carved wares. Willa had seen the proprietor in years past and admired the intricate walking sticks he created. She noticed that Rhys was among the men, with his best mate Neale and others she knew from the village. He caught sight of her.

'Willa.'

'Hi, Rhys; Neale. Congratulations on your engagement, Josh.' Josh smiled and nodded his thanks, then turned to say something to a bloke Willa knew only by sight.

'Have you seen Mollie?'

Rhys tensed his jaw slightly and crossed his arms. Willa was surprised that he seemed so affected just by hearing his sister's name. She'd thought that dating Courtney Williams would've put a lot of distance between him and Mollie.

'No,' he answered. 'But I've been looking for her. So, she is here?'

'Yes. Should I send her here if I find her first?'

Rhys shifted his weight and looked at Neale. Then he said, 'No. There's really nothing much to say, is there? I just wanted to see her.'

'Because he's always had eyes for her,' Neale said, which earned him a punch in the arm from Rhys.

Willa wasn't sure what to say. Did Rhys want to get back together with Mollie? Or was he simply bored and, as young men were apt to do at a village event, maybe they were checking out the females?

'Okay,' Willa said. 'I'll be off.'

'Lovely to see you, Willa. I'd ask how you did on your A levels but I already know.' Rhys smiled and gently squeezed the top of her shoulder like a proud older brother. Willa smiled in return and walked away.

She felt a bit sad then. She'd been sorry for her sister but she hadn't thought too much about Rhys. He'd been the guy who cheated; but Willa could see pain in his eyes. And she realised that, for her own part – even though she didn't really have a part – she'd missed Rhys. He'd always been a friend and a source of comfort and security to her. He was good at calming Mollie, fixing things that were beyond their experience or physical strength, and he'd always treated them well. He'd even taken the time to talk to Phoebe. The episode with Courtney had seemed out of character and now Willa imagined that perhaps he'd been misunderstood in some way. Not in the sense that he had stepped out with Courtney, he'd admitted that and then carried on dating her.

But what had Mollie missed? *Why* had he behaved that way?

After a bit, Willa gave up trying to find her sister. She purchased a sandwich which she ate by herself whilst sitting at one of the tables provided. Then she carried on walking about and looking at things. She came to a stall, at the very end of the row, that drew her attention.

'Hello! Have you seen our soup kits before?' asked a kindly woman with ginger hair. Willa replied that she hadn't. 'Oh, lass, they be wonderful!' The woman picked up a packet and began to explain. 'These be locally grown beans and vegetables. And we added a special blend of seasonings. All you need in one packet, see? Course you can add meat if ye like, most any sort works. Wanna sample, love?'

Willa agreed. The sun was a bit on the warm side, but like most of the summer in the Shropshire Hills, it was mild, so soup wasn't entirely out of the question if you really loved it. 'We got dip mixes, don't miss,' the woman said as she handed Willa a small cup to drink an ounce of soup. 'Dips is nice for raw veg, crisps, bread and such.'

'It really is delicious,' Willa said. She thought it could use a bit of salt, but no doubt the directions inside would indicate that you'd add salt and pepper as desired. 'I'll have a packet of the French Country Vegetable, please.' Willa had very little money to spend, but she loved the woman's enthusiasm for her product. The woman obviously felt about her soup as Willa felt about the goat's cheese products she'd made, and Willa felt inspired not to give up so easily. Perhaps her sister just needed more samples, in order to take Willa's ideas seriously.

'Thanks, me darlin', and you can find us online after the festival ends, alright?'

'Good luck,' Willa replied. She was startled by a woman walking towards her with a smile on her face.

'Willa! Just the girl I hoped to see!'

It took Willa a moment to put a name to the beautifully made-up face. The vicar's wife, Mrs Hayward, was immaculately turned out for an arts festival, wearing a frilly top over slim pants in a cool mint shade. She wore high-heeled sandals and a hat with a wide brim.

'Mrs Hayward, how lovely to see you.'

'Willa, this is my niece, Katie. She's going to stay with us for the remainder of the holiday.'

Katie, taller than her aunt and just as striking in appearance, beamed at Willa and offered her hand.

'How do you do? I hope you're enjoying our little arts festival, Katie.'

'Oh, yes. We live in a city with an art museum, but your festival is so *cute.*'

'Katie is very creative,' Mrs Hayward added, and her niece giggled in agreement. Willa had the sense that Katie was rather accustomed to compliments. 'We hoped to see you, Willa, because we wondered if you may be free to come to lunch next week? No more worries about exam schedules, isn't that right?'

Willa was stunned. She'd never been asked to lunch without her mother and sisters before. She supposed it was because she and Katie seemed to be the same age. 'Yes, I would love to. Whatever day is best for your schedule, Mrs Hayward.'

'Tuesday would be perfect. Yes? Wonderful. We'll see you at the vicarage at noon?'

Willa said an awkward goodbye. She thought it was amazing that she'd been asked on her first date, and asked to her first luncheon, all in the space of a week.

UNLIKE WILLA, Mollie had been popular at school. Her confident good looks and irreverent sense of humour had earned her a wide circle of friends. This currency assured that Mollie got a ride home from an old school mate on the back of his motorcycle. The young man wasn't going in the direction of Hilltop Farm – because there was nothing else at the top of the hill – but he didn't mind, because it was Mollie Purslow who'd asked.

Coming home to the farm in its unoccupied state afforded a rare peace for Mollie. Her Mum and sisters were lovely, but sometimes she imagined what it would be like to be on her own. She didn't really think being lonely would come into it. It was sort of like school. Sure, she'd enjoyed being liked, but she liked being independent more. Most of her school mates had fled Marris Mynd. The boy she rode home with on the motorbike was only home this week visiting. Mollie couldn't conceive of wanting to leave. This hill, this farm, was her home and she wasn't going anywhere.

She walked from room to room in the farmhouse. She opened the door to Mum's room. She'd redecorated a couple of years ago. A few of her father's antiques had been sold off. The room was lighter now, more feminine. She wondered if her mother would ever want to remarry. Lisa treated Mollie as though she was too young to understand. Mothers sometimes had not the faintest sense of reality. By the time her mum was Mollie's twenty-one years, she was married with a toddler, so it was a bit bewildering as to why they didn't really seem about to talk about anything.

Phoebe's room was next to their mum's. What had been the nursery was now completely chaotic with a young teen's clobber. Mollie quickly closed the door.

Willa's door stood open and sunshine from the south facing window came streaming through it and into the passage. Supreme tidiness. She looked on the bedside table. Willa always kept a glass of water there, and scrupulously emptied the leftover water each morning. It was gleaming, and she wondered if Willa got a clean glass every evening or if she rinsed it out and dried it to a shine. Her sister's habits were out of the common, to say the least. There were two books, stacked with the larger on the bottom and the spines in perfect alignment. The top was titled *Half of a Yellow Sun*. Mollie flipped it over. Something about a war in Nigeria, and described as *'tremendously evocative, a searing history lesson in fictional form'*. Whatever. The larger book with a cream cover showing a line drawing of a lobster boasted the French title *La Technique*. By some chap called Jacques Pepin. No wonder Willa slept well.

Mollie continued her tour, looking at the magnificent view rolling out from the back of the house. The sun shone on the olive tops of the hills; the blue sky was full of wheeling birds and streaked with thin white clouds. She sauntered down the stairs, lingered in the dining room, watched the dust motes take ski-lift rides on a shaft of vibrant light.

She was gripped by the need to make plans. Goals. Energised by her solitude and these quiet minutes, she considered the money coming from another modelling job next week. Mollie got a small pad of paper and pen from the drawer in the kitchen dresser and took it into the open air. Tarrant raised his head to watch her and looked rather surprised that she went no further towards the barn. He settled down around her foot while she slouched on the porch and crossed one long leg with an ankle resting on her knee. She was especially excited to write at the top of the list: Order new cheese labels from printer. She savoured the moment and then began a list of preparations. She imagined opening Hilltop Farm for visitors, and having dairy days just like the farms her father had visited for inspiration and information. How much should she charge? Would she send each home with a small sample of cheeses? Or, perhaps it was better to offer cubed cheese for tasting, and then let them purchase their favourite. She'd ask Willa's advice. Her sister would have some idea about a posh way to do the tasting and sales, and how to set up a till.

Mollie looked about the lawn in front of her. She had to admit it was rather a mess. Her mum wasn't very green fingered except when it came to houseplants, and the girls followed suit. The car park area would need more designation for visitors. She wished she'd thought of all this before, and had organised her dairy tour and tasting to coordinate with the arts festival. Well, she'd be ready for next year, and well-experienced by then. Besides, the farmyard and garden hadn't gotten looking so bad overnight, so it would take a bit of time to do it up nicely. And maybe money, too. She'd no idea what flowers, pots and signage would cost, although she planned to do most of the hard labour of removing nettles and things by herself. Maybe Willa knew something about flowers. She seemed to read about everything.

Mollie's thoughts lingered on her sister. She really hadn't been truly bothered by Willa going out with Oliver. She'd just been surprised. No one likes to be put on the back foot; surely Willa could figure that out. She wasn't sure though. For someone so smart, Willa could be so daft. Her sister didn't even grasp the fact that Oliver's mother didn't approve of her. She supposed she ought to stick her nose in and at least warn Willa, to stop her making needless mistakes. But she wouldn't write that on this list, naturally, so, back to more important tasks to be done.

CHAPTER 24

$\mathcal{L}$isa eased into her bubble bath. The seductive scent was both relaxing and rejuvenating. She thought the festival was off to a lovely start. They'd had record numbers. Sam hadn't returned to the arts festival on Sunday, even though the string quartet from France performed a mini-concert on the lawn, along with some other groups. She'd noticed the look of irritation he'd gotten from Ursula the day before, when he failed to confirm his plans to visit her at her home in France. The truth was, Sam could afford to take a holiday, they were well ahead of work deadlines. Perhaps what he couldn't afford was to carry on with a woman he wasn't in love with.

She played the scene in her mind, recalling the way Sam drank in her appearance. Ursula hadn't seemed to notice; Ursula was perhaps a bit self-absorbed. Lisa felt sure she was reading the situation correctly.

Besides discovering that most of the baked goods had been snatched before the Coffee Concert was over, there was an entirely unexpected dilemma. Rhys Davies had sought Lisa out and wanted to speak with her. Her curiosity had been piqued.

'Do you have plans to still be here in an hour?' She explained to Rhys that she had to introduce the performers for the collaboration concert but that she'd be free afterwards.

'I've already heard as much as I care to,' she said to Rhys with a conspiratorial smile. 'As soon as they're onstage, I'll be done with my responsibilities. If you're planning on staying, we could chat then if you'd like?'

They had.

They were settled in her old office at the library. Rhys kindly asked, 'How's the new job?'

'It's going really well. I was a librarian for so long that I didn't think I could be anything else.' *I didn't think I'd ever want to date again*, either, she thought to herself. She was a bit distracted by her thoughts about Sam.

'I suppose this will seem that it's coming quite out of the blue,' Rhys began. 'And it may be something you'll need to consider. You need to know that I don't expect an answer today.'

Intrigued, Lisa said nodded.

Rhys drew a deep breath for courage and it seemed he recited a carefully thought-out script. 'I've been giving quite a bit of thought to my future, in terms of my career. My dad, if he's honest, will have to admit when I speak with him, because I haven't done yet–' Rhys smiled, wiped his face with his hands. 'Sorry. I've messed up my words.'

'It's okay, Rhys.' Lisa assured him. 'Go on.'

'I don't like working with cows. It's not just because the milk prices are so low. It's not because I disrespect what my father's tried to build up. My older brothers, they're fine, they don't mind, and there's enough they can inherit someday. They'll partner up and do well.' He gained momentum as he spoke. 'But that's not for me, going on now. I want to farm. I'm interested in all this old-ways farming done by some here in Shropshire, the slow food movement, if you like. Organically grown produce and specialty foods and such. I've even given a thought to having a flower garden and keeping bees. Anything but cows, Mrs Purslow!'

They laughed together.

'See, I don't know what Mollie'd say,' he continued. 'But I can't afford to buy a place of my own. All our land supports the dairy.' He paused and swallowed. Lisa realised then, what he was coming to. She felt sorry for him because she knew that he was risking a lot in speaking to her. If she said no, it would be quite a blow. Available, affordable land could be very hard to come by.

'Your farm – well, there are so many acres there, some not being tended to. I don't know what your thoughts are about that. I've never spoken of anything like this to anyone. You see, I only really thought it all through for the first time fairly recently. What I am trying to say is, I wonder if there's a chance... an off-chance... that maybe you'd be willing to lease some acreage to me?'

Lisa waited. There would be more he'd want to say, and he'd feel better if he finished. She smiled slightly to encourage him.

'As I said before, I don't know what Mollie would say; she's never been backward when it comes to being forward with her opinion, isn't that so. But I can give you my word that if she isn't easy about it, well, then I'd stay clear of her. Your lower pasture, to the west? It has an access gate through to our farm. I could come and go there, mostly. Maybe even have a little storage for equipment down there by the pump house. Keeping myself out of your drive and out of her line of sight. In fact, Mollie's always pastured the goats in the opposite direction. I wouldn't want to upset her.'

Now he'd finished. He let out a sigh and laughed.

'I think it's a brilliant idea, Rhys.'

'Truly?'

'Yes. And whatever happened to calling me Lisa?'

He smiled.

'I can't really commit to this at the moment, as you said. But I'll give it a think, alright?'

Rhys looked slightly downfallen.

Lisa patted him on the arm. 'I'm not saying no, I just need more time to consider.'

'Of course,' he said, putting on a brave grin.

She'd told him that they could talk through all of the specifics after the festival was finished. She sensed that he needed more time to plan, and now that this step was taken, maybe his thoughts could move on to organising how it could all come about, past staying out of the way. Knowing Rhys as well as she did, she knew he already had lists made in his mind. But he'd have to get even more specific. And, most importantly, Rhys would have to tell his father what his hopes and dreams were for the future.

Lisa's bathwater had grown cold and it was time to leave it. Towelling off, she admitted she'd needed a little time, too. But why? Analysing her thoughts now, she guessed it was because she was moving in a direction she hadn't before. She knew she could've leased out acreage long ago, but she hadn't wanted to deal with the responsibilities, paperwork, and potential problems that could arise. For years, she'd simply put one foot in front of the other. In a sense, she was giving Grant's farm over to another man.

But Rhys felt like the right fit for the farm. Grant had the same dream, to be a farmer. He realised after he'd set up the dairy that he'd wanted both. Grant hadn't had a chance to get started before his death, but that's why he was out on those acres that day.

Lisa had become rather attached to Rhys during his courtship with Mollie. She didn't want him to fail, and she essentially could offer him a phenomenal start as a farmer if she chose.

Taking the long view, there were also financial issues to consider. Edward had offered her a small fortune for Hilltop Farm. Sam had been paying her a generous salary, however, they hadn't discussed a working arrangement past his current projects, expected to take about two years. And perhaps Edward was correct, that she'd need to consider helping Willa, and then Phoebe, to go to university some day.

By the time she slipped on her clothes, Lisa had taken a decision. She would allow Rhys the use of some land, *free of charge*. That way, he could make a strong start of things. Later, they could work out issues like profit sharing and so forth. As for Willa, until she expressed a desire to go to university, there really wasn't any reason to have a plan. Lisa wasn't one to cross bridges before it was time, as things generally took care of themselves. In addition, once, long ago, the girls' grandmother had hinted that their university education and living provisions would be 'looked after'. If Willa suddenly wanted to earn a degree at a posh school, she may be able to count on Granny paying for it, or, at the very least, Granny's guidance regarding student loans.

In the meantime, Lisa would have a talk with Mollie. She had no intention of subjecting Rhys to subterfuge. She hoped Mollie would accept the situation with grace. Lisa didn't care for confrontations, but on certain views she was willing to be rather firm. This was one of those times.

CHAPTER 25

'No, Mollie. I've said, I have plans.'

'Don't you care about our business? You've no proper dedication to the goats, Willa. You can't just swan in, do the easiest part of the milking, and leave me with *everything* else.'

Willa seldom lost her temper but at the moment, she was coming to the boil. They'd just finished the morning milking and were walking back to the house when Mollie began reciting a long list of extra work that Willa would be doing. Beginning today.

'The easiest part of the milking? You're right, Mollie. I do the easiest part of the milking, shooing the goats into the milking parlour, and then I go sit in the sun and read a novel, right? Hardly. You know very well that I'm doing the hard slog of cleaning the goat pens. You know I pull my weight around here, and don't for an *instant* imply that I don't.'

Mollie started to walk away from her, but Willa wasn't finished.

'Excuse me? We're not through.'

'I think we are. I'll simply carry on by myself. In fact, I think I prefer it. Take *every* day off from here on.' Mollie turned again and began to walk away.

Willa was so frustrated that she shrieked and threw a bucket against the barn.

Mollie heard the odd noises and looked over her shoulder. 'Why on earth are you completely having a breakdown?'

'You… don't… understand,' Willa said, catching her breath. Her eyes were suddenly stinging with tears, and her nose was running. 'I wanted to talk to you, Mollie. About Oliver. About me having plans tomorrow. It's not that I don't want to help with your new plans. But you don't see me. You don't… *listen*.'

Mollie had walked back to where her sister was standing. She put her hands on her hips. 'What do you mean, I don't see you? I see you. Your face is all red and you're completely hysterical for no reason. You're not dedicated to moving on with the dairy's goals, so I'll carry on without you. I really don't care.'

'That's just it, really, Mollie. You don't care. You've just said it.'

Mollie stood there, clueless. 'You're getting the day off; you no longer have to work with me at all, so what's the problem now?'

Willa was at a loss to explain. Mollie didn't care about *her*, that was the problem. Her feelings were dreadfully bruised; Willa just couldn't go on arguing. Her calmer nature, her love of order and peace, were already cautioning her to come away. Willa sighed and walked silently to the house. Her older sister followed her in.

Phoebe was home, but thankfully out of sight. Willa went directly to the kettle, filled it with fresh water and flicked the switch. Mollie fell into her usual chair at the kitchen table, watching her.

Willa retrieved a jar of Nutella and two spoons. She sat down at the table opposite her sister. She turned the lid, glanced at Mollie and handed her a spoon. Mollie smirked and dug her spoon into the jar first. They sat in silence, stuffing themselves with spoonfuls of the thick chocolatey spread. When the kettle was ready, Willa made the tea.

Mollie laid down her spoon, reclined in her chair and looked expectant.

Willa began their conversation all over again, calmly. 'I wanted to say that I'm sorry how things came about the morning Oliver turned up. Honestly, I had no idea he was coming. I was as surprised as anyone that he wanted to take me to breakfast that morning.'

Mollie's eyes sharpened a little. Willa wished she could be a bit more generous and try to see her side, but instead it looked like she was wanting another row. Why did everything have to be so difficult?

'I don't believe that's altogether true.'

'It is, Mollie. I swear it.'

'I know you were surprised, that's not what I mean. But you've already admitted that you'd already been to their house. Starting something with Oliver. I suppose you bonded with him by talking to him about me.'

'If I'm honest, there's probably something to that. It was kindly meant, Mollie. I was concerned about you.'

Mollie shook her head and rolled her eyes. Willa felt like giving up. But if she didn't speak now, Mollie may shut her out and not give her another chance.

'Alright, Mollie, you can choose to believe what you like. As far as our schedule goes, I wanted to tell you that I was asked to lunch tomorrow. Milking in the morning as usual, and then I can help with the, uh, *special list*, in the afternoon when I get back.'

'What time?' Mollie asked quietly.

'I don't know. I've been asked for noon, and I expect I'd be there at least an hour? Maybe two.'

'Oliver's actually making you come to his house? Why, to eat with his mother or something?'

'No, it's nothing to do with Oliver.'

'Oh, come on, Willa.'

Willa's frayed temper was heating up again. It was all so

exhausting. 'Yes, I know, Mollie. It's insane to think I went on a date. But just as unbelievable that I've made a new friend, right?'

'Stop snivelling. Who's giving you lunch?'

Willa got up from the table and walked a few steps. Then she turned back to face her sister. 'When exactly did you become so cruel? You've absolutely no manners. This conversation has been so much more difficult than it need be. You're so *mean*, Mollie.'

'I'm not. You're oversensitive.'

'What about the truffles? The goat's milk soap I made? You've never mentioned them again.'

'What about them? I'm happy that you enjoyed your little experiments, but they're nothing to do with me.'

'But they could be. Why can't we expand the business to include products like those?'

Mollie stood from the table and began shouting at Willa. 'Because producing those costs money. Less milk for cheese, and I've been working years to develop *those*. More costs for everything. Refrigerated storage, feed for keeping more goats, new product labels, trying to find shops that will carry weird items like cheese-stuffed-chocolates.'

'They're not weird!'

'Yes, Willa, they are. People around here don't eat truffles made of expensive Belgian chocolate and goat's cheese, they like Maltesers and Kit-Kats. Who d'you think's going to buy them? And why do you think I ought to fund all of it?'

'Very well.' Willa said tartly. 'I can live without making truffles and soaps and being creative. I can just keep helping you for no pay and no personal fulfilment. But I thought we were at least friends.'

'Personal fulfilment? From making smelly soap?'

'It's no more silly than gaining personal fulfilment from making cheese, Mollie.'

Willa's cutting remark hit home and now Mollie was clearly hurt. *But not quite as miserable as she's made me*, thought Willa.

'We've never been friends, Willa. Only sisters, who are *vastly* different to one another, with few benefits beyond survival. Apparently one benefit is getting yourself a new boyfriend by acting sweetly concerned about a sister's welfare, you know the sort of thing.'

'You don't care for Oliver. You don't want him,' Willa said quietly. 'So why are you so angry that he took me on one breakfast date? Why can't you be happy for me? Why can't we talk? I don't have any other friends, Mollie.'

Surprisingly, Mollie's eyes filled with tears. 'Do you think I do?'

Willa stared back, her eyes beginning to sting as well.

Just then Phoebe popped down the stairs. 'What are you two on about? Tara could hear you through my laptop just now!'

Mollie cleared her throat. 'Willa was just telling me about her plans for tomorrow. And I'm actually really excited for her, even though I behave sometimes – okay, a lot of times – like I don't care.'

Willa got up from her chair and gave Mollie a hug.

'Whatever,' Phoebe replied, as she took the jar of Nutella and Mollie's spoon and bounded up the stairs.

CHAPTER 26

Willa Purslow drew in a quick breath and woke herself. The row with Mollie had upset her, even though they'd made peace afterwards. They'd said cutting words.

Finally, in the wee hours of the morning, Willa had fallen into a deep sleep. She'd been out of sorts last evening and neglected to bring her handbag upstairs, meaning that her mobile – and morning alarm – was downstairs.

Consequently, Willa missed the morning milking. It was unintentional. But she knew that Mollie would remember telling Willa that she could do the work by herself, and think Willa had stood her up.

Willa ought to check the time and dash out to the barn if it wasn't too late. But the sun seemed high in the sky. She'd wanted to take her time getting ready to go to lunch today at Mrs Hayward's home. Willa had no feeling of wanting to spite Mollie, but if a bit of the 'breathing room' she'd inadvertently given Mollie this morning would help, then it would be worth it. Willa turned over in her bed and gave herself permission to lie there just another minute.

But then she heard rapid stomping up the stairs and almost

before she could recognise her sister's steps, Mollie burst into her room.

Her whole body when rigid under the covers, anxiety licked a cold path across her abdomen. Mollie could be rude, but she didn't generally coming running through the house and violently throwing open doors. Willa actually knew a moment of being frightened of her.

Mollie spoke in a hoarse whisper. 'They're dying.'

Willa sat up, slowly. The room felt a little like the sea.

'What?'

Mollie shuffled over and sat on the side of Willa's bed.

'The little goaties. My little Princess!' Mollie's body wracked with a sob and she leaned over to put her face in her hands. Willa rubbed her back, trying to give a little solace. She thought of the dear little goats, their floppy ears, and how they bleated and wagged their paintbrush tails and played with one another. They were so adorable, with swirly little waves of silky fur, tiny hooves, no bigger than puppies.

Willa scooted around Mollie and got out of bed. Willa dressed, started down the steps and heard Mollie behind her. She glanced at the clock in the hall, which read nine. They went to the goat barn. Instead of Willa trotting to keep up with Mollie, they walked in tandem, Mollie taking shorter strides to stay in step with her younger sister.

Coming into the barn, Willa immediately sensed that all was far from normal. The goats were stressed. Pearl was positively wild-eyed and bleating like mad, as though she were giving an account of some horrendous crime she'd witnessed. Several goats from the middle pen were walking in blind circles, almost trampling their pen mates. Primrose was yelling to raise the dead, her voice sounding eerily human.

The baby pen was empty.

Willa turned and faced her sister. *Do not cry.* Be strong for Mollie.

'What's happened, Mollie?'

Mollie was pale and looked like she was in shock. Dean Scott, the veterinarian, had most certainly been here and gone.

'What did Dean say, Mollie?'

'I… I called him because Princess was sick. *But he took them all.*'

'Are the other goats safe?' Willa barely recognised her own voice.

'Yes. Well, maybe not. Dean's running tests. They may be sick, too.' Mollie began to shake.

Willa grabbed her by her elbows. 'Mollie. Did you do the milking? Everything's been cleaned?'

'Y-yes. I found Princess after, when I–' Mollie began sobbing, and wiping her nose on her sleeve.

'Good. Then we're going back to the house.'

'But, the goats…'

'I'll come back out in a few minutes. Right now, you're only making them worse.'

Mollie nodded and obediently followed Willa back to the house.

Willa installed her sister at the kitchen table. Now to find something for both of them to eat. *Toast.* She popped bread in the toaster, set the kettle to boil and poured Mollie a small glass of orange juice. Then she began making calls. First to the veterinarian.

'Hi Dean, it's Willa.'

'How's Mollie?'

'Terribly upset. I'm so sorry to bother you, but if you could shed any light?'

'The little ones succumbed to an infection. Pretty rare, and I've already reported it. Hopefully, the larger goats won't be affected, but if they are then the herd will be euthanised. I'll be back tomorrow. So sorry, Willa.'

'Anything we should watch out for?'

'Just keep an eye on them as you usually do and call me if you see any obvious distress. Those were eight fine little kids and quite a loss – the possibility of culling the whole herd doesn't bear thinking about. At this point, I'd be more concerned about Mollie. She promised she'd come to the house as soon as I'd gone.'

'She did.' Willa cradled the phone on her shoulder whilst she buttered Mollie's toast. She put it on a plate and set it in front of her and went to make tea.

'Good. I hated leaving her but I've got a full day of calls.'

'I understand.'

'I'm coming back early tomorrow, but I may or may not have all the test results by then. Plus, someone governmental will be signing off on the treatment.'

'Okay, Dean, I'll tell her. See you tomorrow. Thanks.'

They rang off.

Mollie sat listless at the table, tears streaming down her face.

Willa went into the boot room and phoned her mum, who'd gone into the office for some reason, even though it was the week of the arts festival. Her mother answered a moment before the call would've gone to voice mail.

'Willa? Is everyone okay, love?'

Willa wasn't one to phone her mother at work and she didn't like alarming her. 'No, Mum. The little goats got sick with some weird infection. I'm not sure how many died or how many Dean put down, but the babies are all gone, Mum. Eight of them.'

Willa was surprised to see a man coming onto the front porch. Perhaps he was someone from the government, who wanted to examine the older goats? Her mother said something, but Willa was distracted by his soft knock.

'Mum, there's some man here. What did you say?'

'Is Mollie alright?'

'Not very.'

'Should I come home?'

'That's up to you, Mum. I'll stay with her if you'd like,' Willa said, feeling a pang of regret that she would miss the luncheon at Mrs Hayward's house. Her mother may come home early, but probably not immediately, and Willa should've been through the shower by now. 'Mum, I've got to go answer the door.'

'Okay, love. Call back if you need to.'

Willa went to the front door and opened it.

'Rhys!'

'Hello there, Willa. Would your mum be home? She said she's been working at home.'

Willa couldn't fathom why her mother had told Rhys that, or why he wanted to see her. She stood there for a moment, dumbfounded.

'Actually, she's gone to the office this morning, but, well, she may be back rather soon, as we've had a bit of a crisis here.'

Rhys's face clouded. 'Anything I can do, love?'

'Well, it's Mollie, really. Her baby goats died of some infection–'

With that bit of news Rhys was coming through the door, saying, 'Is she here in the house?'

Willa stepped aside but didn't have a chance to answer.

'Rhys?' Mollie called feebly from the kitchen.

Willa closed the door and then walked into the kitchen.

Mollie was already in Rhys's arms. He was stroking her hair and saying, 'I am so sorry, sweetie.' Mollie seemed to be crying but Willa couldn't really tell. She wandered into the dining room and rang Mrs Hayward. Although it was quite shocking to see Rhys and Mollie have a tender moment after everything that had happened, she didn't count on him staying on through the day. And Willa needed to check on the goats again, soon, so Mollie wouldn't worry.

'The vicarage.'

'Mrs Hayward? It's Willa Purslow.'

'Good morning. How are you, Willa?'

'Well, I'm fine. But my sister's having a challenging day and I need to stay here with her. I'm so sorry, but I won't be able to come to lunch.'

'That's quite all right. How kind of you to put Mollie's needs first.'

'Oh, well, that's what sisters do, I suppose.'

'Willa, are you free tomorrow? Or any day this week. We can easily adjust our plans around yours.'

'Thank you so much. Perhaps Thursday?' Willa didn't want to chance making plans tomorrow should things continue to go pear-shaped with the goats.

'Yes, that would be fine. For noon on Thursday. We'll look forward to seeing you then.'

Willa came back and found the kitchen empty. She then realised that Rhys had taken Mollie out to the barn so that they could check on the goats together. Perhaps she hadn't needed to cancel lunch after all, but it was done now.

Willa wasn't sure what to do next. She felt displaced. Sad for Mollie, curious about her mother and why she'd been speaking to Rhys, and a bit envious that Phoebe had apparently slept through the whole episode.

SAM HAD FINISHED GIVING Lisa some details about an upcoming project. His manner was friendly, his words courteous and professional. But Lisa sensed a slight tension and decided that he definitely didn't want to talk about his relationship with Ursula Schwarz, or explain why he'd missed Ursula's recent concert at the arts festival. Perhaps it was for the best.

She was just about to suggest tea when her mobile rang. Her conversation with Willa was brief and the news wasn't good.

'Everything okay?'

Lisa laid her mobile on the desk. 'My daughter, Mollie, lost some livestock this morning. She's rather shaken. I should probably take my work home.'

'Of course, Lisa. You know you have all the flexibility you need, and–' Sam stopped. She guessed that he was about to comment how their work was ahead of the publisher's schedule and time off was no problem if she required it. *Well-established facts.*

Instead, he turned to fill the kettle.

Lisa busied herself getting her handbag from her desk drawer.

'I do appreciate it, Sam. I'll focus on the edits you mentioned and of course I'll be available by email to take on anything else that may come up.' She simply couldn't resist adding, 'Especially since you'll soon be away in France.'

Sam stood aside while she softly brushed by him and left the office. As she pulled the office door to a close she heard a muffled sigh.

On the drive home, Lisa wondered how Mollie was doing. She was certainly having a tough year. And Willa – usually so compassionate – had failed to help Mollie with the milking this morning. She knew the girls had had a row but she hadn't realised Willa was so immature. Milking the goats was too difficult for one person. She didn't like to poke her nose in too much, but she'd have a word with Willa about the necessity of helping her sister.

In the meantime, she'd realised that she'd never had a chat with Phoebe. After having Charlotte helping around the farm in Mollie's absence, Lisa had come to realise that Phoebe was old enough now to have some consistent responsibilities.

As Lisa drove into Marris Mynd, she smiled. Perhaps she did spoil Phoebe a bit, but she remembered how lovely it'd been to be Phoebe's age. Work and responsibilities all happened soon enough, and then the rest of one's life was plagued with them.

She pulled into the drive of Hilltop Farm and was surprised to see Rhys's truck out front. He must have come by to see her, to ask if she was ready to give him a final answer about using some of her land for his crops. Poor lad, Lisa thought, he'd probably been on pins all weekend. She parked her vehicle and went through the boot room.

Willa was at the sink, washing some dishes. The air smelled heavenly. 'What's that baking?'

'Hi, Mum. It's a loaf of sourdough.' Willa finished the washing-up and began drying the dishes in the drainer.

Lisa dropped her handbag, files and laptop onto the dresser. Then she realised Willa had propped herself against the back of the sink and was unusually quiet.

'How's Mollie?'

'Being well looked after by Rhys – it was quite a surprise to have him show up this morning! They were out to the goat barn. But now I've just seen them going into the dairy.'

'Willa, I was thinking. I must say, I felt it was rather uncalled for that you stood Mollie up this morning. You of all people understand how difficult it is for one person to do the milking. I expect you not to let her down in the future.'

Willa pulled a face that let Lisa know she thought she was being rather unfair, but she said nothing.

Lisa gathered her things,walked out of the kitchen and up the stairs. There wasn't much Willa could say, Lisa reasoned. She was wrong and she knew it. Mollie worked incredibly hard to make cheeses and sell off her goats' milk, and she should be able to count on her own sister for a little help. Especially since Willa neglected to make any plans for university, she certainly didn't have anything else on. She could continue to pull a little of the weight.

Lisa put her daughters out of her mind and sat down at her bedroom desk to work.

ollie followed Dean from pen to pen.

'They look fine, Mols. They really do.' He laid a fatherly hand on her shoulder. 'It's a pity about the babies. But it's just one of those really odd, horrible things.'

'No one else has had any problems?'

'Yes; several farmers had to cull baby goats in the last ten days. Investigations will continue but there's no recommendation about changing any of your present habits. And please remember, there's nothing you could've done. Sometimes animals just get sick. Alright?'

'I suppose you're right.' She trusted his opinion as both her father's former friend and as an excellent veterinarian. 'Thanks, Dean.'

'Anytime. We're going to the arts festival again this evening. I suppose you've been?'

'Yes. I went with Mum at the weekend. I'm not really interested in going again.'

'What about the specialty foods competition?'

'I didn't enter.'

Mollie decided to leave off talking further about why she'd

failed to enter and changed the subject. 'My sister has all sorts of strange ideas. Goat soap and the like.'

'Goat soap?' Dean leaned his head slightly to the side. 'You mean for washing a goat, before showing it?'

Mollie giggled. Dean laughed with her. Her merriment increased as his confusion grew and she laughed until she doubled over.

'Oh. Wait. I think I get it,' he said, laughing again.

'Are you sure?' Mollie asked, wiping tears away. 'Ah. Thanks for that. You can bill me extra for allowing me to laugh at you. Oh, my goodness, that was funny.' She was slightly gasping and chuckling.

Dean turned to go. 'Please, don't mention it. To anyone.' They laughed again.

She returned to the farmhouse, and found her mother and sisters eating lunch. Lisa asked, 'The goats are all right?'

'Yes. Dean says there's nothing to worry about.'

'My word, Mollie, you look more than relieved. In fact, you look as though you're ready to burst with happiness.'

Mollie giggled again. 'I just had a massively good laugh with Dean. I was telling him about Willa's goat soap. He said, "What, for washing them before a show?".' Mollie collapsed in a fit of laughter all over again, joined by Lisa and Phoebe.

Willa was none too pleased.

'Oh, c'mon, Willa,' Mollie said. 'It's funny.'

'It's not. It's just silly.'

'That's what funny things are, you twit!' shrieked Phoebe.

'Sorry, Willa. It wasn't about your soap, really, he just couldn't get his head round it.'

'I know.' Willa's offence melted a little in the light-hearted atmosphere. She smiled at Mollie. 'I'm glad to see you're so happy, Mollie.'

'Me too.'

'We've eaten all the leftovers but I'd be happy to make you a sandwich.'

'That'd be lovely, Willa. Thanks.'

Mollie filled a glass with water and handed down out a plate for Willa on which she could deposit the sandwich. 'I have to say, I was really glad you were back helping me milk this morning. And I'm really sorry about our row.'

'Fine, Mollie. As long as it's worked out for you.' Willa said, dead-pan. She turned and left the room.

'Someone's a bit touchy.' Mollie said to her mum and Phoebe. She came and sat down at the table with them and began eating her sandwich.

'That's not like Willa. What did you do to her, Mollie?' Phoebe loved drama, as long as it wasn't too real.

Lisa cut in. 'Willa knows that she needs to help Mollie with the milking. That's the way a farm works. Speaking of which, Phoebe, we need to have a talk about your taking on some responsibilities around here.'

Phoebe sighed audibly. 'Alright. I knew Charlotte would show me in a bad light. Mum, I ought to check on Willa.'

'Yes, but we will talk this evening. After you've looked in on Willa, you can come back downstairs to do the washing-up.' Lisa got out her laptop and began to sift through emails.

Phoebe got up from the table with slumped shoulders and shuffled upstairs.

Mollie finished her sandwich. 'Mum?'

'Yes?' Lisa looked up from her laptop.

'It's not Willa's fault. She works really hard around here and she gets nothing out of it.'

'That's not exactly true, Mollie. You're both living here, eating meals, and you're both old enough to have responsibilities.'

Mollie hadn't heard her mother talk this way before. In fact, she had thought her mum would be in agreement with Granny, that Mollie ought to work out some sort of payment or profit sharing with Willa.

Mollie decided her mum must be frustrated about something else entirely. And it was not the right time to ask her what it was.

WILLA WAS LOOKING out of the window of her room. Mum hadn't even asked her *why* she'd let Mollie down yesterday morning; she'd just assumed it had been intentional. She would be the first to admit that it was the worst possible morning to oversleep; Willa ought to have been in the barn, then she would've been the one to discover the dead baby goats instead of Mollie.

And she wasn't sure why her mum supported her creativity, but only until Mollie shot her down. Last year, Willa had pitched the idea to Mollie that they put together gift baskets, offering a trio of Mollie's best cheeses. Two years ago, Willa had wanted to knit items featuring the likenesses of little baby goats, and sell them with a tag that showed a picture of the real goat, its name, and a little story about the baby goat's personality. She had the idea that families would like to come and visit the baby goats and follow their progress on a blog.

Mollie hadn't liked those ideas either. But Willa and Mum had; why could no one else's opinion be considered?

Willa's thoughts were interrupted by Phoebe standing in the doorway of her room.

'Willa?'

Willa turned from the window. Phoebe's timing was often horrible. She probably wanted Willa to drive her somewhere. Or, she wanted Willa to bake cupcakes for Phoebe and her friends.

'I just came to see how you are.' Phoebe flounced onto the bed, cradled her hands beneath her head and crossed her ankles. 'Mum's asked me to do the washing-up, but I wanted to come and talk to you first.'

'But what do you actually want, Phoebe? Is one of your friends coming over?'

'Who said I was here to ask for a favour?' Phoebe sat up on Willa's bed, a mollified expression on her face.

'I mustn't do the washing-up for you, Phoebe. You heard Mum, she thinks no one is pulling their weight, so you'd only get in more trouble if I did the kitchen.'

Phoebe let out an agitated sigh. 'For the last time, Willa, I didn't come up here to ask you to do anything. I wanted to talk to you.'

Willa crossed her arms, her brows pressed together. 'About what?'

'Just talk.'

Willa sat down on the bed. Phoebe must have a tricky problem, or something to confess. 'Okay,' Willa answered. 'So talk.'

Phoebe scooted back towards the headboard of Willa's bed and crossed her legs in front of her. Putting her elbows on her thighs, she began tracing the flowers on Willa's duvet with one of her fingertips.

'I just wanted to say that I like your ideas.'

'You mean about the goat soap?'

Phoebe started giggling. 'Sorry,' she tried to wipe the smile from her face. 'Dean thought it was for washing goats. Can't you see that's hilarious, Willa?'

'Of course I can.' She felt tired, and it wouldn't be long before she needed to get out to the barn for the evening milking.

'But I meant to say, that I like all your ideas.'

'Thanks, Phoebe.'

'And I thought that maybe you could share them with me.'

'What do you mean?'

'Well,' Phoebe returned to tracing the flowers on the duvet madly. She was trying to say something, but Willa couldn't fathom where this was going.

'It's always you and Mollie. Working together. Rowing about

something or planning something or going out in the car to buy something.'

'You feel left out? Is that what you're trying to say?'

'Not exactly. Being in the middle of the pair of you would be hideous.' Phoebe stopped tracing and now looked out the window to find her words. 'But I wouldn't mind baking sometimes.'

'Really?'

Phoebe became cross. 'Yes, *really*.'

'Well, alright.' Willa considered this. 'Is there something in particular you want to learn to make?'

'No.' Now Phoebe seemed irritated. But Willa understood. It was difficult being thirteen. She imagined that Phoebe wanted to be closer to Willa and included in doing things but didn't know how it should be engineered. Willa could also see that she may have to be a little firm with Phoebe to pull her into the kitchen and get her going, even though Phoebe had expressed an interest.

'I've got an idea.'

'You do?'

'Yes.' Willa sat on the bed. 'I've been invited to a lunch tomorrow.'

Phoebe was delighted. 'And you're taking me with you?'

'I'm sorry, Phebs, it would be bad manners to have you tag along when you've not been invited. It's at the vicarage with Mrs Hayward. I've been asked because she has a niece my age, so it would be a bit boring for you.'

'No it wouldn't. Couldn't you just ask? I'd be quiet, you wouldn't know I was there.' There was a mountain of evidence to the contrary.

'The problem is, I ought to take Mrs Hayward a little thank-you gift. You know, since she's giving me lunch and I'm making a new friend of Katie. But I'm not sure what I should do. What do you think?'

Phoebe's face screwed up in concentration and Willa had to focus on not smiling. As Willa hoped, Phoebe was throwing herself into the problem. It would be important to take her suggestion seriously.

A few moments later, Phoebe clapped her hands together. 'I've got it!' She bounced up and down on the bed. 'It's brilliant!'

Willa laughed. 'Okay, what is it?'

Phoebe stuck both arms out straight, fingers flexed to the ceiling, preparing Willa for a big announcement. 'What you should do, is make those cool friendship bracelets, like the ones that you gave to me and Tara last summer! We loved them so much!'

A bit childish. Willa said, 'Oh, those!'

'Yes!' Phoebe was over the moon. 'Because, like you said, you and Katie are going to be mates. I'll help you pick good colours. We've still got a whole bag of those stretchy loopy things.'

'I think that sounds like one of your most brilliant ideas, Phebs. Will you help me with it after milking tonight?'

'Why not?' Phoebe gave out an exaggerated sigh. 'It'll take me until then to clean the kitchen.'

illa parked the old Land Rover alongside the vicarage. As soon as she opened the door to climb out, the delicious fragrance of roses wafted up to greet her. The flower garden looked beautiful and Willa longed to go and sit in the sunshine on the warm lawn. Perhaps she could talk Phoebe into helping her create a new flower bed at the farm. It would give them something different to do out of doors and wouldn't be as fiddly as having Phoebe underfoot in the kitchen. They may even grow some veg. Or herbs. Fresh herbs would be lovely. She'd always confined herself to one pot of basil which was a bit witless since she lived on a farm.

With these happy plans in her thoughts, Willa took herself up to the vicarage door and rang the bell. She heard pattering steps on the other side and remembered the day that she'd gone to Myndcroft Hall to see Oliver Corbett.

The door opened. It was Mrs Hayward's niece, sheaved in a hot pink dress.

'Willa, so lovely to see you!'

'Hi Katie, how are you?'

'Please come into the sitting room. My aunt is on her way down.'

Katie beamed a million-watt, television-hostess smile at Willa. Like her aunt, Katie looked impeccably turned out, wearing a string of white pearls. Her voluminous auburn hair fell in perfect curls, as though she'd just stepped out of a salon. She paused in the hall and made a grand gesture for Willa to pass into the sitting room. Willa wished now that she'd dried her hair all of the way, as she smoothed a slightly damp tress behind one ear.

Willa hadn't been in the house since the old vicar passed away. Much had changed in the last two years. The vicarage was ancient, almost as old as the church and the library, which dated back to Tudor times. The room was brighter than the front hall. The curtains were minimal, just scarves of cream wound with cocoa-coloured pieces of fabric along the top. Willa took a seat on the sofa slipcovered in cream linen, one piece of a matching suite. Her eyes took in a low dark wood table in front of her and a pair of brass floor lamps. Opposite to the cream coloured suite was a pair of Parsons chairs – how fitting, thought Willa – that were done in a greyish-blue.

Mrs Hayward entered the room. 'Hello, Willa!' She took Willa's hand, gave it a shake and then sat in one of the cream chairs, opposite Katie, while Willa was alone on the large sofa. A big grey cat with luxurious cream and cocoa fur and startling blue eyes jumped up and joined her. The cat colour-coordinated with the room and Willa wondered if that was planned.

'I do hope you don't mind, Willa.'

'Oh no, not at all. She's beautiful, Mrs Hayward.' The cat wore a delicate pink bell on a hidden collar.

'Thank you. Her name is Misty. And mine is Veronica.' She smiled warmly.

Willa stroked the purring cat. And tried to think what to say. 'Where do you live, Katie?'

Katie laughed lightly, a bit like the cat's tinkling bell. 'I live with my parents and brother in Ely, in east Cambridgeshire.'

'Oh, yes! My friend, Oliver, told me about Ely. He was recently there. His friend lives quite close to your gorgeous cathedral. My Oliver got to visit your Oliver's home – that is, Cromwell's I mean.' Willa said this as a joke, but then found herself blushing. What would Mrs Hayward – Veronica, that is – think of her, calling their mutual friend 'my Oliver'?

Katie laughed, 'We've taken lots of family and visiting friends to Oliver Cromwell's house. But I think Aunt Veronica's house is nearly as old, isn't it?'

Veronica's eyes twinkled. 'Yes, but sadly not with quite such an interesting history. Not much intrigue, as few royals, politicians or high ranking military have found their way to our little village. Are you girls ready for lunch?'

Katie and Willa followed Veronica Hayward down a narrow, rather creaky passage. The original black beams of the house appeared here and there, in a sort of haphazard architecture. Willa could see light pouring around the figures of Mrs Hayward and her niece. In a moment they turned a corner and Willa stepped into the dazzling white kitchen. The black beams were in sharp contrast to the white walls. There was a nook with a trio of bright windows, and in it stood a table with a white cloth, set with black and white dishes. On each plate was a red napkin. The fabric above the window blinds were a pattern of vibrant red poppy flowers with black centres. A red pottery collection hung on a wall facing the black cooker, and oak and white cupboards. Willa admired the punchy decorating, except she thought that no kitchen was perfect without the lovely houseplants that her mother kept. She was shown her seat at the table, between Veronica and Katie.

Conversation was easy. Their lunch was perfect for summer: a chicken salad with rolls. The vicar's wife was an accomplished hostess and Willa hardly noticed when she swept away their plates, whilst Katie chatted about beginning university in the autumn. Veronica joined them again, and explained their pudding was alternating layers of fruit mousse and cream. Willa loved the presentation of the stunning pink and white striped dessert in tall, pedestaled glasses with long spoons.

'What will you read?' Willa had just asked Katie.

Katie smiled proudly and said, 'The same as Auntie Veronica. She said she'd tutor me as needed.'

Willa was embarrassed. She hadn't really thought of Mrs Hayward having any sort of degree; she'd only ever known her as the vicar's wife.

Veronica immediately realised Willa's discomfort and said, 'Willa and I are hardly acquainted, Katie.' She turned her penetrating gaze toward Willa and said, 'I am a psychologist. I specialise in helping people with learning challenges, career issues, and figuring out their gifts. I'm sure Katie wouldn't be content with such a breezy specialty, but the area of psychology appeals, doesn't it, darling?'

'Oh, yes!' Then Katie added, 'But I'd rather delve into the minds of criminals. Abnormal psychology is massively interesting. Probing the minds of psychopaths, terrorists and other deviants would most certainly be my cup of tea!' Katie's trilling laughter sounded out, as though she'd just related the most delightful anecdote.

Willa was stunned into silence and took a sip of tea. Katie rattled on about criminal anthropology. Willa was a little relieved when Veronica caught Katie taking a breath. 'Willa's interests seem to be in the culinary arts,' she said, with a tactful smile at Katie.

'So you're a good cook, Willa?' Katie asked, spooning up the last of her pudding. Her question seemed so forcefully put that Willa stammered a bit.

'Well, I don't know–'

'No need to be shy about your talent, Willa,' Veronica said. 'I've sampled her baking at the arts festival last weekend and I must confess, your pastries were divine.'

'They were really just some very simple recipes,' Willa mumbled. She hardly knew what to say. Cooking was something she'd begun to do because no one else in her family wanted to and they were hungry. The more competent Willa became the more she enjoyed it, but she didn't quite know if it was something to make a career around.

'But doing simple baking to *perfection* isn't something that everyone does, Willa, you must know that.'

'That's right,' Katie chimed in, eager to side with her aunt's opinion in all things. 'Haven't you seen the shows on television? Baking competitions?'

'Sometimes,' Willa said. Usually, she was helping to do the milking and cleaning the barn, then doing some *actual* cooking in the kitchen. There hadn't been much time to sit around watching it done. And Phoebe seemed to own the television, by some divine right of being the youngest in the family.

'I hope you'll give it some thought, Willa. There's a wonderful regional college offering cookery, catering and hospitality in Cambridge,' Veronica said, eyebrows raised with possibility. 'Maybe it would be just the place to take a few courses and see how you get on.'

Willa felt increasingly uncomfortable. 'Oh, well. I'm not sure I have the money to move away, especially in the next month or so, surely–'

Veronica looked at her in a dubious way, as though Willa was making excuses. Katie simply blinked at her and the distance between them gaped wider. Willa felt nervous and didn't want to discuss college any longer.

'My sister keeps goats.'

Katie and her aunt were aghast following this random change of topic.

Katie was the first to respond. '*Why?*'

Willa was prepared for, *what breed? How many does she have?* But Katie's bewildered response threw Willa completely. Her throat felt dry.

Katie was looking at her as though she wondered if Willa was on drugs. Or perhaps criminally insane. Which, Willa thought, might serve to make her more interesting to Katie.

Willa suddenly remembered. 'Mollie's ambition is to be a great cheesemaker. And she's well on her way.'

A moment passed. Veronica graciously added, 'Yes, she is! Katie, I sampled some of Mollie's delicious cheese at a party up at the big house. Remember, I told you?'

'Certainly. How could I forget?' Katie picked up the thread enthusiastically. She leaned towards Willa and said in a conspiratorial tone, 'I met the dishy lad who lives there. His name is Oliver Corbett. He happens to be going to *my* uni and said that he would see me there this autumn. Isn't that brilliant?'

'Yes.' Willa could think of nothing else to say. Naturally, Katie would never imagine that Willa's earlier reference to 'my Oliver' could, in fact, be the same person.

'Leave it to my niece to make *that* connection when we were talking about chèvre!' Veronica laughed as though Katie was hilarious.

Willa was desperate to leave but wasn't sure how. Can you simply say thanks, stand up from the table and begin to walk out? She suddenly had an epiphany.

'Lunch has been so lovely. I wonder, where is the loo?'

'Oh, yes, dear, of course. The door opposite the kitchen.'

Willa concentrated on standing without bringing the table cloth with her or any other horrendous social mistake. She hoped her action of leaving the table would break up the little luncheon, and thus she took her handbag with her.

She slipped across the hall and into a cramped white cloakroom. She pressed a button for the light and a rather loud fan came on as well. There was a black lacquered shelf with some pretty glass bottles which Willa thought were precariously placed; she imagined a large man having been sitting there for some time, then standing up from the toilet and toppling the shelf. The thought sent her into irrepressible giggles. Willa caught sight of herself in the mirror over the basin and threatened herself to be quiet. She couldn't very well have a psychologist and her protégée hearing her overcome with hilarity in the loo and think her completely crackers. Thank heavens for the overly-loud fan.

She flushed the toilet for authenticity, turned on the tap and slapped a bit of cool water on her face to shock her into a dignified self-control, and opened the door.

As she hoped, the pair had left the kitchen. Willa hoped to make her goodbyes and leave.

The thing was, *she couldn't find them.*

She went down the narrow passage and found the sitting room empty. In a panic, she somehow thought she'd missed them in some corner of the black and white kitchen. She trotted back up the corridor and peered in. No, the kitchen was empty of Veronica and her niece. In fact, the kitchen looked startling now – a rather clinical, hospital white, with accents of blood red. She turned and sped back toward the sitting room.

Willa returned to the front hall and stood still a moment, listening. Nothing. She called out, 'Hello?'

No answer. She called out again, louder this time. Crickets.

The rose garden. Of course that's where they'd gone.

Willa clutched her handbag and pulled open the ancient wooden door. She went around the side of the house by the patio and roses.

The garden was empty.

CHAPTER 29

It was Friday. The weather was dry for the remaining day of the arts festival, but the bursts of sunshine were erratic and the sky was frequently gloomy. Lisa sat in the dining room of Hilltop Farm. She glanced at the clock on her computer. She'd check her email, and then soon she'd be off to Marris Mynd to help with the last concert and attend the end-of-the-festival meeting.

She was glad that Colleen Corbett had taken on more responsibilities this year. Lisa lacked her usual interest in how many visitors had come, whether or not the vendors were pleased with the arrangements, and what comments had been dropped into the suggestion box. She fancied a nap rather than going back to the village, but she should press through the final evening event. She promised herself that she would sleep late tomorrow.

Checking her email, Lisa saw a message from Sam Lloyd, titled 'holiday'. She took a deep breath to quench a little nervous flutter in her tummy. She hadn't seen him since spending a few hours in the office the day Mollie's little goats had passed away.

She opened the message and read:

Lisa,

Hope the festival has been a smashing success and that Mollie hasn't had any further issues with her animals.

I've decided to take a holiday beginning next week, through to the end of the month. Of course, if you have any questions, don't hesitate to ring me. I'll send along a few other emails today regarding the next batch of revisions.

Thank you,

Sam

So he was traveling to France after all. She certainly couldn't blame him. Ursula was beautiful and talented and they probably enjoyed each other's company. She'd been silly to fan a spark of hope simply because Sam was a bit muddled during their meeting and he'd missed one of Ursula's performances. Every relationship has its 'off' days.

Lisa's chest ached with loneliness. Michael Ferrington had been a bad sort, but he'd reintroduced her to the world of couple-dom. She realised with unexpected intensity that she no longer cared for being on her own.

She closed her laptop and held her head in her hands. No, of course she wouldn't contact Michael. Based on Sally's comments, Michael had most likely moved on – or perhaps he'd even continued dating whilst seeing her. He'd never bothered to respond to her furious voice message. She'd never heard from him again.

Lisa felt better about other issues. She was rather glad that Rhys Davies had wanted to work here on the farm. She supposed no self-respecting feminist would admit it, but Lisa thought it would be lovely to have a man on the property, even if it was nothing personal for Mollie. Just having him about would bring a certain element of security that Lisa missed.

Soon, her daughters would probably marry or leave the farm for other reasons. Lisa would be on her own. She would miss mothering them; they'd been her life and her greatest joy.

'Mum!'

She heard Phoebe's voice from upstairs. Not alone just yet.

'In the dining room!' she called back.

She heard Phoebe's feet hammering down the staircase. 'What are you doing?' her youngest daughter asked, wrapping her arms about Lisa's shoulders.

'Just checking in with work. Then I need to go back to the festival.'

'You look tired.'

'I feel tired, love.'

'Can I go with you?'

'Of course. Are you meeting friends today?'

'Not until four. Which leaves hours and hours to get through, but if I don't go with you, I'm not sure Mollie or Willa will drive me over later. I don't want to ride my bike because no one else does, so that'd be the absolute apex of awkwardness.'

They heard the boot room door; Mollie and Willa, in from a morning of milking, feeding and mucking out the barn. Lisa and Phoebe left the dining room to join them. Lisa brought her laptop along and plugged it in to charge at the kitchen table.

'You've simply got to make a big, gorgeous breakfast, Willa, I'm famished. Jenny and I went to that new restaurant last night and it was simply horrible. We left half our meals. I'm still hungry.'

'What did you order?' Phoebe asked. She always needed details. She'd decide if Mollie had made the right decision.

'Nothing special. Chicken.'

'What could be so horrible you didn't finish it?'

Mollie put her hands on her hips for emphasis. 'It was pink in the middle. *Raw chicken.* Still think I should've eaten it?'

'Oh, Mollie, you didn't pay for it, did you?' Lisa asked.

'No, Mum, of course not. Jenny had a proper go at the manager and then we left.'

Willa got an enormous frying pan from the cupboard for Mollie's favourites: bacon, fried eggs, mushrooms, tomato, and baked beans. 'Anyone else?'

'Yes, please!' Phoebe answered.

'No,' her mum corrected. 'We really shouldn't delay getting to the festival in case there have been any problems.'

'Wouldn't they ring you if there were?' Willa answered. Lisa felt the twinge of guilt, realising that Willa wanted she and Phoebe to stay for a late breakfast. They'd seen so little of each other this week and Willa hadn't even told them about lunching at the vicarage yet, as everyone had gone different directions last evening.

'Yes, I suppose. That'll be breakfast for me, too!'

The girls smiled and Mollie went to lay the table. Lisa prompted Phoebe, 'Perhaps you could get the tea, love.'

There was talk about the festival, how the goats were doing, and Phoebe's plans with her friends for later that day. 'We're going to eat and then I want to go home with Vanya, if that's alright with you, Mum? Her mother already said yes.'

Lisa nodded. Mollie and Willa brought the food to the table. Phoebe poured tea and proudly added a plate of toast to the meal. They were quiet over the first few bites, then praised Willa's cooking skills.

'You haven't told us how your luncheon went yesterday.'

Looking at her plate, Willa's broad smile enticed Phoebe to say, 'Oh, this'll be super satisfactory. Tell us *everything*, Willa!'

Mollie put down her knife and fork and glanced at her mother. Lisa met her eyes, enjoying the fact that they were around the table together. Suddenly Lisa became teary. Of all the silly times to be sentimental! Fortunately, Willa had begun describing the inside of the vicarage and being introduced to a cat, so no one noticed.

'Then Mrs Hayward, or rather, "Veronica", told me that she was a psychiatrist. Or psychologist. I don't remember. And Katie went on to say that she wants to be one as well, only she adores the criminally insane and wants to specialise in working with them.'

'She's sectionable herself!' Phoebe said. 'I guess the friendship bracelets we made were, like, totally unsuitable.' Lisa had an inkling she might've chosen stronger words if her mother weren't there. She thought she'd heard a few choice expressions coming from Phoebe's room of late.

Willa nodded. 'It gets better.'

'You mean it gets worse,' Mollie astutely observed.

'You've no idea,' Willa agreed.

'Then tell us!' Phoebe said, standing half-way out of her chair and making everyone laugh.

'So then Dr Veronica says that she specialises in helping people find their calling and careers, and *that* seemed to be the chief reason she'd asked me round!'

'Honestly? She had you over to analyse you?' Mollie gawped in surprise.

'Yes!' Willa looked at Lisa. 'She said I ought to learn cookery and catering, and then Katie agreed–'

'*Creepy* Katie,' supplied Phoebe.

'–And she'd even chosen a school for me in Cambridge, Mum!'

'She's so cheeky, handing down opinions like that,' Mollie said. 'But why, exactly, did she say cookery? You're clever and could do any number of brainy things. You could be a shrink like she and Creepy.'

'Because she tried my custard tarts or something at the festival. I mean, they were the most basic tarts known to mankind, nothing at all special–'

'They are really good, though, Willa.' Phoebe looked a bit wistful. A pudding to follow-up their huge breakfast would clearly be spot-on.

'Then what?' Mollie asked.

'Well…' Willa's smile dropped.

They all waited, watching Willa's face. A fleeting look of pain. Lisa wondered if Veronica Hayward had said something unkind to her daughter.

Willa carried on with her story. 'I thought to myself, "I must get out of here", right? So I asked where the loo was, and it was across the corridor from the kitchen. You see, I was sort of hoping that lunch would break-up while I was in there, and actually it did. They weren't at the table when I came out.'

'So, then what? Did they have university enrolment papers on hand?'

'No, she gave me a brochure. But that's not *the* most ghastly thing!' Willa said, eyes wide.

The Purslow women collectively held their breath.

Willa looked around the table, and burst out with, 'I never saw them again!'

'What?' Mollie couldn't take it in. 'What do you mean?'

'Exactly that. They weren't in the kitchen or the sitting room. I called out. No one answered.'

'They've that lovely garden—'

'I checked, Mum. They weren't there either!'

Phoebe came out of her chair and leaned into Willa's face. 'So scary! What did you do?'

Willa threw up her hands. 'What I desperately wanted to do. *I left.*'

Shocked silence hung around the breakfast table.

'Oh dear. Willa, that doesn't seem a nice way to end a lunch.'

'What did you want her to do, Mum?' Mollie countered. 'It seems to me she didn't have any choice. She couldn't very well sit around the house hoping they'd come back.'

Lisa sighed and raised her eyebrows. 'How very strange.' Then she folded her arms and looked at Willa. 'So, have you gone online to check out the cookery school yet?'

Her daughter's surprised face gave them all another great laugh.

CHAPTER 30

*R*hys had never had a row with his father. Until today.

Huw Davies had stormed out of the farmhouse, leaving Rhys pacing the kitchen. His mother stood over the sink, hugging her middle, gazing out of the window. Rhys suspected she was crying. He felt badly about that, but he also believed that it wasn't his fault. His father was a stubborn man. And his father had completely snapped.

Rhys suspected that his da wouldn't like his plan, but he didn't expect his father to *disown* him. He realised he ought to be doing something besides wearing out the kitchen floor.

'What'll you do, son?' His mother's voice was shaky.

Rhys couldn't articulate any thoughts. He stopped his furious pacing and stood with his hands on his hips. To his horror, he began to cry. Thankfully, his mother kept her distance. He wiped his dripping nose with the back of his fist and brushed his shirt-sleeve over his eyes.

The casual meeting with his father, outside, under the big oak, had begun well. He'd waited until his brothers had dispersed after lunch and he'd asked to speak with his dad. His father had clapped him on the back and had grinned. He probably thought Rhys would tell him about a new girlfriend, or one of Rhys's ideas to benefit their farm, since he'd had a few of those in the past.

'Dad, I've been thinking.'

'Oh?' Huw Davies had seated himself on a garden bench. He filled his pipe, which meant he was settling in to listen. Huw wasn't a man to speak his affection, but these sorts of quiet, attentive actions complemented his sons. It gave Rhys the confidence to continue. All the same, he stayed on his feet.

'I've been thinking. Reading a lot, and speaking with some neighbours. And well, the thing is, I'll always want to be a farmer. That's in me, like you.' He paused and his eyes locked with his father's. 'But I don't want to work with a dairy herd, as such.'

Huw lowered his pipe. 'What's that, then? You're saying nothing, bach.'

'Dad, I want to farm. But no cows for me. I want to raise crops. Be an organic farmer.'

Huw Davies rapidly came to his feet. His face was red. 'This farm isn't good enough for you, is what you're saying, is it?' His father swore in Welsh. Rhys was stunned.

'But, you've got the others.' Rhys was the youngest of four sons.

'You've always been big about yourself, you have.' In a fit of rage, Huw threw his pipe long and hard. Rhys never saw where it landed, his eyes were glued on his father. 'Always wanting more, you are. Always having ideas. Alright, I used some of 'em and they worked, they came on. You're more 'an clever. But a more ungrateful arse I've never seen. Do as you please, but you'll not do it here. Off my land, out of my house you go! *Today.*'

With that proclamation, Huw Davies charged past Rhys, nearly knocking him down. Rhys's mother had been in the kitchen, window open to every word.

Now she repeated her question. 'What'll you do, bach?'

He sniffed. The tears had been humiliating but they'd loosened him up a fair bit. 'He won't change his mind.'

'No.' She looked embarrassed. Rhys knew that although she didn't agree with his father, she'd go along with his decision. The only way to get on with Huw was to go Huw's way. No one knew that better than she.

'I have a bit of money, Mam. I'll be all right.'

He hugged her then. Within the hour, he'd packed his things and left home.

MOLLIE HAD ALWAYS SAID that Willa should go to university. Yet now, Mollie couldn't think why Willa would want to go. It didn't seem possible her sister would actually leave.

But she'd thought Natalie would always be there. And Nat was gone for good.

They were moving bales around in the loft, bringing the older ones forward for an easy reach. Willa's stack was perfectly squared up.

Everything Willa did for Mollie's goats was a thorough job, because that was Willa. Fastidious. What a perfect, brainy word to describe her sister.

Mollie laughed. 'You are *fastidious*.'

Willa was surprised at this random observation. 'Hmm. Yes, Mollie. I am.'

Mollie stopped raking. Miserably, she turned to look at Willa. 'I expect that's just the sort of thing, for being a chef.'

Willa's head leaned to one side. 'Oh, Mollie. I don't know.'

'Why don't you know, Willa? You're anything but stupid and a rare talent in the kitchen.'

'She's met Oliver, you know. She even said they planned to meet up in Cambridge.'

'Creepy Katie? No way, Willa. Oliver would never go for the likes of her.'

'She's very pretty. And perhaps he doesn't know she loves deviancy.'

Mollie giggled. 'It sounds like Katie is rather obvious.' Mollie stood up over the newly arranged bales and took off her gloves. 'Have you heard from him?'

Willa sighed. 'No. But he's been very busy. Riding his bikecycle.'

Mollie walked over to the ladder, shaking her head. 'Only you would fall for a genius who spends weeks riding a bicycle.'

Willa laughed with her, knowing that Mollie thought the world of Oliver.

Mollie suddenly became serious. 'I don't want you to go. Isn't that enough to keep you here mucking out goats forever?'

'That's a mean trick, Mollie. You'd like me to feel guilty, feel sorry that you'd have all this work to do without me. But you won't let me act as your partner. I do all of this for nothing.'

'You don't choose to do anything else. At least this is important.' Mollie hated herself for saying that, even if there was a bit of truth in it, to her thinking. Inwardly, she begged Willa to overlook her bad behaviour like she normally did. *Please, Willa. Stay home.*

'Well, I suppose you're right, Mollie. I haven't focused much on myself or made plans. But I'll tell you what I do want.'

An uneasy feeling crept up in Mollie's chest. She wasn't sure she had the courage to hear. Willa could make up her mind for decisive action, and then she always saw it through to the end.

Mollie said, 'Alright, Willa. I'm listening.' She promised herself to agree with whatever demands her sister placed on her. If she wanted an equal share of the goats, and all that came from them, then so be it.

'I want Oliver.'

Mollie was taken aback. 'I thought you were going to demand we do some weird goat product thing again!' Mollie smiled. 'You really are that keen?'

Willa blushed. 'Oh, yes.'

Mollie felt affection for her sister come bubbling up. She'd felt that way about her Rhys. In truth, she still did. She gave her sister an enormous hug. 'He'd be lucky to have you, Willa.'

Willa laughed. 'I thought you liked Oliver.'

Mollie released her and shook her slightly by the shoulders. 'I do! And he's a crashing bore like you. You're perfect for each other.'

A rush of anxiety welled up within Mollie. 'Wait – the penny's just dropped.'

Willa looked away for a moment. 'Yes. You've got it in one. If I go to cookery school I'll be on a different campus. But I'll still be *near* him.'

'And you'd do that?'

'For Oliver, of course I would. Mucking out goats isn't really as glamorous as you think it is, Mollie. I think you'd make an interesting case study for Creepy.'

Mollie giggled with her sister. 'How will I manage without you?'

'I don't know. But you will.'

'I hope you don't mind the odd meeting place,' Lisa said, welcoming Rhys into the chilly library. They made their way to her old office, where there still stood three or four guest chairs, with her chair on the business side. She'd brought her laptop to work on, but, as usual, Rhys was punctual.

There was something oppressive about his manner. 'Rhys, are you alright?'

Avoiding her gaze, he said, 'More or less. But I'm keen to know what you've decided.'

She clasped her hands together on the desk and said in an encouraging, cheerful voice. 'I'm happy to offer you the land, Rhys.'

Surprisingly, he put both hands over his face. A moment later, he dropped his hands and Lisa saw his eyes were a bit shiny. She had, of course, realised that his asking her for a lease was very important to him, but she hadn't understood it was *this* important. Guilt pulsed through her; she shouldn't have made him wait a week for a final decision, poor man.

'Thank you, Lisa.'

'You're quite welcome, Rhys. Now, about the terms. You indicated that you'd be willing to lease the land and then we'd discuss profit sharing?'

'Yes.' He shifted in his seat. She was quite concerned now. After receiving such good news, it would be more like Rhys to look her in the eye and begin outlining his plans. She wondered what troubled him. Hopefully, from a farming perspective, he'd done the planning she'd given him a week to do. Suddenly she considered the possibility that perhaps he wasn't as mature as she'd thought. Maybe this was a mistake. If so, time would tell.

'I've been doing a lot of careful thinking, Rhys. Our family has always thought so highly of you, and I feel as though I know you quite well.' Inwardly, she hoped this was still true. 'Because of our friendship,' she was determined not to mention Mollie, 'I would like you to have use of the land for a year. What I mean to say, Rhys, is that I don't want to have a lease agreement.'

He raised his eyes and stared at her unbelievingly. 'You're saying, I think… you're giving me the land to work, for free?'

'Yes, love.' She felt herself getting teary. Fumbling with the pencil on her desk. This wasn't meant to be a blubbering sort of discussion.

The young man reached both hands across the desk and covered Lisa's hands beneath his own. 'Thank you, Lisa.'

'Rhys. You must see that the land has been sitting there, not earning me a penny for many years, so you mustn't feel unduly spoilt. In fact, Grant's brother has pressured me to sell it to him for years. I'll quite enjoy telling him those acres are under use and he has no share in it.'

They smiled at each other. Rhys had met Edward once. Lisa remembered, at the time, Rhys had said to Mollie, 'He's nothing like your father, is he?'

Rhys withdrew his hands and Lisa became businesslike. 'So, it's quite easy for me to allow you to farm it, experiment, perhaps get some profits going and so forth. I don't know what we'll do following on the first year, but I expect we'll both have a greater understanding later on.'

Rhys smiled for the first time since arriving. She knew he was getting his fire back. This was the Rhys she trusted and loved, and Lisa was as proud of him as if he'd been her own son.

'It's staggering. And wonderful. I can't thank you enough.'

'You mustn't say that again, Rhys, alright? Any questions?'

'Will you tell Mollie?'

'Of course. It was never meant to stay a secret, but we deserved to get organised first, without my daughters weighing in.'

Another smile.

'I've nowhere to keep tools at the moment,' Rhys said. His voice was stronger now, quite normal.

'I've been thinking about that. I think that you ought to take the space you need in the small barn for now. I know it's a distance from the field, but knocking up a shed, however basic, is an expense.'

'There's a saying, money pays for convenience. Until you have the money, put up with the inconvenience.'

'Quite right, Rhys. Especially since Mollie–'

A shadow came and went across his face and he looked away, no doubt imagining crossing her path at the farm.

Lisa tried again. 'Even though Mollie calls it the small barn, it's quite a big space. Since there's no billy goat living in at the moment, you could even keep some things in that pen as well.'

There was a flicker of something still troubling him, but she chalked it up to his thinking about Mollie and embarking on a new career. In considering all of this, Lisa realised that she had to trust Rhys; if he'd not been up to seeing Mollie on a regular basis, he wouldn't have approached her about her land.

But perhaps she should've asked Mollie. She blurted out her thoughts to Rhys. He was a young man but usually quite sensible. 'I hope Mollie can deal with this arrangement. She broke her heart over you, Rhys.'

'No worries. She'll be alright, as soon as she gets some free labour out of me.'

Wise indeed. Lisa knew that Rhys was right. She felt like some of her recent decisions had been a little off, so she trusted him and dismissed the thought. The festival and the situation with Sam had really exhausted her recently, and she was glad to have this business with Rhys sorted.

'Anything else?' She asked the new farmer, whose fortune was his own for the making.

'No, Lisa. Only, I couldn't be more grateful.'

She reached across the desk and patted his shoulder. 'No need, Rhys. You'll make a go of it, and in a few years you'll have a prosperous farming concern.'

They shook hands like old business partners.

THE KETTLE HAD COME to a boil when Mollie and Willa both came in from the morning milking. 'Sit down, girls. We need to have a little chat.'

She saw concerned looks pass over their faces. After having been through the meeting with Rhys, Lisa hardly felt strong enough for another session of young people trying to manage their emotional states. Oh well, she told herself. She would power up on tea, say her piece and listen to their side, and then she could go to her room and relax with a book. Both this situation and the arts festival would be tidied away.

Lisa filled a proper teapot, added her best loose tea, and brought a tray with three china cups and saucers to the table. Very grown-up and setting the tone, as it were. Mollie eased into a chair while Willa popped up and went to get matching china plates, forks and a knife so that they could enjoy the rest of the lemon thyme cake she'd made.

All assembled and with a cup of tea and slice of cake, Lisa noticed that Willa's brow was crinkled slightly. 'This isn't about your going to school, or not going,' she assured her daughter, winning an expression of relief from Willa. 'In fact, I'm hoping you'll both view this as a bit of good news, especially you, Mollie.'

'Me?' Mollie said through a mouth full of cake.

'You know, you really are irritating, darling?' Lisa said.

Mollie covered her mouth with her hand. 'Sorry, Mum.'

'Actually, I don't mean that, although you ought to stop talking when your mouth is full. I meant that, here you are, going off to a modelling assignment this weekend, and you're stuffing yourself with cake, not worrying about gaining an ounce. I've been doing extra duties at the festival and, obviously, I still need to watch my calories.'

'I watch, too,' said Willa.

'Now that Oliver's watching your figure!' Mollie teased.

Lisa perked up at that revelation. 'Oh? Have you seen him again, Willa?'

Willa's smile faded. 'No. I'd just like to, but he's away at the moment.'

Lisa jumped in straightaway. 'Well, speaking of young men, I've made an agreement with one to allow him to farm some of Daddy's old fields at the bottom of the hills. Rather far away from the house, actually, but Grant always said those were the best farming acres.'

The girls listened. Lisa could see that Mollie hadn't even considered Rhys. When she was dating him, he'd been expected to stay in the dairy business with his father.

'I've decided to give Rhys access to some of those fields. His aim is to grow vegetables and crops, and of course, all of his father's farmland is given over to grazing cows.'

Lisa looked at Mollie as she said this, wondering if there would be a row.

'Rhys?'

'Yes, Mollie. Is that a problem?'

'I guess it doesn't matter if it is, since you didn't ask me.'

Lisa decided just to nip it in the bud. 'You're quite right, it was my decision, and that's why I didn't ask you.'

'I think it's brilliant, Mum,' said Willa, always the peacemaker. 'How else would Rhys have a chance to begin a career as a farmer? People must have a huge chunk of money to even be allowed to borrow any.' Willa turned to her sister. 'Surely you wish him well, Mollie?'

Willa had successfully appealed to Mollie's finer feelings. Mollie generously replied, 'Of course I do.'

Lisa was proud that her eldest daughter rose to the occasion. And that Willa was ever the voice of reason.

'Alright then, that's settled. Rhys will be using the small barn as storage, Mollie. Of course, if you purchase another billy than he'll be obliged to make sure the large pen is empty.'

'But does he have anything to store? Does Rhys have supplies or any farming equipment?'

An image of equipment flashed through Lisa's mind: Grant, beneath his tractor. She hadn't been allowed to see him; the men insisted she stay inside the house with the girls. But her imagination had recreated the horrible scene of his death. Lisa cleared her throat. 'I don't know about his equipment or his plans. I'm sure Rhys has that all sorted.'

'Yes, he will have,' said Mollie with obvious pride. 'He likes to have a plan.' Her voice thinned. 'Speaking of plans. Willa, don't you have something to tell Mum?'

So, Willa has been thinking about university, thought Lisa.

But she truly needed a short break in the little dramas ebbing and flowing through her life. 'It'll have to wait, girls. I'm having a little rest and then I need to do a bit of work. We'll talk soon, Willa, I promise.'

That afternoon, Willa was in the process of measuring out where she and Mollie had decided to dig a new flower bed, alongside and in front of the farmhouse. Mollie wanted to host some dairy days, opening the farm up to visitors for tours. Willa thought it was a cracking idea and agreed that their garden needed some brightening up. They also envisioned a small car park on the flat lawn opposite the barns. Perhaps now that Rhys was coming on as a farmer he would have equipment to churn up the new bed and save them hours of backbreaking work.

Willa had been researching what sort of bushes and flowers ought to go in but that was a bit more tricky. She liked flowers and didn't know much about them, and she wanted a scheme that would look quite professional. She was in deep contemplation of these details when her mobile rang.

It was Oliver. Her heart lurched.

'Willa, are you busy at the moment?' He spoke casually, as though they'd seen one another only yesterday.

'No, not at all. I'm trying to plan our landscaping, but I think I'm going to need to do a bit more research.'

'You ought to have a chat with our gardener, Laurence. He knows everything.'

'I'd hoped you'd say that. As long as he doesn't mind giving a bit of free advice?'

'No, I'm sure not. He'll talk about herbaceous borders all day if you like, and maybe even give you some of the plants he's divided, to help get things going. I'd be happy to introduce you. He's brilliant at design, so perhaps bring him measurements of the area and he may just sketch something for you as well.'

'Oh, Oliver, that would be wonderful. I don't mind the work in the least, but of course I want a really good, professional looking outcome. I'm afraid I won't get that without some direction. How are you?'

'I've been better, actually.' He sighed and sort of chuckled, the kind of noises made when a person's trying to make a challenge seem amusing.

'What's happened?'

'A car came off the road and so did we.'

'On your bicycle?' Willa imagined Oliver in hospital. 'Oliver, are you alright?'

'Yes, sweetie, I'm fine, really.'

Sweetie? She was flustered with worry and pleasure. 'You're at home then?'

'I am. I was in hospital for a few days, and that's why I haven't called. You see, my mobile was broken when I came off the bike. And I've been given a lot of medicine.'

'Oh my goodness! Sod the mobile, are *you* broken?' It was an oddly put question and Willa heard him laugh. She didn't care if he thought she was daft, if it brought him a moment of amusement in his suffering.

'My wrist and ankle took the worst of it. Had a bit of surgery and now I'm well on the mend.'

'What happened, exactly?'

'We were trail biking on the designated path, the Jack Mytton

Way. Close to Carding Mill Valley, this bloke came barrelling from nowhere in a four-by-four as though he was going off-road or something, which was insane. He turned directly in front of us, so we ended up in a grass verge. We found out later he was ten sheets to the wind and had mown down bits of a roundabout several miles up the road. He was so out of control he hadn't noticed, apparently. It was all caught on CCTV in the village.'

'You could've been killed!'

'Yes. He was way above the drink-driving limits.'

'And your mate? How's he?'

'Patrick was a bit worse for wear. Broken leg and a knock on the head. But he's doing well. You know, we'd thought if we were riding on trails, it'd be a lot safer. You hear of so many road accidents, you know? On a more interesting note, I wondered if you're free today?'

'I'd love to see you!' Willa gushed.

'Alright. I can't drive myself but I'm sure I can find someone to give me a lift over.'

'Don't be silly, Oliver, I'll come to you. I'm sure you're meant to be resting.'

'It was mentioned.'

'I'm free now as it happens. I'll have to come back this afternoon and help Mollie with the milking but we'll have a few hours. Unless you'd prefer a shorter visit, of course.' Oh dear, she was bungling this.

'The sooner the better and I'll be glad of having you here until the very minute you must go.'

'Really?'

'Of course, Willa. See you soon.'

Elated, she went to the farmhouse to freshen up and change clothes. She texted a message to Mollie, who was somewhere inspecting the goats' grazing field, and took the key to the old Land Rover from the hook in the kitchen. As Willa drove the short distance, she thought about how quickly things could change. She'd been on pins for over a week, wishing Oliver would get in touch. Suddenly he'd rung and now in two or three minutes, she would be with him.

She wondered if she simply amused him. Perhaps he was just so incredibly bored in his convalescence that he wanted a visit from anyone that would come.

Willa swung the vehicle into the gates at Myndcroft Hall and began the ascent to the top. The drive seemed longer than she remembered. Finally she crested the hill and the big house loomed in front of her. She parked the dilapidated old vehicle as out of the way as possible and then made her way to the front door. This time Oliver opened the door himself, wearing a rather large sort of orthopaedic boot on his left foot.

'Willa, so lovely to see you, come in!'

She followed him into the house and he hopped around a bit in order to close the monstrous door. Then he gestured left, towards the front sitting room. She hadn't been in this room for years but imagined that it must be closer to his room or something than the sitting room in the back of the house. She saw that he'd been spending a bit of time in here. There was a television in a large armoire, its channel set to sports. She saw some textbooks and newspapers scattered on a low table by a sofa. There was a large square cushion on the leather sofa that was covered in a sheepskin. She turned to him and said, 'I suppose you'd be best here and putting your foot back up on the cushion.' She stood a moment, not knowing if she ought to help him prop up his leg.

'Are you sure you didn't miss your vocation as a nurse?' he teased and took a seat on the sofa. 'Please, sit here with me. I can keep my foot on the floor like a normal person, alright?'

They laughed and she sat down gingerly beside him. He scooted closer to her on the sofa. She thought his legs looked enormously long and muscular bent at the knees beside her own.

'Would you like something? Tea? Coffee or other?'

'No, thank you.' She was unsure of how he would've accomplished getting drinks and didn't want to be without him for even a moment.

'We talked a lot about me on the phone. I want to hear how you've been.' He smiled encouragingly. Willa couldn't think of a thing to say. Or, even more importantly, what she could tell him versus what she ought not to say.

'Um. Well, I've been alright.'

Oliver drew her out. 'When I saw you last, you were baking for the festival. I suppose your baking turned out perfectly, but how did you get it all transported?'

'Thank you. Everything did turn out nicely.' Referring to their date, she added, 'I had a rather nice breakfast that morning to energise me through the hours in the kitchen.' They smiled at each other and Willa became embarrassed and looked away. 'Delivery wasn't difficult since we each of us carried a box of something, otherwise, you're quite right, it would've been a challenge. Something odd did happen, though.'

'What's that?'

'Naturally the tarts and so forth were meant for the people attending the concert. But the majority of them were gone when the concert ended.'

'Really? Do you think people came into the library and nicked them?'

'I don't know. Unless the first groups of people exiting the concert took extras? We've never figured it out.'

Willa then remembered coming across Mrs Hayward and her niece at the stalls and receiving an invitation to lunch. She told Oliver.

'Ah, Mrs Hayward.'

'Do you know her?'

'I know *of* her. Has she taken you on as her next protégée?'

Willa was stunned. 'It did sort of seem so. You mean she does this regularly?'

Oliver laughed. 'Well, she tried it on with my sister, which I thought was kind of odd. Not to sound patronising, but you know my mother. And, of course, I know yours. In my opinion, they've done a lovely job raising their daughters. My mum wasn't sure why Mrs Hayward thought Penelope was so in need of guidance, if you see what I mean?'

'This was before Penelope went to university?'

'It was. During her gap year. But when Mrs Hayward latched on, Penelope had already been accepted at school and chosen her degree.' Oliver paused. 'Except, well, now that I think about it, there was more to it than that.'

'How so?' Willa hoped she wasn't prying, gossiping or otherwise disappointing Oliver with her curiosity.

'Well, as it happens, Pen ended up taking the woman's advice after all. You see, Mrs Hayward thought that Penelope couldn't possibly excel in life until she'd worked in an orphanage. It was rather strange at the time, but, actually, in hindsight it's made perfect sense.'

'I don't understand how?' Willa couldn't remember much at all about Penelope. They'd never been friends growing up as Penelope had always been away at school. She hadn't been home this summer.

'My sister aims to be a paediatrician. I suppose Mrs Hayward wanted her to have a clear vision of what children are like when they've had very few advantages. I remember Pen saying that children given up for adoption can have associated health risks, and Mrs Hayward wanted my sister to see them first hand.'

'Wouldn't Penelope have encountered all sorts as she moved through her schooling and clinical experience?'

'Yes, but it was pointed out to her that spending twenty minutes gathering a case history and treating a diagnosis isn't the same as working full days amongst children. Penelope volunteered at an orphan camp in South America. It did change her views tremendously.'

'That's interesting.'

'Willa, do you mind my asking what Mrs Hayward said to you?'

'Not at all. To be fair, I suppose it was my fault I didn't make much use of counsellors at school, so I'd been wondering what to do with myself. I'm actually considering Mrs Hayward's advice. She said I ought to go to school for catering and hospitality and cookery. She mentioned there are courses of that variety in a building in the city centre... in Cambridge.' Willa flushed deeply and couldn't look at Oliver.

'Wouldn't that be splendid?' He sounded quite excited. Willa looked up, surprised. Oliver took one of her hands in his. 'We could see each other more often.' He squeezed her hand slightly. Willa felt a fizz of excitement bubble through her body. Looking into her eyes he said, 'Tell me more.'

Her words came quickly. 'I looked at the website and did some research. I'm interested in a specific course offered, it's connected with the Royal Academy of Culinary Arts. I'd learn professional cookery with a pastry specialism. There are business and management courses included in the curriculum, as well as maths and science.'

'That sounds brilliant, Willa. Above anything else, is that where your interest lies?'

'Oh, yes. Baking is what I think about when I'm working in the barn. It's what I do for my family, and friends,' she smiled significantly, thinking of his birthday cake. 'And for fun, as well.'

'Then you absolutely need to do this.'

'You think so?'

'I just hope they'll be able to teach you something. Personally, I think you're quite brilliant a baker already.'

'Oliver, thank you. But I know I have so much to learn.'

'I guess Mrs Hayward isn't altogether off the mark, is she?'

'No, but I've not told you how strange it was being there for lunch.'

'Oh?'

Willa told him about excusing herself and coming out of the loo to find herself alone in the house. 'They were simply gone.'

'They? Who was there besides Mrs Hayworth?'

'Her niece. Katie.'

Oliver's expression was amused. 'Oh, yes. Katie.'

'Yes, I believe you've been introduced?' Willa tried to control her reaction. 'She's rather looking forward to meeting up with you on campus, she said.'

'She won't be part of my plans,' Oliver replied. 'What did you do? Ring her on the phone to ask where she'd taken herself off to?'

Willa giggled. 'No. I looked about and when I couldn't find them, I simply left.'

'Outrageous.'

'Isn't it?'

'Despite it being a ridiculous experience, I'm glad you'll be coming with me to Cambridge. I've missed you since our breakfast, you know.'

'No, I didn't know,' Willa whispered.

He leaned forward, caressing her cheek in his hand. 'I was thinking about how I'd manage to get home more often.' He kissed her. 'But since you won't be in Marris Mynd, I'll only be coming back as often as you need to visit your mum.'

CHAPTER 33

Coming into the barn, Willa called out. Mollie answered from the milking parlour where she was pouring a bit of grain in the troughs for the first group of goats that would be coming in.

'Mollie, I've just been to see Oliver.' Her cheeks were flushed and her eyes were shining.

'Yes, I can see that,' Mollie said, laughing at her.

'We talked and talked about all sorts of things. Including me going to the regional school to do cookery. He's very excited at the possibility of me coming to Cambridge!'

'That's wonderful, Willa.'

'Mollie? Did Oliver ever say anything to you? I mean, about me.'

Mollie put her grain scoop back in the bin. 'Yes, now you mention it.'

'Really?'

'Uh-huh. I'll tell you all about it as soon as we've finished milking. Off you go.'

'I despise you.'

'See you soon.'

While Mollie was preparing the goats and putting on the teat cups, she thought about her conversations with Oliver. He had shown an interest in Willa, and Mollie realised now that she'd been too consumed with her grief over losing Rhys to recognise it.

And now Rhys would be coming back to her. At least, back to the farm. She hoped they could have a new start. Surely Rhys felt the same way or he would partner with someone else who had land nearby; although, she couldn't really think of anyone with acreage that wasn't already under use. She admired him for stepping out on his own. Warmth spread across Mollie's chest; she couldn't recall the hurt he'd caused her. Instead, she thought of how lovely he was, trying to console her the morning her baby goats died. She'd see him soon, maybe even today or tomorrow.

The last group of goats had been milked and Mollie began washing and sanitising the parlour and the milking implements. Willa popped in to help her.

'You can't be done with the bedding,' Mollie said, pretending to be irritated.

'Let's go for a walk,' Willa said a few minutes later.

They finished their work and started down a path that led through the goats' grazing field. It was a hilly pasture and had a few overhanging hedgerows, which a half-dozen goats were nibbling on. They bleated and ran by them and then came to nuzzle, looking for treats.

Mollie sighed and said, 'Think of how big Princess and the other babies would've been by now.'

'No,' Willa replied. 'We're not being depressive. Now give up the goods. What did Oliver say about me when the pair of you had your therapy chats on the rock?'

'I didn't think much of it at the time. But when I was talking about Rhys going out with Courtney, he casually asked me did you date very often.'

'Oh, no.'

'No, Willa, don't worry. I didn't say anything about your not having a boyfriend before.'

'What else?'

'He said he'd always heard you were a very bright girl and had you any plans for university.'

'I'm flattered. But how did he work that into conversation?'

'Actually, some of my problem was that I felt so disconnected from all of you. I could feel the vibe in our house was one of "trying not to upset Mollie". Everyone watching me for signs of distress, noticing whether I'd eaten anything or not. I told him we'd always been close, despite being very different people.'

'It's true, isn't it?'

Willa knew Mollie had told her everything, but she hoped for more. They walked in silence for a moment, climbing, and they crested the highest hill in the pasture. The view of the Shropshire hills was stunning. They stood for a moment taking it in.

Mollie said, 'I think Oliver was asking questions because he'd seen you at the party and hadn't gotten a chance to speak with you. It's my fault, of course; you were so busy with the cheese samples, and then of course the rain came. I'm sorry, Willa.'

They stopped and looked at each other.

'It's alright, Mollie, obviously.'

'No, I don't mean just about Oliver. After I'd come out of my rough patch, I was determined to do better with taking your suggestions. But I haven't, and now you'll be going off to school. It's too late.'

Willa stepped forward and hugged her sister. 'There's another way to look at all of this.'

'How?' Mollie asked.

'If you'd been thrilled and said, "Yes, Willa, this is marvellous, your lot in life is to make goat soap" then maybe I wouldn't have considered leaving home and pursuing my real passion, which is baking and cooking. And maybe even more than that, it wouldn't have fitted in with what Oliver is doing.'

'True. And you're really that potty about him? I mean, I've spent more time with him than you have.'

'And you'll always be brutishly honest won't you, Mollie?' But Willa smiled. 'Somehow, despite all my silliness, inexperience, and absolute cluelessness about many things in life, I know that it's the same way with him. I don't know how on earth I'm so lucky.'

'All that "silliness" pleases him. I don't know Oliver terribly well, but I know him well enough to see you're perfect for each other.'

'Really Mollie?'

'Yes, really. I could tell you that every hour on the hour, couldn't I, and you'd want to hear it again.'

'Only until I actually hear it from him.'

Mollie looked at her with understanding. They turned to descend the hill back to the farm.

AT THE STATION, Mollie stepped into her grandmother's car, driven by Granny's "sometimes" driver, Dorothy.

'You alright?' Dorothy asked. They'd become fast friends through Mollie's frequent visits to Birmingham for her modelling assignments. Mollie had never imagined the modelling would continue, but the money was too good to stop, despite having to take the train and all of the bother of the commute. On the other hand, she could hardly complain about the commute, could she, sitting in the back of a luxury car and being taken to her destination by a driver.

'I'm better now, but I didn't even get to bathe. Goat problems.'

Dorothy had grown up in the city and loved to hear about Mollie's country life.

'What sort of problems do goats have?'

Mollie laughed. 'All sorts. They're like misbehaved children.' She told Dorothy about how they'd somehow managed an escape from the pasture. 'They were easy enough to lure back with food, but it took so much time. I hardly realised I was on the train for twenty minutes. Then I realised although I'd fed the goats, I hadn't eaten at all.'

Dorothy threw a small bag of crisps over her shoulder. 'Help yourself to these.'

'Oh, brilliant. Cheers,' Mollie said, eagerly digging in.

A minute later, the car pulled up at the kerb. Mollie thanked Dorothy and got out. She was finishing the crisps – and licking salt from her fingers – when the other two models found her in the dressing area, which was actually an office for one of the restaurant staff.

'How can you eat those horrid things?' This from Margaret Self, a girl who was aptly named, as it seemed she seldom had anyone else on her mind.

'It's all that hard farming labour, keeps her thin, doesn't it, Mollie?' This from Faith, a warm-hearted girl with blonde hair the same shade as Mollie's mum and sisters. She rather liked Faith, who helped jolly things along and told Mollie jokes just before they were to step out. Because of Faith, there was usually a genuine smile on Mollie's face, which had caused her to be warmly received by the luncheon ladies gathered for the fashion shows. Mollie had learnt, on that very first walk, this was a key secret to success. If she was having fun, so were the punters. Mollie had also discovered that she gained a small commission from clothes purchased that she'd modelled and so she endeavoured to look as though wearing the outfits had put her on top of the world.

Margaret added yet another coat of heavy black eye-liner to her Asian eyes. She was striking and worldly. The Self family had moved to England from Hong Kong several years ago, as Margaret's father had been sent to Birmingham to oversee some financial situation. Margaret was determined to return to Hong Kong as soon as she finished college and could personally fund the level of upscale living to which she was accustomed. She told

Mollie as much within the first three minutes of their meeting, and hadn't bothered to speak anything but mild insults to Mollie since. Mollie guessed that Margaret would never really be happy wherever in the world she lived, since she relished making others miserable. Despite making less money, Margaret refused to smile when she modelled, always assuming an air of being on a catwalk somewhere in Paris.

'Girls, it's time.' Mollie followed Faith and Margaret to the temporary curtain. They stood in the order that they'd be modelling and waited for their cue. Mollie wondered why they allowed Margaret to go first, when Faith would certainly 'warm up' the crowd were she to come soaring out first.

Music played and Margaret launched out into the dining area while an announcer described her clothing. Faith would walk out as soon as Margaret's outfit was described, while Margaret would carry on visiting each large round table of ladies. Faith turned and made a funny face at Mollie and then walked out on cue.

Then it was Mollie's turn. She copied Faith's buoyant attitude and smiled grandly. She took a few slow turns as the restaurant manager described her outfit 'in this season's delectable colour, *spa*,' which Mollie answered in her thoughts, *it's aqua, whatever you want to call it, lady*. The thought gave a little more lift to her smile as Mollie made her way towards the first table, just as Faith was modelling for the third table, and Margaret finished and left the room.

It was then that Mollie first saw her, and her smile faltered. *Courtney Williams. The girl Rhys had been dating.*

'So it's true, Mollie, you're a model!'

One of Courtney's companions sneered and said, 'Darling, you've got a bit of straw in your hair!' As everyone at the table laughed, and Mollie gave a slight shake to her hair, just in case. She'd been in such a rush as she'd left the farm that it may've been the truth. Mollie's pulse quickened as she surveyed the table full of laughing women, with Courtney seated in the centre. Courtney made other jokes, but with the music and other conversations going on around her, she couldn't hear what Courtney had said. Just as well. She walked away on shaking legs to the next table, her face frozen in a grin.

How could she return to Courtney's table throughout the show?

Mollie caught sight of Faith, giggling at some remark by one of the ladies. Faith mouthed a thank you at the punters and turned to show clothes at the next table. Faith was enjoying herself.

Mollie decided she would enjoy herself as well. She wasn't going to miss out on the money even if Courtney and her cronies showed up at every single show and threw food at her. As hungry as I am, thought Mollie, their sandwiches would be appreciated.

At the end of the evening she and Faith were changing back into their own clothing, while Margaret had sailed out in full-face and wearing stiletto heels.

'Is she clubbing again?' Mollie asked.

Faith shook her head. 'Yes, I don't know how she has the energy.'

Mollie and Faith looked at each other and said in unison, 'But she never pays for her own drinks!' They giggled, remembering how offended Margaret had been when Mollie asked if clubbing wasn't a bit expensive whilst she was saving up to go back to Hong Kong.

Faith said, 'I gathered you had a bit of unpleasantness.'

Mollie smiled. She was proud of the way she returned to Courtney's table. The second visit was non-eventful. Whatever pleasure Courtney and her friends enjoyed at Mollie's expense had grown dull within the space of seven minutes.

'I did. A girl who is dating my ex-boyfriend showed up. She and her mates had a few laughs at my expense.'

'That's what I gathered. Well done, Mollie, for going back out there. We've got to live our own lives and make our own luck, haven't we?'

'Yes. I was glad you were here, Faith. You have a brilliant atti-tude, you really do. A real encouragement.'

'Glad to be of service,' Faith said, as she passed a paper napkin to Mollie which held two dinner rolls. 'I almost forgot this. Pinched from the buffet, just for the starving goat farmer. See you next time!'

Willa reflected that, though it had been a rough spring, the summer had been golden.

She and Oliver had plans for the weekend. As icing on the cake, she was also getting on well with Mollie.

With a long list of errands, Willa took the old farm vehicle into Marris Mynd and parked on the high street. There she came across Charlotte Seabury, outside the pharmacy. Charlotte had been such a good worker while Mollie had been away on modelling assignments that Willa spontaneously decided they ought to treat the girl to something special. She invited Charlotte to tea the following week. All smiles, Charlotte had readily, if not rather sheepishly, accepted.

Not everyone was pleased with Willa's idea.

Phoebe was included, as she and Charlotte were the same age. But Phoebe was incensed. She clutched her hands in her waist-length golden hair as though she might tear it out. 'Willa! Just because I had this tiny mo and confessed that I'd like to spend time with you – being sisterly and all that – now you're going to make me be all matey to someone I don't like?'

'Charlotte's not that bad, Phebs. For heaven's sake.'

'She is. She's strange. She wants to be Mollie, and she'd rather milk animals than *anything* – than talking, eating, shopping, or anything normative.'

'Did you just say "normative"?'

'It's a proper word. I thought you more than anyone else in this house would appreciate a sophisticated vocabulary. Shall I think of a few words to describe Charlotte Seabury?'

Willa crossed her arms and chose her next words carefully. She refused to lose her temper, making allowances for her younger sister's immaturity. 'Phoebe, I realised when you wanted to go with me to the luncheon at Mrs Hayward's that we haven't entertained very much. Obviously it isn't Mum's favourite thing to do–'

'I'd say it's on her "never" list.'

'Just so. Since I couldn't ask you to join me at Mrs Hayward's, I decided we could do a bit of entertaining ourselves. When I ran into Charlotte – who does the sort of work on this farm that you refuse to do, so you ought to be grateful – I thought, "I shall ask Charlotte to tea as a thank you". She deserves a bit of kindness, and she thinks the world of Mollie. That's why Mollie will be joining us. But I shan't force you. You're quite right, Phoebe. The tea party is for Charlotte – a girl you can't abide; given by me and Mollie, who appreciate her. So really, you don't factor in, do you?'

Phoebe was appalled to be excluded. Willa turned her back to hide a smile and began consulting her cookery books. She pulled one of her favourite titles from the shelf, Sarah Randell's *Weekend Baking*, and turned to face Phoebe. 'You did say something about wanting to bake with me, Phoebe. Will you be helping me with this tea or perhaps another time would be better for you? Especially since you won't be eating it with us.'

Phoebe's inward struggle was great. She drummed her fingers on the cupboard, blew out a breath and said, 'Alright. I'll help you.'

All efficiency, Willa simply said, 'Excellent. Let's plan our menu.' She picked up a notepad and a pencil, and led her sister to the kitchen table, knowing that not only would Phoebe help her with the baking, but she'd be present and correct to eat her share of the tea as well.

LISA WAS out on the lawn, pegging out the family's washing. The earth smelt sweet and birds were wheeling above her in a blue sky. There was a bit of a breeze, perfect for fluffing up her linens and towels and drying them quickly. The smell of lilies wafted on the air. Willa had brought home pots of them from the greengrocers and set them on either side of the front porch. Lisa was amazed that their fragrance was strong enough to carry this far. She was nearly done with her task when her mobile buzzed.

It was Sam. Lisa couldn't imagine why he was calling her from France.

'Hello?' she said uncertainly. She hoped he hadn't had an accident, and some foreign medical person was using his mobile.

'Lisa, it's Sam Lloyd. I hope I'm not catching you at an inconvenient moment?'

She flooded with relief. He was alright, then. She quickly secured a pillowslip, hung sideways on the line. She picked up her basket and walked towards the house.

'Sam, how are you? How's France?' She set down her basket and lowered herself onto the bench. From here she could see the lilies. They were a pristine white; perfect but not cold, the stuff of wedding gowns and bridal cakes. She wondered if her middle daughter had the same impression of them when she bought them. Surely she and Oliver Corbett had several years of courtship ahead of them? But why was she thinking of that, now? She'd waited days, hoping for some word from Sam. He always seemed distressed about ringing her at home, perhaps because he imagined non-stop excitement happening with all of the girls.

'No, honestly, it's a perfect time,' she insisted. 'I've just popped outside to hang washing on the line, it's simply beautiful here today.'

'Lovely. I'm glad you're taking advantage.'

'What's on your mind, Sam? I've got my computer close by if you want me to check on anything?'

'No, that wasn't at all my reason for calling. You see, well, I'm at home, actually.'

'You haven't gone to France?'

'No. No, I didn't. And, well, I was wondering, if you'd be free for dinner this evening?'

Lisa was gobsmacked. He wasn't with Ursula. They weren't meeting her friends from her musical college at some chic cafe, or strolling along the Seine.

But why? He'd made it clear, albeit gently, that he wasn't interested in Lisa. Then the dinner must be for a business purpose. Which made her more than a little nervous.

'Have the publishers changed their minds about the project?' she asked him.

'What?'

'If you no longer need my services, I completely understand. No need to stand me dinner.'

'No, Lisa. I'm sorry, I've been obtuse. I'm asking you out to dinner, to talk.' Suddenly an impression surfaced, of his looking at her, with obvious appreciation, while they were at the arts festival. She hadn't been mistaken about their mutual attraction, after all.

Sam must've felt as uncertain as she, because he added, 'But perhaps since we've worked together a bit longer, you're not interested?'

'Oh, no, that's not at all true. I'm so sorry. I've been a little muddled lately, with the festival and keeping up with the girls and all of their happenings. I would love to go to dinner. Really, I would.'

They shared halting laughter and awkwardly made plans to

meet at the Italian restaurant in Church Stretton. Lisa had insisted, since it was a bit far to come to the farm from the city where he lived.

'But you drive the distance often, when you come to the office,' he'd said. She assured him that another reason was to keep her girls out of the loop, for now. She'd been glad that they hadn't met Michael Ferrington and although they'd already seen Sam briefly at the festival, she still felt protective of them, despite their ages. He understood, and he clarified the time they were to meet at the restaurant. They rang off. Lisa snatched a dishcloth from the washing and pressed its damp coolness onto her lips, stifling a giggle.

* * *

LISA ARRIVED PROMPTLY and saw Sam's vehicle in the car park, with its university sticker in the window. She went around the back of the restaurant, certain that he'd be on the patio on such a lovely evening. He was.

Sam stood and kissed her cheek. 'Hello. I've already ordered some wine.'

He pushed in her chair and came to sit across from her. She took in the view across the verdant valley, and of the high hills surrounding them. 'Even though I live here, I still find the view magnificent.'

'I agree. There are few nice spots around my neighbourhood for an expansive view like this, but at least I've got my garden out the back.'

The waiter took their orders. Lisa responded by asking Sam about gardening. Her confidence had begun to disintegrate during the drive. Perhaps, even though he was attracted to her, that wasn't the sole reason she was here with him. Perhaps his inclination was more friendship based than romance.

He smiled. 'I'm not exactly green fingered. I've killed my fair share of plants, but I do enjoy it. A few things have managed to survive the last several years and so now they're looking very nice indeed, particularly the lavender.'

The waiter came with their starters. Sam paused while Lisa accepted freshly milled black pepper. He went again, and Sam continued. 'I wanted to explain about my cancelled trip to France.'

'There's no need, Sam. I don't want you to feel as though you have to, you know.' She was concerned now that he was ill. He was breaking the news to her gently, and she worried that she'd let him down by blubbing instead of being strong. Why did these glum thoughts keep coming on? She took a deep breath and willed herself to relax.

'Yes, well, if you wouldn't mind, it would do me good to talk about it. It's important. It's important because, the bottom line is, I haven't been quite as enthusiastic about my relationship with Ursula for some time.'

'Oh?' Lisa ate mechanically, not tasting her food.

'Ever since you asked me to join you for the event in the village. I felt I couldn't go, you see. Ursula and I hadn't talked about being... well, exclusive. But I'm just not the sort of chap who plays around when I am seeing someone.'

'That's lovely, Sam, and I'm so relieved.'

'Relieved?'

'Yes! I've been worrying over what you wanted to say. I thought you were going to tell me you were ill, or my job has come to an early end, or something.'

He laughed. 'No, no, love. You're a real credit to the work we're doing. And I'm quite alright.' He took a sip of wine and his eyes lingered over her face. 'I feel better than alright.'

Lisa blushed. 'My curiosity is piqued. Tell me all of the details.'

Sam laughed and their main course arrived. 'Well, I'd only been seeing Ursula for about three months and, honestly, the long distance thing was never easy. And she was never easy, in the sense that she's a terribly serious person. Must be the artistic temperament one always hears about? She rather stressed me out, if I'm honest.' He laughed again. 'But we... well, we've gotten along a treat, haven't we? I really enjoy you, Lisa. And of course when I saw you at the arts festival, looking like a vision in that dress. I hope it doesn't sound incredibly hard-hearted, but I decided in that moment that I no longer wanted to be with Ursula, if there was a chance that I could get to know you better.'

'I'd be lying if I said that I wasn't flattered. Especially since Ursula is a very beautiful and talented lady. And obviously so sophisticated and European in her tastes–'

'One does wonder what she was doing with a sod like me!'

'You know that's not at all what I meant. You're so intelligent, kind, and good looking, Sam; I knew exactly why she wanted to be with you.'

'I wasn't fishing, but thank you. And I hope it won't be a problem for you, as we're co-workers?'

'Not at all. But I may be coming into the office more regularly!'

'I wanted to phone you earlier, but I've wasted a whole week of my holiday feeling rather guilty. Ursula was quite upset with me for breaking our plans. I felt that I needed to be as miserable as she was for a while, I suppose. It's rather idiotic, but that's how it was. So, I put in my self-directed time of penance. I cleared out my garage, cleaned my house, went through stuff and made three trips to the charity shop, and finally, here we are.'

The waiting staff began quietly clearing up inside the dining room and Lisa checked the time on her phone. 'Oh my goodness, I had no idea we'd talked that long.'

They left their table. Sam thanked her profusely for coming and said he did hope she'd make it into the office more often. 'You've no idea how much I've looked forward to the days when you've come in, even those times I've been in a quandary, attempting to convince myself that Ursula and I were somehow good together.'

Lisa was contented by the time she pulled into the drive of

Hilltop Farm. She liked Sam enormously, and she couldn't imagine how she'd been distracted by Michael Ferrington after she'd begun working for Sam. Well, she did know; Michael was gorgeous and charming and altogether too smooth. He'd probably worked his way through five other women by now. Such a contrast to Sam being a man who prefers one woman. She came into the kitchen, and all three of her rather nosy daughters where lying in wait – well, sitting – at the kitchen table.

'How was your date?' Mollie asked, ever the spokesperson.

'Who said I was on a date?'

'Oh, please, Mum,' Phoebe retorted. 'Even I know that. You're scented and dressed and you have a dreamy look in your eyes. You must be carrying a humungous torch for this bloke.'

'I think I do, rather!' Lisa blurted out, and all of them were giggling. 'It's my boss, Sam.'

'He's lovely, Mum,' Willa said. 'I liked him straightaway when we met at the festival.'

'Yeah, you can tell by looking at him that he's not a prat.'

'Language, Mollie. But thank you.'

'Why didn't I get to meet him? Why does everyone keep everything from me?'

'You went off almost before the car stopped, Phoebe. It was Saturday morning, the first day of the festival.'

'Oh, the morning of those dreadful concerts.'

'That's the one,' Mollie assured her with a look that she hadn't missed anything else.

'Will you see him again, Mum?' Willa asked. Lisa thought Willa was rather a romantic.

'I'll have to. I work for him, remember.'

Willa let out a sigh. 'You know what I mean.'

Lisa smiled. 'Yes, I definitely will. The truth is, I asked him out first.'

Her girls stared at her, stunned. Lisa enjoyed shocking them.

'You are joking,' Phoebe declared. 'I thought men were meant to do the asking.'

'Usually, but I thought he was a terribly nice man. Very attractive–'

'Mum!' Phoebe looked as though she may be sick.

'And I knew as well that he was a bit shy of approaching women. I had it on good authority that he'd been widowed. His wife, Angie, died about the same time that your father passed away. He was tired of being alone but rather out of practise. I understand. It just becomes easier to carry on by yourself.'

Willa laid a hand on Lisa's shoulder and she was looking rather teary.

'Oh, Willa, don't be so sentimental.' Mollie rolled her eyes. 'Mum's been happy with us, haven't you, Mum?'

How does a mother inform her children that she would very much like to have a love life? She didn't want them to resent Sam in any way, even if they were well old enough to get beyond that sort of jealousy.

'Of course I've been happy, darling. I love you all so very much.'

It was true, Lisa thought. It just wasn't *enough* any longer.

CHAPTER 35

Mollie was dumping sacks of grain into the large bin by the milking parlour when Rhys arrived. Hearing his pickup, she quickly finished the task, put the grain bags away in an old dustbin, and smashed the lid down on them. She sped into the small barn, to find him inspecting a large roll of white material.

'Rhys!' She came to stand within hugging distance but kept her arms pressed to her sides. He was more fit and gorgeous than Mollie remembered, so lean and muscular in his jeans and T-shirt. But he didn't raise his eyes to look at her.

'Hello, Mollie.'

'What are you doing with that stuff?'

'It's for the poly tunnel.'

'What's that?'

'Tunnels can produce a range of seasonal vegetables, all year around. Like a greenhouse or a conservatory. There'll be a Mypex membrane floor in each, where I'll use trickle irrigation from the natural water source in the lower field.'

Rhys was brilliant. She knew that he'd learnt all of these things by reading, asking questions, and observing other farmers. His voice was not unfriendly, but that's the way Rhys always spoke to everyone. She'd missed his rhythmic, Welsh accent and the way he could explain something like a schoolmaster. It made her feel special that he was taking the time to share his knowledge with her.

'That's wonderful, Rhys. I never thought of using a poly tunnel to grow anything. But you're going to grow things in the fields, too?'

'Definitely. As soon as I get these sorted. I'm leasing an old tractor and implements, although some day I want to experiment with horse traction.'

'You mean horses pulling the plough, like the old days?'

'Yes. I think it would be quite interesting, and less of a footprint, so to speak.'

She wondered if he'd discussed his ideas with his girlfriend, Courtney. Mollie immediately boiled at the thought. Having a jealous temper wouldn't help and she needed to think of something, as now Rhys was busy with the materials and walking away from her. Tomorrow she was scheduled to make cheeses, so she had to make the most of the opportunity at hand.

'Can I help?'

Rhys turned and looked at her. 'I do need help, Mollie, but you can't offer just because, well, you know, our history.'

Of course that's why she was offering. She was in love with him, stupid bloody man.

'Of course not, Rhys. This is my land, isn't it? I want you to make a go of this, like my father was doing. It's business. I know what it's like to need help but not be able to pay for it.'

She wished she hadn't said that part about owning the place. Especially given the fact that, technically, she didn't. But he seemed to accept her help nevertheless.

'Very well. Grab those tools, will you? We'll be using them to connect the frame of the tunnel together.'

She quickly gathered up the tools and prepared to work hard alongside Rhys until it was time to do the evening milking.

WILLA WAS STANDING at her wardrobe, wondering what to wear on her date with Oliver. Clearing out her school uniforms had created a huge empty space. There wasn't much remaining to choose from.

They were going to run an errand first, and then on to eat a meal at a bistro in Ludlow. Oliver was apologetic asking Willa to drive, but she didn't mind. What she minded more was asking him to ride in their old Land Rover. She told him this. He laughed and said that in that case she could drive herself to his house and then they would take his car from there. Thus everything was planned.

She chose the dress she'd worn to luncheon at Mrs Hayward's and chuckled. Her Mum had seen Veronica Hayward in the village since then, and although she'd expressed interest in how Willa was getting on, she hadn't said where she and Katie were at the time that Willa left without saying goodbye. Perhaps it was a mystery that would go forever unsolved.

Her mobile rang. It was Oliver.

'Hello.'

'Willa. Doing well today?'

'Yes. How's the leg?'

'Alright. I'm afraid I have some news, though. I won't be able to make it this afternoon. Something's come up, you see. I'm needed elsewhere. Can't be helped.'

Willa felt terribly disappointed. 'No worries, Oliver. I understand. You'll let me know when you can reschedule?'

'Thanks for understanding. I appreciate it. Must dash, alright?'

They rang off. Why had he sounded so odd? What did "needed elsewhere" refer to? A sinking feeling settled over her and she knew that something was wrong. She took off the dress and slipped back into her jeans and jumper. She went outside but couldn't find Mollie anywhere. She must be working with Rhys. Phoebe was away with her friends, her Mum had gone to the office. Willa felt quite alone.

She decided to work on planning the flower bed. She'd never spoken with Oliver's gardener and wondered if she could reach him by phone.

She rang Myndcroft Hall and Mrs Jenkins, the Corbett's cook, answered. Willa remembered that she'd been cross with Willa for supplying Oliver's birthday treat this year. Without identifying herself, she briskly requested Laurence be asked to come to the phone. Mrs Jenkins wasn't that easily assuaged.

'May I ask who this is, please?'

'Um, yes, of course. This is Willa Purslow. I have a few pressing gardening questions for Laurence and Oliver said that he'd be happy to help.'

'I can't say that I can locate him, miss,' Mrs Jenkins replied. 'He's out, somewhere on the grounds and so it's best if I write down your number, then let him know that he's to ring you back, alright?'

'That would be lovely, thank you.' Willa gave her the number.

She wandered about the kitchen, pulling cookbooks, not seeing them, and putting them back. She was eating a slice of cheese about ten minutes later when Laurence phoned her.

'Hullo, there, miss?' he said. 'I'm calling from my mobile, as I was told you wished to speak with me.'

Willa explained.

'Oh, yes, right. I wouldn't mind to help, pet, but I'm in the middle of something just now. Could you come by for tea a bit later on, and we can sit down for a mo? Come around four o'clock to the big greenhouse. Do you know where that is? Nearest the old horse stable? Door's painted blue.'

'Yes, sir. I'll be there. Thank you very much.'

'Now, we'll not get on with you callin' me sir. Just Laurence'll do. See you soon, love.'

Willa arrived at Myndcroft Hall and pointed her vehicle up the hill towards the house. When she crested the top of the drive, she looked to the left and noticed a white Mercedes parked alongside Oliver's sports car. In moments the view was obscured, as she took a slight right turning and drove behind a hedge, past the house, and around yet another curve towards the right. Willa parked her car in a space in the large, gravelled yard in front of the stable. She slammed the creaky vehicle door shut and walked towards the large greenhouse. She found Laurence – she realised that she didn't know if that was his Christian name or surname – sitting in the sun at the side of the greenhouse door. Laurence was a jovial fellow with a tanned face. He wore tan dungarees made of cotton drill, with a denim shirt beneath. His hat was the best kind – long-loved and entirely disreputable – and the smile lines on his old face were deep and reassuring. The delicious smell of citrus was coming from inside the plant house, which combined with the smell of his strong black tea. Laurence stood up to greet her and waved her to a canvas lawn chair beside his own. There was a small table with a teapot, and a mug, sugar, and a small jug of milk for her. There were several fingers of roughly-sliced homemade shortbread on a pretty pottery plate.

'I've got electrics and a cupboard in there, where I can put on the kettle,' Laurence said proudly as Willa poured tea into her mug. 'And Mrs Jenkins keeps my tin full of biscuits. She's a dear one, is Mrs Jenkins.'

Willa smiled. 'Thank you for the tea, Laurence.'

'Mind you take a shortbread, too, love. They're that good.'

Willa took a bite. 'Oh, yes, you're quite right.' Mrs Jenkins was a lovely baker. 'As I explained on the telephone, I'm trying to figure out how to do a bit of landscaping around our farmhouse. Every time I think I've got the right plant, I read something that makes it sound a horror!'

Laurence laughed. 'And how big is the plot?'

Willa pulled out a picture she'd taken of the front of the house and printed out for him, with the measurements written beneath. 'I want to begin here.' She told him that she'd love to do up the whole front garden, but that she and her sister didn't have much to spend on the project.

He studied the paper carefully, sipping his tea and making a 'humph' noise as his brain worked through the design. 'I think the shrub you need close to the house is a Philadelphus, which grows about this high, or up to that window ledge in your photo. You'll want the "Manteau d'Hermine" if you'll pardon my poor French!' He laughed. Willa could see that he enjoyed solving the puzzle of her garden plot, just as Oliver said he would. 'That's a Philadelphus that has a sweet scent and double, cream-white flowers.

'Now, we don't go in for tired old flowers that lean on the spade come July,' Laurence said. 'We want real performers and ones that come back next year, right?' He pulled a nub of a pencil out of the pocket of his bib. Writing down the selections on the paper she'd supplied, he jotted: *Tall, back row: Illumination Pink Foxglove.*

'I saw that one at the Chelsea Flower Show last year. A real stunner.'

'Really? The name sounds gorgeous.' Willa was impressed that he'd travelled that far to look at flowers. She wondered if that's how he chose to spend his holiday, or if Lord Ranson funded the trip as a sort of continued-learning experience. He wrote others, naming them as he went, as though looking at an old photograph and remembering lovely girls he'd known in school. *Centre row: Salvia, use the variety called 'Caradonna'. Low planting for the front row, Dianthus, 'Memories'. Along the sides of the front porch, Geranium 'Rozanne'.*

Laurence gave her a few instructions on how to amend the soil, prepare the site for planting and how often to water. 'And it just so happens I have a number of plantsI can share with you.

You just leave this list here with me and come back tomorrow at tea time. Can you do that?'

'Oh, yes. I'm so grateful for your help!'

Laurence wasn't interested in her praise or thanks. He was still adding thoughts to his design, carrying on a bit past the flower bed by the farmhouse.

'And along this fence, you'll want to plant "A Shropshire Lad", of course. That's a proper English rose, named for Houseman's poem, and she's a beauty. Peachy-pink, and hardly any thorns at all. Next to that, along the car park, a couple or three "Black Knight" Buddleja will do nicely. Bring in lots of butterflies, they will.'

As Willa listened to him, she planned what she would bake for him, in trade for the plant starts he was giving her, and for all of his invaluable advice.

Laurence's tea time was over and their business concluded. 'I'll see you tomorrow, pet, when you come for your cuttings. Meantime, you'll get some good compost and ready the site, alright?'

'Yes. I'll be ready. Cheers!'

Willa returned to her vehicle. She reversed and drove slowly down the path in front of the stables and onto the main drive. She glanced towards the house.

A beautiful young woman stood by the white car. She was kissing Oliver.

Willa quickly corrected the steering just inches before coming off the drive. Her heart was pounding. Although part of her brain calmly reminded her the situation may not be as it appeared, she felt seized with humiliation as she remembered Oliver cancelling his plans with her earlier. She looked in her rear-view mirror and saw the girl getting into her car, and Oliver slowly moving away, using his cane, then the hedge loomed up and blocked the view. She would stay calm and not cause herself to be in an accident and be discovered on Oliver's property.

For a mad moment, she considered waiting at the end of the

lane in a lay-by, and following the girl to try to find out who she was. But that would be ridiculous.

She pulled out carefully onto the road. She felt certain that she hadn't been noticed. Willa hoped that Mollie would be home when she arrived. Perhaps Mollie would suggest she simply ring Oliver and ask about the woman. Willa felt another tremor of fear at the thought. No, she wouldn't do that; although her reasons for being at Oliver's house were innocent, she mustn't tell him she'd seen him outside with the girl and have him imagine she was spying. In fact, she ought to tell no one; she didn't want to have to defend Oliver's actions to anyone else, and then begin to seriously doubt him herself.

Willa's mind was in chaos and when she arrived home she could scarcely remember having driven herself.

THE FOLLOWING DAY, Mollie brought in the post. Lisa sat at the kitchen table, steadily typing on her laptop to finish a bit of research. Mollie sifted through the stack of junk mail and bills, and found an envelope addressed to herself. It was from the modelling agency in Birmingham. Mollie sliced open the cream coloured envelope, and found a generous cheque inside, her payment from last month's luncheon fashion show. There was a handwritten note as well:

Mollie,

We've put together a special autumn fashion show for a fundraising dinner next month. Could you model additional to the usual Saturday, on Thursday evening, the 18th? Please contact me for details if you're interested. Payment would be as usual, but we'd need you from 5 till 8, since a portion of the clothes will be shown before as well as after the silent auction.

It was signed by Mrs Royce, the coordinator. Mollie was thrilled for the chance to earn extra income to help Willa with her school expenses.

She then came across a pale blue envelope with gold embossing at the top. Very smart indeed. Mollie read the sender's address and noticed that it was from a solicitor in London.

'Mum.'

'Hmm?' Lisa finished the document a few seconds later and took a deep stretch.

'Mum, this looks important.'

'What is it?'

Mollie handed over the letter and Lisa opened it. Mollie saw her mother's brows push together and it made her curiosity overwhelming. 'What?'

Lisa removed her reading glasses. 'I'm fed up to the back teeth with him, and now look at the mess he's landed me in.'

'With what?'

'I didn't like to say anything to you girls, especially with your little cousin Remi coming to visit us occasionally. It's certainly not her fault. Your uncle Edward has been pressuring me for years to give up the farm to him.'

'Give it up? What do you mean? I thought the farm was paid for, outright.'

'Yes, it is. We're extremely fortunate. But your uncle Edward has tried every means to coerce me to sell to him.'

'You're joking! Why on earth would a Londoner like him want a farm on top of a great hill in Shropshire? Aside from Lord Ranson occasionally throwing a party, nothing the least bit exciting happens here.'

'That's been the puzzle. I've no idea.'

'What's he said?'

'Usually some tripe about how he wants a bit of his brother's legacy. Or even more unbelievable, that his family needs a country place. I honestly think that's the reason he sends poor Remi to us, to try to convince me that his whole family wants to escape to the countryside.'

'So, what's the letter? Has he made you another offer?'

'No. His lawyer is threatening me. The latest is that supposedly Grant verbally promised his brother a portion of this hallowed ground.'

'Dad never did!'

'Apparently, if I don't sell him most of the acreage then they'll take me to court.'

'Mum, he hasn't any proof; it'll never go to court.'

'Well, I can't imagine he actually has any legal ground to stand on. But it is a bit worrying that he's become so aggressive. Do you think I ought to ring your grandmother?'

'Yes. Granny knows a bit about everything, including legal stuff. And she certainly knows Edward. She may have some insight, Mum. It couldn't hurt.'

'Well, it could, actually. That's why I've never said anything. And I'm sure Edward is counting on me to continue to suffer in silence.'

'What do you mean?'

'Just that it could harm family relations.'

Mollie snorted. 'Do you actually imagine that things could be more awkward on Christmas Day, Mum? It's already so tense. They're totally different people to us. Surely not even a lawsuit could make it worse. Perhaps clearing the air once and for all with regards to the farm would help? Edward may feel that he and his family needn't show up at all, and we could have Granny to ourselves!'

Lisa smiled at Mollie. She still had a bit of growing up to do, but Lisa couldn't fault her. She'd thought the same, and had been tempted to reveal Edward's nasty behaviour in recent years.

'I think, Mollie, that you're probably on to a good idea. I'll consider having a chat with your grandmother, soon.'

CHAPTER 36

*S*am joined Lisa in the car.

'They're lovely, but of course you already know.'

'Thank you. The girls enjoying talking with you.'

'Oh, I don't know about that. Mollie isn't one for musty old men who write textbooks, is she? But Willa was certainly sweet and Phoebe seems interested in anyone who lives in a place with a larger population than Marris Mynd.'

Lisa laughed. 'It's amazing how quickly you read each one of them, Sam. You're spot on, I have to say.'

'Years of interacting with students, I suppose.' Sam turned the car and drove from Hilltop Farm, turning right onto the road that wound its way down toward the village.

'Must be. They'd giggle if they could hear you. And you mustn't mind Mollie, of course. She likes you well enough.'

'Well, it's obvious she was distracted by the young man you have working at the place. Didn't you say they used to go out?'

'Good memory. Yes, that's Rhys Davies. I was afraid it'd be a disaster allowing him to farm a few acres of our land. But instead, Mollie follows him out to the field and works alongside him as often as she can. She says he's a good friend and she wants him to make a go of it.'

Sam smiled. 'Few people consider their "friends" worthy of that sort of hard slog. She's still in love with him.'

'There, you've done it again. I'm sure you're right.'

'You weren't matchmaking with Rhys and Mollie?'

'Now that's a bother. You can see straightaway who my girls are, but I'm a bit of a mystery, is that it?' Lisa reached over to Sam and gently stroked the back of his neck.

'You are. I suppose it's because I'm not a parent. A little more tricky to put myself in your shoes. I'm not used to the machinations of mums.'

'Honestly, I wasn't trying to pair them up again. Mollie was gutted when Rhys broke things off. They've had to live in a small community though. I thought, well, lending him acreage doesn't seem as awful as them being thrown together socially, which has happened. What harm can it do her having Rhys turning up now and then to retrieve something from our barn storage? However, I must admit, I've had a few selfish reasons for wanting Rhys about.'

'You're more mysterious than I reckoned. Do tell.'

Sam's vehicle joined up with the main highway as Lisa confided in him. 'Basically, it's lovely having a man's presence around the place again. Not terribly modern, am I?' He exchanged a grin with her.

'But Rhys isn't trying to take over the place,' Lisa said with a sigh. 'I haven't told you, but it's been a bit of a worry to me that my husband's brother has been very aggressive in the last two or three years about taking over our farm.'

'But surely he doesn't have any legal right to it?'

'No. Grant had a trust fund and borrowed some money from his father to secure the farm. Everything was paid in full following his death. Including the initial loan being paid back to my mother-in-law, as Grant's father died shortly after we moved here, so Grant used some of the inheritance. We were completely in the clear financially. Absolutely nothing to do with my brother-in-law, as far as I can see.'

'People do get strange ideas about property when loved ones pass on. Does the brother – what's his name – want to pay you a fair price, then, or is he seeing it as some sort of inheritance?'

'Edward. Yes, it began that way, he felt very entitled. Edward's first notion was that I was to keep the house, but allow him to "maintain" the land.'

'He's a farmer?'

Lisa chuckled. 'No. A confirmed city dweller. In London, with the sort of wife who wants nothing to do with the countryside. Especially out here, where it isn't terribly smart.'

'Has he said what he wants to do with the land?'

'Oh, he hints at things. Ridiculous things, like his children needing fresh air or a pony or other such things. He brings his youngest daughter to visit us some times, she really is quite sweet, not at all like his other child. But it gives him an excuse to come visit us at the farm.'

'And did he offer to buy the land, to begin his maintenance programme?'

'Eventually. When he saw that I wasn't just going to allow him to take over. Very inexpensive offers to start. But lately, he's offered me a price that's actually realistic. Although the property hasn't been valued in many years, of course, so perhaps I'm mistaken. The problem is, the higher his price goes, the more pressure he applies.'

'It's baffling,' Sam said. 'He could buy a smaller country place much closer to London. And I have to say, I don't like that he's been rude to you.'

Lisa smiled at him and when he didn't hear a response from her he took his eyes from the road a minute. 'Well, it's true, isn't it?' he said, a bit self-consciously.

'Yes, he could find another place to maintain, as he puts it. And thank you for being offended on my behalf. I'm used to facing these sorts of issues alone.'

'So the girls don't know?'

'Only Mollie, I just spoke with her today. I've been tempted to tell them about Edward, to warn them before we see him during the odd visits or at Christmas.'

'They might have an idea about his motivation. I find young people to be very perceptive. But I'm sure you'll do what's best.'

A half-hour had passed. Sam made several turns from the A49 and in a mile they arrived on the tree lined streets of Steventon, where he parked the car in his private garage situated on a gravel drive. Lisa remembered Michael Ferrington's shiny new bachelor flat, less than ten minutes' drive from here, but Sam's home seemed to be a contrast in every respect. The garden around the Victorian red-brick house was lovely.

Sam gestured at the buildings towards the back of the property, nestled in beech trees and covered in vine. 'I've got a garage, a workshop and a small, old barn, there.' She wondered if he made things of wood from the workshop but she didn't ask. It was enough at the moment to take in the wonderful patio and conservatory surrounded by an expansive lawn at the back of the detached house. It was made private by a large hedge. They came in through the black front door and stepped into a sitting room washed with light from large sash windows. Everything was neat and tidy, and the walls were painted a soothing blue. He invited her on a tour and Lisa admired the quarry tile floor in the kitchen and the utility room adjoining it, facing a cosy snug. The conservatory was larger than the sitting room and was furnished with a wooden table and chairs, and two sofas, and lots of potted plants.

'The house has three bedrooms,' Sam said. He led her upstairs for a look about and seemed to be feeling a bit shy when he showed her where he slept. The master bedroom was a nice size, and the bed was made up in a masculine colour combination of navy and pine green. She knew he'd done as she had, eventually changing his bedroom to look differently than when there was a spouse in residence. Lisa felt a sort of kinship with Sam; widowhood could better be understood by someone who'd gone through it. She said nothing but smiled in an approving way, and she saw him relax as he led her back down the stairs.

In the kitchen, he began assembling their meal. 'We had a small table,' Sam gestured to the corner of the kitchen. 'But I found after losing Angie that I didn't like eating at that table on my own. At some point I sold it off, bought a bigger one for having friends round, and now have sit-down dinners in the conservatory. Honestly, though, I eat in front of the TV a fair bit when I'm on my own.'

She'd noticed the table in the conservatory had been laid for two, candles ready to be lit, and there was a rose in a small blue vase. It was a pleasure having a man cook for her; there were delicious smells of mushrooms, garlic, onions and steak. There were several handfuls of asparagus, dressed in lemon and salt. A carafe of seasoned oil and vinegar stood beside a salad which was coming to room temperature on the countertop. As he opened a bottle of wine, Lisa asked about Angie.

'She'd been ill even as a younger person. Our biggest regret was not being able to have children as a result.'

'I'm so sorry. It was absolutely dreadful losing Grant, but I can't imagine not having my children. They kept me going most days.'

'We'd wanted a family life. My sister and her husband have two sons and I'm quite close to them, and they live just up the road,' Sam said, popping bread in the oven to warm. 'Although I see Patty and her family fairly often, I've been otherwise buried in my work for a number of years now. And I've succeeded in burying you in it as well.'

She laughed. 'I'm enjoying it. I didn't think I'd find something I liked so well as the library but it suits me to down to the ground.'

Lisa helped him with the food, taking the salad and dressing the short distance to the conservatory. They sat down and she discovered he was a fabulous cook. 'I'm usually a person who needs sauce because I can't properly season anything, but this is fabulous, Sam.'

They ate in silence for a moment, enjoying the flavours.

'I'd better rescue the rolls,' he said, as they heard a timer buzz in the kitchen. 'Excuse me for a moment.'

While he was absent, she put a match to the candles, as they'd forgotten to light them. In their warm glow she sat motionless, listening to him open the oven door and transfer the bread to an empty basket that she'd seen was ready and waiting. She felt content. More than that, she felt loved, even though he wasn't in the room, and it was an odd moment to feel so overwhelmed with gratitude and companionship. It was a different sort of feeling to what she experienced being with Michael, but no less exciting. It was real. She didn't feel as though she was playing the role of someone on a date. Being here with Sam felt like being at home. He returned with the bread smelling like a bit of heaven, and he leaned over it and kissed her before seating himself at the table. If his cooking is as delicious as his kiss, Lisa thought, I'm in for the best meal of my life.

CHAPTER 37

The white car belonging to the mysterious woman hadn't been at Myndcroft Hall this afternoon. And Willa hadn't heard from Oliver.

Yesterday, Willa had purchased the preparation items told to her by Laurence. She splurged on some plant food recommended to her at the garden centre, to help the plants develop their root systems and settle in nicely. She had a list and moved through the whole process rather mechanically. But she hadn't prepared the planting bed as promised. She'd spent too long wandering about, first in the kitchen, baking, then sitting on her bed, thinking. Her energy seemed to vanish and she'd gone to bed early.

Today Laurence had been lovely, giving her many items to plant in the new flower bed. But more than that, he was kind and inspired her confidence about planting the garden. Most importantly, he provided her an excuse to come very near Oliver's home.

'Oh, it's no trouble, love,' Laurence said, pleased with Willa's quiet astonishment when he gifted her the plant starts. 'As you keep gardening – and you will, mind, now that you're getting a taste for it – you're most welcome to come and see me from time to time. I'd have thrown these away if it weren't for you making use of them.'

He'd shown her his seed collection, kept in a big binder full of plastic sleeves where he'd shoved the seed packets in, along with notes scribbled on paper of where the plants were placed, and how they'd got on. As she listened to Laurence speak about his favourite plants, she imagined Oliver and his sister, Penelope, as children, trailing along behind him, asking him questions. He'd probably fed them biscuits, too.

They walked out to her vehicle, and Willa produced a tin of lemon bars. 'For all of your help. They won't be as good as Mrs Jenkin's.' The old gardener was delighted, telling her he was very fond of lemon and would enjoy them. Willa supposed he could put his mind to enjoying just about anything. Laurence reminded her of the planting instructions and then she was on her way.

She slowed the Land Rover and stared up at the house for a few seconds before driving alongside the hedge. She saw no one. Oliver's car stood lonely in the drive. She assumed the rest of the family kept their vehicles in the garages, as she'd seldom seen any others about on other visits.

After arriving home Willa went to the garden to plant her first-ever flower bed. She dug into the dark earth and thought the soil looked as good there as what could be purchased at the garden centre. The blessing of Shropshire, she thought, rich tilth. She knocked the plastic container from the first of a trio of Philadelphus, and stuck it into the hole that she prepared per Laurence's instructions. She'd gotten a little too deep, actually, and had to add a bit of dirt back into it. But now it had come right, and the plant was level with the ground. The two others went in, and possibly the one on the right a bit too close to centre, but Willa wasn't about to dig it up. She wiped perspiration from her face.

Mollie arrived just as Willa was stretching her back and looking at all of the plants Laurence had given her.

'Those aren't spaced evenly.'

'Thanks, Mollie. You're welcome to replant them to your satisfaction.'

'Sorry. We've both worked through lunch, I think. Come in.'

'Is Rhys coming?'

'Why? He never does.'

'What does he eat?'

'I don't know. Whatever he brings with him or buys in the village.'

'Have you asked him?'

Mollie sighed and held the door to the boot room open for Willa, whose hands were caked in earth. 'I haven't, actually. He has been very cross, or cold, or both. I do as he says, and I'm rewarded by being allowed to slave alongside him. But inviting him to lunch seems a bit much. I don't think he'd come.'

'Why is he acting that way? It can't be just because of your history. Rhys isn't one to hold a grudge.'

'I agree. There's something else, but I don't know what it is, and he's not talking. At this point, I'm just carrying on as the traffic allows.'

Willa went to the sink and scrubbed. Mollie heated up a leftover casserole in the microwave and put two servings of it out on a pair of plates. 'This was rather good, by the way.'

'Thanks,' Willa replied, smoothing skin cream on her clean hands.

They grabbed a jug of Willa's old-fashioned cordial, glasses, and plates and sat down to eat.

'Rhys isn't the only one,' Mollie said, a sombre note in her voice. 'I ought not to have insulted your gardening, but you've been off since yesterday. What's wrong?'

Willa had been constantly thinking about what she'd seen. Now that it was time to tell, she found it nearly impossible to say aloud. She remembered how Mollie went so quiet after her breakup with Rhys. She understood better, now. Willa often got through disagreements and unpleasantness by keeping her mouth shut, but this was different. Instead of trying not to make matters worse, she was keeping her fears buried and festering.

Mollie said, 'Tell me. I know it's hard, but you'll feel better. I promise.'

Willa took a deep breath and pushed away her half-eaten lunch. 'Oliver cancelled our plans quite at the last minute. I decided that I'd work on my next project, which was to meet with Oliver's gardener. When I drove past the big house, Oliver was in the drive. Kissing a girl.'

'Kissing kissing or just being polite kissing?'

'Somewhere in between I suppose. Lips, not cheeks. They were holding hands and it was a bit lingering. So definitely more romantic.'

'How many times have you played that over in your mind since yesterday?'

'About a thousand, I'd say.' Willa felt hot tears well up in her eyes. 'If he'd phoned today and explained–'

Mollie put a consoling hand on her sister's arm. 'He doesn't know he's meant to explain. He doesn't know you were there and saw them.'

Willa made a noise that sounded like she'd been punched in the gut. 'So the fact that it was meant to be kept from me is supposed to help?'

'I'm sorry,' Mollie whispered.

'Setting *her* aside, and supposing I hadn't seen anything, I still expected him to ring. I thought he'd reschedule.'

'Did he give a reason for cancelling?'

'No. Just that something had come up. Couldn't be helped, he said. Then he rang off.'

Mollie's face screwed up in confusion. 'That's odd. Most people would give a reason. Or if not a reason, then they'd say something along the lines of "I'll ring soon" or another promise of making it up to you.'

'You are trying to help, right?' Willa said, her tummy aching.

'Maybe there's another explanation. Perhaps his mum was listening and he didn't want to be questioned so he was vague.'

'Because he needs to hide me – or her – from his mother? Really, Mollie. This is making it worse.'

'I think you ought to just ring him up and casually ask how're things and when does he want to see you.'

'The way you casually ask Rhys to lunch, perhaps? You know I can't do that. He's not exactly my boyfriend. He isn't obligated to reschedule our date, or even to speak to me again.'

'So what are you going to do?' Mollie stared at her sister. 'Does this mean you'll not go to school in Cambridge?'

'I've been thinking about that, too,' Willa said. 'I will go to uni and learn to be a pastry chef. But I may not go to Cambridge. The thing is, after Mrs Hayward said that, I did some research and found a school that's closer, by Mum's work. And it doesn't cost nearly as much, especially if I continue living here and make the drive. After all, I need to do what's right for me, not simply following Oliver to Cambridge. Him being so close would've just been icing on the cake.'

'Oh, please, not baking metaphors already!' Mollie thumped her sister on the arm. 'Seriously though, I'm proud of you, Willa. I hope you'll stay home, even if you don't help me do the milking.'

'Gee, Mollie. Thanks a lot,' Willa said. 'Now I've got to sort out how I'd make the commute. You need the Land Rover for deliveries. Mum isn't going to give up her car, even if I can schedule all of the classes for three days a week, it would be asking her too much.'

'Maybe Granny would help?'

'I loathe asking her. It's more likely I need to find a paying job, and buy a car,' Willa said, her tummy burning hot again.

'I wish we were open for dairy days already, or something else for extra income. My saved-up modelling money isn't quite enough, yet. I'm not saying your other ideas weren't brilliant,

Willa, but can you imagine how many truffles you'd have to sell, or bars of soap you'd have to shift, in order to buy a car?'

'I'm begging now. Stop trying to make me feel better, Mollie. You're utter rubbish.'

'Alright. Well, I'm going back out to help Rhys, unless you'd rather I help you with planting the cuttings?'

'No, getting the bed ready, which is the hard bit, is finished. The plants are small and should go quickly. And if we're chatting, I'm liable to get them all confused and plant the tallest ones in the front or something.'

Mollie looked baffled but left her chair and was gone. Willa hoped that things would work out between Mollie and Rhys. Obviously, Mollie had completely lost her heart to him all over again. Willa had thought she felt the same way about Oliver, but at the moment he seemed like a stranger. His rejection hurt, but she could hardly claim the same affection for him as Mollie could for Rhys. At least, that would be the logical conclusion.

ollie felt edgy having to face the whole weekend without Rhys coming by. He'd said he needed to work on something away from the farm. She tried to stay busy by helping Willa spread mulch on the planted-up flower bed.

'I'm afraid they'll suffocate, Mollie. The Corbett's gardener, Laurence, said to be sure the mulch isn't touching the stem of the plant, but just gathered around it. Like this.'

Mollie had decided that she loved farming with Rhys, but despised gardening with her sister. Apparently, she enjoyed doing activities that required more 'expansive gestures' to quote Mrs Hayward, who'd assured Mollie in the village last week that Mollie'd definitely found her calling. As though she'd asked for her opinion. Making cheese did require a bit of patience, but Mollie didn't consider it to be so fussy. Or maybe it was just Willa that was so fussy.

Mollie wondered what Veronica Hayward would make of Phoebe.

'What do you suppose Phoebe ought to do? With her life, I mean,' Mollie asked as Willa tied bits of the new butterfly bush to the fencepost.

'There's a question. Personal shopper? Trophy wife?' The girls giggled.

'Did you manage to get the diva into the kitchen with you, or did everything for Charlotte's tea come down to you?'

'I'm pleased to say that Phoebe actually baked something on her own. She wanted bragging rights, so she warned me off.'

'But will it be edible?' Mollie asked, feigning trepidation.

Willa laughed. 'I think so. She made a wonderful looking loaf flavoured with molasses, marmalade and ginger. It seems a bit wintry for a summer tea, but it appealed to her so I didn't comment. She needed to be excited about the recipe.'

'Speaking of which, we'd better go inside and get ready.'

Mollie said, 'You go ahead and I'll do the watering. It's meant to be rather warm today.'

A few minutes later, Mollie was winding up the hose pipe when Rhys drove into the farm yard and parked his pickup by the small barn. In her typical long strides, she was following him into the barn in moments. She knew immediately that he was upset.

'What's wrong, love?' she asked gently. She hadn't meant to sound so warm and personal, her words just tumbled out that way.

'My landlord's said I've done something that I haven't and has asked me to leave. The lady above didn't like the look of me, doesn't like Welsh good-for-nothings I heard her say to the boyfriend. They lied about me.'

'Landlord? Rhys, what are you talking about?'

'Da kicked me out when I told him I didn't want to be a dairy farmer.' Rhys looked away from her. Mollie could see he was struggling with his emotions, but she knew he wouldn't like it if she dared touch him.

'And where've you been living?'

'There's a story. Of course there's nothing to rent in the village, so I've got the let of a single room in town.'

'Couldn't you complain? Surely you've got a tenancy agreement to fall back on?'

'The landlord's got a friend that's decided to come in as a tenant, and so he and the old biddy upstairs are set on evicting me. I don't want any trouble. I don't know anyone around there, and as I've always paid cash it follows that I didn't have a credit history, so it was hard to get in anywhere.'

Mollie looked at the tarp in the back of the grey pick-up. No doubt Rhys's few earthly possessions were tucked beneath it.

'What will you do?'

'I've been pricing out those tiny cabins. I was sure that Lisa would allow me to build one by the pump house, out in the lower fields.' Rhys smiled wryly. 'No more commute, huh Mollie?' He fell silent a moment. 'I have enough in savings for one of those, the inexpensive kit. They're sort of a flat-pack that builds into a people-shed. But that means I'd have no reserve cash. Talk about eating what you can grow. I'm not sure I can make a profit that soon.' He turned and smacked his work gloves on the side of the truck.

Mollie wanted to speak, but waited for a minute. Her emotions were tightly strung. Rhys assumed their conversation about lodging was over and he began unloading some irrigation tubing into the small, empty paddock where Billy Goat Gruff used to live. Feeling overly emotional, she warned herself that she mustn't think of Gruff, or the dead baby goaties, either.

Watching him, Mollie realised her hesitation reaped a reward: Rhys had had a few minutes to calm down a bit. He looked noticeably better since sharing his troubles with someone, even if his problems weren't solved. *He needs me*, Mollie thought, and it gave her courage.

'I know of a private let in the village, and the rate is really good. No deposit required.'

Rhys had been so preoccupied that he hadn't seen where she was taking the conversation.

'It's a loft. It's been redone, you know the type? Spacious enough for one person, light and airy. The downside is the kitchen and bath are shared.'

'No worries there. I'm desperate. Is there a letting agent? The only person I know of is Mr Cary, the solicitor in Marris Mynd.'

Here was the moment it could all go pear-shaped. But she was this far.

'My father occupied the loft. It was his office, you see.'

Rhys stared at her blankly. At least he hadn't said no.

Mollie continued. 'Upstairs. In our house. No one's using it. Why shouldn't you?' She made the last phrase sound as impersonal as possible – just delivering the facts.

He stared at her, considering. Weighing his options. As Mollie had already sussed out, he didn't have any. At least, not many that didn't require going broke; using the woods for a loo; bathing in a freezing cold river.

'The truth is, Mollie, I'd be grateful. Assuming your mother doesn't mind. Please let her know that none of this was my idea?'

'She'll know it was mine, and I'll be careful to tell her how I trapped you.'

He smiled at her. A normal, natural smile. But she was careful not to step near him or say anything to spook him.

'I'll ring her immediately.' He didn't feel threatened any more, she could tell, but she wouldn't press her luck. Businesslike she added, 'It'll have to be cleaned, though. And I'm busy this afternoon.'

He actually responded to her with a laugh and a question. 'What, some goat needs your attention, is that it? I do know my place in the priority of things.'

'As it happens, I'm attending a tea party.'

'Another modelling gig?'

Now he was just flirting with her. Mollie's heart was rushing and she wasn't able to keep up the cool distance. She came closer and swatted him playfully on the arm. 'No, silly. Willa's hosting. Well, we both are. For Phoebe and Charlotte Seabury.'

'What? Yes, that is quite the social obligation. I'm not even going to ask how you got stuck with that one.'

Mollie pulled her mobile from her pocket and asked Lisa for the necessary permission. Lisa was in a permanent state of joy and generosity since she and Sam had been dating. She was quick to give the attic over to Rhys.

'You'll have to let the postman know your new address, Mr Davies.'

'Really? That's mighty. Thanks, Mollie. And how do I direct my mail? "Hilltop Farm's Amazing Attic Abode" has a nice ring.'

'Don't start rhyming and singing, boyo. Let's take some of your kit and go have a look.'

'What's the reasonable rate you referred to?'

'Helping to pay the grocery bill. Mum knows how it is when your appetite meets Willa's cooking.'

CHAPTER 39

$\mathcal{M}$ollie left Rhys vacuuming thick dust and went to fetch a bucket and cleaning supplies for the floor. As Mollie went striding down the passage, a hand came from Willa's room onto Mollie's shoulder and pulled her right in.

'What on earth is going on up there?' Willa demanded, not quite zipped into her tea dress. She'd gotten a bit blue thinking of how she had planned to wear it when going out with Oliver. The noise from the attic had been a welcome distraction.

'Rhys is moving into the attic loft.'

'Are you serious?'

'Yes. His dad kicked him out of their house when Rhys told him he'd like to be a different sort of farmer. He told me upstairs that he'd slept in his truck until he could find a room to rent in the town. But the landlord wanted Rhys out, in favour of a friend moving in, and so Rhys had nowhere to go. Mum doesn't mind.'

'No wonder he's been so edgy. It all came without a warning, didn't it? And his dad was none too pleased, apparently, so it must've been an ugly row.'

'He didn't say, but I can imagine. And his mum caught in the middle, I shouldn't wonder.'

Willa's face was a picture of compassion. Mollie knew she loved him like a brother and wouldn't mind having him about.

'He's more relaxed now, I think. He's always been so close with his family, that I think it's made him happy to think of living with us. He's not the sort to like solitary dinners and being on his own too much.'

'I'm sure you're right,' Willa said, stepping into a pair of heeled sandals. 'Poor Rhys, he's been through a lot of changes this summer, too. I mean, besides your relationship. Breaking with his parents is an awfully huge change.'

'I'd thought he was angry but now I realise he was stressed and reeling with the shock of everything. Rhys is rather an organised person, so it probably annoyed him immensely for his life to be that out of control.' Mollie sighed. And then she smiled. 'I'm so excited, Willa!'

'I know.' Willa giggled with her. 'We've got to get downstairs. Are you going to change?'

'Must I?'

'Oh, Mollie.' Willa gave her a look that was their mum all over again. 'For Phoebe's sake. She's put a skirt on, you know.'

'Alright. I'll be down in a tick.'

A few minutes later, Mollie joined the others. The windows were open in the dining room, inviting warm, summery-smelling breezes to waft in. Phoebe and Charlotte were hovering around the chairs and Willa was seeing to the tea.

'Hello, Charlotte!' Charlotte had made an effort at looking special. A thin cotton dress clung to her thick body, making her look dowdier than usual.

Charlotte pushed her heavy glasses up on her nose. 'Hi, Mollie. Thank you for inviting me.'

'Our pleasure. We appreciate how you've mucked in around here this summer. Don't know where I'd be without you!' Mollie was careful not to give a disparaging look at Phoebe, but she could see Phoebe's guilty fluttering from the corner of her eye. *No one's fault but her own*, Mollie thought.

Willa arrived, teapot in hand. 'Let's everyone sit, shall we?' She prompted Phoebe with a look.

Phoebe said, 'Shall I be mother?' and slowly picked up the heavy teapot. She misjudged the length of the spout and accidentally flipped the strainer onto the table. Phoebe sighed, mumbled to herself and set the teapot back down. Having properly put the strainer across the mouth of the cup, she reached again for the teapot. Her concentration was almost painful to watch as she filled Charlotte's teacup.

Charlotte, being as sensible as she was sweet, didn't smirk or laugh at Phoebe. She whispered a lady-like 'thank you' when Phoebe had finished. Having poured once without mishap seemed to give her confidence, and Phoebe made her way around to each guests' cup before filling her own. Mentally, Mollie commended Willa for suggesting the tea to help Phoebe along with her confidence and social graces, and hoped she'd remember to say something to Willa later.

Phoebe offered food to Charlotte, explaining, as Willa had insisted, each item. Abandoning proper food descriptions, Phoebe said, 'You *must* eat a slice of this cake, Charlotte, because I made it.'

Willa and Mollie exchanged a look over Phoebe's rudeness.

Soon, everyone was enjoying the delicious food, tea and conversation.

Charlotte was talking about the last time she had a nice tea with all of the fancy trimmings, at the Granger's home.

'I didn't know you had been to Gemma Granger's house,' Phoebe said, obviously impressed.

'Well of course I have,' Charlotte replied. 'She's my cousin.'

'*Your* cousin? But, you're nothing alike!'

Charlotte had the self-confidence to laugh at this.

'Who is Gemma Granger?' Mollie asked.

'Like only *the* most popular girl in the sixth form,' Phoebe declared. 'She wouldn't be caught out shovelling goat poo.'

Charlotte pursed her lips together in a smile.

'What?' Phoebe asked.

'She's my cousin, so of course I love her. But, basically, Gemma's a bore.'

Phoebe stared at Charlotte, scrutinising her. 'Well, what sort of things do *you* like to do, Charlotte?' Her tone was suddenly conciliatory. Mollie and Willa shared another look.

Charlotte said. 'Oh, the usual things. I like to craft.'

'Craft? What do you mean?'

'You know, Phoebe. I make things. Scrapbooks. I paint sometimes. And I make greetings cards.'

'I've never done anything like that! No wait, I've lied. I've *crafted* friendship bracelets. They were achingly cool.'

Charlotte didn't reply. Phoebe changed tack. 'But your projects sound ever cooler. Especially making those books.'

'I'd be happy to show you.'

'Really?' Phoebe said with an eagerness that shocked her older sisters. Phoebe looked at Willa and said, 'Baking was just the beginning of my creative life.'

'So it would seem,' Willa replied.

The younger girls realised they also shared a love of film. Thus began a long comparison of every movie they'd ever seen, leaving Willa and Mollie to their own thoughts. The girls then moved on to a not so riveting discussion about how often they managed to leave Marris Mynd and how often their siblings escaped to the city. Phoebe bragged about Mollie's foray into modelling, while Mollie scarcely noticed, since her ex-boyfriend was moving into the loft space above their very heads.

Willa got up from the table with the empty teapot and was just about to start the kettle, when a comment from Charlotte stopped her in her tracks.

'Yes. My older cousin, Gwen, that's Gemma's older sister, and her friend have gone to Birmingham.'

'Who is Gwen's friend?' Phoebe asked. It was quite a nosy question, Willa thought and she would speak to Phoebe later about minding her own business.

But then Charlotte had replied, 'Arabella Stockton. Her boyfriend is Oliver Corbett, so she's been to see him and that's why they weren't going to Birmingham until today.'

Willa froze and her jaw dropped. Mollie reached up and rescued the teapot from Willa's loosening fingers.

Phoebe looked at Willa with a puzzled expression. 'That can't be true, Charlotte,' Phoebe said. 'Because my sister is Oliver's girlfriend.'

Charlotte looked at Willa with a horrified expression. 'I'm so sorry, Willa. Obviously I've made a mistake!'

Mollie intervened. 'It's alright, Charlotte. Willa and I are going to put the kettle on. Shall we bring more food?'

'Mollie–'

'No, Phoebe, let's not discuss Oliver Corbett's personal life over our tea table. There must be some simple explanation.' She gave Phoebe a terse look.

Ten minutes later, Charlotte and Phoebe had gone off to visit one of Charlotte's mates down the road, chattering contently as they walked down the drive.

For once, Willa didn't immediately begin clearing the dishes. 'Mollie! Is that the girl that Oliver dated at university?'

'Yes.'

'And so possibly the same woman I saw kissing him yesterday?'

'Of course, Willa. How many women do you think Oliver goes about kissing? But you said it wasn't necessarily a romantic kiss, didn't you?'

Willa slumped into a chair at the kitchen table. She reviewed the clip in her memory once again. 'I just couldn't be sure. Oh, Mollie, who am I kidding? Of course it was.'

'Maybe she visited Oliver and tried to get back together with him?'

'Yes. Probably. Why else would she want to see him? Unless they never broke up and he's been having me on.'

Mollie went to set the teapot on the cupboard. She walked back to the kitchen table and sat across from Willa. 'No, Willa, they definitely broke up. Oliver said he was gutted for months. It was all a long time ago. There could be dozens of reasons to explain the situation.'

Willa looked doubtful. 'Dozens?'

'Yes. One of their friends from university could have had some bad news from the doctor, for example. I mean, Oliver himself was just in a dreadful accident in which he could've been killed, right? Maybe Arabella came to deliver some news in person.'

'But Charlotte referred to Oliver as Arabella's boyfriend.'

'She could've got it wrong, Willa. Phoebe called you Oliver's girlfriend, but would you really say that's accurate? I'm sorry, Willa, don't look so pained!'

'I don't know why I talk to you about anything.'

Mollie pressed on, trying to help Willa consider the possibilities. 'But you know you've only been out a few times with Oliver. Okay, forget that example. Look at it this way: Phoebe is Charlotte's age. Phoebe would probably tell Charlotte that Rhys is my boyfriend.'

'And is that what you call me, Mollie?' Asked a deep, masculine voice.

Both sisters jumped and turned to find Rhys propped against the doorway of the kitchen, grinning at them.

'Sorry,' he said. 'Obviously I've walked in on a good natter. Mollie, love, I'm starving as usual and there seems to be quite a bit of tea left in there. Do you mind if I plunder a bit?'

'Of course not, Rhys. I'll get you a plate and a mug.' Mollie beamed at him.

Willa bolted from the lovebirds and their quickly mending

courtship. Had Rhys still been seeing Courtney? It was astonishing that Mollie didn't seem to care, so of course she couldn't be trusted in reassuring her about Oliver's relationship with Arabella.

She wandered out to the new flower bed. Everything looked the same as she'd left it, naturally, except there were wet streaks on the ground where Mollie had watered. Willa reflected on how long it would take before the cuttings began looking like a garden. And she wondered what sort of shape her life would take in the meantime.

CHAPTER 40

*L*isa sat with her daughters and Rhys around the kitchen table. They were enjoying her speciality, which wasn't really that special, spicy sausage sauce over pasta, alongside a fresh garden salad. But this time the meal was prepared – quite surprisingly – by Phoebe. The conversation and laughter was brisk. Lisa was glad that Rhys had come to live with them. In the past weeks, they'd fallen into a peaceful routine and everyone in the household was content.

Everyone, of course, except Lisa. She'd been keeping a secret.

She didn't like to upset the lovely family harmony that the children were enjoying. Particularly Mollie, who was absolutely radiant. Rhys had made it abundantly clear that his relationship with Courtney had ended within a fortnight, practically over before it began. His discontent was finally sorted, with a new career direction. Perhaps she and Rhys weren't exactly back to where they'd been before their break-up, but it was obvious they were falling in love again. Lisa couldn't imagine two people better suited for one another.

She only wished she could say the same about her relationship with Sam. Lisa pushed the thought away and tuned into the conversation.

'I've looked over the cookery course fees. I could get a loan to pay for it.'

'Then what are you waiting for? Why didn't you register?' Mollie demanded.

'I told you before, I haven't got a car to get there, and you and Mum need yours.'

Rhys turned to Willa, seated next to him. 'Why didn't you say? You could have the use of my pickup.'

They all fell silent. Lisa felt tears spring to her eyes. It was so sweet of Rhys.

Willa muttered, 'But it's very smart, Rhys. What if I had an accident? And of course you need it.'

Rhys put his arm around Willa. 'Don't be silly, love. My commute here is enviable, isn't it? I walk out the door to go to work. And you've even said your classes are only held three days a week. Not to mention, I can borrow the old Land Rover from Mollie if I'm needing something unexpected.'

'Even you can't find a problem there, Willa,' Mollie added, beaming at Rhys for his generosity.

Lisa pulled together her composure and piped up. 'Of course, darling, you'll give Rhys fuel money, and make sure the insurance is in order.'

'My insurance covers other drivers,' Rhys responded, sweeping away any hindrance.

'Oh, Rhys, I'd be so grateful,' Willa said.

'Then it's done and dusted. You're to register, soonest.'

Willa kissed his cheek. 'I'm glad I made one of your favourite desserts, Rhys. A summer pudding, with fresh cream.'

'Top of your class, Willa, you'll see.'

Lisa helped with the washing-up, which flew by with so many hands sharing the work. She was astonished at how Phoebe pitched in without being asked. She'd grown up so much lately, and this thought threatened to make Lisa teary again. Phoebe and Charlotte had become constant friends, always crafting something, meeting in the village to look about or haunt boys, or talking for hours. Most shocking, Phoebe had trailed out to the barn on the days that Charlotte helped Mollie with the milking. She'd heard that Phoebe and Charlotte were a fine team and could probably do the milking on their own with a little more practise. Lisa could see Phoebe's influence on Charlotte as well. The girl who'd cared nothing for her appearance was now wearing pink lip gloss, Phoebe's best shade.

Lisa aimlessly followed the kids out onto the front porch, where the summer sun was lowering in the sky and washing the clouds in pink lemonade. They each found a seat on the bench or lawn chairs, cradling bowls of magenta-coloured berry pudding in their hands. Rhys was telling funny stories about his father's dairy cows. Lisa knew from Mollie that he'd been to see his mother, but his father was still nursing a powerful grudge against him.

She listened and grew a little tired as dusk rolled in. She'd been up early and had been driving to the office daily, grasping every opportunity to spend a bit of time with Sam. He'd been lovely about suggesting again that she work at home to provide Willa the car, and he promised he'd collect her several evenings a week for dinner. Lisa had considered it and felt rather selfish in both keeping her car from Willa and wanting to see Sam no matter what the inconvenience for herself. She was grateful that Rhys had come up with a solution and thus spared Lisa having to arrange her own life differently. Interrupting the chat about goings-on in the village, Lisa bade them all good night and headed off early to bed.

Whilst cleansing her face, she determined that she wouldn't lie in bed for hours thinking. She needn't have worried. Once she was tucked in the covers, she drifted to sleep almost immediately.

WILLA WAS SITTING on the porch eating summer pudding with her family, except her mum, who'd taken herself off to bed. Phoebe was talking about a film she'd seen with Charlotte when Willa's mobile rang from inside the house. She hated being drawn away, such was the cosy mood but she popped up to take the call.

The kitchen seemed bright. Willa hadn't realised how dark it had grown outside.

Blinking, she answered. 'Hello.'

'Willa, it's Oliver.'

Instinctively, Willa moved toward the Aga for support. She had wished with all of her heart for him to contact her after he'd cancelled their date and had heard nothing. Now, suddenly, he was asking her if she were still there.

'Um, yes. Just a little surprised to hear from you.'

He sighed. A few seconds slipped by. 'I know. I feel really badly about not being in touch. I was wondering... if I could see you tomorrow?'

'No.' Her reply had fairly flown out of her mouth. Calmly. Flatly. She tried to feel regret but it didn't come to summons.

'Willa,' he seemed a bit knocked sideways by her reply, 'I have some things I'd like to explain to you. It's rather complicated and I was hoping we could talk in a place we wouldn't be interrupted. Perhaps a walk. Or meeting on the rock, where I used to chat with Mollie when she was so low.'

Had he mentioned that last bit to manipulate her? Willa had one image of Oliver in her mind. And that was a picture of him kissing Arabella Stockton.

'I'm sorry, Oliver, but suppose you just tell me, *now*, why you cancelled our date and I've not heard from you since?'

He sighed. 'Alright. I suppose that'll have to suffice.'

Willa pressed a bit harder. 'Just the bottom line, please. I was having a lovely time here and I'd like to get back.' *Who was this Willa?* She smiled at her new found ferocity. Perhaps Phoebe wasn't the only person in the house to have grown up a bit this summer.

'Yes, of course,' Oliver was saying. 'The bare bones of it are these: I received a visit from my ex-girlfriend. The one that I spoke a lot about to Mollie, I'm sure you've heard something of our story.'

Willa chose not to confirm that. She merely said, 'And?'

Oliver continued. 'And I wanted nothing to do with her.'

Was he lying? 'Go on.'

'Even though she wanted to get back together, and I didn't, I suddenly went off the idea of beginning another relationship, with you. I mean to say–'

'Thank you very much!'

'No, Willa, don't. I mean to say that seeing Arabella brought it all back. I didn't fancy being hurt again. And I already care about you; I can't really see us going about our relationship casually. I can't say I was altogether comfortable with feeling vulnerable again. Arabella, she was working on me; I admit, I felt a bit confused. She kissed me, thinking she'd bring me around. I felt nothing.' Oliver paused and sighed out a breath. 'The thing is, it sort of destroyed my confidence in... *us*. How could've I have been having that conversation with her? Later, I realised that she'd had an advantage, catching me off guard as she did. But now...' He seemed, then, to run out of words. Willa didn't speak, either.

The door opened and in wandered Phoebe, with Mollie and Rhys following, casually holding hands. They walked by her, unaware of the momentous conversation she was having.

Willa walked over to the kitchen sink, where the window was a square of darkness. 'Alright, then I need to say something to you as well.'

'Yes, of course,' Oliver said.

'I'm not going to Cambridge. So before your mind goes on to planning our future, consider that you won't see me there, during your remaining time at university.'

'You've decided not to attend the cookery course?' he asked. His interest seemed genuine and respectful of her decisions.

'I'm taking a similar course, but at another school. I'll live at home and commute. It's better for me financially, and I don't really want to leave home. I know that doesn't sound very independent or impressive, but that's my decision.' She'd said the last bit firmly, as though expecting him to disapprove.

'No, no, I quite understand. And I think you're tremendously independent to do what you like.' His voice was tender and sweet. Willa felt complimented and a bit melty.

'I have to return to Cambridge of course, and finish. Not just for my parents, but I'm rather interested in the study involved in getting my doctorate. Finally, I've gotten to the more interesting part.'

'Yes, I imagine so.'

'But I hope that I'll be able to see you. Before I leave and when I come home. Which could be a bit more frequently, should you allow me to see you. In some ways, my work is a bit more independent at this point, and so I'll be able to snatch a few more days at home than before.'

'I don't know what to say, Oliver.'

'Well at least you've heard me out. Please understand – I had to decide if I could fully commit to you. There have been some other things happening here, but that's for another time, I suppose.'

Wisely, he said that he'd ring her back tomorrow.

CHAPTER 41

She'd decided to share her news with Sam first, and tell the girls when Mollie had finished her modelling work and was back from Birmingham at the weekend.

Lisa hadn't warned Sam that she needed to discuss a delicate matter with him, preferring not to cause any concern. Now, she wished she'd alluded to something. As they threaded through traffic on their way to a restaurant in Ludlow, she realised that had she asked him to stay in then she could leave abruptly if necessary, and without making a scene.

'We're nearly there,' he said, smiling at her. He drove alongside the River Teme, now hidden in the flourish of summer trees, hedgerows, and the businesses situated around the water housed in their ancient dwellings. Looking up through the car's open sunroof, Lisa saw the crumbly turrets of Ludlow Castle holding up the heavens.

She knew that Sam had noticed how quiet she'd been thus far. She made an attempt to be jolly, remembering that Willa had sent along a treat for Sam. 'Oh, I nearly forgot. Willa wanted you to try one of her truffles. It has goat's cheese and caramel with some sort of herb or something? Sorry, I've forgotten the recipe already.' She unwrapped the sweet and stuck her open palm close to the steering wheel.

Sam popped the unusual truffle in his mouth and hummed an energetic, 'Mmm.' He finished chewing and said, 'Really, that's surprisingly good.'

'No wonder my girls approved of you immediately,' Lisa said to Sam with a chuckle. 'If you'll eat Mollie's cheese and Willa's cooking then you get a gold star at our house.'

'Not very difficult to earn. They both do really well.'

'Yes, they do, don't they? Mollie has stuck with what's tried and tested regarding her cheese recipes, but Willa is becoming quite the gourmet. Over the last few months, she's been trying more challenging things.' Lisa folded up the cling film that she'd brought the chocolate sample in and stashed it in her handbag.

'I follow her new food blog,' Sam said with a smile. 'I was rather impressed with her salad yesterday. Pears and chicory with Roquefort cheese, dressed in walnut oil.'

'Was that what it was?'

'Doesn't she give you a bit of the description? Or are you saying that you've come to the point where you just gladly eat whatever she puts in front of you?'

'Actually, you're quite right, she does sort of introduce every-thing. But to be honest, the smell of the cheese rather put me off, so I wasn't paying attention.'

Sam found a space in the car park and they walked into the restaurant. Lisa felt comforted immediately, as the place had dim lights and a hushed, intimate atmosphere.

'Very romantic, Sam,' she whispered and they shared a steamy glance. Things had recently become more physical between them, but she hadn't allowed herself to rush in this time. All the same, she was seeing a very sexy side to Sam these days, and it made what she had to say – rather what she was about to lose – this evening all the more difficult.

They were led up narrow stairs to a smaller dining area and

seated in a cosy corner. The thick carpets absorbed the noise of other diners and staff. Sam helped her with her chair, and Lisa smoothed her dress and slipped beneath a heavy white tablecloth. He sat across from her and smiled again, looking very handsome. There was a white rose on the table whose full petals looked about to drop; Lisa felt rather the same, as her time with Sam was running out.

They ordered. Lisa managed to keep her mind on the conversation about a friend of Sam's, who was leaving unexpectedly and going to live in Finland.

'You just never know about people,' Sam was saying as he sipped his wine. 'I thought Terence was the type to stay in the same job until he keeled over at his desk. Now suddenly he's buying all manner of down-filled outerwear and learning conversational Finnish.'

She felt that she'd never get a better segue to telling him her news.

Lisa cleared her throat and absently rearranged the cutlery by her plate. 'Actually, I'm about to embark on something totally new as well. Perhaps not totally new, it's something I've done before, but it certainly was as unexpected as Terrence slipping off to Helsinki!' She laughed nervously and Sam leaned in close.

'Lisa, are you alright? You seem a bit flushed, even though you haven't had any wine.'

'I must tell you, before I lose my nerve, Sam. Please.'

He nodded.

Lisa sucked in a deep breath. Her heart fluttered. 'Sam, if you want to… stop seeing me after I share my news, I'll understand.' Unable to look at him, her eyes fell to her plate. 'In fact, I rather expect it.'

But Lisa glanced up at him and found his eyebrows raised in a horrified expression. In a moment, her eyes were shining with tears. With impeccable timing, a waitress came bearing their starters. She set them down and started chirping questions. *Did they care for a sprinkling of cheese? Was there anything else she could do for them?*

Sam pulled a comical face, suggesting that he thought she'd never leave. Then he reached over and took one of her hands. 'I'm listening.'

'Alright. Naturally, you'll recall my *brief* relationship, if one could even call it that, with Michael Ferrington. You'll also recall that I was wildly infatuated with him. You see, Sam… Well, what I'm trying, badly, to say is that I hadn't been on a date in nearly twelve years, and perhaps I didn't handle it all very maturely?'

Sam nodded.

'I'm pregnant.'

To Sam's credit, although he leaned back in his chair and looked rather stunned, he managed to keep hold of her hand. Lisa laughed again nervously and this time tears dripped unchecked down her cheeks, so intent was she on Sam's reaction. She could say nothing else; she only shook her head and emitted slightly-hysterical, laughing sobs.

'Staggering news, Lisa. But wonderful!'

'Honestly?'

'Yes.'

She sobbed into her napkin, streaking mascara all over the fine white linen. 'Excuse me.' She stood, a bit unsteady, causing Sam to leap to his feet. His hand was beneath her elbow, and he was leading her to the Ladies. He left her at the door and was about to go, but not without first startling a woman that came out.

A few minutes later, still shaking but more in control, she returned to the table. Their dinner had arrived and Sam hadn't taken a bite. The food sat steaming and Lisa caught the eye of their overzealous waitress, who looked a bit concerned. Lisa couldn't make sense of this now, and was simply relieved to find herself tucked by Sam back into her chair.

'Darling, had I known what you were going through, I

certainly wouldn't have chosen to eat here this evening. I can't think you're wanting a duck liver custard?'

Lisa laughed. 'No, it doesn't really appeal.'

Sam raised his hand and summoned the waitress, who'd been watching Lisa's dramatics.

'I'm so sorry, Tanya, was it? Yes, well, Tanya, my partner and I need to leave rather unexpectedly. We'll pay for all we've ordered, of course. But if you wouldn't mind packing up what's here for my lunch, and we'll be off as soon as possible?'

Lisa audibly sighed after she'd gone. 'You're wonderful, Sam, thank you.'

'No worries. It's silly to sit here while they bring course after course when you're wanting to be away.'

'But I've ruined it for you and you've been waiting so long to eat here. I remember you mentioned it to me early on, when I'd just met you. I remembered the setting, by the river, and thought it sounded lovely.'

Sam laughed. 'I didn't tell you, though, that I'd been here to eat with Ursula recently. I didn't enjoy the meal because we got into quite a difficult conversation. As it happens, I broke things off with her during the dessert course. So you can imagine how I thought, the way you were talking, that karma was going to properly fix me, with you dumping me in turn.'

'Oh, Sam!' Lisa couldn't help but laugh with him at the coincidence. The efficient waitress returned, bearing their bill and a bag full of savoury smelling boxes.

'Don't worry, I won't send you home with this lot,' Sam promised. 'It's for my supper tomorrow.'

'I'm glad you're not sharing. My appetite has been fine, but only for ordinary types of food, nothing rich.'

They drove to his home. Sam offered to make a simple supper for them of eggs and toast, which Lisa relished. They enjoyed the warm evening on the patio, secluded behind his home and surrounded by his rather large garden.

'We might be out in the country instead of in town,' Lisa remarked.

'Yes. I'm fortunate to have so much garden space.'

She leaned back on the chair's puffy cushions and stretched.

'Coffee?'

'Decaf tea, if you don't mind,' she said, so happy to have finally shared her secret with him.

He came back a few minutes later with their hot drinks and a few biscuits.

'Lisa, I know this may seem to be rushing things on a bit, but I won't be sleeping at night unless we discuss our future in a practical way.'

He'd been looking at her with loving eyes all evening, and she wasn't afraid of talking things over. In fact, he couldn't have been more supportive. And he'd done it by simply by being calm and kind. Oddly, she imagined what a very good husband he'd been to poor Angie, especially when she had been ill.

Sam leaned over the table toward her on his elbows. 'I'd already thought of proposing to you, do you know that?'

She was truly surprised. 'Had you really?'

'Yes. It was one of the reasons breaking up with Ursula came so easily, because I realised that not only did I want to date you, but that I could entertain thoughts of sharing a life with you.'

'Sam, I had no idea. But I'd thought of that, too. I guess it's inevitable when you've been as happily married to other people as we've been. You start to wonder if you could be that lucky twice in a lifetime.'

'Well put.' He smiled and said, 'I love you, Lisa. I'd love to marry you. We could raise the baby as ours.'

'Oh, Sam. I love you, too! And I think that sounds like heaven.' She began crying again and laughing through her tears. They sat in his garden until late in the night, making special plans.

IT HADN'T BEEN VERY difficult, with Mollie's help, to get the first poly tunnel planted in. Rhys had chosen a variety of nice lettuces and herbs that he thought would sell well at the farmers' market. Mollie had told a few of the owners of small shops where she sold cheese, and they'd expressed interest in getting some veg from him.

His first customers, thanks to Mollie.

Following a few phone calls, they also discovered a chef in Ludlow who wanted some specialty items for his smart restaurant. Rhys was happy to oblige him. Today he'd be sowing seeds for chards, peas, radishes, spinach, and, for the chef, a type of striking, magenta coloured onion with the dramatic name, 'North Holland Blood Red'. The chef also requested 'Heartsease' Viola, an edible purple and yellow flower used to decorate his salads and puds. Rhys was glad to learn that they were easy-growers, and added them to the list. Mollie had laughed at this and told him that Willa had been using them for ages, and the flowers grew by the metre on the shady side of the house.

He was in the small goat barn sorting out supplies when he heard a vehicle pull into the drive. Lisa was working; it was too early for Mollie to return from her deliveries and Willa had gone to her new college for a meeting of some sort. Rhys came from the barn, expecting a delivery to sign for.

He noticed the car first. He'd never seen an Aston Martin in real life, and it was a beauty. The silver saloon car squelched to a stop. A tall man got out, and Rhys knew immediately from the shape of his nose, chin, and slim height that he must be a relative of Mollie's. He shut his car door and spent a moment surveying the farmhouse and grounds. Then he noticed Rhys standing in the doorway of the barn and gave him a slight nod of the head. Rhys was about to call out to tell him there was no one home, but the gentleman dismissed him with a frowning face and began striding towards the house. Rhys stood still, watching him.

After his knock went unanswered, the man actually had the nerve to enter the house. Rhys followed.

'Lisa!'

'No one is expected back for a couple of hours.'

'Who are you?' The stranger looked angry. Rhys guessed he'd made a long drive and was sorry to waste his time.

'I could ask the same of you.'

He looked Rhys up and down. Adopting a friendlier tone he said, 'Lisa works in the village. I'll just pop around there.'

'She doesn't. The library's closed.'

'Oh.'

'You have a message for her?'

'Why should I leave it with you? I'm family. I hardly need your help.'

'It would seem you do. You don't even know where Lisa works. Or that no one would be home.'

The man took a step toward Rhys, and then seemed to think better of it. 'Quite right. We don't speak very often.' He stuck out a hand. 'I'm Edward Purslow, Lisa was married to my brother.'

'Rhys Davies.'

'What do you do here, Mr Davies?'

'I work here.' Rhys wasn't in the mood to elaborate. Purslow's pompous attitude was annoying, and he sensed trouble.

'Well, you may be a person that could prove to be of value to me. You see, my brother always wanted to share this farm with me. But his wife doesn't care. Look at all these acres. Completely wasted. Farmland is meant to be farmed, isn't that right?'

Rhys looked at the man's posh clothes. Imagined him going to the seed store in his Aston. Rhys pulled himself up and said, 'I think it's time you left.'

'I'll go when I'm damned ready.'

Rhys stepped toward Edward. 'And I think you're ready now.'

The two men stood eye to eye. A moment later, Edward stepped back, raising his palms toward Rhys. 'I have no quarrel with you, son. But if you want to keep your job here, you'll mind your attitude. Remember, you'll work for me soon.'

Rhys stepped aside and Edward wasted no time in leaving the confines of the kitchen. Rhys trailed him out to the car.

Before easing himself into his vehicle he said, 'You tell Lisa that she may have lost a husband, but I lost a brother. And blood is thicker. You tell her that.'

With that, he got in his car and drove away. Rhys wished the bastard would've thrown a punch.

CHAPTER 42

The following week, Lisa made a lunch date with Sally Andrews. She'd meant to get in touch long before now, but it seemed so much had been happening. Now that the summer was drawing to a close, Lisa couldn't believe how much had transpired in her life since the day she bought the bath salts and learned what a fool she'd been with Michael Ferrington. Lisa remembered Sally's unexpected compassion. Although Sally wasn't a stranger, it was quite touching that she would look out for her interests in the way Sally had done. Lisa needed friends and Sally was a woman who could be trusted. She was fun and creative and very bright as well.

Not wanting to sit in the village pub, they met a bit further from home at a tea room in Church Stretton, which had a homely, friendly atmosphere. Lisa noticed a paper in the window; the tea room was looking for kitchen help. She must remember to tell Willa.

Sally came in a moment after Lisa, and they settled on a sofa with a low table in front of them. It was rather like being in one's own sitting room. The closest tables were unoccupied, so they had a bit of privacy as well. Lisa had a taste for a hearty ploughman's lunch, and Sally a club sandwich, along with pots of tea. While waiting for their food they sat sideways on the sofa, facing one another.

'This is a relaxing treat, Lisa. I'm so glad that you invited me.'

'I've been meaning to meet with you for weeks. I have a bit of news to share. Well, *a lot* of news, actually!'

'Really?' Sally's face was hopeful and smiling.

'Yes. Sam and I are finally together, just as you'd hoped!'

'Oh, Lisa, that's marvellous!' Sally leaned over and grasped Lisa's hand.

Their tea arrived. The steaming cuppa helped Lisa deliver her most stunning news.

'But there's more.'

'Do tell!' Sally giggled like a school girl. She was quite different to the village pharmacist role in which Lisa usually saw her and it was fun to have so much news.

'Well, you'll recall our discussion at the shop that day, and my confession about getting… a bit carried away with Michael.'

Sally made a face, as though to suggest they needn't cover old ground again.

'I'm expecting. And before you ask, yes, it's *his*.'

This time Sally wasn't very jubilant, so great was her shock at the news. Lisa was certainly glad that Sam hadn't reacted this way, although she could appreciate how surprised Sally was. Her own daughters had been dumbfounded.

Sally said, 'Oh, Lisa, I'm so thrilled for you. I know Sam well enough to know that he's delighted about the baby.'

'You're right, thank God. I think he'll perhaps even forget that it isn't our baby when he or she arrives. Can you stand more news?'

Sally laughed. 'There's more? Oh, goodness!'

'Sam proposed.'

'And?'

'I accepted!'

This time Sally hugged her. Lisa was touched that she actually had tears in her eyes. 'Lisa, that's simply wonderful. Really, you both deserve the greatest happiness.'

'Thank you. I knew that Sam was lovely, but to be honest, I thought he'd break up with me when I learnt I was having a baby. But I couldn't have been more wrong.'

'And as many years as I've known him, it doesn't surprise me that he wants to marry. He really is a darling man.'

Their food arrived and Sally had lots of questions for Lisa. 'How will this put things with your daughters?'

'Well, the youngest, Phoebe, will move with me to Sam's home in Ludlow. She's over the moon. She's always been quite like her grandmother. Meaning, she's always wanted to live in a city environs, away from the farm. Now, she'll have it.'

'But yet it shouldn't be too much of a shock, since Sam's property is a bit of the country in the middle of town,' Sally supplied.

'That's true. It's a beautiful place, and just the right size for us. Mollie and Willa will stay on the farm for now. Rhys Davies has taken over the loft and is farming a few of the acres. They'll need a bit of financial help the first year or so, but as all three of them begin to earn a bit more, it'll work out just fine. I think Mollie will want to stay on permanently. I feel certain she'll marry Rhys and they'll farm it together.'

'It couldn't have worked out more beautifully.'

'No, it couldn't,' Lisa agreed. 'Although I'd really appreciate your advice. Regarding Michael.'

Sally laid a hand on Lisa's arm. 'You're not to worry about that. Remember I told you that I know all about his checkered past? Well, he's been in this position before. Unfortunately, the other woman had *wanted* him to be involved, and expected him to want some sort of fatherly role. But he was completely disinterested, which is no surprise, as he never wanted a relationship with my nephew.'

'That's a relief. I didn't like to ask Sam what he thought. We've been enjoying discussing our own plans.'

'Sam probably hasn't given Michael any thought. And neither should you, in my opinion.'

'Surely you don't mean to not even tell him?'

'I wouldn't. But you should do as your conscience dictates. If he decides to be a bother, Sam would sort him. So, perhaps think about it for a while, alright?'

'Thanks, Sally.'

They made plans for dinner together, with Sam and Sally's husband, Tom Andrews. They talked then of Lisa's exciting calendar: wedding dates, moving dates, and, of course, her due date. Sally reassured her that hundreds of women aged forty-one had healthy babies every day, and Lisa shouldn't worry. She surprised Lisa by quoting current statistics, that more women in their forties were having babies in Britain than woman under twenty for the first time since World War II.

As they finished their tea, Lisa said, 'It's all going to be happening very quickly, and rather quietly.' Sally smiled and agreed that she and Sam ought to do exactly as they please. No one in the village would learn about their plans from her.

CHAPTER 43

'Willa, you've outdone yourself!' Sam leaned back in his chair and smiled warmly at Lisa's middle daughter. 'You may find yourself teaching those cookery courses instead of being a student!'

Everyone around the table laughed and added their compliments to Sam's. Granny had surprised them all by coming for a visit. She pulled Rhys aside before supper.

'I understand that you've moved yourself right into the house and begun to work the land.'

'Yes.' Rhys met her steady gaze and hoped she didn't disapprove.

'What are your intentions towards Mollie?'

'Well, we've both been quite busy sorting out–'

'Oh, come, young man. Answer my question.'

Rhys had felt the warmth of embarrassment on his cheeks. There was something both disarming and intimidating about Granny Phoebe. She could see right through him.

'I hope that when… when I start earning some money, that she'll marry me.'

'What's wrong with right now? Money is the only impediment?'

'Yes. Without Lisa's generosity, I'd have less than nothing. No good for Mollie, for certain.'

Suddenly Granny had smiled and laid a hand on his shoulder. 'Oh, I think you do Mollie a great deal of good. You can't put a price on everything. But I appreciate your wanting to be an independent man before you marry.'

'I'm going to give everything I've got to make a go of it.'

Granny had seemed pleased with his initiative and Rhys sighed in relief. It was true that it felt his future depended on this foray into farming. He loved Mollie and the dream of his heart was that somehow Lisa would allow them to go on living and working here together. He'd come to love Hilltop Farm, too, although he couldn't imagine how he'd ever be able to afford to buy it from Lisa. Especially now that he'd learned its true worth.

He'd been reading – with Lisa's permission – through Grant's old papers about the farm. And what he'd discovered had surprised him. Perhaps tonight, he'd get a moment alone with Lisa to tell her what he'd learnt.

Instead of things quieting down, the house party seemed to take on more energy after dinner. The women were busying themselves in the kitchen putting away food and doing the washing-up. Rhys slipped out to the barn to check on Mollie's goats. He'd begun doing that recently and she seemed relieved to let him. The animals were happy and lazing about, having enjoyed another summer's day out to pasture. Milk production had slowed a bit and Mollie was glad to be caught up on making cheese. She'd discussed wanting to try a sort of new hard cheese next week. Rhys was glad to see her passion and creativity returning. He wouldn't have thought her new modelling job would've done that for her, but it seemed to have reenergised her.

Walking back to the farmhouse, he enjoyed looking at it from the outside. Light was pouring out of the large windows. He could smell the fresh scent of flowers that had tripled in size in the weeks since Willa had planted them. Laughter could be heard after Granny made one of her unerring observations.

Rhys thought of his parents. He could imagine them sitting around the kitchen table with his brothers. He missed them, yet he loved Mollie's family, too. Somehow he felt in between them both, not entirely belonging to one or the other. Maybe it was time to pay another visit to his mother, and if he happened to see his da, so be it. Rhys had spoken with two of his brothers recently in the village, and heard from them that his name was never mentioned by their father. All the same, his dad hadn't actually forbidden him to come round, so he would.

Rhys came up the steps and, unusually, through the front door, having on a clean pair of boots. Granny was laughing with Sam, and Rhys was glad that he'd also appeared to have Granny's acceptance. Rhys knew that Lisa had come to be like a natural daughter than a widowed daughter-in-law to Phoebe, and Rhys figured if Sam wasn't right for Lisa then Granny would've had something to say.

Young Phoebe – who'd grown taller over the summer – jumped up with her phone and headed for the dining room. Mollie and Willa had decided that it was time for pudding and were in the kitchen.

Rhys came to stand with Sam, Lisa and Granny. He saw that Lisa had taken advantage of her daughters being gone from the room, and she said to Granny, 'I've something a bit distressing to tell you, Phoebe.'

'Oh?'

'I'm sorry to say that Edward has threatened me with legal action.'

'If such a vague letter could be called that,' Sam added.

'For heaven's sakes, whatever for?' Granny demanded.

Mollie and Willa had arrived with dessert and a few coffee cups, but they knew something serious was being discussed and kept quiet. They put the dishes down and stepped towards the circle, eager not to miss any of the conversation.

'Well, you see, for the last few years,' Lisa became distressed. Her eyes welled with tears. She stopped speaking and crossed her arms. She'd stopped apologising for being over-emotional, now that everyone knew she was expecting.

Sam finished for her. 'He wants the farm. Says his brother wanted him to have it.'

'That's ridiculous. What does he imagine he'd do with it?' Rhys heard a note of raw irritation in Granny's voice.

Lisa mopped her eyes. 'I don't know. He's said different things at different times. It began with his claim that his family needed a place in the country. At that time, it didn't seem so fantastical, as his youngest was visiting us and simply adored being here. But then I realised that we're too far from London for that to be the case, and it still didn't justify us leaving our home. More recently, Edward claims that Grant had wanted him to have the farm, and he's tried to make me feel rather guilty.'

'There must be another reason. One we haven't yet come to,' Granny said, obviously perturbed with her younger son. She'd adored Grant, who was headstrong and favoured her own family. Greedy Edward had always taken after his father, which led him to financial success, but he had little else to endear him.

Rhys hadn't planned on things taking this turn, but obviously it was time to speak. 'I know why he wants the farm.'

All eyes turned to him. He hoped he wasn't about to fall out of good graces, when he'd only just secured them. 'I was going to speak with you this evening, Lisa. As you know, I've been having a look through Grant's files. I was interested in his crops of course, not intending to pry into any family business.'

'It's alright, Rhys.' Mollie said, and he felt her supportive hand on his back.

'I found a few documents from the British Geological Society. A few days before his death, Grant had received information on some boreholes drilled here at the farm. Apparently, there's a wealth of building stone and gravel on the northern acres, above the ridge line. As I understand it, Grant had never farmed up there, or even grazed the goats.'

'And you think somehow Edward has discovered this?' Granny asked.

Rhys nodded. 'I'd imagine you could make a small fortune, selling it to an aggregate company, for construction use. It's one of the natural resources not automatically owned by the crown, such as oil.'

'Yes, that sounds right,' Granny smacked her palm on the kitchen cupboard. 'Follow the money. And there you'll always find Edward.'

'But what am I to do?' Lisa asked. Sam put an arm around her shoulders and squeezed gently. 'I don't want to go to court.'

'With regards to Edward,' said Granny Phoebe, 'Do absolutely nothing. If you desire to open up the land for pulling all of that gravel out of here, that's another matter entirely.'

Lisa shook her head, indicating that she wanted no part of such a scheme.

'The way I see it,' Rhys began, noticing the look of respect on Mollie's face. *How long he'd waited for that look in her eyes.* 'Doing so could cause a lot of upset in the community. Large trucks tearing up and down the road and so forth. On the other hand, it would provide a lot of jobs and wealth for men who do that sort of work, men who would be brought in.'

'Why didn't Daddy tell you, Mum?' Willa seemed hurt, thinking her father had kept a valuable secret.

'I wasn't home, love. I'd gone to be with my sister for a few days when she brought her baby home. You'll remember perhaps, hearing that little Stephen had been very sick that week, and they finally allowed him to come home from hospital. That's when they lived a bit closer to us, instead of so far south, in Cornwall.

I'd come in on the train, and was at home, waiting for your father to finish up and join us for lunch.'

'At any rate, Uncle Edward came across the news some other way, because you said he hasn't been keen on the farm until recent years, right, Mum?'

'That's right,' Lisa said, 'Well, I hope no one will be disappointed if I say that I don't intend on doing anything.'

'It's your right to do whatever you wish, dear,' Granny said.

'When the farm comes to you girls then you can mine up the whole of it. I'm sure beginning an enterprise like that is expensive at the start. And right now, I want to begin my life with Sam and Phoebe in Ludlow, and leave you kids to enjoy the farm as you have been.'

Mollie leaned over and hugged her mother. 'Thanks, Mum. We'll all be terribly successful, you'll see!'

Phoebe entered the room. 'I can't believe you haven't started on the pudding yet. What is everyone waiting for?'

'You, naturally,' Rhys said, tickling her until she giggled.

SHE HADN'T REALISED how hard it was to get what you want. Not that she didn't want to flee the countryside – she couldn't wait to be closer to civilisation – but Hilltop Farm was home.

'You must be excited.'

'Of course!' Phoebe had too much pride to let Charlotte know how afraid she really was.

They were walking, carefully, through the goat pasture. It was sort of a stupid place to walk, but they were tired of their other routes. Phoebe had been finding it oddly difficult to stay indoors. She just wanted to walk and walk and walk.

What if she hated living in town? Sam's house was a lot smaller, and her own bedroom would be half the size. Not to mention the horrors of starting at a new school. With that thought, her tummy felt quivery. She hadn't wanted to eat much, but fortunately no one seemed to notice.

The girls came to a fence and paused, looking out over the Shropshire hills. Several goats were cropping grass nearby. 'I know you've always wanted to leave Marris Mynd and I'm happy for you,' Charlotte said. Seemingly inspired by the goats, she was picking apart a weed clump that she'd snatched up from the ground. 'But I'm totally miserable that you're going. You're my very best friend that I've had ever, Phoebe. I'll miss you so much!' At this, Charlotte's voice broke and her eyes filled with tears. Phoebe stared at their shoes. 'You're so brave,' Charlotte squeaked, tears unchecked.

'I'm not!' Phoebe looked at her friend. Now she began crying, too. 'You're the one who is brave, Charlotte.'

'How can you say that?'

'Because, well, because, you're *real*. You're just standing there telling me, like, all of your feelings.'

'So?' Charlotte wiped her eyes with her fingers. She wore a puzzled expression.

'So, that's really… I've been acting like I can't wait to leave. But my life is falling into heaps, obviously… Because I'm too uncourageous to admit I'm so scared. Of *everything*.'

'Is that a word?'

Phoebe stepped back and crossed her arms. 'Really, Charlotte, you're as bad as Willa! It's a word because I've just said it.' Phoebe felt strengthened. She still had a bit of cheek rising to the rescue, helping her save face. 'Anyway, when will you be coming to visit?'

'I didn't know if you wanted me to.'

Phoebe was taken aback. Charlotte didn't usually present difficulties. Phoebe was suddenly reminded of Charlotte's dignity.

Phoebe acquiesced. 'Of course you must visit. I'll *need* you to visit. I'll miss you, too, Charlotte!'

With that, they were hugging, crying loud tears into one

another's hair. A minute later, the misery subsided and both were preoccupied with drying their noses on the hems of their T-shirts.

'I hoped that you'd come with me during the move, actually,' Phoebe said, sniffing. 'Maybe you can help me sort out my new room? And we could have a good look round Sam's neighbourhood. There's some shops and a place that does pizza and sandwiches, only five minutes' walk.'

'That nearby? How exciting!'

'Yes, and that's not even the high street,' Phoebe boasted, feeling hopeful once more. 'There's lots more and a theatre where they sometimes show films, that's only about ten minutes' walk. I'll bet you've never had Japanese food? There's a French bakery, so there'll be no need for pining over Willa's cakes. And an open air market, too, where we could get brilliant craft ideas.'

They giggled, their laughter scattering the goats. Phoebe stuck her toe in the fence and was quickly copied by Charlotte. They raised themselves up and over, and raced each other back to the farmhouse.

EPILOGUE

$\mathcal{A}$utumn

The washing was the worst – the weekly loads went majorly off course when Lisa left Hill Top farm. There were considerably less clothes in the queue with Phoebe gone, since she had changed her outfits constantly and preferred her school uniforms nearly sanitised. The other household chores had already been parcelled out to the girls for years, but it had taken a few days of having nothing clean left to wear for Willa, Mollie and Rhys to work out a proper schedule.

Hearing the dryer buzz, Willa went downstairs in her dressing gown. She doubted very much if Rhys would keel over in shock should he come into the house and find her in a Gap t-shirt and pyjama shorts, but she covered up for her own sense of modesty. She didn't care a jot about comparisons to how much swimwear showed versus undergarments, she wasn't going to be caught out roaming around in her smalls. Willa sorted through the miscellaneous warm clothes in the dryer, pulled out what was hers and enjoyed slamming the door against the rest. They could wait or be claimed as needed by her housemates.

Then she'd had a wonderful Saturday morning reading by the

fire in her soft, freshly laundered jeans and favourite jumper. She went to the kitchen window over the sink and looked out, amazed by the brilliant blue autumnal sky and the golden leaves. Willa hugged herself and laughed aloud. It was the end of September and Oliver would be calling for her in a couple of hours, after a leisurely morning spent with his parents and sister. Then they'd have the whole day to themselves, to have lunch and go for a walk and visit a new bookstore where Oliver had promised to buy for her whatever cookbook she wanted. Then, this evening, they were meeting up in Ludlow with Mollie and Rhys to have dinner with their mum, Sam and Phoebe. Sam insisted on doing a barbecue for them. They would enjoy their family time and laugh and play cards and she knew that Oliver was looking forward to joining them. He'd had dinner – Oliver said 'supper' which made Willa smile – with her family at Hilltop Farm before he returned to university, but this would be his first time at Sam's home.

At the end of summer, Willa's life had changed rather dramatically. She was relieved when Rhys told her that he'd be helping Mollie with the goats most of the time, and in turn, Mollie was delighted to work alongside Rhys in keeping the veg and herbs growing. Willa felt free, for the first time in her life, to focus on herself. It had been slightly terrifying, until she began to imagine all the possibilities. She got a part-time job in Church Stretton at the tea room and had been given the responsibility of baking, job sharing with their usual chef who'd just had a baby. The owner of the tea room had even allowed her to change the menu for autumn, which, surprisingly, was something they'd not done before. Willa was challenged by her college curriculum, but not overly so. It had all been so exciting.

Her better instincts led her to fold the fresh washing, leaving neat stacks of clothes for Rhys and Mollie on the kitchen table. She heard Oliver's car on the drive, and rushed out of the house to meet him. He stepped out of the car and she ran toward him. Oliver scooped her up in his arms, kissing her. They laughed and stood glued to one another for some time, till finally he helped Willa into the passenger's seat and they drove away.

'I've a bad suggestion for lunch,' Oliver said, turning the heater on high for Willa.

'What? You're so funny. What sort of lunch could be a bad suggestion?'

'I'd really like to have tea where you work. Meet everyone that you've told me about. Try the baking, and insult everything that you haven't personally made. What do you think?'

Willa laughed. 'It's the last place I thought we'd go, but actually, I'd enjoy it. It may be sort of interesting. I haven't been there as a patron, you know.'

'Really? How'd you manage that?'

'Well, my mum would meet friends there, for the library, or for her mum's circle. But my treats have been with Granny in Birmingham or away somewhere lovely. I didn't have many girlfriends, and of course Mollie's never said, "Gee, sister, let's go for a delicious lunch!" It's always been, "Willa, I want scones, make some, would you". So, there are lots of places that would count as my first visit.'

'Then I've got my work cut out,' Oliver said, grabbing her hand and kissing it. He'd done that the first time they were alone, and she'd noticed it happened to be the same way Sam took her mother's hand and kissed it.

They met Willa's co-workers with much excitement on both sides. Roni, the owner of the tea room, leaned over and whispered into Willa's ear. 'Now you're a dark one! Dating an earl's son, and he's good looking and rather nice as well. Well done, Willa!'

They were shown to the best spot in the tea room for conversation, which was a sofa in front of the window on the second floor. Willa recalled her mum liking the spot and telling her about it, but she'd only ever peeked into the room on the tour given to her on her first day of employment.

She and Oliver ordered and he made jokes about everything.

The food was excellent and Willa was proud, even though she hadn't been in to bake and prepare any dishes since Wednesday and could take no personal credit.

An hour later they made their way down the high street to the new bookstore.

'Oh, it's lovely, Oliver!' Willa said, as they stepped into a former church, appropriately called Chapel Books. The floor was gorgeously old, creaking wood covered in a variety of coloured rugs, and the huge windows bathed the whole place in light. There were orderly rows of shelves, with rare volumes living in glass-fronted cabinets close to the till. A little reading area was situated towards the front. There were several sofas, some sweet children looking quietly at picture books and one little girl assembling a wooden puzzle with large pieces. 'Oh, we must bring my mum,' Willa said. 'She'd love it.'

'Yes, I thought of her, too. And Sam as well. I was in here for a moment before going back to school, but they weren't officially opened yet and I had to leave. But even in the few seconds I was here, it had the same warm atmosphere that Lisa's old library had in the village. I used to love going there as a child.'

He'd located the cookbooks and they were walking in that direction when a woman said, 'Willa? Is that you?'

They turned to see Mrs Hayward standing behind them with an amused look. Immediately Willa's thoughts flew back to her niece, who'd planned on seeing Oliver at Cambridge, and she was glad that Creepy Katie wasn't with her aunt today.

'Oh, hello, Mrs Hayward,' Willa said quietly, trying to rebalance from the surprise. 'You'll remember Oliver, of course.'

'Yes, hello, Oliver; but you've forgotten to call me Veronica,' Mrs Hayward said with a chiding smile.

'My apologies. Our last vicar and his wife were rather formal, so it takes some getting used to for me.'

Veronica Hayward turned to Oliver. 'You'll have to bring her out of her shyness a bit, won't you?'

Oliver said. 'Do you think so?' He looked at Willa and smiled. 'Willa is a bit too timid – even at my home.'

'Oh?'

Willa glanced at Oliver. Not only was it annoying that Veronica spoke about her as though she wasn't present, but Willa was in utter confusion as to what the woman was on about.

Veronica laughed. 'Obviously, she hasn't told you she was too bashful to come upstairs to look at Katie's new wardrobe. My niece bought a lot of new dresses to impress all of the young men at Cambridge, including you!' She laughed, stepped forward and caught up Willa by the shoulders. 'But I understand, dear. Since then, I've learnt that the village children used to circulate silly stories about the vicarage being haunted. We all have moments of feeling like a child again, don't we? Well, I've taken enough of your afternoon, and I'll say goodbye. Do come look in on me for tea one day, Willa.' And with that, she floated away.

'Well, that's a mystery solved,' Willa said. 'You know, the fan was very loud, and I suppose I only caught the end of the message, telling me not to hurry.'

Oliver laughed and steered her back towards the cookery books. Willa struggled over her decision, and in the end, Oliver bought her two.

As MOLLIE SUSPECTED, Phoebe was thriving in her new school, and had made many new friends in the past three weeks. Mollie had missed her bubbling presence in the farmhouse, even though there was much less tidying to do after Phoebe was no longer there to scatter all and sundry all over the house.

They heard car doors. Willa and Oliver had arrived, and Lisa came sailing out of the kitchen to welcome them in. Like Mollie, Willa was surprised at how Mum's tummy bump had grown. Sam was out at his barbecue, so Willa and Oliver went through to greet their host. Mollie followed them.

'Lovely property,' Oliver said, shaking hands.

'Thank you,' Sam said with a smile. 'It suits, and Phoebe's school is only five minutes away.'

'And I've done up a home office in the old workshop building,' Lisa said, coming out onto the chilly patio. 'Remind me to show you later.'

'I didn't know it was anything but machinery and such, Mum,' Willa replied.

'Oh, no, love. It's finished out rather nicely.'

Mollie followed Rhys and Willa back inside, followed by Sam bearing tongs, and promising that the food would only need ten more minutes. Mollie felt slightly removed from all of the commotion around her, as though she were an outsider, observing her own family for the first time. Willa stood lovingly stroking Phoebe's long golden hair, while teasing her about a new boy she was carrying a torch for, Phoebe's first. Lisa complimented Willa on a new blouse that Mollie had brought home to her after a modelling assignment. Willa could see how pleased Mollie was that their mum had noticed, and saw the tender way Oliver's hand rested around Willa's shoulder.

Mollie was grateful; this was her family, and there would be more little ones joining them in the coming years, growing up alongside her mum's baby. Her heart squeezed with love for Rhys, who happened to turn his head while talking to Lisa, and catch her eye. He winked at her.

Rhys turned to Lisa and said, 'I don't think Mollie's told you. We've got a plan in place for our first series of dairy days at the farm.'

Mollie felt her cheeks flush with excitement.

'How lovely, Rhys!' Her mum turned to hug her. 'Your father would be so proud!'